The
DISAPPEARANCE

Katherine Webb was born in 1977 and grew up in rural Hampshire before reading History at Durham University. She has since spent time living in London and Venice, and now lives in Wiltshire. Having worked as a waitress, au pair, personal assistant, book binder, library assistant, seller of fairy costumes and housekeeper, she now writes full time.

katherinewebbauthor.com
@KWebbAuthor

Also by Katherine Webb

The Hiding Places
The English Girl
The Night Falling
The Misbegotten
A Half Forgotten Song
The Unseen
The Legacy

The DISAPPEARANCE

KATHERINE WEBB

ORION

First published in Great Britain in 2019 by Orion Fiction,
an imprint of The Orion Publishing Group Ltd
Carmelite House, 50 Victoria Embankment
London EC4Y 0DZ

An Hachette UK Company

1 3 5 7 9 10 8 6 4 2

A CIP catalogue record for this book is
available from the British Library.

ISBN (Hardback) 978 1 4091 4860 9
ISBN (Export Trade Paperback) 978 1 4091 4861 6

Typeset at The Spartan Press Ltd,
Lymington, Hants

Printed and bound in Great Britain by Clays Ltd,
Elcograf S.p.A.

www.orionbooks.co.uk

The DISAPPEARANCE

I

Saturday

1942 – First Day of Bombing

That Saturday, the twenty-fifth of April, would have been Wyn's birthday. Frances was distracted by her memory all day long, and as evening fell she grew even more restless, sitting in the front room with her mother after supper, Davy drowsing in her lap. It was well past the time that his mother, Carys, might be expected to turn up to collect him; she would just leave him with Frances – she'd done so many times before. Davy was small for his six years, but even so his weight pressed down on Frances, and he radiated heat until she began to sweat, and feel suffocated. It was impossible to think, with that and the wireless muttering, and her mother tutting as she struggled to mend a shirt by the light of a single lamp, turned down low. She refused to use the overhead lights during the blackout, even though Frances's father had made sure of their precautions. The room began to crowd in on Frances; too hot, too close, too populous.

She looked down at Davy's face, drooping softly in sleep. The skin of his eyelids was pale lilac, with a waxy sheen, and Frances felt a familiar tug of dismay: he always looked so worn out.

'I might go out for a bit of fresh air,' she said, shifting her position, trying to ease Davy's weight against her thighs and ribs. Her mother, Susan, looked up sharply.

'What, *now*?' she said, sounding worried. 'But it's almost bedtime.'

'I'm not tired.'

'Well, I am. And you know Davy'll wake up as soon as you move, in spite of his medicine. You can't just go off and leave him with me, and I bet Carys is in no fit state by now,' she said. Frances stifled a desperate feeling, the *need* to escape. She struggled up out of her chair; Davy stirred, rubbing his face against her shoulder.

'It's all right, go back to sleep,' she whispered to him. 'No, I expect you're right about Carys; he can't go home. I'll take him along to the Landys,' she told her mother. 'They'll be up for hours yet.' Susan gave her a disapproving look.

'It's not right, you know; passing him around, pillar to post.'

'I just . . . I can't breathe. I have to get some air.'

Davy was squirming by the time she got up the hill to the Landys, pressing his knuckles into his eyes. Frances felt his ribs, each no thicker than a pencil, fanning against her own as he yawned. 'Hush, hush,' she told him. 'You're going to sit with Mr and Mrs Landy for a while. You'll like that, won't you? She'll give you a cup of cocoa, I bet.' Davy shook his head.

'Stay with you,' he said, very quietly, as Mrs Landy opened the door. She was in her housecoat, with her white hair up in rollers, but she smiled when she saw them. She and her husband had no children of their own, no grandchildren.

'Is it all right? Just for a couple of hours?' said Frances.

'Course it's all right,' said Mrs Landy. 'Come on in, my little lamb. You can let him stop here with us if it gets very late, Frances, it's no bother.'

'Thank you. He's had supper, and his dose.'

'Frances,' said Davy, still groggy. He didn't say anything else, but Frances knew it was a protest.

'There's a good boy,' she said, guiltily. As the door closed she caught a final glimpse of his face — pale, bewildered; dark shadows under his eyes as he struggled to focus them on her. Later, she would be tormented by that last look he gave her, and by the ease with which she set her guilt aside. How easily she abandoned him there.

But it was Wyn's birthday, and Frances needed to breathe. She climbed to the top of Beechen Cliff, high above Bath, and sat on a bench looking down at the dark city. She'd come to love the peace and solitude of the blackout. The way that, if you let your eyes get used to it and didn't carry a torch, nobody would even know you were there. You could be completely invisible. She wasn't the only one to make use of it — she was often aware of hushed voices in the park, the furtive movements and snatched breaths of courting couples. Frances liked the silhouettes of things against the gauzy sky, and the way sounds and scents seemed sharper. In daylight she didn't notice the musky horse chestnut blossoms or the too-sweet lilacs, or the damp smells of grass and earth in the park. So different to the stone, soot and people smells of the streets below. She felt no danger, except perhaps the same faint frisson they all felt, every night: the possibility of a danger that seemed remote. She looked down and imagined how other people were spending their Saturday nights. All those lives, loves and arguments; all that talk, going on and on. It was a relief to step away from it.

She thought about children, and what made a child a child. Sometimes, Davy got a look in his eye like that of an old, old man — a weary resignation to the inevitability of whatever was to come. He was only six; definitely still a child, but somehow old beyond his years. A bit like Wyn had been. Frances had been looking after him for two years, since she'd gone back to live with her parents. He'd been tiny when his mother, Carys

Noyle, had first shoved him into Frances's arms — a scrap of a boy wearing filthy, sagging shorts, scratching at an infected flea bite on his arm and stinking of long-term grime. She hadn't wanted to look after a child — *any* child — but Carys was hard to say no to, and harder for Frances than for anyone. So that one-off favour was repeated, and became a routine of three or four times weekly, never with any notice beforehand. Carys took it for granted that Frances would have nothing better to do with her time.

It was a still, clear night, the air just mild enough not to show Frances's breath. Wyn should have turned thirty-two that day, the same age as Frances. Every year, Frances tried to imagine her as a grown woman, married, with children of her own. She tried to imagine how she would have looked, and all the things she might have done, and she wondered whether they'd have remained friends. Frances hoped so, but they'd been very different people, and friendship seemed to get more complicated for adults. She would never know. Wyn had vanished on an August day twenty-four years before, and hadn't been seen since. She'd stayed a child of eight years old. On her birthday, Wyn haunted Frances mercilessly, cluttering her mind with echoes and half-remembered things, and a sense of loss like an ache in her bones.

A lone plane flew over, eastwards near Sham Castle, and left a sparkle of light behind. Chandelier flares, falling with slow grace. Frances waited, and sure enough the air raid sirens set up their wailing down below. The first planes usually came over between eleven and midnight; Frances realised with a start that hours must have slipped by without her noticing. She ought to hurry home and go down into the cellar with her mother, to get backache in a deckchair and feel the air turning turgid as the hours crept by. Sleep was impossible down there, and playing I-spy in the dark had stopped being funny months ago. The prospect was as welcome as a wet weekend. Lately, Frances had stopped bothering to move when the sirens went off, and she wasn't the only one. They'd gone off too many times – hundreds of times – and no bombs had fallen.

Moonlight slid along Holloway, the ancient street at the foot of the hill, and found the roof of St Mary Magdalen Chapel. It lit the roof of the old leper hospital next door to it, too: a narrow box of a cottage, couched in darkness like the rest. In the blackout, there was nothing to show that it was empty. Empty of the living, anyway. It had a rough, stone-tiled roof; small, Gothic windows; and a chimney stack on one side. Frances couldn't look at it without steeling herself first – almost daring herself; and once she had, it was hard to look away. The sight of it took her back to her childhood, abruptly, painfully. She stared at it, and didn't notice the sound of the planes at once – they came gradually, gently overwhelming the quiet rustle of the trees. A dog started barking somewhere down on Lyncombe Hill. As the sound grew louder Frances picked out the particular, two-tone throb of German propellers, so different to the smooth roar of British ones. They'd all got used to telling the difference.

Night after night, for months, the people of Bath had hidden away as the planes went over on their way to Bristol, to batter its docks and wharves and warehouses. Frances had watched from Beechen Cliff as the western sky lit up with explosions and anti-aircraft fire; she'd watched as people died in the neighbouring city. The odd stray bomb had been dropped around Bath by nervous pilots unsure of their location, or dumping unshed load on the way back to the continent. A barn on fire here, a crater to be gawped at there. On Good Friday the year before, four bombs had been dropped with random malice by one pilot, killing eleven people down in Dolemeads. It was hard to picture those young German pilots, cold with sweat in their cockpits, delivering death and mayhem. Frances found herself wondering what their favourite food had been when they were growing up, or what they'd wanted to be when they were twelve years old; whether they'd enjoyed their first kisses, or rubbed them away in surprised disgust. She was supposed to hate them; to not hate them was to hate England. You *had* to hate them, just like before, in the last war. She'd been afraid of that hatred then, and she despised it now.

The racket got louder. It was coming from two directions – from the east, along the River Avon from Box, and from the south, behind Frances. She lit a cigarette, carefully shielding the tiny flame of her match, and thought back, trying to work out when Davy had got his old man's expression. That first time she'd looked after him she'd been unsure what to do with him. She'd gone back to scrubbing carrots in the lean-to scullery round the back, and had virtually forgotten he was there until she turned and saw him peering at her from around the door jamb. He had light eyes and matted blond hair, and pale skin smudged with dirt. His expression hadn't been scared, or curious; more dogged. Quietly determined to find something to eat, she soon found out. The look of weary resignation must have come later. Frances wasn't good with children, and at first she hadn't known what to say to him. She'd said, 'You all right, then?' and, 'You can go and play in the yard, you know', and she'd been embarrassed, even a bit put out, when he didn't reply.

The planes were low, lower than she'd ever seen them; it seemed as though she might reach up and touch them. Their black shapes filled the sky – more numerous than ever before. Frances dropped her cigarette in shock, and clapped her hands over her ears as she looked up. They were like a swarm of giant insects; the sound of them went right through her chest and rattled her heart. They seemed to move too slowly, like they might drop out of the sky, and suddenly Frances realised why it was all different: they weren't heading for Bristol, they were coming for Bath. Blameless, defenceless Bath. She sat stupefied for a moment, too stunned to move, as the planes began to dive and she heard the tell-tale whistle of incendiaries, and saw the white flashes as they went off – setting buildings on fire, lighting up the city, making a mockery of the blackout. Then came the vast, incredible thump of a high-explosive bomb. The last thought she was able to have, before the noise obliterated everything, was of little Davy Noyle, with his blond hair just like his Aunt Wyn's.

Frances scrambled forwards off the bench, huddling on the damp grass with her arms wrapped over her head. She couldn't seem to fill her lungs; the air tore and shrieked around her, the ground shook, and all thought abandoned her. It was a moment of pure fear – fear that made her muscles tremble and turned her weak and stupid. She'd felt it before but not for a long, long time; not since she'd first seen the ghost in the old leper hospital. This was the same debilitating fear – a feeling of free-fall, of having seconds left in which to exist before hitting the ground. Frances shut her eyes tight, clenching her teeth until it hurt as wave after wave of planes went over, swooping low over the city, dropping bomb after bomb. It seemed to go on forever: the roar of engines, the shudder and crump of explosions. The springtime smells of grass and trees vanished into the stink of burning; smoke filled the air, and when Frances finally made herself look up she saw fires all over Bath. The gasworks were an inferno. Holloway was on fire. The road she lived on – the road her parents lived on.

Panic jolted her up; she felt horribly exposed and, with a cry, she ran for the top of Jacob's Ladder – steep steps that cut down the side of Beechen Cliff to the back of Alexandra Road, where her Aunt Pam lived. It was the nearest place of safety she could think of. She heard the rattle of machine-gun fire – never heard before but somehow instantly recognisable – as she flung herself down the steps, swinging between the railings, desperate for the deeper darkness of the laurels and undergrowth as fire banished the night. Frances ran blindly, out of control, and halfway down she missed a step, lurched and fell hard against the railings, turning her ankle and giving her head a whack that made white spots scud across her eyes. Another bomb dropped, nearby. It fell with a whistle that became a banshee scream, then landed with a noise that sucked in everything else, consuming it utterly, just for a second or two. It was staggering. Frances stayed where she was, gripping the railings as though they might save her, feeling like her head was being crushed. She thought of her mother, down in the cellar, and how frightened she would be; she thought of her father, out in a public shelter somewhere. She thought of ghosts. Then she didn't think for a while, because there was nothing to do but exist.

Sunday

1942 – Second Day of Bombing

The sun shone, pallid through the lingering smoke. Frances squinted up into the sky. Her head throbbed, and she felt a little drunk; her thoughts were moving with an odd, deliberate slowness, like high clouds on a hot day. She'd cut her forehead when she fell and it had bled all down her face, but she hadn't done anything about it other than to scratch it when it itched. She had a worrying feeling that she was forgetting something important, and the sequence of the previous night wouldn't make sense, no matter how hard she tried to order it. She knew from listening to people talk that there'd been a lull of a few hours after the first raid, and then another attack in the small hours of the morning. To Frances, it had seemed as though the bombings had gone on and on, unrelenting, for half a lifetime. She'd woken with the rising sun, still on the steps where she'd fallen, and made her way home slowly.

Now she was helping a civil defence team clear rubble from the house at the end of Magdalen Cottages, the row of three where she and her parents lived, which had taken a direct hit from an incendiary and gone up like tinder. The roof, chimney stack and upper floor had slumped through the ground floor into the cellar; a whole house reduced to a charred heap, hissing gently with steam.

'Frances! Don't just stand there like a clot, love,' said her father, Derek, and she was so relieved to hear his voice that she didn't mind the reprimand. The Hinckleys, an elderly couple who'd lived there since before Frances was born, were still inside somewhere. They had a Morrison table shelter in their kitchen, Frances knew, but she also knew they were both a bit doddery and had stopped getting out of bed for the air raid warnings. On the other side of the street, Paradise Row was gone – a four-storey Georgian terrace, flattened. Its absence kept drawing her eye – the fascinating, horrifying strangeness of it. Frances could see the whole of Bath through the gap – the river at the foot of the hill, the abbey, the lofty crescents to the north. Smoke was rising everywhere.

Rousing herself, Frances took a piece of a door from her father and passed it to the lad behind her. They were trying to clear the top of the cellar steps. Not many women were digging; they were bringing out tea, or fetching water from the static tank by Magdalen Chapel, wiping their children's faces or standing about in huddles, looking bewildered. But Frances was tall and wore slacks, and her hair was short, and people sometimes forgot to think of her as a woman.

'The bastards were shooting at the fire crews while they worked,' said Derek, to nobody in particular. 'That's the filthy Boche for you, isn't it?'

'They've hit Civil Defence HQ an' all,' said the lad behind Frances. 'It's bloody chaos.'

'The cemetery's been hit, along to Oldfield Park,' said a woman as she passed, pushing her pram briskly down Holloway. 'There's bodies all over the place! Bodies long since buried – I saw them!' she said, urgently. 'I saw the bones, and I had to . . .' She shook her head and walked past without finishing.

'Well, we can't do much to help those 'uns, can we?' one of the men called after her, with black humour.

'Shh!' said the rescuer at the front, up to his knees in the ruins of the house. He crouched down, holding up a hand for silence. 'I swear I heard something, then,' he said. 'Someone's tapping down there!' There was a smattering of applause. 'Come on, lads, put your backs into it.'

But both of the Hinckleys were dead, in fact, when they were dug out an hour or so later. Mrs Hinckley's face was so white with plaster dust, and her husband's so black from the fire, that they could have been anybody. Frances stared at them distantly; her ears were ringing, and she kept thinking she could still hear bombs falling. She felt odd and not at all well, as though she might faint.

'Frances!' She heard her mother shout. 'Oh, Frances! Do come away, love.'

'Who do we report this to, then?' asked one of the men. 'The deaths, I mean. Who are we supposed to tell? The police?' Derek gave him a blank look, then shook his head, confounded.

Frances blinked, and found herself sitting on a kitchen chair at home, with her mother dipping a rag in water and dabbing at the cut on her head.

'Frances was out in it all night, if you can believe that,' her mother, Susan, was saying. A breeze nudged through the glassless windows, and the front door was gone. A crack ran from the corner of the jamb to the ceiling; the linoleum floor had been swept but dust was already resettling. The abnormalities were small but nonetheless disturbing, like in a dream where everything was slightly off kilter.

'Front row seat, eh, Frances?' said her aunt, Pam.

'Pam? Are you all right?' said Frances. Her aunt gave her a quizzical look, and Frances felt a rush of joy at seeing her safe.

'Am *I* all right? Course I am. It'll take more than a few fireworks to finish me off.' Pam's thick, grey hair was held back by a yellow scarf, and her jacket was smudged with soot. Frances glanced down at the floor and there was Dog,

Pam's wire-haired mongrel, appearing quite calm. 'Him, too. Though you should have heard him howl as the bombs fell!' Pam smiled briefly.

'I was coming to your house,' said Frances, frowning as she attempted to marshal her thoughts. 'I think. I was coming down Jacob's Ladder, and I fell.'

'What on *earth* were you still doing up on Beechen Cliff at that hour, that's what I'd like to know,' said Susan. 'A "bit of fresh air", you said.' Pam gave Susan a weary sort of look.

'Nothing much,' said Frances. She didn't dare remind them it had been Wyn's birthday, not when her mother was already so fraught. 'Just sitting and thinking. Enjoying the peace and quiet.' Her mother made a dismissive sound.

'Well, the top of the cliff's a good spot for that,' said Pam.

'Please don't encourage her, Pam,' said Susan. 'She put herself in terrible danger.'

'Encourage her? She's a grown woman, Sue. And besides, were the folk under all the brick and steel any safer? The shelter opposite the Scala on Shaftesbury Road took a direct hit, I heard, and they're all as dead as you like. Seventeen of them.'

'Pam!' said Susan, horrified. She was pale, and looked a bit sick, and Frances wished her head would clear so she would know the right thing to say. She was still certain there was something important she'd forgotten to do.

The three of them were quiet for a while, listening to the drip of water, to shouting voices and the racket of a generator pump. The smell of smoke and wet ash seemed to come from everywhere. Dog growled softly, then sighed and lay down across Pam's feet. He was black and white, with legs too short for his body and a collie's flag for a tail; the offspring of an unscheduled coupling up at Topcombe Farm. Frances had given him to Pam when her old fox terrier died, and at first

Pam had refused to love him, or even to name him. 'That dog,' she'd said, and it had stuck. That had been back when Frances was a married woman, a farmer's wife, instead of . . . whatever she was now. An outsized cuckoo, back in her parents' nest.

She looked around the familiar kitchen, with its flimsy cupboards, tin-topped table and ancient stove. The electricity was off, like the gas and the water. There was a frying pan abandoned on the side, holding three sad-looking slices of bread. The kitchen clock had come off the wall and was lying in pieces on the table. The face, without its hands, looked startled and bare.

'They'll be back, folk are saying,' said Susan, tightly. There was real fear in her voice; her face was pinched, her eyes too bright. The blotting had reopened the cut on Frances's head, and was making it sting. The water in the bowl had turned pink. Frances shut her eyes, trying to put her finger on what it was she'd forgotten to do. It was maddening. 'They'll be back tonight,' Susan went on, 'and we'll get it again. We've to get out of the city – they're emptying the rest centres already; they've been taking people in buses. We'll go as soon as Derek gets off duty – they're putting people up at the Withyditch Baptist chapel, Marjorie says. We'll not stay here to face it again, none of us.'

'I'm not going anywhere,' said Pam, with a shrug. 'Buggered if I'll let a bunch of boys without a chest hair between them drive me out of my own home.' Susan shot her an incredulous look.

'Did *you* hit your head as well? It isn't a game, Pam – they mean to murder us all! You'd be mad to stay. And there'll be no more wandering around in the middle of the night all by yourself, Frances . . . People talk, you know. Could be getting up to all sorts, that's what they say about you.' Frances drew breath to retort, but then she noticed that her mother's hands were shaking. She reached up and took one, meshing their fingers for a moment.

'It's all right, Mum,' she said, gently. 'Don't take on.'

'It's not all right! If I lost you . . .' Susan shook her head, then sighed, and tucked a strand of ashy blond hair behind her ear. 'Frances. If I lost you . . .' She dropped the rag into the bowl and set it down on the table.

Frances needed to think but the ache in her head made it all but impossible; her eyes slid out of focus and she saw the night sky again, lit up orange with fire and swarming with huge black flies. Bombs screamed like injured animals; hands reached down for her and she came to with a jolt, woken by her father plodding into the kitchen, clumsy with fatigue.

'Derek! You're trailing the streets in with you!' said Susan, fussing at his filthy bootprints, the fragments of plaster and ash dropping from his Air Raid Patrol uniform. Derek looked wearily at his wife.

'Susan, love, if I don't get a cuppa in the next two minutes you'll find yourself a widow,' he said. Frances got up and turned the tap to fill the kettle, forgetting that the water was off, and that the stove was dead.

'There's water in the pail,' said Susan. 'We'll be fetching it from the tank up the way for the time being, I suppose.'

'Well, at least it's not too far,' said Frances, absently, feeling for her matches to light the fire, but not finding them. Somewhere halfway up Jacob's Ladder, no doubt. But there was something else, too – something else she was missing.

'Are you off duty now, then? Can we leave?' said Susan. It was not yet noon, but she seemed to expect the planes back at any moment. Derek shook his head.

'Off duty? No, love, not for a good long while. This is what they trained us for, after all. You girls pack up what you can comfortably carry, and go on ahead. I'll make the house secure, then I'm to go up to Bear Flat and help guard against looters at the bank. There's a hole in it wide enough for Ali Baba and his forty thieves, and—'

'Bear Flat? But . . . how long for?'

'I don't know, love.'

'Sit down before you fall down, Derek,' said Pam, giving her brother's arm a squeeze. He nodded heavily.

'But they're coming back! They'll be coming back!' Susan cried.

'And you three'll be far away when they do,' said Derek.

'Well, I won't be,' said Pam.

'What about you, Dad?' said Frances.

'I'll get to a shelter, don't you worry, but I can't just abandon my post now I'm actually needed, can I? How's that head, anyway?'

'It's all right, I think,' said Frances.

'We've been very lucky, all of us. The poor Hinckleys, and that lot up the hill at Springfield . . .' He shook his head.

Frances went cold. She tried to speak but her voice got stuck in her throat. She coughed, and tried again.

'What?' she said.

'What do you mean, what?' said Pam.

'Oh . . .' said Frances, her thoughts coming into sudden, terrible focus. She knew exactly what she'd been forgetting. '*Davy* . . .'

'What? Oh! Oh no,' said Susan.

'I . . . I took him up to the Landys!' Frances cried. She ran out of her doorless home, ignoring the calls that followed her. Pain shot through her head when she moved and she felt nauseous, horrified that she could have forgotten to ask, to check, to go and fetch him. The dreamlike veil disappeared from the day, from the world, and she saw the horrible reality of it for the first time. People were dead; homes were destroyed; more was coming. She ran on, gasping for breath as Springfield Place came into view further up the hill, where Holloway curved up and away to the south. Or at least, what remained of Springfield Place. She slowed, filling with incredulous dread.

There was no smoke, no charred beams or blackened stone. The near end of the row, where the Landys had lived, had simply collapsed like a house of cards. Roof timbers poked up here and there, looking like snapped bones. The damage got lighter towards the far end of the row, but Frances didn't care. She came to a halt outside number one, and a shiver poured down her spine. The place where she'd left Davy had been obliterated. She could only stare, stunned, until an ARP man with smuts in the creases of his face stopped to see if she was all right.

'Knew 'em, did you, love?' he said.

'Where are they now?' she asked, numbly. The man shrugged.

'Dunno, love, sorry. I heard they was planning on using the church crypts as mortuaries, but I don't know. They was down in the cellar – Mr and Mrs Landy, weren't it? They survived the blast all right, they was even talking to the rescuers for a while. But the water pipe had split and it flooded the place . . . drowned 'em before they could be got out, and if that ain't a cruel twist of fate I don't know what is. Bad business,' he said, offering her a cigarette. Frances took it, and couldn't hold it steady as he lit it. She shut her eyes and steeled herself. Would it be better to know the exact details? The particulars? Or better not to have a clear mental image of it? She decided that knowing was better than imagining, yet she could still hardly bring herself to ask. A terrible chill was creeping through her, and her legs felt weak. She was supposed to have been minding Davy; she was supposed to have kept him safe. Instead she'd abandoned him to go up Beechen Cliff and sit in the dark, alone with her thoughts. Davy had wanted to stay with her.

'And the little boy?' she whispered.

'What's that?'

'The little boy . . . was he in the cellar with Mr and Mrs Landy? Did he . . . drown too?'

'Two came out dead, that's all I know,' said the ARP man. 'Are you saying there's a third?'

'What?' Frances turned on him, heart jumping. She grabbed his sleeve. 'A little boy was in there too – David Noyle? Did they find him? Is he alive? He's only small – just six.'

'Steady on . . .' The man rubbed at his chin. 'Hold on. The rescue team went along to Hayesfield Park, I think. Come along with me, and let's ask 'em.'

The sun was dropping in the west by the time the men decided to give up. Frances's back was aching, her hands were scraped and bruised. They'd cleared as much rubble from the Landys' flooded cellar as they could, shoring it up with wooden beams and jacks. Mrs Landy's pink eiderdown was hooked over the back railings, caked with dirt. Frances had helped where she could, though the men mostly wanted her out of the way. The stone walls of the cottage had disintegrated with the blast; everything and everyone was covered in the white dust. Now and then Frances thought she saw things – familiar shapes in the alien whiteness: an arm or a hand; a mop of hair; a small shoe. Her stomach dropped every time, but it was never Davy. There was no sign of him at all, and though her head was still thumping and it was hard to think clearly, Frances began to hope.

The rescuers picked up their tools to move on, and one of them paused to pat Frances's shoulder.

'If he was right under the bomb, there might well be nothing left to find,' he said, as kindly as he could.

'But . . . the Landys were still alive after the bomb,' she said. 'And they'd gone down into the cellar – if they'd had Davy with them, they'd have taken him with them. We should keep looking – he might still be in there . . . he might still be alive in there!'

'No, pet, he's not,' said the man. 'There's no one else in there.'

'Then he might . . . he might have managed to get out by himself, mightn't he? After the bomb? Or before it, even. He might have run off. He'd have been so scared when it started.' She swallowed a sudden sob at the thought.

'I heard a child got thrown out of a shelter down by Stothert's,' said a woman Frances hadn't noticed standing beside her. She had dust in her hair, and was shaking uncontrollably. 'She was the only one to survive it; them that stayed in the shelter all died.'

'He has fits, sometimes . . . he loses track of where he is, and what he's doing,' said Frances, staring at the wreckage and trying – or trying not – to see a little boy there. 'If he was scared, he might have tried to go home . . . or to find me. Don't you see? He might be somewhere else altogether!'

'That's right, he might,' said the rescuer, in a placatory tone she didn't like.

'Well, what should I do? Should I report him missing?'

'We'll put it in our report,' said the man. 'Davy Noyle, you said?'

'David, yes.'

'Right you are. Well, I'd start with his home address, if I was you. Then at the hospitals, and maybe the rest centres, once all this has blown over. If he was thrown clear then someone might have picked him up and taken him in. Best you get on out of the city now, missus; I don't reckon we're in for a quiet night.'

'I can't go now.' Frances remembered the scream of falling bombs, the guttering roar of fire as it banished the night, and fear turned her stomach. She tried to ignore it.

'Suit yourself,' said the rescuer, losing patience.

Frances stayed a while longer, paralysed by the thought of having lost Davy, of having caused his death. The terrifying, unbearable irrevocability of that. Not long after Carys had first brought him round he'd started turning up at Frances's house of his own accord – appearing silently at the back door, or waiting on the step when Frances got back from work. She always gave him a glass of milk or a biscuit and, like a stray cat, he kept coming back. She got used to his small, silent presence as she did laundry, or peeled potatoes, or just sat outside at the end of the day, smoking a cigarette. She was surprised by how quickly she began to look out for him, and stopped minding that she often smelt him before she saw him. Her mother said they should ask Carys for money.

'If Carys had money she wouldn't need me to watch or feed him,' Frances replied.

'If she didn't drink like a fish, she would have money. And I don't see why we should have an extra mouth to feed,' Susan pointed out, but with no real rancour. 'Besides, she's managed to look after all her others, hasn't she? It's because he's simple, and she's bone idle. That's all it is.'

'Not *all* her others – little Denise still lives with Owen and Maggie, don't forget. And Davy's not simple,' said Frances, to which her mother tutted. Susan might complain, but she'd make Davy a jam sandwich all the same.

Frances wasn't sure if Davy was simple, or simply different. He was far too small and skinny for his age; his ears were too big for his head and stood out like the handles of a trophy

– which was what his classmates called him. He didn't speak much, and his attention drifted easily. His focus didn't leap constantly to the next interesting thing, like with most children; instead he seemed quite happy to focus on nothing at all. Since he'd been prescribed phenobarbital he'd had fewer of his seizures, and Davy's dad paid the doctor quarterly in advance for the medicine, so there was no chance of the money being spent elsewhere. The seizures ranged in severity, from his awareness shutting off for a few minutes, even as his feet kept moving, from which he returned confused and frightened, to sudden full collapses into spasms and unconsciousness. The latter had scared Frances half to death the first time she'd seen it happen, but the drug seemed to prevent them, even if it did make him groggy as a result. He had his biggest dose at bedtime, because of that.

One sunny day, early on, Frances had heated some water in the big copper, put the tin tub out in the yard, tipped in a few inches of water and suds, and beckoned Davy over. He trusted her by then, and let her strip off his filthy clothes and drop him in. He thought it was a game. Frances took the opportunity to scrub him top to toe, but he laughed and splashed the whole time, until she was soaked. That was the first time she heard him laugh. She washed his clothes too, and while they hung to dry on the warm tiles of the outhouse roof, Davy wandered about the yard as naked as the day he was born, playing some game with twigs and pebbles that Frances couldn't fathom. He was all ribs and vertebrae, his arms like sticks, a bit like Wyn's had been. It had been worth the roasting Carys gave her – she couldn't stand the implied criticism of Frances having bathed her child – to see him so jolly.

Thinking about it now made Frances feel hollow. She made her way slowly to Beechen Cliff Place and stood outside Carys Noyle's house at number thirty-three, waiting for the courage to go to the door. While she stayed outside, the hope remained that Davy had run home after the blast; the hope remained that she wouldn't have to tell his mother he was gone. Her pulse ticked in the back of her throat. Beechen Cliff Place was a narrow street of terraces that led off Holloway, part of the tangle of houses at the bottom of the hill. The walls were blackened with soot, and streaks wept down from the gutters and sills. The window frames were spongy with rot, the chimney pots were cracked, and weeds grew from the roofs. The front yards were for dustbins and broken things; there was a shared backyard, criss-crossed by washing lines, with a trio of privies and a washhouse. It was always damp – water sprang out of Beechen Cliff in hundreds of places, and trickled down to the river whichever way it could. Even the rats pottering around the bins were damp, their fur dark and spiked with wet.

Dry-mouthed, Frances took hold of herself and knocked. Fred Noyle, one of Davy's older brothers, opened the door wearing his gas mask. Fred was twelve years old, a bony boy, all angles and awkward levers. He had his mother's dark colouring, and through the goggles of his gas mask Frances saw his eyes alight with a strange hunger – the thrill of the young to change, and to destruction.

'Mum's out the back,' he said, the words muffled. 'I'm off out for a gander.' He bumped past Frances on the step, tugging his cap down over his forehead.

'Hang on, Fred – is your little brother around?' said Frances.

'Davy?' Fred shook his head. 'Don't think so. I'n't he with you?'

'No,' said Frances, heavily, to his retreating back.

On slow feet, she made her way through to the backyard. Carys was snatching vests and socks down from the washing line and hurling them into a bundle on the ground. She glanced up as Frances approached.

'These'll all have to be washed again,' she said, without preamble. 'Covered in bloody dust. Like I haven't got enough to do.' She raked strands of her greying hair back from her forehead. She'd still been Carys Hughes when Frances had first met her: Wyn's big sister. Her hair had been a glossy brunette, the colour of black treacle; her skin had been smooth, with roses in her cheeks. Frances, at the age of six, had thought her as lovely as Snow White. Now drink had burst the capillaries in her cheeks and across her nose, and there were deep wrinkles between her eyebrows and bracketing her mouth, giving her a permanently sour expression. Carys was only forty-two, but could have been ten years older. 'Here. Hold this,' she said, passing Frances the peg bag. 'I expect you've come to ditch Davy, have you? Come to tell me you're too busy to watch him with all this bloody . . .' She waved a hand at the smoking city below them, and the gaps in nearby streets. 'Bloody *nonsense*.' She glared at Frances.

'Carys, I . . .' Frances paused, swallowing hard.

There was no good way to say what she had to say, no way to avoid it, and no way to make it sound any better than it was. For a moment, Frances wasn't sure how to force the words out. She almost wanted to be shouted at. She was furious with herself for taking responsibility for Davy in the first place, and setting herself up to fail so profoundly – it was this exact, unbearable feeling of failure and guilt that had stopped her wanting children of her own. Their vulnerability terrified her. Yet, having ruined her marriage by refusing to have any, she'd somehow – by stealth rather than choice – ended up with a child to care for, a child to love. She hadn't wanted this to happen; she hadn't wanted any of it. The pain in her head was awful. 'Carys, I'm so sorry. I took him up to Mr and Mrs Landy last night. I had to go out, so I took him up to Springfield Place.' Something in her tone made Carys pause. She turned to face Frances, her knuckles white around a grubby shirt, gripping it hard. Frances took a breath. 'They...they're dead. The Landys. Their house is gone, and I...There's no sign of Davy anywhere. I made them look...I made them look right down to the foundations of the place...'

Frances fell silent, and Carys said nothing. She walked closer until she was near enough for Frances to smell the reek of gin that wasn't so much on her breath as leaking from every pore of her body. An unnatural heat, like a fever, rose from her skin. Frances was a full head taller than Carys, but felt small.

'Well, where is he, then?' Carys said in the end, a flicker of fear in her voice.

'I don't know.'

'You were looking after him. So where is he?' Carys spoke through clenched teeth.

'I had to go out!' said Frances. 'He...he should have been fine with the Landys. I couldn't know the raid was coming. I'm so *sorry*, Carys...I'm so sorry. I'll find him. I won't stop looking till I find him, I promise, and—'

'You were supposed to be looking after him!' Carys shouted, shoving Frances so that she stumbled back. 'Is he dead? Is that what you're saying?'

'No! That is, I – I don't know. But I don't think so...They searched and searched, and there was no sign of him – nothing at all. I think he got out, and he's got lost. Wouldn't that be just like him?'

'You *think*? You don't know?' Carys shook her head, as if struggling to follow. There was a pause. 'I...You...Always so bloody *perfect*, weren't you?' she said, breathing fast. 'Telling me I don't know how to look after my own bloody kids. And now you've gone and bloody well *lost* one! Because you "had to go out"! What was so important? Got a new boyfriend, have you?'

'No! I . . .' Frances took a breath. 'You know what day it was, yesterday. The date, I mean. I just wanted a bit of time alone. I just needed . . .'

'What day? What are you on about?'

'It . . . it was Wyn's birthday yesterday. You know that.'

Wyn's disappearance was the watershed point around which Frances's whole life divided, into everything before, and everything afterwards. Sometimes she forgot that the same wasn't necessarily true of everyone who'd known her. She'd thought that Carys would remember her sister's birthday, though, since she'd been the one, at the age of ten, to pull Wyn from their mother onto the kitchen floor, but a sneer contorted Carys's face, and Frances realised she hadn't had a clue of the date. Her expression grew even more furious, her colour even darker.

'That's your excuse? That you're still moping about something that happened donkey's years ago?'

'No, it's no excuse. I just . . .' Frances didn't know what to say. Carys glared up at her, her mouth framing words she was too angry, for a moment, to articulate. 'You know what Davy's like,' Frances said, wretchedly. 'Losing track of where he is. And everything looks so different now . . . I expect he's just wandered off somewhere, that's all.' Something flickered in Carys's eyes then, but Frances couldn't tell if it was hope, pain, guilt, or what. It didn't last long – the anger flared again, and burnt it away.

'You'd better hope so, hadn't you?' she said. 'And you'd better have him with you next time I set eyes on you, or I'll . . .' Carys shook her head, shoulders drooping. 'You'd better have him with you,' she mumbled, swaying slightly. Then she dropped her face into her hands, and sobbed. Frances watched helplessly, shocked.

'I'm so sorry, Carys,' she said. She took a step forwards,

holding out one hand, but Carys's head came up in an instant, her eyes dangerous.

'Get out of my sight! Go and find him,' she said. Frances fled.

As Frances went back out to the front, Nora Hughes, Carys and Wyn's mother, emerged from number thirty-four and came down the path in the rolling, awkward gait her arthritic hips gave her.

'You all right, Frances?' She smiled in her vague way. 'Bit of a business, isn't it all? A few houses down in Dolemeads have gone, but Owen's fine, thank God,' she said. Frances nodded, feeling the slight jolt she always felt at the mention of Owen's name. She paused, but then couldn't face having to talk to Davy's grandmother too, and carried on walking. 'You all right? And your lot?' Nora called.

'Yes. Thank you. I think . . . I think maybe Carys needs you,' said Frances, despising her own cowardice. Mrs Hughes's face fell, and behind her Mr Hughes came to stand in the doorway, as inscrutable and threatening as he'd ever been. Frances didn't meet his eye. The shame was unbearable; her mistake was so huge, so terrible, she knew it could never be forgiven. Her feet faltered. Bewildered, she realised that she already knew that *exact* feeling; that she had felt it before. The pavement blurred in front of her, and instead of grey slabs and gravel she saw a pair of small feet in dusty shoes; a narrow back, walking away; a long pennant of blond hair, lit with sunshine. 'Wyn,' said Frances, but when she blinked the drab pavement was back, and Wyn's mother was still watching her, uneasily. Nora Hughes insisted that her daughter was still alive, but she was alone in that. Frances knew differently. Though there'd never been a body or a confession, the whole world knew differently. A man had been caught, and tried, and hanged for her murder.

Frances hurried away, back up towards Springfield Place, in case Davy had reappeared there. She didn't know where else to go, or what else to do. The city was in chaos; *she* was in chaos. Her feet felt leaden. Halfway up Holloway the ground seemed to tilt and she staggered to a halt, swaying.

'You all right, love?' said a voice, and a hand clasped her arm. 'Had anything to eat today, have you? That cut could use a stitch, I reckon. Where's home? Come and sit yourself down over here.' Frances let herself be moved; it suddenly all seemed to be happening a long way away. When she shut her eyes the world spun, and she saw Davy's pale face, just as she'd last seen it; she heard his mumbled words: 'Stay with you.' She should have kept him with her but she'd left him, and now the best she could hope was that he was lost somewhere, with strangers or all alone. She'd thrown him his first ever birthday party the year before, with a Victoria sponge cake with jam in the middle, and presents of a yo-yo and a bag of sherbet. He'd been astonished, thrilled, even though she couldn't quite make him understand what it was all for. In about six weeks' time he would have been seven, and she'd wanted to get him a catapult to deter his classmates from bullying him. The thought that he might have had his one and only birthday celebration caused a physical pain that shocked her. She wrapped her arms around her ribs, unable to pinpoint where it was in her body. It was everywhere.

Susan Elliot slapped the palm of her hand down on the table where Frances was sitting, making it shudder on its rickety legs. A teacup wobbled. Frances looked up at her miserably.

'Have we any aspirin?' she asked. 'My head's splitting.'

'What do you mean you're not coming? You *are* coming. It'll be getting dark soon, and they'll be back! You go upstairs *right* now and put together some things, and then we're setting off.' Susan drew in a sharp breath through her nostrils, watching for her daughter's reaction. Frances sighed, and got up. She was taller than her mother, and broader. They had never looked alike. Her mother's hair and nails were always tidy, and she never left the house without lipstick on. 'Go on, Frances,' she said.

'How can I just go off when Davy's out there, all by himself?'

'You don't *know* he's gone anywhere! He's... he's most likely *dead*, Frances. This is... it's what's *happened*. People are dead!'

'But he isn't! I mean... there's a fair chance he isn't. And he's likely to come home, isn't he, if he's lost somewhere? He'll try to come home, and find me.'

'I know you want to think he might, Frances, but he's *gone*. And in any case, he's not *yours*! This isn't his home, and he's not your boy, is he?'

'What does that matter, Mum? I was supposed to be looking after him! And if I had been, he wouldn't be lost now. I've promised Carys I'll find him.'

'Well, perhaps you shouldn't have. And he's not mine to worry about, Frances, *you* are. You were barely with it when those kind people brought you back just now! Now, go upstairs and get your things. I've packed your brother's letters, and all the other papers. You just need clothes and your hairbrush and the like. And you'll want a book to read, no doubt.' Susan stood and straightened the chairs, pushing them tight beneath the table, refusing to look at her daughter.

'Mum, please. I *can't* go.'

Frances pictured the bombs and madness of the night before, the fires and the deafening noise. The thought of it all happening again was terrifying; the oncoming night was like something creeping up on her in a childhood nightmare, and the urge to run for safety was powerful, but Frances knew she wouldn't be able live with herself if she did. She got up and went to the foot of the stairs, which were littered with the remains of the stairwell ceiling. Plaster and powder and splinters of lath. 'I'll pack my things and go and stay with Pam tonight,' she said. 'Then I can keep checking the places Davy might be. Once I've found him, I'll come out to South Stoke.' In the kitchen, her mother's silence rang.

As she left the house later, Frances halted at the top of the front steps. A stream of people were walking up Holloway in silence. They carried their children on their hips, and suitcases, bundles of clothing and blankets; some were struggling to push loaded prams and handcarts up the hill. Old and young, men and women, slack faces and unbrushed hair. A strange, quiet procession of the scared and dispossessed, trudging out of the city. It was an eerie sight, and as Frances walked down Holloway she was the only one going against the flow. On Calton Road she passed a huge bomb crater in which a group of people were cooking a makeshift Sunday roast. Their frantic jollity looked, to Frances, a bit mad. Two women were peeling potatoes into a pan over a brazier, while children explored the ruins and an old woman turned a charred rabbit on an improvised spit. A Sally Army trolley was doling out cups of stewed tea, and everyone was smiling, up to their knees in the remains of their homes.

'Jerry'll not see us downhearted,' a man was telling a reporter. 'Hitler'll learn, Bath folk's made of sterner stuff.' He had a crust of dried spit and ash in the corners of his mouth, and his eyes weren't quite focused. Frances wondered what would happen when all this strangeness and fear and odd elation passed, and it was just another weary slog of a day for people who had lost every last thing they possessed. She wondered how things could ever be put right.

Pam lived in a cottage called Woodlands, which was dug into the side of Beechen Cliff, above Alexandra Road. There was no road to it, just a steep flight of stone steps covered in moss and campanula, and it gazed northwards over the smoking expanse of Bath. The blackened shell of St Andrew's church, over a mile away on Julian Road, was clearly visible. Woodlands was a double-fronted house, more spacious than many, with a steep, terraced front garden where Pam grew vegetables and towering sunflowers. She had lived there alone since her friend Cecily had died, on New Year's Day in 1930. Cecily simply didn't wake up that morning, staying cold and peaceful on her pillows with Pam beside her, dumbstruck by grief. Woodlands had been Cecily's, and now it was Pam's, and she was very selective about with whom she would share it. She got by with the little money Cecily had left her, and by working four shifts a week in Woolworth's, selling goldfish, toffees, and bobby pins to Bath's schoolgirls.

There were plants on every window sill inside Woodlands – African violets, waxy begonias, peppery geraniums. Dead flies lay scattered between the pots. The tongue-and-groove wainscoting was painted in shades of green and grey. Frances followed Dog's clicking toenails across the parquet of the sitting room and into the kitchen. It was a room she'd always loved, with quarry tiles on the floor, a deep sink with a brass tap that dripped, a coal-fired stove, and wall lamps with fluted glass shades. Frances had sat for countless teas at the scrubbed wooden table over the years – gorging herself on whatever Pam had baked. Currant buns, or coconut macaroons, or cheese scones, always with real butter instead of margarine, except now because of the war. She'd often taken Wyn with her, who'd reacted with awestruck delight every time. Wyn had always been hungry. One summer's day she literally ate herself sick there – Frances remembered the rhubarb being high, and the buddleia alive with red admirals, as Wyn threw up in the privy.

Pam was out in the narrow backyard, wrestling with one of the tall poles between which her radio aerial was strung. It had sagged to one side, and Frances dropped her bag by the door to go and help.

'Can't get the bugger in deep enough,' Pam muttered.

'Let me have a go.' Frances gripped the pole, leant her weight on it and felt it sink.

'That's the ticket, well done.'

'I've come to stay, Pam. If that's all right?'

'Course it is. Did she calm down? Your mum?' said Pam. Frances shook her head, brushing off her hands. 'Well, it's hard on her, but I don't blame you for staying put. Come on, let's get the kettle on. It's been a while since I had a house guest, but I remember it's supposed to start with tea.'

They sat on a bench on the front terrace to drink their tea, as the sun began to drop, blooming gold through the drifting smoke. High above them the sky was a clear green-blue. Frances stared down into the twisting streets. It was impossible to follow a specific one, there were too many of them; too many buildings, on too many different levels. How would she ever find one small boy, in all of that? How could she even begin? In just a couple of hours' time he was due his phenobarbital, and she had no idea how quickly the effects of him missing a dose might manifest. She felt impatient, desperate to act. Carys had sent her away before there'd been any mention of an organised search for Davy, but she assumed they would be looking, too – Carys and Mrs Hughes, and young Fred. Looking, and no doubt feeling the same despair that she was.

'Do you think they'll be back again? The bombers, I mean,' she said. Pam shrugged, turning her unlovely face to the sky, where the light softened it.

'They know where we are now, and so much for the black-out. And they know we've no defences. Miserable bastards.' She studied Frances for a moment. 'It all seems so ridiculous, doesn't it? I know I should take it very seriously, but how can I when all I want to do is knock their heads together? All these bloody men. What will you do? Can I convince you to stay here with me, and come down into the cellar?'

'No. I should be out looking now, I know I should, but . . . I don't know where to start. And I think he's more likely to come and find me, isn't he? He'll make his way home, or to our house. I'm sure of it.' Frances let herself believe it; she let herself imagine him safe and well, just for a moment. A brief respite from the fear.

'Yes, possibly,' said Pam, sounding unconvinced. She took a deep breath and let it out slowly. 'Strange little lad, that Davy Noyle. He always made me think of a story I was told as a child, of a changeling. Half human, half woodland creature or fairy, or something like that. And such a tiny scrap of a thing.' She patted her lap, and Dog hopped up onto it.

'He's strange enough to have run away somewhere, and got lost,' said Frances, quietly, thinking that Davy had never seen a woodland until the first time she took him up Smallcombe Vale. 'He'll make his way back. I just need to make sure he can find me.'

'So you'll go back down to Holloway?' said Pam, and Frances nodded. 'And if the bombers do come back? You'll come back here, or go into the cellar at your parents' house? I'm going to need your word on it, Frances. If you're blown to bits they'll hold me to blame.'

'Of course they—'

'They will hold me to blame, and I'll hold myself to blame as well. You can stay here for as long as you like, but if the sirens go off, you get yourself to a safe place. The last thing I need is a *real* reason for Susan to scold me for the rest of my life. Do you promise?'

'I promise.'

They had a supper of corned beef sandwiches, and shared a bottle of beer, then Frances borrowed some matches from her aunt and dug a torch out of the cupboard under the stairs. The batteries were nearly flat so she stuck them in the oven to revive them, and went to change into warmer clothes. Her stomach was uneasy, full of butterflies. She left Pam fiddling with the dial of her wireless as *It's That Man Again* disappeared into static, but at least she'd have an early warning if the planes did come back. Her set was one of the 'magic eye' kind, and whenever aircraft approached the needle went wild, jerking to and fro. Frances went back down the steep steps to Alexandra Road, and along to where Calton Road joined Holloway, feeling better for doing something, for moving, for acting.

The lilacs were still in blossom; pigeons still roosted on rooftops, feathers puffed out. There was no sign of the group who'd been making Sunday dinner in the ruins; they'd vanished completely, leaving a deep hush in their wake. Frances wondered if everybody had gone – if she had the city to herself. A huge wave of loneliness engulfed her at the thought of being left behind to face the danger and her own terrible mistake all by herself. But then a door slammed and Frances heard a baby crying. A Home Guard officer strode past her, showing no sign of noticing her. Plenty of people had stayed behind, in fact, and were now holding their collective breath, hoping to escape whatever was coming. Frances's heart was beating too hard, and she found that she was holding her breath, too.

'You get yourself home, love. Sharpish like,' said a special constable, as he passed.

'I am home,' she told him.

Frances went around to the back of her parents' house first of all, thinking of the time she'd found Davy tucked away in the privy one morning after a night of heavy rain. Carys hadn't come home, and he'd had nothing to eat, so he'd come to find Frances. Life had already taught him to expect to be shut out, forgotten about, and the unfairness of that had enraged Frances. There was no sign of him in the backyard this time, though, so she went indoors. The house was gloomy inside, nearly dark, so she lit the gas lamp in the lean-to, and carried it into the kitchen. There was nothing to see at first, and as she paused to listen, nothing but silence. But then she noticed that the floor-level doors of the dresser were ajar, and the biscuit tin was down from the shelf, and empty. She caught her breath. 'Davy? Davy!' she called, her heart surging up. She ran into each of their four rooms, checking behind every door and under all the beds, but didn't find him. Back in the kitchen she crouched down and angled the light until she could make out shapes and marks in the dust on the floor. They were so disordered it was hard to say who or what had made them, or when. But over by the abandoned biscuit tin there was a scuff on the cupboard door, as though someone had kicked it, or climbed up, and on the floor below was a single small, perfect footprint. Frances stared at it, and she smiled. He was alive – he had made it out of the Landys' place, and come looking for her. Relief made her dizzy for a moment.

But even if Davy had been there, he wasn't there any longer. Frances turned out the lamp and hurried away, unnerved by the silent emptiness of the house. She carried on up Holloway, eyes darting eagerly into every shadow, certain that she would see him at any moment. She pictured him sitting on the front steps of the Landys' house – steps that now led nowhere – with his chin on his knees, looking up as she approached. Or perhaps perched on the window sill of the plumber's shop opposite, staring, bewildered, at the ruins. Far too small for his age, dressed in threadbare trousers and hand-me-down boots without laces, watching the world with eyes as grey and lustrous as wet stone. Hope made these imaginings as clear as day; Frances convinced herself, utterly, that she *would* see him. So when she reached the ruins of Springfield Place and he wasn't there after all, she was crushed. Tears flooded her eyes but she rubbed them away. He was alive; he hadn't died with the Landys, she had proof of it. So she *would* find him. She checked all around, scraping her shins as she picked through the rubble, calling for him, over and over. Then she sat herself down on the plumber's window sill to begin her vigil. The plumber had pinned a hastily scribbled sign on his door. *Got a leaking pipe? Form an orderly queue!*

Frances tried to keep watching, but she'd barely slept for thirty-six hours, and fatigue ached behind her eyes. She drifted into sketchy sleep for a while, with her head tipped back against a broken shutter and her shoulder wedged into the embrasure. Her dreams were hurried and disjointed, and when the air raid siren woke her she was stiff and cold, and uncertain where she was. It was pitch dark, and she realised she'd forgotten to bring Pam's torch – she'd left the batteries in the oven, where Pam would find them when the stink of melting tar filled the house. She stood up, cursing herself. Fear sank heavily into the pit of her stomach. It was one thing to walk blindly in the dark when she would have known the way blindfolded, quite another to do it when there was rubble and craters and broken glass everywhere. And a little boy, still lost, who knew only too well how to blend into shadow.

'Christ,' Frances swore, trying to think clearly as her fear mounted and she started to shake. She could hear the planes already, getting louder – they'd almost beaten the sirens.

'Davy! Are you there?' she called, crossing to the ruins on unsteady legs. 'Come along, Davy – it's all right,' she said, but there was no reply. The sky began to buzz, the ground vibrated; the stars above vanished as flares bloomed, and then she saw the deeper black of the planes, swooping down towards the river. They moved so smoothly; as quick and sure as birds.

Seconds later the explosions began, seeming louder than before, closer; none the less terrifying for being expected. Panic grabbed Frances and she ran down Holloway, thinking to keep her promise to Pam, but a wall of sound and burning air cut her off – a huge wave, knocking her off her feet and sending her sprawling to the ground. She lay winded and bewildered for a moment, as fire blossomed somewhere to her left; she felt its heat and light on her face and for a second she was grateful to be able to see. Then bullets began to pepper the road, shattering roof tiles and hitting the stone slabs of the pavement with a zinging, popping sound, until the din of a plane drowned them out, roaring in Frances's head. Scrambling up, electrified by fear, she turned and ran back up Holloway. A spectral echo of the flames danced across her vision, confusing her; she felt chips of stone fly up and cut her legs, and waited to feel a bullet hit her in the back.

'Over here, love! Come on, quick!' a man's voice shouted. Frances ran towards him and hands reached for her, pulling her into the shadow of a large doorway. 'Hang on!' the man said. She felt bodies close around her, more people sheltering there. She smelled their breath, laden with cigarettes and fear, and felt the rough fabric of army uniforms. For a while they stood in silence, and Frances tried to catch her breath, to steady her heart. Then the ground heaved, and her ears popped; there was a shower of earth and debris, and a man grunted, loosening his grip on her. Another toppled sideways without a sound, and the smell of blood joined all the others.

'Fuck!' someone cried, his voice shaking. 'Jesus fucking Christ!' Frances stayed where she was, not knowing whether she could have moved if she'd wanted to. Her body felt numb, wooden. She pressed her back hard against the door and shut her eyes, and the hours crept slowly by, seeming to take an eternity. She tried to picture herself a hundred miles away, in another place altogether.

In the morning, Frances sat in the kitchen at Woodlands and tried to stop shivering. She had the same feeling of disconnection as after the first night, the same sense that her head was not quite attached to her body, made worse by the muffled ringing in her ears. She was adrift in unreality, unable to get back to herself. There were small, stinging shrapnel cuts up her legs to the thigh. Pam put yet another cup of tea down beside her.

'Were you *trying* to get hurt? Is that it? Trying to ... to punish yourself for leaving Davy with the Landys?' she said.

'I don't know. No,' said Frances. 'I just fell asleep waiting for him to appear, and then ... then there wasn't time ...'

'Rubbish,' Pam muttered. Fresh fires were burning all over the city; the stink of smoke and ash was worse than ever, and every few minutes came the rumble of a building being pulled down, or coming down of its own accord. Woodlands hadn't lost a single roof tile. Frances felt a wheeze in her lungs, and she coughed. She was deafened, yet every small sound made her flinch. 'I don't know what to say to you, Frances. Thank God you're all right.' Pam sighed again. 'I wish to God Cecily was here. She'd know what to say,' she said.

'I hope ... I hope Mum and Dad are all right,' said Frances.

'So do I.' Pam looked worried. 'My brother's got good sense. He'll have found a safe place; and your mum's a long way out of it. I'm sure we don't need to worry too much. I'm sure Derek will send word soon.'

Frances took a sip of tea that tasted of dust. Everything tasted of dust.

'The men I was with... they were from the Gloucester Regiment,' she said. 'They only got here yesterday, to help out after Saturday night. The one who died, he... he...' Frances shook her head. She wondered if the dead man had been the one who'd spotted her, called her over and pulled her into the doorway of Magdalen Chapel, where he'd been sheltering with two comrades. He had probably saved her life. The blast up in Magdalen Gardens had sent debris from the previous night flying. She hadn't been harmed, and neither had one of the trio of soldiers. Another had sustained a minor injury, but the dead man's head had been severed clean away. Frances was confounded by that. It seemed ludicrous that fate could point the finger that way, at some but not at others. The sight of his body slumped on the pavement, as the sun rose, was one she would never, ever forget – he'd lain in a nimbus of clotted blood, sticky and dark. Frances hadn't known a human body could hold so much blood. She'd squeezed the shoulder of the uninjured man when he started to cry, and realised that she was at least a decade older than him. At least a decade older than the dead boy, too. She'd felt old, and tired, and frightened to realise that the fate of the country – of the world – was in the hands of children. 'But Davy's alive – he'd been at our house, looking for me, and for food.'

'Can you really be sure it was him, Frances? All sorts of looting has been going on...'

'This wasn't looting; a child had been in and looked in the cupboards for food. Nothing else had been touched, or moved. It was him, Pam, I *know* it was. But... all those bombs... I'll go round the hospitals this morning. And the rest centres.'

'The hospitals will be chaos.'

'I know. Could I have a bath, do you think?' said Frances.

'Course. Good idea,' said Pam.

They stood up and then paused, exchanging a look when they heard heavy, hurried footsteps coming up the path, and the sound of a man trying to catch his breath. Dog growled.

'Oh,' said Pam, reaching out to grasp Frances's hand. 'Is that Derek? It could be Derek.'

'Well, it can't be bad news. Not that quickly,' said Frances, wishing she was sure about that. The footsteps ended with a hurried knocking at the back door.

'Come in, for goodness' sake, whoever you are,' Pam called. A tall man took a few uneven steps into the kitchen. He was rangy, not yet forty, dark-haired and unshaven, with a long, crooked nose and tired blue eyes. Sweat had made rings under the arms of his shirt, and he was filthy with dust and smuts. Frances knew him at once – Owen Hughes, Wyn's and Carys's brother. The air in her lungs seemed to swell at the sight of him.

'I'm looking for Frances,' he said, fighting for breath, chest heaving like bellows. 'Is she here?' Frances stepped into his line of sight, and dismissed the brief notion that he might have brought news of Davy. She suddenly felt very, very calm. The kind of calm that came before a violent storm.

'I'm here,' she said, seeing two people at once, standing there in Pam's kitchen – a grown man, and the lanky boy he'd been when she'd first known him. Owen steadied himself; he took a breath but didn't speak at once, and Frances's heart beat harder, until it almost hurt. Somehow, she knew exactly why he'd come. She'd been waiting for it for years and years.

'We've found her, Frances,' he said, without blinking. 'We've found Wyn.'

1915

The first time she ever saw Bronwyn Hughes, Frances had just turned six, which Wyn wouldn't for another five months. Frances had been concentrating on scrunching up her toes inside her boots, as tightly as the space allowed, then stretching them out again. They itched and ached as she did it, and it was a bit like pressing on a bruise – painful but also irresistible. Her mother said the scrunching would help her not to get chilblains, but by the end of the day her toes would be burning red, and would throb horribly when she was made to sit with them in Epsom salts for twenty minutes before tea. The schoolroom had a coal burner and a couple of big radiators that ticked and hissed but gave off little heat; Frances's feet got frozen on the short walk from home to school, and stayed frozen all day as her shoes leached damp into her stockings. She was supposed to go directly to school in the mornings, and directly home again at the end of the day, but she liked to take a meandering route and peer at the broken cobwebs between the railings, swinging with drops of water. She marvelled at how the crust of ice on a puddle could be so thin it was thinner than the thinnest glass, and perfectly clear no matter how dirty the puddle; and the way the jackdaws along the rooftops puffed out their feathers, and gave off tiny belches of steam when they cawed.

The schoolroom smelled strongly of wet wool, wet hair and wet wood. Their teacher, Miss Bertram, wore a thick felt jacket with a scarf wound round and round her neck. She sucked Formamint throat lozenges that made her breath smell like pickling liquid, and had chapped cheeks and a drip at the end of her nose that she blotted at continually – with her cuff when her handkerchief was sodden. She was a kind but slightly watery teacher. Her fiancé was on the Western Front, Frances's mother had told her. Frances knew that was to do with the war, and pictured the Western Front as a big ship, full of all the brothers and cousins and fiancés who had disappeared from Bath's streets. She knew boats were dangerous; she knew they could sink. And some of the men who came back to be treated in Bath's hospitals hardly had any faces left at all – they went out for walks, sometimes, in their bright blue suits – so Frances didn't blame Miss Bertram for being weepy about it. She wouldn't have wanted to marry a man with no face either.

Frances sat at the end of a row, quite near the tall windows that reached right up to the ceiling. Her wooden desk was smooth from years of being leaned across, and blotched with ink here and there. When it was arithmetic, which Frances hated, she began to see shapes in the blotches: a whale, a paw print, a dog with pointed ears and a very small body. She knew she ought to pay attention, because the horror of being asked to go up and solve the sum on the board was a constant threat, but it was difficult because she often didn't realise she wasn't paying attention until it was pointed out to her. So she was scrunching her toes and staring at a duck on her desk, which even had some pencil shavings for feet, when there was a knock at the door and a tiny blonde girl entered, wearing clothes far too big for her and boots that wouldn't stay on her feet, the heels scuffing along the floor.

'Ah, yes. Girls, this is Bronwyn Hughes, who has come to join us. Let's all bid her a good morning, shall we?' said Miss Bertram.

'Good morning, Bronwyn,' twenty-four girls' voices chimed

obediently, dragging out the 'morning', hesitating slightly over the unfamiliar name.

Frances looked at the newcomer's long, fair hair, her grey eyes and protruding upper lip, and guessed that even though she was smaller than the rest of them, she wasn't that much younger. There was something knowing and confident in her face that made her look older, in fact. She didn't flinch, or hang back, or look at the floor, as Frances would have done in front of that many curious strangers. Bronwyn's eyes swept the room, sizing up her new classmates. When Miss Bertram touched her on the shoulder and suggested she take the empty desk towards the back, Bronwyn gave her a smile that revealed her upper teeth poking out over the lower. She looked a bit goofy, but somehow it didn't make her any less pretty. Then Bronwyn looked directly at Frances, and caught Frances studying her. Frances looked away hurriedly, and fiddled with the dog-eared corner of her copybook. She wished she could be bold, like the new girl. Bold and pretty, and small, instead of shy and too tall. Bronwyn marched to her new desk with a quick, peculiar gait, as though she might break into a run at any moment.

In the yard at lunchtime, where the frost had all melted and the girls were reassembling after going home to eat, Bronwyn began to make new friends.

'Everyone calls me Wyn, by the way,' she said, as though it ought to have been obvious. There was no question of her being teased or interrogated by the bigger girls, as any other new starter might have been; she was far too assured. She asked the questions, in fact – demanding to know how strict Miss Bertram was, and whether she used the cane or the slipper, and how often; boasting that she'd been caned three times at her old school, for various daring acts of rebellion, and that she'd had to move schools when her dad had got into a fight with the headmaster. Frances expected to be overlooked. The shy girls usually were — they huddled together at the edge of things, safe in numbers and happy to watch without the pressure of joining in. But as the bell was rung for them to go back inside, Wyn marched over to Frances, and looked up. Frances was a good head taller, and her wrists, ankles and knees were twice the circumference of the new girl's.

'Why are you so tall?' said Wyn. There was no aggression in the question, particularly, just a frank demand for information. Up close, Frances saw that the corners of Wyn's mouth were cracked and sore, her fingernails were bitten right off, and blue veins showed through the white skin at her temples.

'I don't know,' she replied, nervously.

'Have you always drunk the cabbage water? My mum says I have to drink it to make me grow, but it tastes like farts, so I won't. Do you drink it, though?'

'No,' Frances lied. Her mother regularly made her and her brother Keith drink the water in which she'd cooked their vegetables, cooled and strained. Frances shut her eyes and gulped it down, but she wasn't going to admit that when Wyn had just said it tasted like farts.

'You're shy, aren't you? I knew a shy girl in my last school. She was called Betty, and she used to cry when she had to stand up and do her reading. Is that what you do?'

'No,' said Frances, though she'd felt close to tears many times. Never with reading though.

'Good. I always thought it was so silly when she cried over *that*.' Wyn studied her for a bit longer, then shrugged one skinny shoulder and moved on. And for the rest of the day Frances had the uncertain but pleasing feeling of having been measured in some way, and found not completely wanting.

2

Monday

One Day After the Bombings

Wyn was lying face down with her head turned to one side and tipped back. She didn't look comfortable, and Frances fought the urge to settle her into a better position.

'But you can't know it's her,' Carys was saying to her mother. Nora Hughes was sitting on a broken wall nearby with her hands clasped together, shaking her white face side to side. Frances stared at Carys and thought how absurd that statement was. Of course it was Wyn. She was just the same size she'd been when Frances last saw her; skin and bone in life, now simply bone. Fragile little bones the same colour as the masonry and dust all around her – a set of pale sticks, she seemed, her head looking far too big for her now. Her face gave Frances a strange ache in her knees, as though she were about to fall. There was her slight overbite, her splayed front teeth with the gap in between them. Deep black pits where her eyes should have been. There were scraps of fabric around her ribs, and her fingers were curled into fists; the long, golden fall of her hair had been reduced to a few colourless strands, and she was still wearing one cracked leather shoe.

Twenty-four years before, the shoe's partner had been found in the dank yard behind the leper hospital, and Frances wondered what had happened to it. Perhaps Mrs Hughes had kept it, or the police. The pair could be reunited now, if so. 'There's no way of saying it's her,' Carys said again. 'Not for sure.'

'Shut up,' said Frances, before she knew she was going to speak. Her voice was a whisper. She looked over at them. 'Just bloody well shut up,' she said, louder. Carys shot her a startled, hostile look, and Nora met Frances's eye for a moment. Grief had aged her; she wore her life's hardships on her face, and the look in her eyes told Frances that she recognised the small corpse as readily as Frances did. Frances took a breath and glanced around. The Hughes' house was still standing, as was Carys's – just about – but their neighbours' had been obliterated in the night; the crater Wyn lay beside was somewhere in the backyard, but it was hard to pinpoint the exact spot because nothing in the wasteland looked right any more. 'Of course it's her,' said Frances. 'Of course it is.'

'Don't you to talk to *me* like that!' said Carys. 'Why are you even here? You've no business being here. You should be out looking for my boy!'

Frances absorbed the words like blows. Even if it was true, she couldn't go. She had to see Wyn. Stumbling, she went closer to the skeleton, arms out for balance. She was sure the ground was moving; she felt like she was walking on a crust of flotsam, over deep water far from land. It was hard to look at Wyn's bones, but impossible not to look. The blast that had levelled so much of Beechen Cliff Place had scoured away the contents of the shared backyard – all the sheds and the washhouse and privies. A bicycle saddle stood proud of the mess, but there was no way of knowing if the rest of the bike was buried beneath it, or simply gone. Yet Wyn's bones weren't disarranged – each one was in its proper place. They hadn't been lifted or moved by the blast, they'd simply been unearthed. This was where she had been all along. All the long, long time they'd looked for her, and in all the far and unlikely places, and here she had been all the time. At home.

Owen was standing over his sister's remains with his arms

folded and his long legs apart, and Frances went to stand beside him. The years had carved slight hollows into his cheeks, and drawn lines across his forehead. Precious few laughter lines, Frances noticed, but a vertical line between his brows that gave him a perplexed, almost wounded expression. His stance was ready for some kind of action but his face was blank, his eyes undecided. He glanced at Frances as she reached his side, and took a breath as if to speak. Frances felt the stress radiating from him, a slight tremor, like an animal tensed for flight. It was as close as she had been to him in a long time, and she could feel his nearness without turning to look – the air he displaced, the slight change in sound.

'Thank you for coming to get me,' she said.

'I thought you'd want to know.'

'What should we do?' She wasn't sure why she asked; she didn't expect him to know. Owen shook his head.

'I've no clue,' he said. 'Got a smoke?' Frances passed him one, taking one for herself too, but then couldn't find the matches she'd borrowed from Pam. Owen shrugged and put the cigarette into his shirt pocket. 'I mean, we knew she was dead. All but Mum, of course.' He took a deep breath and shook his head again. 'We all knew. But... We can give her a funeral now, I suppose. But now? With all of this going on?' He waved a hand around at the destruction. 'They're not going to want her at the funeral home, are they? They've enough on their plates. So... what the hell are we supposed to do?'

'Has somebody told the police?'

'What do you expect the police to do?'

'I don't know,' said Frances. 'But don't you think we should?' She glanced at Owen's profile, seeing a little grey appearing in his dark hair. The breeze pushed it into his eyes and he brushed it away, and didn't turn to look at her. After a while it seemed that he deliberately wouldn't, or couldn't. Frances wanted to ask him more, but she couldn't think what, exactly. It had been months since she'd had the chance to speak to him, but her mind emptied of words. She had the growing feeling that something was very, very wrong.

The sun shone down on them from a pretty spring sky. People picked their way through the ruins all around, trying to salvage personal possessions, reminding Frances of seagulls sifting through the high-tide line. In due course, a tired-looking policeman did arrive. He spoke to Nora Hughes while she stared blankly ahead; there was no sign of Bill Hughes, Wyn's father, or of Carys's husband, Clive – but then, there hardly ever was. Frances watched but couldn't overhear, and in the end two elderly men turned up, and one of them took some photographs of Wyn's bones as the other began to unfold a large piece of canvas next to her. Frances thought they were going to cover her, but then the one with the camera crouched down by her feet, while the other man went to her head, and Frances realised.

'You can't just take her!' she shouted. The men jumped like they'd been caught thieving.

'Now then, madam, try not to upset yourself,' said the policeman, stepping forward and looking relieved to revert to a script he knew.

'Mrs Hughes – tell them! You can't just move her – look, the bomb hasn't thrown her about, it's only uncovered her! This is where she's been all along! Right *here*!'

'What are you saying, Frances?' said Nora, shaking her head. 'Let them take her ... my poor Wynnie ... my poor girl. Let her come inside at last.'

'But ... isn't it evidence? Where she's been found, I mean? Isn't it important?'

'Important?' said Mrs Hughes. 'She's *dead*, Frances! She's

been . . . she's been dead all these years, when I so hoped . . . I *so* hoped someone had snatched her, see, and she was growing up somewhere else . . .' Nora's face sagged, and she staggered against the policeman with an awful moan, pressing her fingers into her chest, over her heart.

'Come here, Mum,' said Owen, going to her side and wrapping an arm around her.

'We can hardly leave the . . . the child out here. That's hardly decent, is it?' said the policeman. 'And if the bombers come back tonight she might be lost all over again, mightn't she?' He nodded to the elderly men, and they began, gingerly, to inch their fingers beneath Wyn's bones, ready to lift her.

Frances shut her eyes, sure that her friend would come apart in their hands – her head from her neck; hands from her wrists; legs from her hips. Thoughts swarmed in on her, crowding each other out, and panic began to build. She felt she had seconds left to do the right thing, to say the right thing, before something crucial was lost again, forever.

'Wait! Please wait!' she cried, stumbling back to where the men were crouching. She stood beside Wyn and looked to the north, at the back of what remained of Beechen Cliff Place. Then she turned through one hundred and eighty degrees to look south, at the steep rise of Beechen Cliff. The view – the angle from which she was looking at it – was familiar to her. 'Please take some photos of where she is before you move her. Please. North, south, east and west. So we can say exactly where she was buried. Please!' she begged the man with the camera. He glanced at the policeman, who gave a reluctant nod, then did as she asked.

When he'd finished, they moved Wyn onto the canvas. Her skeleton hung together, making small, alarming shifts here and there. The men lifted it with little effort, as though it weighed less than bird bones. As they were about to cover her over, Frances held out her hand. She felt unsteady, and short of breath. The breeze was gentle enough, but she felt it might blow her off balance. She looked down and saw Wyn's quick grey eyes, and the flash of her grin, and the way her hair would trail behind her when she moved; then that lovely ghost faded, and Frances saw the cable-knit pattern in the colourless remnants of her cardigan, still clinging to her ribs. She remembered the cardigan exactly – it had been mustard yellow. Wyn had always worn it, with her daffodil brooch pinned to it. She'd been stuck in that outfit, and in that day – in that *very* day – for over twenty years, but now there she was at Frances's feet, and Frances realised it would be the very last time she ever saw her best friend.

She reached out and touched Wyn's hand. Tiny finger bones, tapering at the ends; the bones of her palms and wrist, still held together with some substance stronger than mere memory. Gently, Frances put her index finger beneath Wyn's curled fingers, where her warm, grubby palm would have been. Through tears she saw how huge her own finger was in comparison, how fleshy and worn, how aged. Even when they were children, Frances's had been bigger – Wyn had had the kind of fingers that could pick locks. Frances thought of all the years she herself had lived but Wyn had missed out on; all the things she had touched and felt and done with her hands, when Wyn had done nothing, and felt nothing; *there* was the injustice she couldn't bear – the terrible, furious unfairness of it all.

'I'm sorry, Wyn. Forgive me,' she whispered, the words unbidden, speaking themselves.

'Come along now, missus,' said one of the men, stiffly. He began to fold the cloth over the bones, and in her final glimpse Frances saw the black empty eye sockets again, and the gap between the upper incisors. The newly grown adult teeth Wyn had been so proud of. Frances sat down where she was. The breeze cooled the tears on her face, and she had no idea what to do – she simply sat there as they took Wyn away, until Owen pulled her to her feet a short while later.

The policeman was talking to a reporter as they passed.

'This discovery concludes a very old case, and solves a mystery that has haunted our city. I'm sure many Bath residents will remember the search for little Bronwyn Hughes; some may even have joined in the search for her. This is a sorry end to the story, but perhaps it is one that will bring her family some peace at last.'

'Yes, indeed,' said the reporter, nodding, scribbling fast. 'And was the child's place of residence not searched by the police at the time of her disappearance?'

'Of course it was.' The officer sounded affronted. 'No stone was left unturned, I can assure you.'

'What?' said Frances, interrupting them. The memory of a shaded place flickered behind her eyes; lines of sunlight streaming in through cracks, a smell of wet stone and rotting wood. She blinked, trying to focus. 'What did you just say?' she said. The reporter glanced up at her, his look quick, calm, calculating. '"No stone was left unturned",' he quoted from his notes. 'Do you remember the case, madam? Would you like to comment?'

'Yes,' said Frances, vaguely. The damp place receded, back to the furthest part of her mind. Her memory of that summer was like black water into which some things had sunk without trace, whilst others floated near the top, startlingly bright and clear. The surface of the water was flat, glossy, hard to see past, and the deeper she tried to look, the darker and more distorted things became. But the policeman's choice of words had caused a furtive ripple of movement. 'Yes, I remember her,' she said.

'Have you any comment on finding her after all this time?' said the reporter. 'And with the help of a German bomb, too — isn't that a bitter irony, of a sort?'

'She was at home this whole time,' said Frances.

'What are you telling him?' Carys interrupted them. 'You don't need to be talking about us to strangers.' She appeared beside Frances, glaring at her, then turned hard eyes on the two men. 'Why don't the pair of you just clear off? I've just put Mum to bed — she's been near enough finished off by all this. My house's got no roof on it, I've one boy missing and one to find a bed for tonight. I've no time to stand around talking, and there's nothing to say about it anyway. We've found my sister and now we can bury her. That's that.'

'You're Bronwyn Hughes's sister? And your name, if I may?' The reporter hovered his pencil.

'Clear off!' Carys repeated, setting her jaw.

'Steady on, Carys,' said Owen. 'They've a job to do, after all.'

'Well, haven't we all?'

'Carys Hughes, is it?' said the reporter.

'No, it bloody well isn't!'

'She was in her own backyard,' said Frances, so quietly that Carys didn't seem to hear her. 'We looked everywhere for her. We looked everywhere. And she was in her *own backyard*.'

'The last place anybody expected her to be, I suppose,' said the reporter. 'So perhaps a good hiding place for the villain to choose.'

'But . . . don't you see?' said Frances.

'It's nothing to do with *you*,' said Carys, stabbing a finger into Frances's chest. 'You did enough at the time. Didn't you, Frances? Or little enough, I should say. And oughtn't you to be out looking for my boy instead of idling here, being no help to anyone?'

'What's this?' said Owen, looking at his sister, and then at Frances. 'What boy?'

'Davy,' Frances whispered, brokenly. 'I've lost Davy.'

'Frances,' said the reporter, smiling slightly. 'And your surname, if I may?'

'Come along,' said Owen, pulling at Frances's elbow and giving the reporter a level look. 'We've all had a shock.' Frances was staring into the depths inside her head, trying to see what it was she'd remembered.

'They got it wrong. We all got it wrong,' she said, her thoughts spinning. 'Oh, it was *all* wrong!' she cried, as Owen led her away.

He walked her back to Woodlands, and they sat at the kitchen table as he told Pam what had happened, what had been found. Frances was grateful to him; grateful not to have to talk. Outside, clouds filled the sky, stealthily turning the world flat.

'Of course you're upset,' said Pam, rubbing Frances's hand. 'Who wouldn't be? Last thing we need right now is the raking up of old pain.'

'It's not that,' said Frances. 'It's not just that ... Of course it was awful to see her like that. And of course it brought it all back. But for her to have been right there, all that time ...' She shook her head.

'What is it?' Pam asked. But Frances didn't answer at once. 'I meant to tell you,' Pam went on. 'Your dad dropped in for a quick cup of tea. He's fine; he spent the night in the shelter up by the Bear – not a scratch on him, though he's just about asleep on his feet.'

'Oh, thank God. And Mum?'

'Yes, he'd been out to check on her, and she's all right. Staying put for now.'

'Good. That's good.'

'What's this about Davy?' Owen asked. Frances glanced at him, her heart sinking. The shame was like a dark stain, spreading, consuming everything.

'I'll leave you two to talk,' said Pam, gently. 'It's time I took Dog out.' She reached for her coat as she left the house.

'I was meant to be looking after him, Owen,' said Frances. 'Carys dropped him with me in the afternoon, on Saturday. But I . . . I wanted to be alone. So when she didn't come to pick him up in the evening, I took him up to the Landys.'

She told him about the bomb at Springfield Cottages, the Landys' deaths, and that Davy – Owen's nephew – was nowhere to be found. Owen let out a long breath, his shoulders slumping. He rubbed one dusty hand across his eyes.

'Christ,' he muttered. 'Poor little blighter.'

'He wasn't killed though – I saw his footprints at my parents' house yesterday, and he'd taken some biscuits. I'm going to find him,' said Frances, vehemently.

'But he was out in the bombing last night? Somewhere close to home?'

'I . . . I don't know.'

'Carys didn't say a word to me about it.' Owen sounded too tired to be angry. 'How can you be sure it was him at your folks' place?'

'Who else could it have been? Who else would know exactly where to look for biscuits? I *saw* his footprints . . . If he'd . . . died . . . in the cellar with the Landys, we'd have found him. He got out, I'm certain of it, and I'll find him.'

'Frances—'

'Carys was so . . . she was so . . . She *cried*. I don't think I've ever seen her cry before.' Frances twisted the knife inside herself, letting it hurt. 'Did she even cry when Wyn disappeared? I can't remember.'

'Neither can I.' Owen frowned. He thought for a moment.

'Don't let her... don't let her make it all your fault, will you? She's always been good at that.'

'But it *is* all my fault.'

'Is she helping you look for him?'

'No. I mean... I'm sure she must be looking for him herself. Her and Fred. But not with me.'

'I was in and out of there all day, helping shore up Mum and Dad's place. She's been there all the time, not out searching. And she didn't say a word about Davy,' said Owen. Frances looked up at him incredulously.

'Well... she must have sent Fred, then,' she said. Owen said nothing. He frowned down at his hands on the table, where his long fingers were laced together, thumbs fidgeting uneasily. His shirt was torn and stained, more buttons missing than present, and Frances noticed that the edges of his braces were frayed.

'I'll help you,' he said. 'I've got to do some repairs on my place, but I'll help you look first. Poor little sod.'

'Thank you. Thank you, Owen.' Frances felt suddenly hopeful, and less alone. 'He's missing his pills, two doses now. He could have an episode, and get himself lost, or hurt...'

'He might not... not straight away.' Owen didn't sound as though he believed himself. 'I was glad when I heard you were mucking in with him. Looking after him a bit. It's good of you – I know my sister won't be paying you, whatever she might have said. I was happy you'd be looking out for him.'

'Well, I haven't turned out to be much good, have I? I've let him down. Terribly.' Frances hung her head, assaulted by the physical memory of Davy's ribs pushing against hers as he yawned, and the hot, heavy weight of his sleeping body in her lap. 'He didn't want to go to them,' she said, quietly. 'He wanted to stay with me. If *only* I'd been at home yesterday, when he came looking for food!'

'That's enough of that,' Owen said, keenly. 'You weren't to know what was going to happen, and torturing yourself won't help him one bit.'

'You sound like Pam.'

'Your aunt has always had her head screwed on.'

'Let me make you some tea.'

Once the tea was brewed, they took it outside, sitting on the bench in silence for a while. Frances was still so stunned by the sight of Wyn's bones that she was finding it hard to concentrate on the here and now. The pain of both losses – Wyn, and now Davy – was combining, sending her into confusion. She felt that there was something important, something frightening, just beyond her grasp, and even as she fought to see it clearly, she felt a gathering cloud of guilt. The realisation of a terrible, unforgivable betrayal.

'I can't get used to seeing all the mess they've made,' said Owen. 'All the flattened houses.'

'You know what it means, don't you?' said Frances. Owen's face fell.

'What?'

'Where she was found. Wyn ... where she was buried all this time. You understand what it means, don't you?' she said. Owen was silent. 'Please, say something.' Owen glanced down at her for a moment, and then away over the city's broken teeth. He didn't answer her, but she saw the pain in his eyes, and the stress in his clamped jaw; she saw that he was wrestling with something. Frances took a breath. 'Johannes didn't take her,' she said. 'It wasn't him! He ... he was made to pay for it, but he was innocent. They hanged the wrong person, and I ... I helped them!'

'You can't know that, Frances—'

'I can! I *do* know it. He never came outside, he was scared to. And he ... he never knew where she lived – how could he possibly have buried her there? Anyway, he wasn't like that – he wasn't capable of it.'

'There's no knowing what a man's capable of. It's too long ago now to—'

'Whoever killed her got away with it. They've got away with it all this time!' she said. 'And poor Johannes... Oh, *God*.' Owen turned to her then, staring intently, and she could see thoughts shifting behind his eyes.

'Listen, Frances, losing Wyn back then was *terrible*. What's happening now isn't much better. But, look – we can't know for sure what happened to her, and we can't do anything about it now. We *can't*, Frances. I know that finding her body ... brings it all back; but it's too late. But Davy ... we *can* do something about Davy. We can try to find him, and bring him home.'

'Yes.' Frances felt tears flood her eyes. She nodded. 'I have to find him.' Owen nodded, but she thought he looked uneasy.

'Drink up then, and let's get cracking.'

They spent the afternoon walking a long circuit around as many local rest centres as they could – in church halls and community centres and charitable institutions – asking after unaccompanied children who might meet Davy's description. After two nights of bombing there seemed no reason not to expect a third, and even more people were leaving the city. Everywhere they went they saw scenes of barely contained chaos – fraught, listless people; the walking wounded; children with filthy, streaked faces, crying with exhaustion or fast asleep, curled up under a table or a chair. But none of the children were by themselves, and none of them were Davy. Frances suffered the anguish of disappointment every time they moved on. In one place, a nurse wearing a long, grey habit peered at the cut on her head and told her it ought to have been stitched. She wouldn't let Frances leave until she'd washed it, and covered it with a strip of gauze. Owen waited with no sign of impatience, and Frances was glad of his company; glad of his steadiness and the quiet kindness he'd always had, even when they were little. Even when she was nothing to him but his little sister's shy friend, a person barely worth noticing. Later, as a teenager, she'd longed to be noticed by him, and for a while it had seemed that he did. Somehow, it had all gone wrong, yet even now, when they were both past thirty, she still noticed the lessening of her anxiety when he was around, the subtle easing of her heart.

As the afternoon wore on Owen suggested that they make their way back, and that Frances check at her parents' house one more time, just in case.

'You look done in. You're staying with Pam?' he said. Frances nodded. Exhaustion was dragging at her steps, and muddying her thoughts; partly due to the lack of sleep but also from the raising and crashing of her hopes in each place they'd been to. Owen's eyes were bloodshot.

'We should . . . do you think I should look in the . . . mortuary?' said Frances, the words unreal, terrible to say. 'After last night's bombing, I mean. In case he . . . I heard they were using the crypt of St Mark's for everyone they've found from Holloway.' She pictured the Landys there, perhaps lying next to the Hinckleys; abandoned in darkness, as cold as the stone underneath them. She thought of the soldier who'd died beside her at Magdalen Chapel, and the pool of his blood on Holloway, and she shivered. Owen didn't reply at once. They walked side by side back towards Beechen Cliff Place, where Owen was going to check on his mother before he headed home. He cleared his throat.

'I'll go, Frances,' he said, firmly. 'I'll go in the morning, and I'll go by myself. You're not coming with me. Do you hear?'

'Yes,' she said, grateful to him.

'I'll come and find you tomorrow. That's if we're both still around.' He smiled crookedly, just for a moment. 'Keep yourself safe.'

'Thank you, Owen. Thank you for helping me.' She was finding it a huge effort to speak.

'If he's out there to find, we'll find him.'

'But not tonight,' said Frances, so quietly that Owen didn't seem to hear her. That night Davy would have to fend for himself again, wherever he was. Frances shut her eyes and saw his face, with its strange tranquillity, its soft edges and diffuse gaze. It was easy to think of him as insubstantial, somehow, which had troubled her from time to time. When the feeling had got too much, she'd gathered him in and hugged him tight, feeling the bones beneath his skin, his warmth and the steady thrum of his heart; reassuring herself that he was flesh and blood and wasn't going to disappear. And yet he had, and she had let it happen.

Too tired to take another step, Frances stood awhile outside Wyn's old house and thought about faces, and the ways in which they changed. Bronwyn Hughes had been dead for twenty-four years, but Frances had still recognised her at once. If Davy had gone now, and she saw him again in twenty-four years, would she recognise him? Would it be like seeing Owen, with the sure, steady emergence of childhood familiarity from his adult face? Or would it be like seeing Wyn again had been – sad little remnants, but still undoubtably *her*? She pictured another face then, a boy's face, though to her eight-year-old self, he'd seemed like an adult. Frances only came to appreciate how young he'd been as she grew up herself. The face she remembered was full of fear; it was a face that had haunted her sleep for years, carrying with it such a cargo of conflicting feelings that she would wake exhausted from dreams of it.

'Johannes,' she whispered to herself. Yesterday, she'd

recognised the way she was feeling – the grief and shame, the crushing feeling of having done something terrible that could never, ever be undone. She'd been at a loss as to why she should remember feeling that way, but now she thought about Johannes. She thought about his kindness and his fear, about what she'd said and done, and wondered if she'd found the cause.

She was dizzy, and her heart was stumbling, missing beats here and there then speeding to make it up. Again, the police officer's words sounded in her ears – *no stone was left unturned.* Again, it produced the memory of a dank place, striped with sunshine, long ago. A memory of something she had seen there, but not understood. It was getting dark; the sky was pink and grey in the west, navy blue in the east, with the first faint flicker of a star. It felt like a hundred years since Frances had seen either of her parents, yet it felt like five minutes since she and Wyn had stood outside the leper hospital, steeling them-selves to go inside for the very first time. *Hush, little sisters!* With a gasp, Frances flinched, and fresh tears scattered her face. For the second time that day she found herself begging forgiveness, helplessly, from someone who couldn't possibly hear her. 'Oh, Johannes. I'm so sorry.'

1916–1917

Magdalen Gardens had its own precise smell, which, in spring, was of the laurels with their powdery blossoms, the leaf mulch underneath them, and the faint stink of sewage from the back of Springfield Place, where the privy pipes were cracked and ran too close to the well. The people there were always getting ill. Frances's brother, Keith, was ten, and had no time for his six-and-a-half-year-old sister; he often ditched her in the gardens to go off with his friends. The boys liked trespassing onto the railway at Brougham Hayes, and putting farthings on the tracks in the hope that passing trains would squash them into halfpennies. It never worked, but the fun seemed to be in the endeavour. Frances played quite happily by herself, and that day she was playing at being a deer. She'd seen one in the gardens the week before, all alone and apprehensive. She'd watched it stepping hesitantly through the shadows, until a woman with a crying baby made it bound off up the slope of Beechen Cliff. Frances was the tallest in her class, for which she was teased, and her mother often called her a 'clumsy clot', so she was enjoying pretending to be the deer – moving as quietly as she could, skulking in the undergrowth with the woodlice and the money spiders, peering out at people. And then, suddenly, Bronwyn Hughes was there.

'What are you doing?' she said, loudly. Frances didn't have it in her to bound off up the slope, as the deer had done.

'I was being a deer,' she said, reluctantly, in case Wyn thought it was a stupid game.

'All by yourself?'

'My brother's gone off with his friends.'

'My brother does that too. Mostly to play football. I've got sisters, but Carys is too old, and Annie's too young. She's only a baby.' Wyn seemed to be waiting, but for what Frances had no idea. 'I could play your game with you. If you want,' said Wyn, in an off-hand way. As if she didn't really care either way. Frances nodded again, with a sinking feeling. Playing with other girls usually took a bit more effort, and was a bit less fun, than playing by herself.

Playing with Wyn turned out to be different. She embraced the game wholeheartedly, and even though she made it her own, her changes made it better. As they played, Frances stole glances at her new friend. Wyn's button-down dress had been washed so many times it had faded to a non-committal colour somewhere between green and brown. Her hair looked grubby, but had been combed and plaited neatly. She scratched at the nape of her neck and behind her ears quite often, and she didn't smell very nice – sort of like stale bread. But she was very pretty, especially when she smiled her big, gap-toothed smile; and since she talked a lot, Frances didn't have to, and that seemed to suit them both.

'Did your mother give you a ha'penny for grub? We could go and get scrumps,' said Wyn, as the afternoon wore on.

'No,' Frances confessed. Scrumps were the frazzled bits of batter strained from the chip shop oil; her mouth watered at the thought. 'I'm not supposed to eat between meals,' she explained. Wyn gave her a searching look.

'I'm starving hungry,' she said.

'Oh.' Frances thought for a moment. 'Well, if we go to see my Aunt Pam and Cecily, I expect we'll get a glass of milk. But it's not teatime, really.'

'All right, let's.' Wyn took her hand, waiting to be led.

Wyn went very quiet when they got to Woodlands, which

puzzled Frances because she knew Wyn wasn't the least bit shy. She didn't realise, until she'd had been to Beechen Cliff Place, how different Woodlands must seem to Wyn. Wyn eyed Cecily's easel and the potted plants, the framed pictures on the walls and painted plates in the dresser. At one point she ran her fingers along the edge of Cecily's silk jacket, and she got down on the floor at once to put her arms around the cat, which backed away uncertainly.

'See?' Pam remarked to Cecily. 'I said we should have got a dog. A dog would want to play with the child.' To which Cecily only smiled calmly. She and Pam had lived together since before Frances was born. They'd met when Pam was a kitchen maid at Cecily's family home, one of the big villas on Lyncombe Hill, and made friends at once. 'Thick as thieves,' Frances's mother always said, in an odd tone of voice. Cecily was a tall, lovely wraith of a woman, with milk-white skin and mousy hair. She spoke differently – with a plum in her mouth, Frances's mother said – wore long, diaphanous dresses, drank jasmine tea, and painted huge canvases of sunrises in blues and pinks and golds.

Pam spotted Wyn's insatiable hunger at once, which, Frances soon learnt, stemmed from her never knowing when she would next eat, and gave them a biscuit with the milk. After that they went back to Magdalen Gardens and waited until Keith returned, then Wyn walked back with them as far as Magdalen Cottages before carrying on alone down Holloway, skipping left to right on her stick-thin legs, her knees like bed knobs beneath the skin.

'Where'd you live, then?' Keith called after her.

'Beechen Cliff Place,' Wyn called back. 'See you!'

'Well then,' said Keith, giving Frances a haughty look. 'No wonder she smells like old socks. She's got fleas, you know; I saw her scratching.' Frances felt defensive of her friend, but said nothing.

There was the same tension the first time Wyn came to Frances's home in Magdalen Cottages. Frances's parents seemed to bewilder her.

'It's very nice to meet you,' said Susan Elliot, smiling, with her hands clasped in front of her apron. Her hair was pinned up in a neat bun, she wore a good day dress, with pleats down the front, and a silver locket around her neck. Her hands were always clean. Derek Elliot was a mechanic in the coach works on the Wells Road, which serviced and repaired anything from a bicycle to a Humberette or a Model T Ford. He always had the smell of engine oil and axle grease on his overalls, and his fingernails were black every day of the week but Sunday, but he smiled broadly at Wyn and shook her tiny hand in his.

'Bronwyn, is it? That's pretty. Is that an Irish name?'

'It's Welsh. My dad came from Wales, before.' Wyn's expression was perplexed as she looked up at Frances's father. As though she'd never met his like before.

'Is it Scottish, maybe? Sounds a bit Scottish,' Derek mused, as though Wyn hadn't spoken.

'No, it's Welsh. I told you it was Welsh,' she insisted.

'Could it be Cornish, perhaps? Or – I know!' He snapped his fingers. 'You're French, aren't you?' he said, and Wyn dissolved into giggles.

They played for a while in Frances's room, which she shared with Keith.

'You have your own bed,' said Wyn, in wonderment. On Keith's side of the invisible but much disputed central line was his beloved Meccano, his *Boys' Book of Airships* and his battered old ice skates. There was a small trunk where his spare set of clothes and his winter coat and socks were kept, reeking of camphor to kill the moths. On Frances's side was a similar trunk, her library books — *Queen Silver-Bell* and *Anne of the Island*, which was proving almost too difficult; her teddy bear, and the hairbrush and comb set that had been a Christmas present from Pam and Cecily, the backs inlaid with blue enamel, iridescent like peacock feathers. These Wyn loved. She sat down on the end of the bed and held the brush out to Frances.

'Be my servant, and brush my hair,' she instructed, 'then I'll do yours.' Frances did as she was told, though Wyn's hair was so fine it snagged constantly, and Wyn winced with every stroke. She sat up beautifully, though, hands in her lap like a china doll.

The following Saturday Frances went to call for Wyn, and found that things were very different at her house. The houses at the bottom end of Holloway were shabby, tiny terraces, some of them only accessed by narrow flights of steps. Some dated back hundreds of years, to the time of the civil war, but most were Georgian or Victorian. The only heating they had was a smouldering coal fire in one downstairs room, and upstairs, hot bricks wrapped in rags and stuffed beneath the bedsheets. There were ash pails on the doorsteps, and the constant whiff of the privies in warm weather. Beechen Cliff Place was well populated with Wyn's family. Mr and Mrs Hughes lived with Wyn and her brother Owen at number thirty-four; Wyn's sister Carys, who was too old to share a room with a boy, lived at number thirty-three with their cousin Clare and widowed Aunt Ivy. One set of Wyn's grandparents lived next to another aunt and uncle in Parfitt's Buildings, which was a little way east of Beechen Cliff Place.

Heart hammering, Frances knocked at the door. Mrs Hughes answered, jiggling a drooling baby on her hip. She looked at Frances wearily, and Frances squirmed on the step like a worm on a hook.

'Well, come on then,' Mrs Hughes said at last, standing to one side, holding the door with her elbow and trying to wipe her hands on a cloth without dropping the baby, which Frances guessed was Wyn's little sister, Annie. The front room was cool despite the sunshine outside, and not much light found its way in. Wyn was standing by the fireplace, holding a sheet of newspaper in front of it to help it draw. She was swaying from side to side and singing quietly as she stood there, and grinned cheerfully as Frances came in. Mrs Hughes disappeared into the back room without another word, and before Wyn could speak, a man's voice made Frances jump.

'You'll not stir an inch till that fire's took hold.'

Wyn's father, Mr Hughes, was slumped in a hearthside chair. He managed to be both thin and large – he had big bones, thick knees and wide shoulders, but no spare flesh on them. Only his stomach looked at all soft, and he had ruddy cheeks, like steaks, that rode up and squeezed his eyes into slits. He wasn't that tall, but he gave the impression of size. In all the times Frances was to see him, she only saw him smile five or six times, and on each occasion didn't understand why he was smiling. His Welsh accent sounded foreign, to her ears, and it began to seem strange that Wyn should be so normal. Mr Hughes was in his vest, which let dark tufts of chest hair escape. His braces were off his shoulders, tangled around his hips. Wyn had told her that he worked for the brewery on the Bristol Road, loading barrels onto wagons. The room had a definite smell, unlike any Frances had smelt before, and she wondered if Mr Hughes were part of it.

'It's nearly there, Dad,' said Wyn, of the fire, without a hint of boredom or begrudge. Mrs Hughes poked her head through from the back room. She was pretty, but a ladder of worry lines climbed her forehead.

'You're not to pester your dad, Wynnie,' she said. 'His

back's playing him up something awful again. Once that's going, you girls get on outside to play.'

'We won't pester, Mum. Frances doesn't pester, do you, Frances?' Wyn said, and Frances shook her head, not daring to meet anyone's eye.

Frances had never felt less welcome, more awkward or eager to leave a place. But then she remembered how confounded Wyn had been at Magdalen Cottages, and at Woodlands, and realised that this was where Wyn belonged. This was what she knew, and where she was loved; this was home to her, and the thought gave Frances a strange feeling. She knew she oughtn't dislike it – she shouldn't be repulsed by the house or afraid of Wyn's family – but she couldn't seem to help it. She felt horribly embarrassed, and could feel Mr Hughes watching her, not wanting her there.

Then, in the back room, baby Annie began to wail. Wyn stiffened. 'There! All going nicely, Dad,' she said, abruptly. 'Time to go.' She grabbed Frances's sleeve as she passed, towing her to the door. It slammed behind them just as Mr Hughes began to bellow. 'It's best to clear off when Annie cries – it makes him angry. He says he'll throttle her, but he doesn't mean it,' Wyn explained, with a lopsided shrug.

Outside, they paused to watch Wyn's Aunt Ivy, who was chasing a young man along the pavement with a broom. A curvaceous young woman was watching from the front step of the house next door, a small smile playing on her lips.

'That's Clive. He's going to marry Carys, my other sister,' said Wyn, pointing at the young woman. 'Mum says he's a handsome devil and no mistake.'

'It's you I'm after really, Ivy,' said Clive, grabbing at Ivy's apron strings.

'If I catch you shinning up my drainpipe again, I'll have your guts for garters,' said Ivy.

'Oh, let him alone, Auntie Ivy!' Carys called. 'We all know you're not serious.'

'He'll not have you till you're wed, my girl, or it'll be over my dead body,' Ivy retorted, and Clive laughed, making a final lunge at her. He had a lovely laugh – the kind that made you smile in spite of yourself, and Frances was quite ready to smile because she was so relieved to be away from Mr Hughes. Clive grinned at them as he passed, fitting a cigarette between his teeth and tucking one hand into his pocket. He took out a silver coin, flicked it into the air with his thumb, caught it on the back of his hand and inspected it before slipping it back into his pocket with a shrug.

'All right there, Wynnie,' he said, dipping his shoulder at them as he passed. 'All right there, Wynnie's chum,' he said to Frances.

'Her name's Frances!' Wyn called after him, turning and jumping on the spot as if to make him notice her better.

'Well, all right there, Frances,' said Clive, turning, giving them a wave. Then he winked at Carys and blew her a kiss, and off he went, striking a match for his smoke.

'Once they're married, Clive'll be my brother,' said Wyn, watching him go.

'Brother-in-*law*,' said Owen, tugging one of her plaits as he passed. 'I'll still be your proper brother. I'll still get to boss you about.'

'Will not!'

The girls carried on away, dodging the carts on the corner of Holloway, and the muck the horses left behind, and a pair of drunken men reeling out of the Young Fox in spite of the early hour. They went along to Broad Quay, where the barges were unloaded, and watched a man moving sacks to dry land in a hand-barrow, via a twenty-foot span of narrow plank over the water. The girls cheered every time he wobbled – half wanting him to fall, half terrified that he might. But he never did. Frances wondered whether she should say anything about Wyn's house, or her family, or the fact that she hadn't even been offered a glass of water let alone a glass of milk. She wondered if she ought to say that she liked it, to hide the fact that she didn't. In the end her natural tendency to say nothing when she was unsure won, but Wyn seemed to sense that something wasn't being said.

'What's your Keith going to be when he grows up?' she asked.

'I don't know. A mechanic, I suppose, like Dad. He likes machines.'

'Owen wants to be a footballer.'

'But that's not a *job*.'

'That's what Dad says, but Owen says it can be. Clive's a brickie. He's going to own the business one day, and be the boss of lots of other men, so then he'll give Owen a proper job, that's what Mum says. And when Clive's the boss he'll buy a big house for him and Carys to live in, and we'll go there and have feasts, with more kinds of cake than you've ever seen before. That's if you *want* to come,' she said, as if it were already a reality; as if this were an official invite.

'Yes, please. Thank you,' said Frances. They weren't yet seven years old, and neither one could know how much these two things about them would come to matter: that Wyn could imagine her reality away so easily, and so completely; and that Frances, when uncertain, would say nothing.

Wyn called Frances her best friend. Frances had never had a best friend before, and it made her feel different – better, and somehow more definite. Before, she'd tended to stay close to home, and play mostly by herself. Wyn had bigger ideas, and no boundaries, and she liked to get away from Beechen

Cliff Place. They went to the Theatre Royal to watch the posh people go in and out. They walked along the canal, looking at all the barges, and called at the tea kiosk by the deep lock, because the man who worked there was a soft touch and would sometimes hand out day-old scones, or the crusts from the sandwich bread. Wyn dreamed about her wedding day, and about finding out she was secretly the princess of a far-off country. She loved animals, and would go up to any creature they found and try to pet it – even the Jack Russell terrier at the Workman's Rest, which snarled and bit. She liked to wait at the bottom of Stall Street and watch the trams and the traffic, hoping for the Brooke Bond Tea lorry to get its wheels stuck in the tram tracks again, and to see the hilarious look of panic on the driver's face.

The girls lived where the city of Bath met the countryside of Somerset, and in the summer months they packed picnics and set off out of town, further than Frances had ever been: up onto Beechen Cliff, where a new park was being made and houses were creeping over the western slopes; up to Claverton Down, or to Perrymead, and then onto open farmland. They walked through meadow grasses as high as their hips; they spread their arms to the wind as it seethed through chestnuts and elms, and watched it make distant wheat fields ripple like water. They were bitten by ants and stung by bees; they ate wincingly tart damsons and blackberries before they were ready. And the more time they spent out of the city, the more its familiar streets and crowds of people came to seem, to Frances, like a net in which she'd been caught. Out in the open, where no one could see her, and no one had any expectations of her, she felt released.

They met Joe Parry one day, as they were going along the hedges in Smallcombe, picking whatever they could to eat.

'Hold on, don't eat that!' he said, stepping out through a gap in the hedge and startling them. He was older than them but not as old as Owen; a brown-haired boy with a slightly snub nose, wearing overalls and carrying a shotgun crooked over one arm. Frances simply stared, but Wyn recovered quickly.

'Why can't we?'

'That's spindleberry. They'll make you sick; could even kill you,' he said. Wyn peered at the bright pink berries in her hand then flung them away.

'We weren't going to eat them. We're not *stupid*,' she said, and Joe smiled sceptically.

'Funny. Looked like you were.' He set off down the hill, and after a brief consultation the girls decided to follow him, at a distance, to see where he went. So they found Topcombe Farm, and when he saw them lurking by the gate, Joe shook his head and rolled his eyes, as though they were silly.

'I don't know why he thinks *he's* so clever,' said Wyn, watching him through narrowed eyes. Frances shrugged. She knew Wyn hated to be helped, and to be proved wrong.

After that they added Topcombe Farm to the list of places they went to – places that were theirs. Joe let them stroke the lambs in spring, and dip for tadpoles in the pond, and hunt for eggs in the barn. Sometimes his mother gave them barley water or an apple, but she was a stern woman and they never felt very welcome. Joe was good at building, and sometimes helped with a den in the woods near the farm, or with making stepping stones across the muddy stream that fed the duck pond. He let them help set snares one day, but when they caught a rabbit and it choked itself to death, Wyn was stricken and Frances burst into tears, and he stormed away, calling them 'stupid townies'. They'd both thought the rabbit would be caught alive, and that they could keep it for a pet. Joe went to school in Claverton, so neither Frances's brother Keith nor

Owen Hughes knew him. It was part of his appeal, to Wyn at least – that he was secret, and somehow belonged to them.

In winter Frances's chilblains throbbed mercilessly, and Wyn developed a cough that went on and on, racking her thin body, leaving her listless. She was hungrier than ever. In December, 1917, Frances went shopping in Widcombe with her mother. She'd been saving up her pocket money for weeks to buy Wyn a present, but it still took a long time to find something she could afford, and thought Wyn might like. She wanted to get her something grown up, since what Wyn coveted more than anything were her big sister's clothes and things. At last, when her mother's patience was wearing thin and she was holding her coat closed at the throat against the creeping chill, Frances found a brooch on a market stall. It was only made of tin, but it had been painted brightly – it was of a bunch of daffodils, which her mother said was perfect, since Wyn was Welsh. Yellow paint on the flower heads, pale green on the long, pointed leaves. The pin on the back was wickedly sharp.

On Christmas Eve Wyn came to tea at Frances's house.

'Would you like another, Wyn?' said Derek, offering her the last mince pie because she'd been staring at it so intently. Wyn took it quickly, in case he changed his mind.

'That's *so* unfair,' Keith complained, but Susan hushed him.

'You've had plenty, Keith. And you'll have more tomorrow,' she said, pointedly.

'These are simply *delicious*, Mrs Elliot,' said Wyn, as she levered the top off the pie with her teeth. It was something Cecily often said to Pam, and it made Frances laugh.

'Well, *thank* you, Bronwyn.' Her mother sounded flattered, which made Frances laugh even more.

'Oh no, it's Giggling Gertie,' said Keith, rolling his eyes. They'd made paper chains and hung them up, criss-crossing the room, and they had a small Christmas tree in the front room, wedged into a bucket with rocks. The tree had ribbons and candles and a few precious boiled sweets hidden in the branches, which Frances had to forbid Wyn from pilfering. Instead, she gave Wyn her present, and had the delight of seeing her unwrap the brooch with a gasp, her eyes lighting up.

'Frances, it's the best present *ever*,' she said, and Frances could tell that she meant it. It didn't matter that Wyn hadn't got Frances anything; Frances didn't expect anything, and Wyn didn't need to explain. There was no such thing as pocket money for her; no such thing as going shopping in Widcombe with her mother. 'You're the best friend, ever,' said Wyn, hugging Frances and then peering down as she pinned the brooch to her yellow cardigan.

The pallid light of the gas lantern shone on her hair, and the warmer colour from the fire was on her face; her hair was a bit knotted from the wind that day, and her cheeks a little chapped. Under her dress, her thin chest rose and fell. Frances heard the soft sound of the air in her nostrils, and was suddenly assailed by a rush of feeling, of love, so powerful it was almost unbearable. Wyn was often amused, or bored, or cross, or intrigued, but Frances realised just then how rarely she was delighted. Knowing that she had delighted Wyn made Frances feel like she was swelling up inside, fit to burst. She decided to do it again, if she could, whenever she could. She thought, of course, that they had years ahead of them; she thought she would have lots of chances.

3

Tuesday

Two Days After the Bombings

When Frances woke, it was like swimming up from a long way down, and she couldn't remember where she was. Gradually, squinting at the bright square of the window, she recognised the spare bedroom at Woodlands – the mothy silk eiderdown, a piece of faded glory from Cecily's former life in her family's house on Lyncombe Hill; the washstand and towel rail; the dressing table with its pink padded stool. She could hear sounds of construction coming from outside, some way off, and downstairs Pam was rattling a pan on the stove and talking to Dog, who barked softly now and then in reply. The window was open and cool air moved the curtains, and rustled a trailing spider plant on the sill. There was an overwhelming sense of peace. That was the feeling Frances most associated with Woodlands – of being calmed, of feeling clear, and serene. Like the deep, soothing shade of a tree on a hot day; or, when she was little, the mysterious realm beneath the rhubarb leaves in the garden, hidden away from the world.

For a moment it was as though none of it had happened, but, as Frances rose stiffly, she realised that the sounds of construction were actually sounds of demolition, and that there was still the faint tang of smoke on the air, thick ridges of dirt beneath her nails, and an aching lump on her head. Then came the spasm of anguish when she remembered Davy. The pall of shame, so horribly familiar, that threatened to wipe out everything that made her who she was. She froze for a moment, seeking the flicker of hope that she would find him again, and undo the damage. When she found it, she cradled it close, and felt the desperate need to search overtaking her again. She had no recollection of getting back to Woodlands; she was still fully clothed and had left dirty marks on the sheets; her shoes had been left beside the bed where they'd fallen. Crossing to the mirror, she peeled off the gauze and sticking plaster to examine the cut on her head, and saw her hair stiff with grime, standing up at odd angles. It was brown and loosely curled, getting long at the back of her neck and in need of a trim.

Then, for a worrying moment, her own face shifted and wasn't what she expected to see – the light brown eyes with their faraway look, the curve and dip of her lips and her strong jaw; too strong, her mother lamented, begging her to grow her hair out to soften it. She'd half expected to see a little girl looking back at her, and it took a while to know herself again – the march and alterations of twenty-four years. Shallow hollows in her cheeks and fine lines across her forehead. She'd half expected to still be eight years old, because the way she was feeling now was just the way she had felt back then. When Wyn was taken; when Johannes was arrested. She suddenly felt as though there were things she could have done differently, things she could have done better. Or perhaps things she shouldn't have done at all. The thought of it made her jumpy; it felt like being followed, or being late for something urgent. She almost felt afraid.

In the kitchen she was met by the sight of Pam's rounded shoulders, and the strings of her apron cinching in her broad waist.

'Here she is,' she said, stoutly, looking round as Frances

appeared. 'Large as life and twice as mucky. Frances, dear, please tell me you plan to have a bath before work?'

'Work?'

'Don't you have the Tuesday afternoon shift?' Pam fetched a plate from the dresser and shovelled mushrooms onto a piece of toast. 'Have some breakfast. I've baked a loaf but there's no more butter till the end of the week.' As she spoke, Frances's stomach knotted in hunger, and rumbled loudly. She sat at the table and began to eat, gratefully.

'What time is it?' she asked.

'Coming up for eleven.' Pam dried her hands then came to sit down, smiling. 'On Tuesday, in case you've lost track.'

'*Eleven* o'clock?' said Frances, astonished. Pam nodded, her eyes wary.

'You've been asleep for about fourteen hours. You were so tired when you got back here, you were talking nonsense.' Pam's smile faltered slightly, and Frances wondered what she'd said. 'So it's no surprise you're hungry. And thirsty, I expect – I'll put the kettle on.'

'Fourteen *hours*? But Davy . . . I need to . . .' Frances half rose, but Pam held out a hand.

'You needed the rest, and you need to eat. No arguments,' she said. Frances did as she was told.

'So . . . if I slept right through, that means . . . ?'

'No more bombs,' said Pam, nodding. 'The sirens didn't even go off.' She smiled, and Frances felt relief wash through her.

'So it's over,' she said. 'Thank God.'

'Well, there's not a lot left to bomb, but I suppose we should be thankful for small mercies. People are already starting to make their way back. I think we can safely take it as an all-clear.' Pam sat down opposite Frances. 'How are you feeling, love?'

'I'm fine. But I can't go to work,' said Frances. It seemed a ridiculous idea.

'Why not? Green Park Station's closed – there's a carriage belly-up on the bridge at Brougham Hayes, I hear, and the track's all tangled up like string – but Bath Spa's open. Trains are still running, people still need their luggage put on trolleys. I'd be on at Woolies myself, but they aren't reopening till tomorrow.'

'I've to go round the hospitals and look for Davy. They can manage without me at the station – goodness knows people will need to be a bit flexible for a while.'

'Yes, of course you must look for Davy. I just thought it would do you good to get back to a . . . familiar routine.' Pam studied Frances for a moment. 'Well. Owen dropped by earlier this morning. He said to tell you he hadn't found anything at St Mark's, that he was going up to the EMS hospital before work, and he'll be in the Young Fox after his shift, if you want to see him.'

'Oh. Oh, that's good.' Frances pictured Owen walking along the lines of dead in the church crypt, and was at once ashamed and grateful. He was too gentle a person to have to see such a terrible thing, but at least Davy had not been amongst the bodies. She felt guilty for sleeping in; for being so neglectful. 'All right. Then I'll go to the Royal United, and check there. I'd better get cracking.'

Frances finished her toast and gulped at her tea.

'Hold on.' Pam hesitated, then pushed the new edition of the *Bath & Wilts Chronicle and Herald* towards her. 'You'd better see this first.' Frances stared at it.

'Is it about Wyn?' she asked. Pam nodded, then got up to refill her cup of tea. On the front page was a photo of a smiling boy holding a plate of sloppy food. The caption beneath read: *Kenneth Marr, bombed-out schoolboy, thinks the canteen meals are just fine. We agree.* She turned a few pages, past photographs of the destruction and stories of hope and courage, and found her name on page six. *Human remains presumed to be those of missing Bath schoolgirl, Bronwyn Hughes, found after twenty-four years.* Frances's skin prickled. There was no picture of her, of course. In 1918, only the well-off took photographs of their children. It was a short piece but the reporter's flowery style still grated on her.

> *The criminal responsible for the little girl's untimely death was executed for the crime many years ago, yet, in a final act of cruelty, he died without revealing the location of the corpse, thereby leaving an unresolved ache in the bosom of her family. Now, at last, their sweet daughter has come home; our bitterest enemies, the Germans, have inadvertently resolved a tragic mystery that had haunted the city for more than two decades. This writer can only hope that they will somehow learn of it, and of the many other ways in which the people of Bath have been roused — not cowed — by their cowardly bombings.*

'That's it?' said Frances, incredulous. ' "Sweet daughter"? She wasn't *sweet*. She was brilliant, and brave, and ...'

'I know, I know,' said Pam. 'The man's an idiot, that's plain enough.'

'It doesn't say anything about where she was found! Or what it might mean.'

'And everything's a chance to put one over on the bloody Germans,' Pam sighed. 'Even a murdered child.' Frances flung the paper down in disgust, took a deep breath and pinched the bridge of her nose.

'Mrs Hughes'll probably cut it out and keep it,' she said. 'Do you remember how she kept every mention of Wyn? And everything about the trial. Cut it out, filed it away. Why would she possibly have wanted to read or reread any of it?'

'I don't know.' Pam sat down again. 'Perhaps to feel she was doing something – *any*thing. What else could she do?'

'I should go down and see her. I'll stop off on my way back from the RUH.' Frances pushed back her chair and stood up.

'A bath first? Perhaps a change of clothes?' Pam suggested.

'All right. But I need to hurry.'

Frances hadn't been over the river since before the raids. She crossed via Halfpenny Bridge, the old iron footbridge where what had once been the tollbooth was now a kiosk selling newspapers and cigarettes. It was a couple of miles to the hospital and her pace was halting – she had to take a circuitous route where an unexploded bomb meant the road was taped off, or where there was simply too much rubble to pass. When she turned into a street that hadn't lost any glass from its windows, nor a single petal of apple blossom, it seemed miraculously, impossibly tidy. There were queues outside the Pump Rooms, where a British Restaurant had opened and was exuding the smell of stewed meat and onions; women with bundles at their feet queued by the emergency washing service buses; knots of people stood around the Salvation Army tea trolleys, sipping and looking lost. Thick clouds rolled across the sky, and when one covered the sun the whole city seemed to flinch, like someone had stepped on its grave; as though the sky were now threatening.

The hospital itself was undamaged, but cluttered with people and resonant with tension; voices raised in distress echoed along the corridors. The walls were white, the floors tracked in every direction with dusty footprints, and only clean in the corners. Frances had never been there before; she didn't know the rules – whether she was allowed to just walk in, as she had done, or if there was any such thing as visiting hours at a time like that. Her stomach fluttered with anticipation at the possibility of finding Davy there. She waited impatiently near the entrance for a while, where a tangle of people were trying to get the attention of the harried-looking girl on the front desk. Nurses came and went, always brisk, pursued by ashen relatives and the walking wounded. In the end Frances slipped off to one side and followed signs to the children's ward.

She'd expected it to be noisy – with all the crying and shouting and asking for things that children generally kept up. The hush was a surprise, and it made her skin crawl. The air had the tang of carbolic and urine, with the smell of blood underneath it all like a stubborn stain that refused to be scrubbed out. Frances was aware of her heart thumping, not fast but curiously hard. She walked slowly up the middle of the ward, noting that no number of teddy bears, nor a pattern of clouds on the curtains, could stop the long room being a grim place where no child ought to have been. But then, it would seem comfortable and clean to Davy; he'd never had a teddy bear, and the time Frances had bought him a toy monkey, Carys had thrown it away, saying it was no business of hers to be buying him things. Frances hoped to see him in one of the orderly hospital beds, with a clean sheet pulled up under his armpits and something in his hands to occupy him – a picture book, or a toy soldier. She hoped it so hard it was like an ache.

She focused on the beds against the left wall, planning to turn at the bottom and come up the right-hand side. The first bed went by, then the second, and the little bodies beneath the sheets were neither of them Davy. Some of the children had visible wounds, bandaged up or in plaster; some looked untouched. Some were awake, staring at the ceiling or the walls, or drawing patterns on the bedclothes with idle finger-tips; some lay as still and silent as corpses. A chubby boy with brown hair lay with his eyes shut and both his hands bandaged into white boxing gloves; his mother sat beside him, knitting, with her legs crossed and her back rigid. She looked up and met Frances's eye, then stiffened even more and looked away, as if suspecting criticism of some kind. Another mother sat slumped, her head back in exhausted sleep, mouth drooping open. Her daughter had bandages across her eyes, through which reddish-brown stains were blooming. It was impossible to say if the girl was awake or asleep; she lay quite still, but it was the stillness of a frightened animal, hoping to go un-noticed.

Down the left side Frances went, then up the right. And then down and up again, and this time the mother of the brown-haired boy looked at her with more sympathy. At the end of her second pass, back by the doors, she simply stood for a while, at a loss.

'Excuse me, you really shouldn't be just wandering around, you know.' A nurse appeared at her elbow, short and thin, with a freckled face and a tic of exhaustion tugging at the corner of one eye.

'I ... I was looking for a little boy. He's missing,' said Frances.

'Name?' said the nurse, pencil ready on her clipboard.

'Mrs Parry.'

'No – the patient's name? And age?'

'Oh. David Noyle, and he's six.'

'Noyle?' The nurse glanced at Frances suspiciously. 'You're not his mother?'

'No, I ... I'm his nanny.'

'Description?' said the nurse. Frances gave as good a

description of Davy as she could, and the nurse alternately scribbled and frowned in thought.

'There was a child taken to Bristol, I heard – no identification, and no one's been in asking after them. I never saw him, so I can't say as it's David or not . . . Have you been through the other wards? We couldn't fit them all in here. I shouldn't just send you wandering, but it's probably quickest; heavens knows we're in a bit of a flap just now. I'll call through to Bristol, if you like? By some miracle our phone's still operating.'

'Yes – yes, please.'

Frances was halfway around the men's ward when she stopped in her tracks. A quick glance had already told her that none of the patients were Davy. She'd decided to look closely at each of them regardless, just in case, in spite of the glares she got from some of them, the winks of others, and the fact that she was taut with hope that the nameless child in Bristol was Davy.

'I'm the one you're after, love,' said the man in the bed next to where she'd stopped. He grinned, showing bruised gums. 'An' I'm ready for me sponge bath.' Frances ignored him. She stood at the end of bed five, staring, and wondered why it was suddenly harder to breathe. The patient had dressings around his head and spreading down over the right side of his face as far as his cheek; the exposed part of his face had the peeled, angry look of a freshly boiled ham, puffy and glistening with whatever ointment had been applied to soothe the burnt skin. His visible eye was closed, the lid as dark and swollen as a slug; tufts of greying hair stood up on top of his head, frizzled and burnt at the ends. His right hand and arm were bandaged; his nostrils looked too dark, like they were full of dried blood; his lips were pallid. Above the noise of life and death going on all around, Frances could hear his breath whistling in and out, shallow and even.

She stepped closer to the end of the bed, where the man's chart was hanging from the foot rail. She looked for his name, but when she found it – Percival Clifton – it meant nothing to her. She'd never known a Percy Clifton, she was sure of it. She studied the unconscious man again, wondering if she were mistaken and didn't know him after all. But the feeling remained, and it was growing. A shivery sensation, creeping up from her feet to make her knees ache, that was very like dread. When she looked at him it was like straining her eyes into deep darkness, and just – only just – seeing movement there. The stirring of some unknown thing, far better left alone. She had a sudden memory of being hot, and uncomfortable – of sweat sliding at the backs of her bent knees, a pain in her head, a stab of sharp, bewildered fear.

'Mrs Parry?' The freckled nurse made her jump. She still carried her clipboard in front of her, pencil poised, like a shield.

'Yes?' Frances struggled to focus on her, then remembered Davy and turned her back on Percy Clifton. 'Did you find out? Is it Davy?' she said, but the nurse was already shaking her head.

'Sorry,' she said, briskly. 'It was a little girl, about three years old, found on Henry Street. Still got no idea of her name.'

'Oh,' said Frances. Hope disappeared beneath a wave of disappointment. 'Was?'

'She died of her wounds.'

'Oh. Have . . . have they got any other children from Bath there? Any they don't know the names of, who might—' Frances cut herself off because the nurse was shaking her head again. Her lips were tight and she wrote something on her clipboard, though Frances couldn't think what. The tic in the corner of her eye kept jumping, and Frances wondered how much awful news she'd had to deliver in the past two days. 'Well, thank you for checking. He needs his medicine, you see. He has fits – epileptic seizures. Can you make a note? He needs to have his pills.'

'I'll make a note, but we'd need him identified before we could give him anything, in any case. I'd check back again, if I was you,' said the nurse, attempting to smile at Frances. 'They're still finding people, all the time. All the time, they're bringing them in.'

'Thank you. I will. Wait, Nurse,' she said, as the woman turned to go. Frances nodded towards the unconscious man. 'Do you know . . .' She floundered, unsure what to ask. 'Do you know where this man was found? What happened to him?'

'Regina Hotel,' the nurse said, shortly, keen to move on. 'Down by the Assembly Rooms. It took a direct hit, cut it in half. He's one of the lucky ones,' she said. 'They'd ignored the sirens and most of them were up in their rooms, or still down in the bar. Fetched out far more dead than alive from that mess, they did. Do you know him? No one's been in asking for him.'

'No,' said Frances. 'That is . . . No.'

'Right. Well, I must get on.' The nurse waited to make sure Frances was leaving, and as Frances turned she felt Percy Clifton behind her. It was like being stared at from across a room – an intrusive, prickling feeling that made her want to look back, to be sure of where he was, and that he hadn't moved.

Paths had been cleared through the debris surrounding what remained of Beechen Cliff Place. A green tarpaulin had been stretched across a section of missing roof tiles between numbers thirty-four and thirty-three; there were few signs of life in any of the remaining houses, but a thin curl of smoke rose from the Hughes' chimney. Frances knocked, and her heart sank when it was Carys who opened the door. Her figure had gone to seed, the curves enveloped by the shapeless solidity of a far older woman; her eyes were very bloodshot, and they widened when she saw Frances.

'Have you found him?' she said. In the pause, Frances saw Carys's hope. It was well disguised, as though she was afraid to let it show, or perhaps afraid to feel it. Frances shook her head, her throat squeezing.

'Not yet,' she said, with difficulty.

'I thought I said you weren't to come back until you had?' Straight away the anger was back, jumping up like a flame given air; just as it always had in her father, Bill Hughes.

'I know. I've just come from the hospital, but . . . he wasn't there. But I'm certain he escaped the bomb at the Landys' – when I went to my parents' house on Sunday I saw signs . . . I'm sure he'd been there.'

'What signs?'

'There were footprints, the right size, and he'd been look-ing in the kitchen cupboards and the biscuit tin. Doesn't that sound like him?' She attempted to smile, but couldn't in the face of Carys's blank hostility. 'Has there been any sign of him here? Do you think he's tried to come home, or been looking for you?' As soon as she said it, Frances heard how it might sound to Carys. That her son had tried to find Frances, but not his mother. Carys stared at her in silence. 'Well, there's been so much damage here,' Frances hurried on. 'It all looks very different, doesn't it? It would be . . . very confusing for him. Where have you looked?' she asked. 'You and Fred? I mean, just so I can go to different places, so we can cover more ground.'

'*Me?* I got hit by a bomb, in case you hadn't noticed. You should be worrying about where *you'll* be looking.'

'Yes, but...' Frances paused. 'I mean, is there somewhere in particular he likes to play? Or to hide?'

Carys stared at her again, and a furtive expression hurried across her face. When she spoke, it was through clenched teeth, and Frances realised that she hadn't the first clue where her son liked to play.

'Why are you wasting time standing here, asking *me* questions? Get going, why don't you? Get gone!'

'I just... I wanted to speak to your mum,' said Frances. Carys glanced over her shoulder.

'Well, she doesn't want to speak to you. Can't you leave her in peace, for once? Her heart's been bad since all this started, and it's the stress of it, you mark my words.'

'Carys? Is that Frances?' Nora Hughes called from inside. 'Don't keep her out on the step.' Carys paused, then stepped back, grudgingly, to let Frances pass.

Frances had hated going into number thirty-four even before Wyn vanished, and she'd been loath to ever since. Their sorrow was too much when she had enough of her own, and she hated the way Mrs Hughes had always examined her, over the years – hungry for all the ways in which she was changing and maturing, because she'd believed that the same things would be happening to Wyn, wherever she was. Frances took a breath and looked around the tiny room. It was like going back in time – everything was just as it had always been. Damp peeled back the wallpaper in the corners, and black mould bloomed in a wide swathe under the stairs; the distemper on the ceiling was greyish yellow from tobacco and coal smoke. The same foxed, frameless mirror hung above the fireplace, the same trinkets sat along the mantelpiece – some china thimbles, a brass gas lamp and a Fry's chocolates tin from the coronation in 1911, with a picture of King George on the front. Threadbare chairs still faced the tiny fireplace; a lace panel still hung limp across the window.

In that moment, it seemed as though Wyn had been there only yesterday. Frances's eyelids flickered; she felt off balance, and saw again, as clear as day, a small, blonde figure standing by the fire, thin but smiling. Frances tried to pull herself together as Mrs Hughes appeared in the kitchen doorway, and Carys stalked past her to stand in front of the dormant gas stove, staring down at it, hands on her hips. 'It's nice to see you, Frances,' said Nora, stuffing a handkerchief up her sleeve as she came forwards, slowly, stiffly. She had arthritis in both hips; in spells of damp weather she could hardly move. Her housecoat was stained and she hadn't done her hair; it hung down in unkempt, grey tendrils. Her eyes were swimming, and she blinked far too often. There was no sign of Mr Hughes.

'How are you, Mrs Hughes?'

'Mustn't grumble, I suppose. Bill's taken himself off somewhere, he'll be sorry to have missed you.' There was a small pause after she spoke, as all three of them silently acknowledged that Bill Hughes wouldn't give a damn about missing her.

'He's all right though?' said Frances, feeling deceitful for pretending to care.

'Oh. I'm sure he is. Nine lives, that one,' said Nora. Frances was unsure how to speak, or how to stand. She felt at odds with herself; too big for the place, and as though she were the wrong species. Nothing had changed since she last saw them, and yet everything had.

'I hope you don't mind me dropping round,' she said.

'Do sit down,' said Mrs Hughes. Frances perched on one of the chairs. 'You'll be wondering about Wyn, I suppose. We'll be having a funeral for her, of course. Once all the fuss has calmed down, and all the poor souls bombed to death are buried. Perhaps our Annie'll come down for it. That'd be nice. Though I don't suppose she remembers Wyn at all.'

'Of course she doesn't,' said Carys, from the kitchen. Annie, the youngest Hughes sister, had married a tailor and moved with him to Aberdeen, and Frances wasn't surprised that she didn't visit all that often.

'The undertaker said it was no bother to keep her till we're ready, since she...' Mrs Hughes trailed off, blinking even more. 'Well. She wouldn't mind waiting a bit, in any case. For a proper burial at last, with a nice stone...'

'Oh? And how're we going to pay for that?' said Carys, coming to the doorway. Mrs Hughes shut her eyes tight, perhaps praying for strength.

'We'll find a way!' she said.

'Right. It's not as if the roof needs fixing, or my kids need shoes,' said Carys.

'She'll have a stone if I have to carve one out of Box quarry myself! Not like the bomb dead, all going in a mass grave up at Haycombe.'

'I'd like to help. If I can,' said Frances.

'That's good of you to say,' said Mrs Hughes. 'But we're her family. We'll manage.'

There was a silence that stretched on too long.

'You saw the bit in the newspaper?' said Frances, when she could stand it no longer. Nora Hughes nodded.

'You were always a good friend to her, Frances,' she murmured, her gaze drifting away across the room, to the muted square of daylight that the window let in. 'You weren't to blame. You were only little. You weren't to know the danger, were you?' she said. 'At least I'll always know where she is, from now on. No more wondering. No more... *hoping*,' she said, as though hoping Wyn was alive had been worse than knowing she was dead. But perhaps it had been, in some ways.

'But . . . don't you think—' Frances tried again, but Carys cut her off.

'What *I* think is that you should be out looking for Davy, instead of hanging around here, picking at old scabs.'

'I . . .' said Frances, stricken. 'I really am so very sorry about Davy. I'm sure I'll find him – I'll go on looking, I swear. Perhaps it's good that he wasn't at the hospital? I mean . . . he might not even be hurt at all.'

'Perhaps not,' said Nora. 'But where is he, then? And missing his medication. Poor little lad. He might be a few pence short of a pound, but he's a sweet boy.' Wearing a stifled expression, Carys returned to the stove, and Frances felt panic clawing at her, threatening to take hold. Panic at the thought of not finding him in time. Nora coughed. 'Wyn's with her maker now, in any case,' she went on, a little absently. 'Safe in the hands of the Lord.' She didn't sound as though she really believed it. 'My granny always used to say there's a special bit of heaven kept aside just for children, where they can play all day long and eat nothing but sweets and cake.'

'Oh, for pity's sake!' Carys stalked back into the room. 'I can't hear another second of this. Not another second!' She rounded on them, face knotted and puce. 'She died *years* ago! Decades ago! We've all mourned her, and we've all got enough trouble now without the two of you acting as though it's just happened all over again! I need to go and start packing up. They're pulling my house down, you know,' she shot at Frances.

She marched back to the kitchen and slammed the door, but Frances noticed that she didn't leave, in spite of what she'd said. She stayed well within earshot. Mrs Hughes pressed her fingers into her chest, wincing.

'Are you all right?' said Frances. Nora nodded.

'Just my angina, playing up. Where would I be without my Carys shouting at me and slamming doors? She's as reliable as rain at a picnic, that one.' She lowered her voice. 'As soon as she feels anything, she gets angry about it, you know that. It's not personal. It's shaken her up, her Davy vanishing just like her sister did, and then finding Wyn after all this time. It's shaken all of us up. To think we've been walking past her all this time... walking on her grave. Every time I went out the back... all this time...' Her eyes flooded. 'And her Clive's been away these past three months. That always puts her on edge.'

'He found some work?' said Frances. The war had brought a moratorium on new building work – tricky for those in the trade.

'Up in London, last I heard. All the bomb damage.'

'Silver linings, I suppose,' said Frances, weakly.

'Please, find our Davy, Frances,' said Mrs Hughes, softly. 'It's the not knowing that's unbearable.' There was a pall of ineffable sadness around her, and Frances saw a kind of pleading in her eyes. She wondered if it was only to do with Davy. 'I'd better get on. We've Carys and young Fred staying here with us for now. Lord help me.' Mrs Hughes eased herself out of her chair. 'It was good of you to call, Frances,' she said, not looking at Frances as she tried to usher her to the door.

'Will you let me know when the funeral is, please? I'd like to come,' said Frances, as she got up. Mrs Hughes nodded, still keeping her eyes down.

'Of course; you should be there. It'll be down at St Mark's. Not at Magdalen Chapel. My girl never needs to go back there again.' She shook her head. 'I've clipped that bit out of the newspaper. It didn't say much though, did it? Not much, after all this time.'

'No. And it didn't say anything about... about what it might mean,' said Frances, her pulse picking up. 'Where she was found, I mean – here at home.'

Carys pushed the door open yet again.

'And what do you suggest it *means*?' she said, in a low voice.

'Well...' Frances paused. She knew they hated even to hear his name, but she had to say it. 'Johannes wouldn't have known where she lived. And he wouldn't have... come down here. He'd have been far too afraid. Perhaps... *he* didn't kill her after all – isn't it more likely that she was killed by somebody... closer to home? By somebody who knew her, and knew where she lived?' Nora Hughes looked down at her hands. Carys stared hard at Frances, then drew in a deep breath. Frances braced herself for an angry outburst, but it never came. Instead, Carys seemed frozen. The silence rang.

1918

Wyn Hughes refused to be afraid – Frances learnt that very early on in their friendship. She was so bold, so daring, that Frances occasionally ended up in situations that worried her, like the time Wyn stole two pears from the greengrocer's in Lower Oldfield Park, then legged it while Frances stayed rooted to the spot, and the grocer almost had her before she gathered her wits to flee. Wyn promised she wouldn't do it again, and although she kept her word, Frances got drawn into plenty of other scrapes. She found it very hard to say no to Wyn.

'Of course she's fearless,' said Aunt Pam, when Frances mentioned it to her. 'Growing up where she does, she'd have to be.' Frances thought about that, and it began to make sense. After all, she herself was afraid of Wyn's family, especially her glowering father and her big sister, Carys. If they were an everyday thing to Wyn, then other alarming things might seem everyday as well.

Carys was a grown-up, at eighteen, and she would happily beat her little sister if she caught her in some misdemeanour, but Wyn wasn't afraid of her. In fact, it seemed like Wyn deliberately goaded her sister at times. One of her favourite things was to trespass in Carys's room, in the house next door to where Wyn and Owen lived, and try on her things. Carys would fly into a fury if she caught her at it, yet Wyn always seemed to do it when she was due home from work, and likely to catch her. Frances hated having to go with her; she hated being in Carys's room. Even if she wasn't to blame, she knew she was trespassing, and dreaded discovery. Most of the time they got away with it, but not always.

The house was identical to the one Wyn lived in – same footprint, same measly space, same state of damp and disrepair. The small room Carys shared with their cousin, Clare, had a view of the backyard, rooftops and the railway. Frances liked to watch the passing trains while she waited, reluctantly, for Wyn to finish pulling clothes from the dresser. Clare was twenty-two and rarely seen. She worked long hours at Bayer & Co., the corset factory, and sometimes brought home pieces that hadn't been stitched right, or had spots of machine oil, for herself and for Carys – sophisticated garments of which Wyn was deeply envious. Wyn liked to dress up, and put on powder and paint. She liked to pretend to be eighteen, and engaged, like Carys was. That day, Wyn put on her sister's good blouse – a ruffled, diaphanous thing – and it hung limply from her skinny shoulders as she leant towards the mirror over the fireplace and daubed rouge on her lips and cheeks. She had no skill at it, in spite of practising, so the result was clownish. But she puckered up all the same, blew herself a kiss, then turned to Frances and laughed.

'Don't you want me to put some on you?' she said, but Frances shook her head. 'I think it'd make you look really pretty.' Wyn shrugged.

With her face done she went back to the dresser, tugging off the blouse and fetching out one of Carys's corsets instead. 'Help me do it up, Frances,' she said. Frances pulled the laces as tight as she could around the sharp ridges of Wyn's shoulder blades and the raised knobs of her spine. It was far too big, and the fabric was drab from being washed and worn too many times, but it had a little lace along the top edge, and though the cups sat proud of Wyn's bony chest, there was something exciting about it. Something that spoke of the mysteries of being an adult. Wyn put one hand on her waist, lifted her chin and tilted one ankle, like the model on a dress pattern. 'When I get married, I'm going to look *much* nicer than Carys,' she said. 'Don't you think? Dad says I'm going to be a proper beauty, like a society lady. No one says that about Carys.'

'No,' said Frances, with one eye on the door, ears straining for the sound of footsteps.

'No what?' said Wyn.

In fact, Carys was admired for her figure and her dark, lustrous hair. They'd once overheard the coal man comment that she went in and out in all the right places. What Wyn really envied was her sister's freedom; the fact that she was out from under their father's roof and done with school, and had a job that paid her a little money to go to the pictures with her friends on a Saturday night. Wyn was the pretty one, the only blonde in a family of brunettes, and her father's favourite, but Carys was halfway to having a different life altogether, especially now she had Clive. Her fiancé lit up at the sight of her, and wolf-whistled when she walked into the room – as long as Mr Hughes was out of earshot. Carys had reinvention within her grasp; Wyn only had it in her daydreams.

Usually, their illicit forays into Carys's realm ended with Wyn putting things away none too tidily, as if she wanted her sister to know she'd been there. That day, she was still posing in the corset, while Frances fidgeted in her scuffed boots and navy pinafore, when Carys came pounding up the stairs. She was a waitress in a café near Green Park Station, and wore the long black skirt and high-necked blouse she had for work as she stormed into the room with mottled cheeks and savage eyes.

'You little bugger! What have I said about going through my things? And wasting my bleedin' rouge? What have I told you!' She made a grab at Wyn, who darted away with a yelp, leaping onto the bed and over to stand behind Frances. 'You've no bloody business coming in here, messing about! God in heaven, I moved out of the house to get away from you, but you still plague me . . . Come here! Take it off!' She reached around Frances, caught her sister's arm and yanked it. Frances kept quiet and tried to make it to the doorway. She knew she couldn't actually go until Wyn could come too, but she wanted to be ready. She wished she had the courage to say 'We weren't doing any harm', or something like that. Wyn protested with furious defiance.

'Get off me – ow, Carys! You're hurting my arm!'

'I'll *break* your ruddy arm!'

'Don't let Clive hear you talking like that, when he thinks you're so sweet!'

'You shut your face!'

They wrestled and dodged for a moment, then Carys dealt Wyn a slap around the face that left a bright pink handprint. There was a moment of startled silence before Wyn turned on her heel and fled.

'Wait for me!' Frances cried, going after her.

'Oh, that's right! Run and tell tales!' Carys shouted down the stairs. Which was exactly what Wyn did. Nora Hughes emerged from number thirty-four, leaving baby Annie screaming on her own, and marched next door to confront her eldest daughter. Wyn trailed behind her, furious and absurd in the pilfered corset. Frances dithered, unsure whether to go home and save herself from the awfulness of it all by abandoning her friend, or be loyal and wait, when she was neither needed nor wanted there. In the end she parked herself on the wall outside as their angry voices rang out.

'She's just a kid, Carys! You don't raise your hand to her!'

'She's a pest! And she does it on purpose! Look – she's got rouge all over my best blouse!'

'Wyn, go and take that corset off, for heaven's *sake*, child!'

Secretly, Frances didn't blame Carys for being upset about it, but she wondered if Wyn would be so determined to provoke her if she didn't flare up the way she did. But then there'd been the time, the year before, when Carys actually *had* broken Wyn's arm. There'd been floods of tears and repentance then, as Wyn tottered off, white and shaking, holding the arm out in front of her like it belonged to somebody else. It was splinted and wrapped by a friend of the family who was a nurse, and who tried to make a joke about how thin Wyn was, even though her eyes showed real concern. It didn't matter how many sandwiches or biscuits Frances sneaked her, or how many times she saved her pocket money for chips and handed over the lion's share – Wyn never seemed to get any bigger. There was a hunger at the core of her that titbits couldn't fill.

The row raged on, and Frances watched a veined white butterfly moving steadily from flower to flower along the dandelions in the gutter. Gulls wheeled over Beechen Cliff; an ant came to investigate her boot heel. Her stomach rumbled and she wondered what it would be for supper that night. She heard the churches ring four and decided to go home, but she was still there a short while later when Clive Noyle came sauntering along the lane. He worked as a bricklayer, and wasn't off fighting in the war because his chest was too weak, which Frances had been told not to mention because the burden of not being able to fight for his country was a heavy and terrible one for a man to bear. But Clive always seemed quite cheerful about it, so Frances supposed he must just be good at pretending.

He was quite tall and slim, and had warm brown eyes with a lustre that was almost metallic, a bit like conkers fresh out of the shell. He had thick, straight, tea-coloured hair that shone in the sun, a ready smile, and was so handsome that Frances felt flummoxed in his presence, and disappeared into shyness. She picked up the faint, pungent smell he always had, from the Bosisto's Oil that helped his chest – he put drops of it on a handkerchief, and breathed it in.

'Hello, Frances.' Clive squinted down at her, standing with one hand in his trouser pocket and his shirt undone at the collar. 'How come you're out here guarding the gate?'

'They're having a set-to,' she said, blushing bright pink for no reason.

'The women?' he asked, and sighed when she nodded. He tweaked the knees of his trousers and sat down beside her, lighting up a smoke. 'I bet young Wyn was fiddling about in Carys's room again, am I right? I don't know why you girls are in such a hurry to grow up,' he said, blowing a plume of smoke into the afternoon sky. 'You and Bronwyn, I mean.'

'Wyn wasn't *trying* to annoy her,' said Frances, doubtfully.

'You reckon? Look, Carys has precious little to call her own,' Clive pointed out. 'You wouldn't like it if she came around and played with your toys without asking, would you?' he said. Frances shrugged, not daring to point out that she was too old for toys, really, and was far more interested in books and puzzles. Clive was twenty-six, far too old to be expected to know a thing like that. 'Being a kid's the best thing in the world. I don't suppose you realise that yet, since you are one, but trust me. Once you're a grown-up, it's all about work, work, work. Getting enough money to scrape by. You have your games while you can, Frances. Tell Wyn that from me – you should be making the most of it, not looking ahead all the while, pretending to years you've not grown into yet.'

Clive reached back into his pocket and took out his silver coin. He always carried it with him; he liked to spin it, high in the air, and turn it to and fro between his fingers. 'See this?' he said, holding it out to Frances. 'Take it – look closely.' Frances did as she was told, noticing how warm the metal was from being in his pocket. 'Look at the date,' said Clive.

'It says 1892,' she said, reading the figures underneath the head of a woman.

'That's the year I was born. It's an American dollar, pure silver. My uncle sent it over the pond for my tenth birthday, and he said it was going to be the first of thousands I'd make. Thought I was quite the big man, I did, taking that to school to show my chums. I boasted a good deal about how I was going to go to America and work with my uncle, and be a millionaire. It was all I thought about.'

'And aren't you going to go?'

'Well.' Clive shrugged, taking a long drag on his cigarette. 'My uncle died the year after that, without a penny to his name, so it turns out this might be the only dollar I ever have. There you go. Things don't always turn out how you want them to.' He took back the coin from Frances. 'That's why I don't naysay Owen about being a footballer when he grows up. Let him have his dreams and his fun, I say; he'll find out soon enough. Stay a kid as long as you can, Frances. Oh – here we go,' he said, at the sound of a door opening behind them. They stood up. Clive tossed the dollar into the air and caught it with a slap on the back of his hand. 'Heads she'll bite my head off, tails she'll remember that she loves me,' he said, with a grin. Frances peered at the coin when he uncovered it.

'It's tails!' she said.

'Lucky for me, eh?'

When the Hughes women emerged from number thirty-three – Mrs Hughes weary, Wyn faintly triumphant in spite of the handprint on her cheek – Carys stayed in the doorway behind them with her arms folded and a face like thunder. Clive sauntered over to her, throwing Frances a wink and a farthing as he went, and even though Carys said, 'No, Clive,

I'll not have it—' as he approached, he grabbed her around her hips and hoisted her up, spinning her around and kissing her loudly until she laughed and stopped trying to bat him away.

And whether it was seeing how quickly Carys forgot her anger, or the fact of the handprint, Wyn was restless and morose for the rest of the afternoon. She turned down all of Frances's suggestions, and made none herself, until she finally agreed to go and look for newts in the washhouse round the back. Water was channelled from the hill's many springs into a big stone trough, and the cobbled floor was slippery and uneven with damp. The trough water could be used for cooking or washing, but not for drinking – that had to be got from a pump at the other end of the yard. There was a big copper with a burner underneath; a hand-cranked mangle; a huge wooden washboard; scrubbing brushes and baskets of clothes pegs and the odd lost sock. As was the rule in the communal yard, everyone knew what was theirs and where it went. The door was made of wooden planks, and so rotten at the bottom that there was a big, jagged gap for wet-loving creatures to get in.

Frances liked the newts best. She liked their small mouths and slightly apologetic expressions, and the way they spread their toes for balance when you picked them up, and squeaked with a sound like leather rubbing. Wyn wasn't really bothered either way; she didn't like to touch them, but she didn't mind looking at them once Frances had picked them from the water, or from under the loose cobbles.

'Look at this one! I think it's the same one from before, with the yellow on him, underneath,' said Frances, holding up her latest captive.

'Could be,' said Wyn, not really interested. It was hard work, and Frances was relieved when Owen poked his head around the door, all messy hair and long nose.

'Hello, half-pints. What you up to?'

'Catching newts,' said Frances, holding up yellow-belly to show him. She was never shy around Owen.

'Well, don't eat too many before supper, will you?'

'Don't be *stupid*, Owen,' said Wyn.

'What's up with you, bellyache?' said Owen, rolling his eyes. Wyn didn't smile and she didn't reply, so Frances took a chance and answered for her.

'We went into Carys's room and then Carys slapped Wyn.'

'I don't care about that!' Wyn cried, convincing no one.

'She slapped you?' Owen seemed to think about that for a while. He came into the washhouse and sat down on the edge of the trough. 'What about you, Frances? Did she slap you, too?'

'No, course not.'

'Did she ... bite you? Kick you? Threaten to cut you up and cook you?'

'No!' Frances laughed.

'Huh. Sounds like you got off pretty lightly to me.'

'She's a cow,' Wyn muttered.

'Well. So don't go in her room,' said Owen, shrugging one shoulder. 'Don't you want to know where *I've* been after school?'

'Where?' said Wyn, in spite of herself.

'I've been to one of the most ancient and haunted places in the whole city of Bath – probably in the whole of England, in fact.' He paused for effect and Wyn looked up, one cheek still mottled, her eyes simmering. The newt wriggled, and Frances let it plop back into the trough.

'Where's that, Owen?' she said.

So Owen told them about the old leper hospital on Holloway, and how Holloway had once been the Fosse Way, a Roman road, ancient beyond measure, and how in medieval times the people of Bath didn't want the lepers living anywhere near them, so they built the hospital outside the city walls, near Magdalen Chapel, so that when they died the vicar could say prayers for them, and then bury them in a pit. Over the years, many men and women went into the hospital to die, and they were all crowded in and lived in misery, so of course they would come back after they were dead, as ghosts, to share that misery around.

'Mr Jackson says we ought to know the history of where we live. He says it's one of the oldest buildings in Bath. And it's right here, a stone's throw from our house.'

'But it just looks like a normal cottage,' said Wyn, sounding sceptical.

'It may do. But haven't you noticed that nobody ever lives in it? Haven't you sometimes felt, when you walked past it, that those funny little windows were watching you?' The girls listened, rapt. 'And do you know about leprosy? There's no cure, and your skin and all your meat just rots off your bones and drips down you like candle wax – all while you're still alive. And once there was no more leprosy they shut lunatics up in there instead, because nobody wanted to live there. Madmen and murderers and . . .' Owen dried up, failing to think of anything as bad as a murderer or someone with lique-fied skin. Frances swallowed, feeling sick at the thought of it, but Wyn's expression was avid. She was never squeamish – she looked delicate, and dreamed of wedding dresses, but there was a streak of steel at the core of her. 'So think about that, next time you're walking past it. And never – ever – go there at night. Or . . .' Owen paused, then leapt at Frances with a ghostly wail, his fingers grasping. Frances started backwards so fast she tripped on a cobble and landed on her backside, and Wyn dissolved into laughter as she went to help her up.

The following day, the girls went to sit on the damp grass

in Magdalen Gardens, and stared across at the leper hospital. It was early summer, and the sprawling Judas tree in Magdalen Chapel's yard was raining the last of its pink blossoms over Holloway. Frances had brought Bovril sandwiches for Wyn; they weren't her favourite, but she never complained. The old leper hospital did look different to all the rest – its proportions were slightly off, to twentieth-century eyes. It was too small for a detached building, for one thing; it was too shallow, and its windows were too narrow, and pointed at the top. Nobody lived there, Owen was right about that; nobody had lived there for years and years. Day and night, those Gothic windows remained utterly blank – no movement behind them, no lights, no curtains. Wyn stared and stared at them, as though trying to catch sight of something fleeting. Frances felt uneasy.

They'd always known of the place, of course, but it hadn't particularly inspired them until Owen told them about it. They knew that boys clambered over from the churchyard from time to time. They made dens in the small yard on the hospital's west side, hidden from the road behind a high stone wall, smoking and swapping dirty postcards until the chapel warden caught them and turfed them out. But the building itself was locked, and as far as anybody knew, no one had actually been inside it for years.

'When you think about it, how could it *not* be haunted?' said Wyn, once the sandwiches were gone. 'When so many people have suffered and died right there, locked up inside?' The sun came out from behind a cloud and lit Wyn's blonde hair. It had been washed quite recently, and she'd left it loose down her back – long, thin ribbons of it, almost touching the waistband of her skirt. Frances admired Wyn's hair, and her pretty face, and the quick way she moved. She admired her friend very much, and the sight of her sunlit hair helped dispel the images Owen had conjured. Wyn scratched at the rash she sometimes got on the soft side of her elbows. The windows of the old cottage were beginning to look sinister, and watchful. It was breezy, and Frances heard whispering voices in the hiss through the trees.

'What do you think they look like? The ghosts?' she asked. Wyn shrugged.

'Dead rotten things, who want to steal your flesh to fill in all the holes they've got in them.' Wyn thought for a while. 'Auntie Ivy says the dead are jealous of the living, so maybe that's it. They hate us. They want what we've still got.'

'But that's not fair! It's not our fault.'

'Doesn't matter. That's how ghosts *are*, Frances.' Wyn shrugged again, suddenly an expert. There was a pause, then she turned and squinted at Frances. 'Let's go in.'

Frances stared at her in horror, and shook her head.

'No. I don't want to.'

'Oh, come *on*, Frances! Everybody knows ghosts can't *actually* hurt you, they only *want* to,' Wyn backtracked. But Frances shook her head again, and wrapped her arms around her knees for protection. The thought of it gave her a choking feeling. 'Come on, don't be a cowardy-custard, Frances, or someone will give you the white feather. Please? *Please?*' Wyn pleaded, but Frances would not be moved. The thought of being told off by the church warden or stumbling across a gang of boys was bad enough, without the lepers and the ghosts. Even getting the white feather would be preferable.

Two girls had given Clive the white feather, the year before. He'd been on a tram, coming down Southgate Street, and they'd gone over and handed him one feather each, right there in front of everyone. Never mind that as soon as he got out of breath his lungs packed up, so he'd been declared medically unfit for service – Frances had heard the wheezing sound herself often enough. She overheard her father telling her mother about the feathers, in the hushed voice that told her it was a Terrible Thing; and it must have been bad because Clive went away for weeks afterwards, and Carys cried her eyes out. It was a dreadful thing to be called a coward, but this was different, and Frances tried to stand firm.

'You can go, you don't need me,' she said. Wyn folded her arms and stared silently at the leper hospital. Frances squirmed inside. She already knew Wyn would start up again, and she knew that she would surrender. She almost felt cross about it, because of course Wyn knew she would win. The silence went on; it began to feel like a weight pressing down on Frances. She could hardly stand it. The breeze whispered; a dray horse clopped down Holloway, brakes squealing on the cartwheels behind it. Frances heard the tiny wet sound of Wyn's mouth opening again, and her indrawn breath.

'*Please*, Frances?'

4

Tuesday

Two Days After the Bombings

'They were just so . . . odd about it,' said Frances, frowning, as she picked at her lunch. 'They didn't say a word.' She'd been telling Pam about her visit to Nora and Carys Hughes; her suggestion of Johannes's innocence. There'd been an odd tension in her stomach ever since, something she couldn't unclench that made it hard to eat.

'Well,' said Pam, 'how did you expect them to take it? It's no small thing, is it? I mean . . . the implication of it – if it was someone Wyn knew, then it was someone they all knew, wasn't it? A local.'

'Yes, so I expected Carys to shout, and throw me out, and I expected Mrs Hughes to insist it had been Johannes. Instead they just . . . stared at me.'

'The poor woman hasn't had a chance to get used to the idea that her daughter's been dead all these years. She's barely had the chance to adjust to that, and then you go and suggest that her killer walked free all those years ago.' Pam took a sharp breath through her nose, which she only did when she was angry.

'You don't think I should have said anything?' said Frances.

'Don't you think they've got enough on their plates at the moment?'

Pam watched her sternly, and Frances had to look away.

'Of course,' she said, quietly. Her head was aching again.

'Especially with Davy... nothing's more important than finding Davy. I do know that, more than anybody.'

'I know,' said Pam, softening.

'But isn't this important too?'

'The police investigated. That man was tried by a judge and jury, and he was hanged. There's no question of who did it, Frances.'

'Don't say it like that! Don't say "that man".'

'How else should I talk about a man who kills children?'

'And if it wasn't him?'

'Frances—'

'Johannes would never have buried her in her own backyard! He *couldn't* have.'

'But you can't possibly know that, Frances.'

'I can! I knew him, and I—' She broke off, uncertain what to say.

'You thought you knew him, but you were just a child. And even so, you knew he wasn't... quite right, didn't you? The things you told the police, the things he'd done, and said...'

'But he never would have hurt us! I don't... I don't think I ever believed it, not really. The police took what I said and... and... fitted it to what they wanted to hear!' The tension in her stomach twisted like a snake, holding her tighter.

'No. They simply recognised it for what it was. Which you couldn't have, at that age.'

'I think there are things we never found out about what happened. Things we never knew.'

'Things? What things?'

'I don't know, Pam. I just... Since we found her, I remember... feeling ashamed. I have the feeling that I... that I played some part in it all. Some terrible part.'

'Frances, no. You didn't.' Pam gave her hand a squeeze. 'You played no part in it.'

'How can you be so sure? I remember you and Cecily arguing once, when I was playing out in the garden. Before it all happened. Cecily was arguing for the abolition of the death sentence, and you were arguing that some people are better off dead. And Cecily asked which was the greater travesty – that a guilty man should walk free, or that an innocent one be wrongly executed.'

'Yes. She always thought the latter far outweighed the former. I was never quite as sure.'

'Well, what if *both* happened, back then?'

They were quiet for a while. Pam sat back, deep in thought, her expression grave.

'Frances, dear . . . You've so much weighing on your mind at present. And you have had for a while – leaving Joe like that, and having to come back and live with your mum and dad again. Now with all this, and little Davy disappearing . . .' She shook her head. 'You must be so very worried, and so very . . . distracted.'

'What are you saying, Aunt Pam?' said Frances. Pam leant forwards and took her hand across the table again.

'I'm saying, please don't fly apart, dear girl,' she said. 'You've always felt things deeply; you've always stopped to think when others just plough ahead – and that's a very good thing. But . . . perhaps, right now, a little bit of ploughing ahead would be just the ticket? A little bit of getting back to normal, and sticking with the here and now. Hmm?' She looked at Frances intently, and Frances noticed a distance between them that she never had before. It was frightening; lonely. *Hush, little sisters!* She heard the words in the back of her mind; a voice that wasn't there. *No stone was left unturned.* And then, as clear as day, she heard the last thing Davy had said, as she'd left him with the Landys, a single, sleepy word of protest: *Frances.* She stood abruptly.

'Well,' she said, fighting down tears.

'Oh, I've upset you – Frances, dear—'

'No, no. You're right. I should be doing, not thinking. I should be finding Davy. I'll . . . I'll go to the police now, and make sure they have a record that he's missing, and a good description.'

Frances left before Pam could say anything else, and walked down to the police station on Orange Grove, next to the big, ugly Empire Hotel, now occupied by the Admiralty for the duration of the war. When she paused, just outside, she heard a set of footsteps behind her, of which she'd hardly been aware, also halting. She turned to look, but there was nobody there. Frowning, she carried on inside. The desk sergeant was sympathetic as he helped her fill out a missing persons form for Davy. He became less sympathetic when she then asked to speak to a detective and wouldn't say why. She'd hardly known she was going to ask until she did, and was anxious not to be turned away before she'd had the chance to speak. She waited in the large foyer as ten minutes became half an hour; fretting at the delay to her search for Davy. Messenger Service boys rushed in at regular intervals, and caught their breath as replies were scribbled for them to carry back. The police station was surrounded by bomb damage, and the blown-in windows had been covered with board and canvas. It was gloomy inside, and stuffy with the smells of tobacco, boot polish and men – an over-familiar, unwelcome smell, like someone else's bedsheets left on too long. 'Will he be much longer, do you think?' Frances asked the desk sergeant.

'I expect so, yes,' said the sergeant. He sighed through his nostrils. 'Cup of tea?' he said, relenting.

Eventually, a detective came out to talk to her. Inspector Reese was a tall man, very thin and groomed, with a thick moustache two shades paler than his mahogany hair. He came with a faint scent of stale coffee, and wore an expression of frayed patience as he led her to a panelled room and seated her at a table. A sergeant came to sit beside him – a woman, Frances was surprised to see. She was very fair, with blonde eyelashes and pink, freshly scrubbed skin. She looked older than Frances, perhaps over forty, and had a notebook and pencil at the ready.

'Mrs Parry,' said Inspector Reese. 'I apologise that you've had to wait. We're somewhat busy, as you can doubtless see. So, please be brief, if you can.' He steepled his fingers on the table in front of him. Frances doubted herself then; she had the feeling, before she even began, that it was pointless. But the growing tension when she thought about Johannes was getting hard to bear, and there was the way Carys – *Carys* – had been silenced, earlier, and Mrs Hughes had politely but firmly ejected her.

'I'm here to . . . to talk about new evidence in the disappearance of Bronwyn Hughes,' she said.

'Bronwyn Hughes . . .' Inspector Reese frowned, trying and failing to place the name. He was middle-aged; Frances wondered if he'd been on the force twenty-four years ago, and would remember Wyn. Or perhaps he hadn't even been in Bath; his accent was more Home Counties. 'You'll have to remind me,' he said, eventually.

'She disappeared on August the twelfth, 1918, when she was eight years old, and she was found yesterday. One of the bombs uncovered her body on Sunday night.'

'Ah, yes – yes, I heard about the discovery. It was before my time here, of course. The final piece in an unfinished puzzle. But, surely, there's no mystery there. The case is closed. What new information is it you wish to report?'

'Well . . . it's *where* her body was found. I tried to tell the officer who came up to Beechen Cliff Place, but I don't think he understood me. She was still lying where she was put, you see, and that was in the backyard of her own home. She must have been buried there, perhaps beneath one of the outbuildings.' *No stone was left unturned.* The phrase still niggled Frances, like whispered words she couldn't quite hear.

'And you're an expert in such things, are you? In saying for certain that the bones hadn't been moved from their burial place?'

'Well . . . no.' Frances blinked. She felt a growing desperation to be heard, to be believed. 'But she was . . . the skeleton was very fragile. Yet every bone was in its place. They took photographs, the men who took her – one of them had a camera. Photographs of her bones, and of the surroundings, to orientate them – I asked them to do it. And I think . . . well, don't you think her being so close to home shows she was killed by somebody who . . . somebody who knew her? Knew where she lived, at any rate?'

'Any killer could have waited and watched, and found that information out. That's probably exactly what he did, in fact. The kind of man who'd snatch a child is the very kind to prowl and lurk in the days and weeks beforehand, like the predator he is. And close to home can be the best place to hide something. Not quite in plain sight, but people often forget to look right under their own noses.'

'But . . . the man who was arrested . . . he never knew where she lived. And he would never have gone there, even if he had . . .'

'And how can you possibly know that?'

'Because I knew him. I was . . . I was his friend. He was our friend.'

'A poor friend indeed,' said Reese, but then he paused, and Frances felt the attention of the female officer home in on her. 'You knew Bronwyn Hughes?'

'She was my best friend. I was the one who . . . She . . .'
Frances broke off, feeling their scrutiny like hammer blows.
Blood flared hotly in her cheeks; a flush of pure shame. The
inspector cleared his throat.

'The man was not only arrested, if I recall, but convicted
by a jury of his peers, and hanged.'

'But what if he didn't do it?'

'What would you have me do, Mrs Parry? Un-hang him?'

'He could be pardoned. Posthumously. And the real killer
brought to justice.'

'And who do you imagine this real killer to be?'

'I'm . . . I'm not sure,' Frances was forced to admit. She
said it quietly; his question made her stomach turn, and sweat
prickled under her arms. Something stirred again, in the depths
of her mind. She felt the heat of a summer's day on her skin,
had the smell of nettles in her nose, and she was afraid.

'He was a German, as I recall,' said the inspector. 'An enemy
combatant in the last war. And a man given to befriending little
girls. There was never any question of his guilt, and—'

'He was Austrian.' Frances cleared her throat. 'And there
should have been! There *should* have been questions!' She
hadn't meant to raise her voice. The inspector stiffened; the
sergeant shifted in her seat.

Inspector Reese took a long breath in.

'So what you're suggesting to me is that, at a time when no
one can remember being harder pressed by current events, I
should reopen a case that was solved a long time ago, because
the child's body has now been found, and you have no information further to that?' Frances looked down at her hands,
frustrated, cowed, but also defiant, because however confused
she was about some things, she was suddenly completely sure
of one thing.

'They hanged the wrong man,' she said. The words shook

her. It seemed like she'd waited twenty-four years to say them, and they brought a wave of cold, sickening guilt with them.

'And at this very time — at war, our city under siege by German aggressors — you wish to protest the innocence of just such a man?'

'He wasn't German! But even if he had been, it wouldn't make him a killer.'

'I think a quick look outside might suggest otherwise, Mrs Parry.'

'And what about all the bombs we've dropped over there? I read about what happened to Lübeck. So are we murderers, too?' she said, breathlessly. Reese looked at her coldly.

'I suggest you go home, Mrs Parry, if you're lucky enough to still have one to go to. And if you haven't, then I imagine there are people prepared to offer assistance. It's been an upsetting time, and I'm sure the discovery of your friend's remains has been most distressing . . .'

'You won't do anything?'

'With regards to that unfortunate little girl, there's nothing to be done.' He pushed back his chair and got to his feet. The sergeant looked up from where she'd been scribbling in her notebook.

'Hadn't I ought to take Mrs Parry's details, in case we need to—' she said.

'There's no need, Cummings.' Reese's tone was final. Sergeant Cummings gave Frances an apologetic look as she rose and held the door for her, and Frances had no choice but to allow herself to be ushered out, sunken with failure.

Frances went from the police station to the first of several rest centres, retracing in part the route she and Owen had taken the day before. She glanced back over her shoulder more than once, thinking there was someone there, or that she could hear footsteps behind her, matching her stride exactly. She never saw anybody who seemed the least bit interested in her, yet the feeling of being watched grew and grew, adding to her agitation at finding no sign of Davy. She was tearful with worry and frustration as she turned for home, and paused on her way back over Halfpenny Bridge to steady herself. A thin kind of sun had come out, and the breeze scattered its light on the river, giving it bright scales like a fish. Ten people had drowned there when the original wooden bridge had collapsed, years before, and now Frances had heard that several bombs had been swallowed by the mud at the bottom, without detonating. Down there they would remain, buried like secrets, just waiting to explode. Frances stayed for a while, her thoughts slipping back to when she was eight years old and her life broke – quickly and agonisingly, like a bone. It had been reset but the scar remained; she was knitted together but not like new. She still ached, still moved differently.

Gulls flew low over her head, calling and cussing at each other. By that evening, Davy would have missed six doses of phenobarbital, and would still be lost, and afraid. Likely to have a seizure. It might already have happened – and he might have come back from one of his absences with no idea where he was, or what was happening. He might have fallen and hit his head, or broken a bone. For him to have survived the bomb at the Landys' but still be in such danger was unbearable. She couldn't stand for him to simply vanish as Wyn had done; to know that one day, years ahead, she might also have to stand over *his* tiny bones, knowing her guilt. Abruptly, she thought of Percy Clifton, the unconscious man in the hospital, and felt again an echo of summer heat – too much, suffocating. A memory of the panicked need to breathe. She thought about Percy's purple, bloated eyelid, and the way she'd felt watched and vulnerable when she was near him. She'd felt watched all day, ever since. She raked through her memories for his name again, and was certain she didn't know it. Yet she couldn't dismiss the feeling he gave her, of staring into darkness at something not quite visible, but there all the same, waiting.

She walked on briskly, up to the Young Fox on the corner of Holloway and Old Orchard. The pub was a mishmash of parts, a building with very old bones that had been added to and altered many times, leaving it with various levels and connecting rooms, slanting doorways and gabled windows in a steep stone roof. It was after five and the pub was crowded with men stopping off on their way home; mostly men from the Stothert & Pitt engineering works on the Lower Bristol Road — reserved work that kept them out of the war — and those past call-up age. With the pervasive smell of burning still outside, the ordinary reek of beer and working men inside was welcome. Frances bought a pint of stout, and the barman didn't bat an eyelid at her being there by herself — the war had changed a lot of things. She looked around the two rooms either side of the bar, then saw Owen in a far corner of the club room, his long body tucked onto a bench, all shoulders and elbows.

There was little decoration to the room other than some old maps on the walls, and a stuffed fox that looked anything but young. The taxidermist had fixed its face into a snarl of utmost savagery, at odds with the mournful look in its glass eyes. Owen Hughes was sitting underneath it, and when he smiled she saw even more clearly the boy he'd been, behind the man he was now. His face was grimy, and the dirt made the lines there more visible; his fingernails were black with grease and muck, and he looked tired. He'd been so full of fun when they were little, such a clown. His smile stuttered when their eyes met, then came back stronger. As a boy he'd wanted to be a professional footballer, now he was a machine tool fitter at

Stothert & Pitt. One small human cog in that roaring machine of a place, filing in and out every day with a long line of other men. Frances had heard rumours that they were making things for the army now – tank turrets and gun housings – along with the shipping cranes and machine parts they'd always made.

'Shove up, Baz,' Owen said to the man sitting across from him, making room for Frances to sit down. There was shuffling, then a grudging pause as the men checked their conversation, taking a female presence into account. Frances gulped her drink as the awkward moment passed. Gradually, the others returned to talking amongst themselves. Owen shot her an apologetic look, with half a smile. She saw sadness behind his eyes, and felt its echo in her heart.

'How are you?' she asked him. Owen shrugged.

'Fed up of the mess. But fine. You? I came up to Pam's earlier, but you were asleep.'

'I know. I'm sorry . . . she let me sleep far too long. But I went to the Royal United, and I went to see your mum too.'

'Why should you be sorry? How long had it been since you'd slept? You needed the rest.' He paused. 'Pam told me you were out in it. The raids, that is. Both nights.'

'It wasn't by design, but yes,' said Frances. Owen shook his head slowly. She saw the salt of spent sweat at his hairline, the stiffened strands of his dark hair, falling over his forehead; she imagined the softness of it once it was washed.

'Nothing there, then? At the hospital?' he said.

'No. But I saw—' Frances cut herself off, looking away. A man she didn't know, who sent her spiralling into old, half-forgotten fear.

'Saw what?'

'I . . . Nothing. Was it . . . was it awful at St Mark's?'

'As you'd imagine,' said Owen, his face closing off.

'Are you all right? I mean . . . I hope you are. I should have gone with you.'

'No, you shouldn't.' Owen shook his head emphatically. 'And I'm glad you didn't. Anyway, Davy wasn't there, that's the main thing.'

'Yes.' Frances swallowed against the tightness of her throat. 'How long can he be expected to survive on his own, do you think? Out there, in all that chaos?'

'Frances, stop it. That's not what's happened. Either . . . either he was killed with the Landys, or he ran off and somebody's picked him up. He'll be safe, wherever he is. He'll be looked after till we find him.'

'He wasn't killed with the Landys. He got out, and he tried to find me, but . . . if someone's picked him up, where is he? Why haven't they taken him to a rest centre, or to hospital? He needs his medicine!'

'Well, they won't know that, will they? Davy won't tell them.'

'They wouldn't just . . . keep him, would they? People don't just do that, do they?'

'I'm sure . . .' Owen frowned slightly. 'I'm sure they wouldn't.'

'What is it?'

'Nothing.'

'Owen, tell me.'

Owen looked at her and then away. He sank slightly in his seat, obviously reluctant to speak.

'You remember those stray bombs that dropped on us down in Dolemeads last Easter?' he said, and Frances nodded. 'Well . . . a kid went missing after that – Gordon Payne. The Paynes' house was hit, but they all got out OK. He was with them the morning after, but somehow, in the chaos as they got themselves sorted, they lost sight of him.'

'What do you mean, lost sight of him?'

'He disappeared. One moment he was there, scared but not hurt, as they set about salvaging what they could, the next he was gone.'

'What happened to him?' said Frances, a shiver of threat ghosting up her spine. 'Did somebody take him?' Owen looked across at her, and nodded.

'He . . . There was no sign of Gordon for almost a fortnight. His people went frantic looking for him. Then he came back – made his own way home. What was left of his home, anyway. God, I won't ever forget how his mum wept when she saw him.'

'But where had he been?'

'He couldn't say.' Owen shrugged one shoulder. 'Couldn't or wouldn't. There were signs on him that he'd been . . . kept. And not treated well. Bruises, and the like. All he'd say was that a man had offered to buy him fish and chips and then hadn't let him go home, but that he'd got away.'

'And you think . . . do you think it could have happened to Davy? He could have been kidnapped, I mean? You do, don't you?'

'I don't know, Frances – it's unlikely, but . . .'

'How old was Gordon?'

'Seven or thereabouts, I think. Look, I shouldn't have told you . . . it's probably nothing to do with it.'

'But if Davy's been taken . . . He wouldn't try to escape, not like Gordon did. He's not that kind of boy . . . he wouldn't even cry out for help! Would he? Did they tell the police? The Paynes?'

'They're not the sort of family that talks to the police.'

'Well . . . can I talk to them? Perhaps the little boy can remember something about where he was taken, or where he was kept? I could ask him, and——' She broke off because Owen was shaking his head.

'Their house was a ruin, Frances. They moved away, I don't know where. I shouldn't have told you – please, try not to think about it. I'm sure Davy's just got himself lost, that's all . . .'

'But what if he's——' Frances heard her voice shaking; she couldn't keep it steady.

'Stop it.' Owen reached across and took her hand, brushing his thumb across the back of it to soothe her. 'You can drive yourself mad with "what if".'

Frances rubbed at the cigarette smoke in her eyes, trying to banish the idea of a snatcher from her mind. Davy was so quiet, so gentle. So pliant. He would be the easiest child in the world to steal. She took a deep breath, and tried not to picture it. She looked down at Owen's hand, holding hers. His touch made her notice all her edges – the surface of her skin, and all the places her clothes were touching it. After a moment he let go, dropping his chin self-consciously and clasping his hands on the table. The pause grew strained. She and Owen had once been so at ease together, harmonious in some unspoken way. Frances knew exactly how and when that ease had ended, and even though it was far too late to fix it, she still wished to. It had been a gauzy June night, and they'd walked out along Lyncombe Vale together, to where the road tapered to a muddy track and disappeared under the railway bridge, into a field. They'd been sharing a bottle of cider he'd pilfered from somewhere; she could only have been fourteen, and Owen eighteen or so. By then she was no stranger to kissing, and she knew what men wanted. But it had been different with Owen; so different that they'd never even touched.

The way the road ahead vanished into wildness; the way they hadn't needed any light but the night sky; the way she'd known the exact size and shape of him, without having to look. She'd been certain that they would go on like that, always: side by side. So she'd gathered her courage and kissed him. For a while he returned it, and it had sent a fire scorching through her – it had felt completely safe and utterly thrilling at the same time. But then he'd stepped away, his face obscure in the twilight. He'd said she was too young for that; he'd sounded uneasy, almost amused. Frances had felt sure the humiliation would obliterate her, and she'd hated him for a long time after that; she'd hated the memory of the taste and feel of his mouth, and his skin, but the memory refused to leave her alone. By the time she was old enough to realise he'd broken her heart, it was too late – time had passed and life had changed and they hardly saw each other any more. Out in the street sometimes, just passing, and then not at all for weeks, months, at a time. She didn't let herself cry when Owen got married, though it felt at the time as though somebody had died; and a couple of years later she agreed to marry Joe.

She looked across at Owen now, pressing the familiar deep bruise of what might have been.

'Maggie's still not back, then?' His wife's name always felt peculiar in her mouth, like she was saying it wrong, though it was an easy enough word.

'No. Says she's still not sure it's safe. Plus the dust sets her off, and I need to do some work on the house before they all come back and get under my feet.' He smiled slightly.

'Are you missing the kids, or revelling in the peace and quiet?'

'I revelled the first night, but I'm missing them now. Impossible not to, really – they take up so much room. Nev's fourteen now, and he'd take umbrage if he heard you calling him a kid. Sarah's ten, the spitting image of her mum, and Colin's just turned six.' He'd counted them on his fingers but then let his hand drop, as if feeling foolish. 'They're staying out with Maggie's sister in Bathford.'

'Well, that's good,' said Frances. 'Good that they're safe, anyway. You've still got Carys's daughter Denise as well, haven't you?'

'That's right.' Owen nodded. 'She's no bother at all, good as gold.'

'How old is she now?'

'Seven. She looks just like—' Owen broke off. A shadow flickered over his face. 'She looks just like Wyn at that age. Blonde hair and buck teeth. It's the damnedest thing.'

'Is that why . . . Do you think that's why Carys asked you to look after her?'

'How do you mean? No, she just can't cope. You know how she is these days . . . Denise is better off with us – she and Sarah are more like sisters than cousins. Who did she have to play with at home with her mum? Fred's twelve going on twenty-four, and Davy . . .' He paused, taking a breath. 'Davy's not quite all there. She was having to look after him all the time . . . it wasn't fair, really.'

'But he was left with only Carys to look after him.'

'And you. That's where you came in, wasn't it?' he said. Frances didn't think there was criticism there, or an accusation, but she heard them anyway. 'I didn't mean . . . I didn't mean anything by that, Frances,' he said, gently. 'He should have been fine with the Landys. You weren't to know.'

'But I shouldn't have—'

'You've always been the first to blame yourself, but if anyone's to blame, it's Carys. She's his mum. If she wasn't so drunk all the time she'd be able to look after him better, and wouldn't need to farm her bloody kids out left, right and centre. And maybe Clive would stick around a bit more, too. And if she hadn't been so drunk the whole time she had Davy in the oven, maybe he wouldn't have come out . . . the way he did.'

They were quiet for a while. He was right about Clive staying away most of the time. Frances tried to think when she'd last seen him properly, and it had been years ago, when she was still a teenager herself. She remembered coming out of number thirty-four, having been to visit Mrs Hughes, and Clive being on the step of number thirty-three, filthy from work and holding out a bucket of frogs to four-year-old Howard, his and Carys's first child. Carys had been hugely pregnant with Terry, their second, at the time. She'd stood with her hands wedged into the small of her back, taken one look at the wriggling amphibians, with their bulging eyes and pulsing throats, and paled.

'We had to clear out a pond at the site today. There's hundreds of the blighters,' Clive said.

'I don't see why that means we have to have them here,' Carys replied, catching Frances's eye and pulling a face, but Clive could only smile at Howard's boggle-eyed delight. They'd still seemed relatively happy, back then; Carys hadn't drunk as much, and Clive had only gone away for work a few weeks at a time. That was before he did his first stretch for petty theft – it was harder for him to get work after that, and he'd had to go further afield.

Frances took another mouthful of beer.

'I asked Carys where Davy liked to play, or where he might hide, and she couldn't tell me,' she said, quietly. She looked up at Owen. 'I don't . . . I don't think she's even out looking for him.' She was incredulous, and at the same time noticed the heat of her resentment towards Davy's mother. Owen looked uncomfortable.

'No, well. She's been hard hit, and she is about to lose her home.' He downed the last of his pint. 'And she's bloody useless. We've established that.' His tone told Frances not to say anything else about it. The beer was making it harder to think straight. She watched Owen for a moment, looking straight into his eyes with their particular shade of washed-out blue, like faded cloth. 'I expect your Joe's been worried about you. He'll be back to see you, I suppose,' he said, and Frances pulled her gaze away.

'I don't know,' she said. 'Do you think they'll even have had news of this, up north?' When Joe had got the call-up, he'd opted to go into the coal mines rather than the forces. Frances didn't like to think of him working underground, in darkness. He was so used to far-off horizons and green spaces. She didn't like to acknowledge how easy it was not to think of him at all.

'Of course they'll have had news of it. Haven't you let him know you're all right?' Owen was incredulous.

'I probably should.' Frances didn't want to talk about her husband, least of all with Owen. She was too used to being made to feel she'd done the wrong thing in leaving him, when in fact she knew she'd finally done the right thing. The wrong thing had been marrying him in the first place.

'Joe's a good man,' said Owen, stiffly, as though Frances might not know, or might have forgotten. She turned to look at him but he looked away, embarrassed.

She was relieved when a stranger interrupted them. The man smelled strongly of beer as he pushed past Frances, leaning over towards Owen.

'You found the kiddy yet? Only I heard there's been a gang of 'em kipping in the haystacks up Claverton Down, 'cause the community hall's full up. Could be he's up there?'

'Claverton?' said Owen, looking at Frances.

'I don't think he knows Claverton . . . but then, all those

people walked that way on Sunday, didn't they? He might have followed them . . . or latched on to someone.'

'All right, let's get up there. Thanks, John.' Owen clapped the man on the shoulder as he stood up. 'Night, lads, see you tomorrow,' he said. Frances glanced at the other men, half expecting foolish grins, or suggestive looks, but there was none of that. Perhaps the bombings had changed things, or perhaps they just didn't think of Frances that way, with her slacks and battered sweater, and no make-up on. 'We've an hour or two of light left,' said Owen. 'Should be plenty.'

'We can ask in the community hall too,' said Frances, pushing her hands into her pockets as they went out into the cool evening, and wishing she had her coat.

As they walked up Widcombe Hill, Frances thought about how a person from childhood could feel so known, and be such a figure of trust, even though growing up almost always meant growing apart. She supposed it was because the things seen and felt and done in childhood were indelible; that version of them stayed with you the rest of your days, whatever else happened. She'd been aware of that with Davy, hoping that she was giving him good things to remember alongside the rest. She pictured him in the haystacks, in a tangle of other children – unwashed, with bits in his hair and furred, unbrushed teeth, but warm, safe, not alone. She knew the way gangs of children formed miniature societies: the older ones bossing the younger ones – sometimes too harshly, but ultimately keeping them safe. And there were always one or two of the older ones who were surreptitiously kind, and comforted the persecuted when it went too far. That had been Owen. She looked sideways at his rangy figure, long-striding, frowning in thought. Cheering her and Wyn up when other boys had stolen their sweets or pulled their hair; when Carys had gone too far in a row, or their father had settled a discussion with a slap. Clowning about and jollying them along until a smile returned. She wished he looked happier now; she wished life had been kinder to him, as he'd grown up.

She also knew what children could be like when they singled someone out as different. Would the strangeness of the bombings mitigate that kind of prejudice? Frances hoped so. When Davy had started at the infants' school at the bottom of the hill, his classmates had taken against him at once. They made fun of his ears, and said that he stank, and had fleas. Frances had hated hearing their needless, unthinking cruelty, and the worst of it was that even if Davy was slow, he wasn't stupid. He was perfectly able to grasp that he was being shunned, and that it was because he was bottom of the class, and that he did smell, some of the time, in spite of Frances's efforts. When she trimmed his hair it was always full of nits – she'd caught them from him herself, more than once. On the worst days, when he came out with a bloodied lip or his shirt torn, he'd fly into her arms and wrap his skinny limbs around her, hanging on tight. It always gave Frances a peculiar squeeze of the heart that was by no means pleasurable. A sense of utter powerlessness.

On Claverton Down they found where the children had been sleeping – the hay had been kicked about and strewn over the grass in a wide ring around each stack. There was a mislaid felt cap, some greasy chip papers and empty lemonade bottles. They walked around the area pointlessly, since there was no movement or sound other than the breeze pushing through the elm trees at the field edge. The children had all gone – perhaps back down to their homes, perhaps collected by their parents and taken to safety. The cold air crept in at Frances's collar and cuffs, making her shiver.

'On to the community centre, then?' said Owen. 'We've time, but I should try to get back down to town before dark. The Home Guard's got orders to shoot looters but I don't suppose they'll be bothering to keep watch in Dolemeads. Christ knows we've little enough for anyone to nick, but still. What we've got I'd like to keep.'

'Why did you move to Dolemeads, Owen?' said Frances. 'It's underwater half the year, every time the river floods.' Owen made a face.

'But then we get swans swimming past the kitchen window. Not everybody gets that, do they?' he said. 'I don't know. It's not so bad. Maggie and Carys never saw eye to eye, you see – like cats in a ruddy sack, at times. It seemed a good idea to put a bit of space between them.'

'Carys has never been the easiest to get along with, I suppose.'

'Well, this time it isn't all her fault. Maggie's got some... ideas, about what's proper. She's always been keen to be respectable.'

'So... she doesn't like Carys's drinking?'

'That, and when she found out about Clive having done time, that sealed it. Didn't matter it was only six months here and there for petty theft, nothing too serious. She didn't want to know.'

'Oh, dear.'

'Last time they spoke, Carys called Maggie all sorts of names that amounted to her being a stuck-up so-and-so. It almost came to blows.' He grimaced. 'Reckons she married down, does my Maggie. Perhaps she's right.'

'Perhaps she ought to know where she's lucky.' Frances blushed slightly after she spoke. 'And yet Carys doesn't mind Maggie raising her daughter?'

'My sister doesn't see it that way around. She sees it as Maggie doing her a favour, Maggie paying her dues.'

'A bit like me with Davy, then.'

'What do you owe my sister?' said Owen, puzzled. Frances

didn't reply, hardly knowing how to define it herself. There was just that pall of shame; the resurfacing memory of a terrible guilt. She thought of Wyn and Johannes, both of them long dead, and the feeling twisted like a knife.

The community hall was packed with people and scattered with bedding. They were making onion soup and the smell of it, combined with stale bodies, was rank. But there was no sign of Davy – no unaccompanied children at all, apart from a brother and sister, their faces pinched and white, evacuees down from London who'd now lost their interim home as well.

'Leave us a description, and his name and that,' suggested one of the WVS women running the centre. 'And write down where you can be reached. It's going to be a few days before everyone's back where they're supposed to be – not that everyone will be going back, of course,' she said, heavily. Frances did as she was told, and as they left she was struck by the scale of the chaos, the numbers of injured, dead and displaced people. Finding Davy in amongst it all – small, quiet Davy – seemed more impossible than ever, and she knew it was far more likely that she wouldn't find him at all. And now, as well, there was the spectre of a man who stole children. The thought made her eyes blur. A tide of misery was rising inside her, and she knew she could easily drown in it.

'Steady on,' said Owen, when she stumbled into him. The sky was an inky blue, and thin strips of black cloud streamed across it as the moon rose, tiny, distant and cold.

'What if he's really gone?' said Frances, struggling for the words. 'What if he's been taken? Or he's died?'

Owen put his arms around her and held tight, and the simple warmth of him broke her. For a while she simply cried, full of sorrows old and new, and helplessness, and wrongs that could never be put right. Gradually the storm passed, and she began to feel calm again. She noticed that her head fitted neatly underneath Owen's chin, and that he smelled beautifully human – of work and dirt and shaving soap. She noticed that she wasn't at all embarrassed to have given in and wept; she wasn't embarrassed to be in his arms when they were both married. It felt fundamentally right to be there. She took a deep breath of him, letting herself feel better for a moment because she knew it couldn't last. Sure enough, seconds later, Owen straightened and gently detached himself.

'Don't give up just yet,' he said. 'You heard what that woman said – it'll be a while before everyone's accounted for.'

'Yes. Yes, you're right.'

'That's better. I hate seeing you cry,' he said, awkwardly. Frances wiped her face on her cuff, since she didn't have a handkerchief.

'Come on, then,' she said. 'Looters are probably carrying away your kitchen sink even as we dither here.' Owen hesitated, as though he might say something, but in the end they walked on in silence. Frances noticed that she hadn't told Owen she'd been to the police about Wyn, and that she hadn't told him about Percy Clifton, and it troubled her.

Owen left her at the bottom of the steps up to Woodlands, and Frances climbed wearily. She paused in the deep dark at the top to listen as he walked away. Even when she could no longer hear his footsteps, she stayed still and quiet, in his wake. Feeling his absence grow. Alexandra Road was dimly lit by moonlight, and as she turned away at last a shadow moved, fleetingly, like somebody passing by the bottom of the steps. With a gasp, she turned back and stared at the window of moonlit street below. Nothing moved, and there was no noise. She stared until her eyes began to ache, and she was no longer sure she'd seen anything; but the idea took hold that, like in a child's game, the shadow would move again as soon as she looked away. Grandmother's footsteps. The thought of it made her heart pound as she forced herself to turn at last, and hurry inside. As she did so, she realised that if Wyn's killer had never been caught, and if they had known Wyn and where she lived, then they might still be around, and they almost certainly knew Frances, too.

Later, when she slept, Frances slipped into a nightmare that circled, meeting itself as it ended and beginning again, repeating for what felt like a lifetime. In it, she was down near the ground – crouching with her head held down – and Percy Clifton was standing over her. He was so much bigger than she was. She knew it was him even though she couldn't see his face or body – just his feet, in leather shoes, and the shadow he cast. It was hot; she could smell nettles and she knew she had to run away but her knees were locked, and she couldn't raise her head – she couldn't move. He covered her mouth; she fought to breathe, feeling her head tighten like it might explode. She was utterly powerless. It didn't matter how she panicked – because she did panic – there was nothing she could do but stare at the ground and wait for it to be over. But in the nightmare it was never over.

When she woke, in darkness, it was with her teeth clenched so tightly that her whole jaw ached, and there was sweat on her lip and between her breasts. She'd had the dream before, but not for a long time. The man in it had always been anonymous, but now it was Percy and Frances was sure it had always been him. She sat up, shivering, in the perfect silence of Woodlands. She'd had nightmares as a child, even before Wyn disappeared – she knew that the echoes would fade, eventually. But it took a long time, and what remained – jetsam thrown up by the tide of fear – was an overwhelming feeling of frustration. To have kept still when she needed to run, to have been silent when she should have shouted. Slowly, alone in the dark, Frances realised that it wasn't merely a dream at all; it was a memory.

One she had wilfully let sink into the depths of her mind, so she wouldn't have to think about it any more.

She shut her eyes, concentrating on the air going into her lungs, spreading her ribs; feeling it push out again, warm on her lips and tongue. The warmth of her blood, her life. She was alive, Wyn and Johannes were not. She centred herself on those two incontrovertible facts. They'd been at the heart of her for decades; she had weighed herself down with them for decades. *Hush, little sisters!* A surge of something unbearable rose up inside her, until she thought she might scream. It was the injustice she had witnessed, and caused; it was the pain of loss; and the shame of wrongs done. It was the torment of things unsaid, pent up for far too long. She fought to see the dream clearly – where the place that smelt of nettles had been, when she had been there, and who had been there with her. But it faded and made less sense the more awake she got. In the blackness of her room she saw Wyn walking away from her – storming away in anger, blonde hair swinging, thin body jerking – and she decided, right then, to root the memories out. To force them into the light, and find a way to say what she should have said long before. A way to clear Johannes's name, and find Wyn's killer. Because her nightmare told her that, somewhere deep inside, she knew.

1918

The main door of the old leper hospital fronted the street, so it was far too visible. Besides, the door was a formidable thing, and securely locked. Wyn decided that they should go in around the side, the way the boys went, so they snuck between the graves of St Mary Magdalen's and climbed over the wall into the old hospital's sunken yard. Breathless and smudged with powdery green algae, there they halted and looked around. The yard had a carpet of moss and rotting leaves, and was littered with sweet wrappers and bits of broken stone. There was a smell like pond water, with the faint tang of urine underneath. Frances was rattled and anxious, but Wyn was excited, intent on the adventure. Frances kept behind her, arms folded. She had the notion of there being spores of the disease left behind – from all the liquid skin and bodies that must have been slopped out of the hospital over the years. She didn't want to touch anything; she didn't really want to breathe it in. More than anything, she wanted to turn and go back.

The breeze seemed colder there, and the shadows darker. There was a rickety wooden lean-to along the back of the cottage, and its door hung crooked from the frame. The girls stared at it for a while – peeling white paint, a rusty metal knob and a cobwebbed keyhole. From a yew tree in the graveyard a rook cawed down at them. Holloway and Magdalen Gardens were only yards away, on the other side of the high front wall, but they seemed distant, out of reach, and Frances curled into herself. She saw the place *itself* as a ghost – abandoned in time, in the past; it seemed a place where warm, living things, like little girls, had no business being. No business at all.

'I'm going to try the door,' Wyn whispered.

'No, don't! We said we'd just *look*!' said Frances.

'Well, we're not going to see any of the ghosts from out here, are we?'

'*Please* don't, Wyn,' said Frances. She'd been avoiding looking at the blank windows in case she *did* see something. 'Let's go. I don't like it here.'

'I'm just going to see if it's locked, that's all,' said Wyn.

On tiptoes, Wyn crossed to the door, turned the handle and gave it a shove. Frances's stomach lurched as it opened, grating over twigs and grit on the floor. Then Wyn gasped, freezing as though something unexpected had happened, and at the same moment Frances saw it: a pale face, streaked with gore, with wide eyes couched in dark, dark shadows. It appeared from nowhere in the small, grimed window beside the door, and Frances's heart seemed to stop. Wyn turned to her, uncertainly, and then they both saw the movement inside: a thin shape; a quick, scraped footstep.

With a squeal Wyn spun away, fled back to the wall and started to climb the ivy. Frances tried to follow but her whole body felt clumsy and slow, and she couldn't make her legs work properly. She scrabbled to get back over the wall – it was harder from the yard, which was lower – expecting at any moment to feel spectral hands dragging her back, then set off across the graveyard after Wyn, tripping and stumbling. They ran up Holloway until they had no breath to run any further, then they stood, gasping, in the shadow of the big brewery up on Bear Flat. Frances realised she'd wet her knickers, and felt sick with shame. Wyn looked contrite. 'Don't worry,' she said. 'We'll stay out till they dry. I won't tell anyone.' As though that was the worst thing about what had happened.

Ghosts roamed Frances's dreams for the rest of that week – they leapt out at her from behind doors, and gravestones, and even, one night, from inside her school desk. She woke crying out for her father, since he seemed the best equipped to deal with things like that, but he'd gone off to be trained for war since the draft had been expanded to include men up to the age of fifty. Her mother did her best to soothe her, but she wasn't sleeping well either, without him, and during the day she was either silent or short with them.

'Can't you just grow up and stop upsetting her?' Keith whispered to Frances, as their mother sat crying at the kitchen table. 'You're not a baby any more. Try thinking about someone other than yourself for a change.' Frances was stung, since she couldn't help the nightmares. She didn't really understand why her mother was so upset – Frances missed her father, but she wasn't afraid for him. He was a hero now, and he'd be back when they won the war, which wouldn't be long now – everybody said so.

Bill Hughes was fifty-two, so he hadn't gone off to war.

'It's a pity your dad's too old to fight the Hun,' Frances said to Wyn, on the walk to school one day, and Wyn shot her a look through narrowed eyes. Even though he often hit her, and was usually angry about something, he was still Wyn's father, and she loved him. Frances explained herself hurriedly. 'I only mean...he's so strong. And...you know, he likes to fight, doesn't he? Sometimes. He'd be great against the Hun.' Wyn thought about this for a moment, then grinned, showing the gap in her front teeth.

'He'd wallop them, good and proper,' she agreed. Wyn seemed completely unmoved by what had happened at the leper hospital, and because of what Keith had said, and her mother being sad, Frances tried to emulate her. It was hard to forget about it, though, when she could see the place as soon as she left the house, and had to walk past it time any time she wanted to go up to Bear Flat, or into Magdalen Gardens. She still saw it in her dreams, too.

That weekend was the go-cart race down Holloway, and Frances and Wyn went to watch. Clive had helped Owen build his cart out of a wooden wheelbarrow, pram wheels bought off the scrap metal man, and a real steering wheel they'd filched from a narrowboat half-sunk in the canal on the way out to Bathampton.

'Can't be stealing if it's no use to anyone else, can it?' said Clive, cheerily, when Mrs Hughes raised an eyebrow.

'Yours is definitely the best one,' Frances told Owen. In fact, Keith's looked sleeker, but she didn't feel much sisterly loyalty any more. She far preferred Owen to her own brother.

'She's a winner, for sure,' said Owen, folding his arms proudly as Clive tightened one last screw.

'There,' said Clive. 'That should hold it. Just don't forget to slow down on the bends, even if it means falling back a bit. You can make it up on the straight. Better that than ending up hanging off a chimney pot, right?' He flipped his silver dollar into the air. 'Heads you'll win, tails they're all going to lose,' he said, holding out his hand. It was heads, and Owen grinned.

They shook hands then set off for the start line at the top of Holloway. Wyn and Frances made their way into Magdalen Gardens to watch. The park had its summer smell of trampled grass and warm paving stones, tainted by the faint, swampy whiff of the river below. The finish line of the race was right by Frances's house, before Holloway made its final left-hand curve to join the main road at the bottom of the hill. A series of signals would be given between boys at the start, the finish, and halfway up the hill, to say when no traffic was coming and it was safe to start. The girls could see the finish line from the gardens, and would also have a view of the racers coming around the top bend, and hurtling right past them. But while they waited, what they could see was the old leper hospital. They'd sat down in some dappled shade directly opposite it, and Frances didn't suppose it had happened by chance.

It looked quite ordinary in the sunshine – far less brooding and sinister than before. The sun glinted from its pointed windows, and a pair of pigeons were at it on the roof.

'Who do you think he was?' said Wyn. 'The ghost, I mean. When he was alive.'

'I don't know,' said Frances. 'Just somebody from Bath who turned into a leper, I suppose.' Wyn's curiosity made her uneasy. It generally ended up satisfied, one way or another, and there was only one way any curiosity about the ghost could be satisfied.

'Did you see him properly? I only got a glimpse, really. He didn't look . . . rotten to me. I mean, not disgusting or anything, like I thought he might look,' said Wyn. Frances shook her head, silently urging the race to start and distract her friend.

'We had a letter from my dad,' she said, in desperation. 'He's still in the training camp, and then he's going to France, but he's only B grade, he said, and because of that he won't be in the front.' Frances hadn't really understood the news, but her mother had been all smiles after she read it. Wyn merely put her chin on her bent knees and kept staring across at the leper hospital, and Frances had a sinking feeling. She almost yelped in relief when they heard the race start – a sudden roar of boys' voices, the rattle and squeal of the go-carts.

They came careering around the corner by Springfield Place – nine lads in a selection of motley vehicles, oversteering wildly, veering dangerously close to collision. Their teammates ran alongside them down Holloway, trying to keep up, yelling their support.

'*Come on, Owen!*' Wyn yelled, at the top of her lungs. She leapt to her feet and waved her arms, and Frances scrambled up beside her.

'Come on, Owen!' she echoed. 'Come on, Keith!' she added, out of fairness. Keith was in the middle of the pack, his eyes white in his face, his teeth gritted. He was tugging his steering wheel this way and that but it didn't seem to have any effect on the direction in which he went. Owen was out in front as they sped past the leper hospital: a rush of noise, peril and pounding feet. There was a shout and clatter as the front wheels came off one of the carts, and the driver was pitched onto the cobbles.

'Go *on*, kid!' Clive shouted gleefully as Owen sped away. He'd been running alongside but he'd pulled up, hands round his ribs, fingers gouging in, as if that would make his lungs work any better. '*Yes!*' he cried, as Owen zoomed across the line and began to swerve madly, trying to stop.

'Owen's won!' said Wyn, hopping up and down. She turned to Frances, her face alight. 'I think your Keith was second.'

'Looked like third to me,' said Frances. They ran down to the finish line, where Owen was up on Clive's shoulders, wearing a paper banner and beaming.

Owen was tall and heavy for his twelve years, and Clive soon had to put him down. The four of them walked slowly back to Beechen Cliff Place, where Clive kept a bottle of his Bosisto's Oil, which helped to ease his wheezing. They were having tea and biscuits with Aunt Ivy, to celebrate Owen's victory, when Carys got home from work. She'd lost her job at the café because a man had grabbed her backside, so she'd tipped his pot of tea into his lap. He'd had to go to the hospital to have ointment on the scald, but Carys said he'd finally got what he deserved. When she was sacked, the other waitresses had a whip-round and bought her a hair comb in the shape of a peacock feather. Cecily called it a 'righteous action', when

Frances told her about it. She'd recently been arrested herself, for a midnight foray onto the golf links by Sham Castle, where she and her friends had dug up the greens and tied luggage labels to the pins, with slogans demanding votes for women. Now Carys had to work in the Lotor soap works on Morford Street, and came home sweaty and exhausted, with pink eyes and sore, chapped hands.

'You'll pack it in as soon as we're married,' Clive promised her, as she joined them, pulling her down to sit on his knee and kissing her red fingers. Then he started coughing again, in spite of the Bosisto's, and Carys stood up, wearily.

'Come on,' she said to him.

'I'll be right as rain in a bit,' Clive protested.

'You might, or you might not. And you don't need another chest infection, do you? So, let's go,' she said. As Clive stood up, they all heard the air whistling in and out of him, and saw how hard he had to work to make it happen. He had a thing called a nebuliser, which worked with a pump and a funnel, so he could inhale a drug to help him breathe. It was an expensive thing, and he kept it in a special box at home, for when the eucalyptus wouldn't do. 'Well done on the win, Owen,' said Carys, ruffling her brother's hair as she passed.

Since she ought not worry her mother with it, Frances decided to talk to Pam and Cecily about the leper hospital. She decided not to say that they'd been into the yard, or that Wyn had opened the back door. Instead, she said she thought she'd seen a ghost in one of the windows.

'Really?' said Cecily, leaning towards her eagerly. She had green eyes, the colour of young wheat, and she opened them wide. 'I believe in ghosts, very much. What did it look like?'

'Sissy, *really*,' said Pam. 'Can't you see the child's frightened?'

'She's not,' said Cecily. 'You aren't, are you?' she said to

Frances, who didn't reply because she didn't like to lie. 'Well,' said Cecily. 'In any case, I've always thought people are wrong to assume ghosts are evil, or mean us any harm. Why should they?'

'Wyn says they're jealous and they want our flesh,' said Frances, to which Pam tutted.

'Young Wyn has a flair for the macabre,' she said.

'Well, I don't think that at all,' said Cecily, staunchly. 'If anything, I've always thought they must simply be very lonely, and longing to be seen, or spoken to.'

'Do you really think so?' said Frances.

'Frances Elliot,' Pam said, firmly. 'There's no such thing as ghosts.'

'Oh? And you know that for sure, do you?' said Cecily.

'I know the tricks people's minds will play on them, if they're willing to let them,' said Pam.

'Well, *I* believe you, Frances,' said Cecily, cocking an eyebrow at Pam. 'And Owen's quite right – that cottage was a home for lepers, and it's very old indeed. We live in an ancient city, Frances, and this part of it, Holloway, has always been a bit ... different to the rest. It's always been home to artisans and outcasts—'

'Not to mention thieves and vagabonds and ... women of the night,' Pam interjected.

'The more *colourful* people of Bath. The kind that come home from work grimy and exhausted every day. Some of the poorest, and least fortunate. And who could be less fortunate than the poor lepers?' said Cecily. 'They were just people who caught an illness, Frances; just ordinary people like you and I, not monsters.' She took Frances's hand and gave it a squeeze. 'But one thing I'm sure of, whatever Wyn's brother has filled her head with, is that ghosts cannot harm us.'

'We can agree on that, at least.' Pam seemed to think for a

moment before she spoke again. 'I think you're a deal more sensitive than your friend Wyn, Frances. Don't let her stories frighten you into seeing something that isn't there.'

So, a few days later when Wyn suggested that they went back and tried to see the ghost again, Frances had something with which to temper her fear. She had Pam's reassuring scepticism, and Cecily's certainty of the benign nature of spirits. In fact, she herself had started to feel a gnawing curiosity to see, and to know more. And, thinking back, she'd heard a scrape and a footstep from inside, when Wyn had opened the door. Ghosts didn't make footsteps, did they? And if they did, and there was one in there, the idea that it might be lonely tugged at Frances's heart. She hated to think of anybody being lonely. She was still nervous but she agreed to go back, and Wyn, who'd clearly anticipated a struggle, smiled with surprised delight.

'We'll be ready for him this time,' she said. 'He won't make us jump like before.' Back they went, beneath the arched boughs of the Judas tree, through the dank fallen leaves and furred gravestones of the churchyard, and over the wall again. Wyn's eyes were focused like a hawk's, and Frances had a stomach full of butterflies. Then Wyn – bold, fearless Wyn, how fiercely Frances admired her then – stepped forwards, put her hands on her hips and spoke loudly.

'Show yourself, ghost!' she said. 'We know you're in there, and we're not scared of you.' She paused, and the silence rang.

Wyn waited a while, and then changed tack. 'We'd like to help you, in fact,' she said. 'If you come out, we promise to try and help you find infernal rest in the bosom of God.' The Hughes family didn't go to church very often, but Wyn's declaration came in a lofty, benevolent tone very like the vicar's, and Frances didn't think it the moment to point out that she probably meant 'eternal'. They both gasped when the

face appeared at the window again, peeping up over the sill –
straggling, matted hair; a pale forehead and wild eyes, the irises
ringed all around by the whites. Frances braced everything,
ready to run, but the ghost flinched at the sight of them and
looked frightened, which didn't seem very ghostlike. And then
it became obvious that it wasn't a ghost at all, but a person.
Flesh and blood, and full of fear. He looked about the same
age as Clive or Carys – it was hard to tell with all the dirt, on
him and on the window. Wyn stepped back to Frances's side
and took her hand uncertainly.

'Well?' said Wyn, to the man. And then they heard his
voice, strained, muffled by the glass.

'*Hush*, little sisters!'

5
Wednesday

Three Days After the Bombings

Frances worked her morning shift at the station because she could no longer claim a reason to stay away. Everyone uninjured and with a roof over their heads was expected to behave as though nothing out of the ordinary had happened. She'd stayed awake after her night terrors, and was heavy with fatigue as she fretted about the time spent not looking for Davy. Picturing him wandering lost after a seizure – or worse, taken by some faceless man – caused pressure to build inside her skull, and behind her ribs. As though she might come apart. She worked in distracted silence. There wasn't a women's version of the porter's uniform, so she wore the men's without the waistcoat – trousers, shirt, tie and peaked cap, all in black except for the shirt. It suddenly seemed appropriately funereal. Since Frances was married, the war hadn't required her to work or to volunteer, as it had single women all across the country, but she'd worked since leaving Joe and the farm anyway, to pay her parents for her keep, and she'd been drawn to the idea of taking on a man's job, just to show it could be done.

She was the only female porter. During her first week there, her colleagues had invented a problem with one of the loading pulleys, and had tried to send her to the engineer's shed to ask for a long weight to fix it. *A long wait*. Frances hadn't known whether to go along with the prank, let them laugh at her and think themselves cleverer than her, or to explain that she'd rumbled them, and try to laugh it off. In the end she'd said, more coolly than she'd intended, that she hadn't been born yesterday. She'd meant to show them that she wasn't completely useless, but in fact she'd spoilt their fun and made them feel stupid, and made herself even more of an outsider, apparently irrevocably. She sat to one side of the little room where they waited between trains; furthest from the stove in winter, furthest from the window in summer, and always required to make the tea. But on the whole she liked working there – watching the people coming and going from the trains with all their different faces and clothes and demeanours. Sometimes, they caused her to imagine all the many lives she could have been born into, instead of the one she had been.

At lunchtime, consumed with hope in spite of herself, she caught the train to Bristol and went to the Royal Infirmary, but no unidentified child patients had been brought in. She returned to Bath and to the Royal United Hospital, but there was no sign of Davy there either. This time, the disappointment had a physical effect on her. She felt enervated, so utterly weak that she was forced to sit down for a while in the foyer, staring, unable to speak or move. For almost half an hour her body felt as heavy and unresponsive as wet sand. She was dimly aware of another person sitting not far away, off to her right, as immobile as she herself was. It seemed to Frances that the other person was watching her – she thought she saw the blurred, pale shape of a face, turned towards her – but she couldn't bring herself to look. She didn't care. A nurse brought her a cup of sweet tea, which helped, and after a while she felt enough resolve to get up. She glanced to her right but the seated figure had gone. There was nobody else there, yet the skin between her shoulder blades tightened all the same. She'd planned to go directly back to Woodlands to collect the notices she'd drawn up, with Davy's details, and take them around some rest centres further afield, but the memory of her nightmare made her pause.

Reluctantly, she returned to the foot of Percy Clifton's bed, trying to see him clearly, to work out why he'd appeared in her dream when she wasn't even sure she knew him. She was relieved to find him still unconscious; she wasn't sure she'd have been able to go near him otherwise. She felt odd, looking down at him; almost absent from herself, as though some vital inner part refused to be near him. She couldn't tell if it was caused by the lingering shock of the bombings, or her nightmare, or something more specific. But still, she felt the maddening certainty that there was something – *something* – about him. Something that wasn't right – or maybe something that was? She stared, and he slept, and no insight came. The skin of his face looked a bit less angry, though it still looked sore and shiny. An ugly bruise had spread out from beneath the bandage around his head, seeping wider like an ink stain under his skin. Stubble had sprouted along his jaw.

He was slightly over average height, Frances reckoned, and averagely built; perhaps fifty years old, perhaps less, perhaps more – it was hard to tell with his face swollen, obscured by injury and wrappings. Similarly hard to tell if he was a nice-looking man, with his jaw hanging slack and his lips cracked.

'Percy Clifton,' Frances whispered, as though saying the name aloud would strike a spark, and tell her why she was there.

'Hello, are you his wife?' said a nurse who looked too young, like a schoolgirl.

'No,' said Frances. She thought quickly, wondering if she should invent some lie to excuse her being there, and excuse her coming back again. When no story presented itself she decided to be honest. 'No, I'm not his wife. I just have the oddest feeling that I know him from somewhere. Has anybody else been in to visit him, do you know?'

'Not as far as I know. That's a pity, I was hoping he had a missus,' said the nurse. 'We've tried to find out his address from the book, but the only Percival Clifton listed for Bath is fit as a fiddle, up in Larkhall.'

'It's not on his ID card?'

'It was near enough burnt away,' said the nurse. 'It was in his wallet, which saved part of it, enough to see his name and date of birth, and—'

'How old is he?' Frances interrupted her. The nurse tapped the chart at the foot of the bed.

'Born June twentieth, 1890, so he's coming up for fifty-two,' she said. Frances thought hard about that, waiting for anything that might ring a bell.

'Could you read his occupation on his ID?' she asked. The nurse shook her head.

'No, but it must be something quite fancy, I reckon,' she said. She glanced around before lowering her voice. 'He had a huge stack of cash on him. Over sixty pounds, I heard! Some of it too burnt to use, more's the pity. He'll be needing new clothes, once he's out of here – we had to throw his suit away. All he's got left are his shoes, down there in the locker.' She nodded at the bedside cabinet. 'He was in the Regina Hotel, see. Most likely a guest there, so he could be from anywhere.' She paused, and noticed Frances staring at the cabinet. 'The money's locked away in the ward sister's room, for safe keeping,' she said, pointedly.

'Has he woken up at all?' Frances asked, and again the nurse shook her head. 'Will he, do you think?'

'Dr Phipps seems to think so. Sometimes, in a fire, the body's starved of air – the brain in particular. That's what causes the stupor. But everything's holding steady – heart and lungs and all, and he'll most likely keep the eye that's under that dressing, though he'll have some scars. He's just not ready to wake up yet. Shall we contact you if he does?'

'No!' Frances replied, before she'd had a chance to think. The nurse blinked at her. 'That is, no, thank you. Perhaps I don't know him at all, you see,' she said.

'Right you are,' said the nurse, dubiously.

Frances walked out of the ward, conscious of the nurse watching her go. But she waited by the doors until the girl had moved on, then doubled back. Taking a breath, she crouched down beside Percy Clifton's bed, opened the bedside cabinet and took out his shoes. They were black brogues, made of good leather but heavily creased across the toes, and with two different knobs where the end of the big toe had rested. As though they'd been moulded to more than one pair of feet. The laces were frayed and the heels worn right down, unevenly. Whoever Percy was, he walked with his weight in the outer edges of his feet. The soles were badly worn too. Frances put her hand inside to feel, and found the insoles gritty and perished. She pressed her index finger to the roughest part, then turned the shoe over. Sure enough, she could see a fleck of pink – a glimpse of her own finger. So Percy had been wearing a suit and carrying a large sum of money, but his shoes were most likely second-hand and so badly worn they wouldn't have kept out the rain.

Frances pulled out her hand and found bits of insole and fluff from his sock on her fingers. A smell was rising from them, and from the shoes – a smell of burning, but underneath that the stale, slightly acrid tang of feet. Revolted, she dropped the shoe. It clattered to the floor and she looked around anxiously, then up at the bed above her. She could only see his right arm and hand, resting on the sheets, but she froze, suddenly struck with horror at the thought of that hand moving, of him waking up while she was crouching down beside him, vulnerable, unable to see him. For a second she was paralysed and couldn't get up, then she stood abruptly, taller than him again, looking down on him again. Her throat felt knotted, her knees shaky. She wiped the debris from his shoe against the seat of her trousers, then turned and hurried away.

Back at Woodlands, Frances was through the door and into the kitchen before she realised that Pam had company. There was another woman sitting with her aunt at the kitchen table, a pot of tea between them. The visitor had her back to Frances, so that all she could see was a set of sturdy shoulders in a dark jacket, and a mass of frizzy blonde hair. Pam's expression, when she looked up, was serious but intrigued.

'Oh! Sorry to just barge in,' said Frances. Pam smiled briefly.

'Not to worry. We've been waiting for you,' she said.

'For me?' Frances went over to the table as the blonde woman looked around, and began to get up. With a start, she recognised Sergeant Cummings, who she'd met during her brief interview at the police station. The policewoman smiled in a wary, faintly apologetic way.

'Hello again, Mrs Parry, I hope you don't mind me visiting you like this. I got your address from the missing person report you filed about David Noyle.'

'You're here about Davy? Is there news?' said Frances, catching her breath.

'Oh,' said Sergeant Cummings, her face falling. 'Oh, no. There isn't. I'm so sorry, I didn't mean to . . .' She closed her mouth, flustered. 'No, I'm afraid I haven't heard anything about young David. I've come about another matter.'

'Sit down, both of you,' said Pam. 'I'll make a fresh pot.'

Frances did as she was told, and Sergeant Cummings took

out her notebook and pencil, tucking a few strands of hair behind her ears. Her peaked cap was on the table beside her. She had a broad face with large blue eyes and a wide mouth; not a pretty face by any means, but with a good complexion and an expression so open, so ready to approve and to smile, that it was instantly disarming. Frances imagined it would be very hard to lie to such a face, and very hard to see disappointment there. The sergeant cleared her throat.

'In fact, I've come to talk to you about Bronwyn Hughes,' she said. Her pencil hovered above her notebook. At the top of the page, upside down, Frances could see the words *Bronwyn Hughes*, *Johannes Ebner*, and *Frances Parry née Elliot* written in a neat, sloping hand. 'I'm not really supposed to be here, you understand,' said Cummings. She looked up at Frances, and there was obvious intelligence behind that disarming frankness. Her frizzy hair was so fair at her temples it looked white. 'We're snowed under after the bombings. It's chaos, and certain types will always take advantage of that. This wouldn't be the first time a serious crime went undetected – or unsolved – because it happened in chaotic circumstances. Not an acceptable state of affairs, in my opinion.'

'No,' Frances agreed, the words jarring her. She thought of young Gordon Payne, who'd also disappeared during a time of chaos, and who'd managed to escape. Just like the man who'd taken him. 'Owen Hughes told me about another little boy who went missing, after the bombings down in Dolemeads last Easter,' she said. Cummings raised her brows, so Frances repeated everything Owen had told her, including the impossibility of talking to the Paynes. 'Perhaps... you could ask your colleagues, or check in the records... Perhaps more children have gone missing, since Wyn did, and somebody's taken Davy. A proper search would—'

'Mrs Parry, forgive me, but the chances of us mounting an

organised search for one little boy at the present time are nil. Especially when by far the most likely explanation is that he has got lost, or has been taken in somewhere.' Cummings took a breath, softening. 'I'm sorry, I really am, but it's just not possible. I'll look into it as far as I can – other disappearances, I mean. And I'll make a note of your concern on the missing persons report,' she said, and Frances nodded, defeated. 'I've come to talk to you about Bronwyn because . . . well, you convinced me. You were there when it happened, after all. You knew the victim . . . Bronwyn. You knew Bronwyn, you knew the Hughes family, and you knew Ebner. In my book, that means we ought, at the very least, to listen to you. It does strike me as significant that she has been found so close to home – it would seem to suggest she was put there by someone with a strong local connection . . . And when I heard you talk about it, when I heard your *certainty* . . . I don't know. Call it intuition, if you want, but you got my attention. And since I only live along in Oldfield Park, I thought I'd come by on my way home.'

'Thank you. Thank you for coming and—'

'I shouldn't be here,' Cummings repeated, carefully. 'Inspector Reese would be very unhappy about it, were he to hear. You understand? This all happened a very long time ago, and the case is closed. A man was hanged. I can't reopen the investigation on a hunch. I can't go and talk to the Hughes family about any of it. At best I can look into the old case report, and, with whatever else you can tell me, I can look for grounds to ask for the case to be reopened. So,' she said, looking up again, her pencil poised, 'what can you tell me?'

Frances sat silent for a moment. She felt on a knife edge; she felt things in the depths of her mind stirring, shifting away as she reached for them. Crouching, hot, with her head down; a smell of nettles in her nostrils; sunlit yellow hair; *hush, little sisters!* She could feel Pam and Cummings watching her as she spread her hands on the table top to hide how her mind was racing. She knew she must deal only in facts; only in things she knew for certain.

'Wyn. She was known to everyone as Wyn, not Bronwyn,' she began. Sergeant Cummings made a note. 'She was my best friend. We met Johannes Ebner early in the summer of 1918, when we went exploring in the old leper hospital. We were ... looking for ghosts. He was starving, and very afraid. He was so young ... He seemed like a grown-up to us, but he was only nineteen. We started to take him food, and we became friends. He spoke good English. It was exciting, having a secret like that. And he really needed the food we took him because – this is the thing, Sergeant Cummings – he couldn't leave the cottage. He was so afraid. He was terrified of being outside, of being seen, and recaptured. He nearly starved to death in there because he wouldn't go out. He *couldn't*. So, you see, he would have had no idea where Wyn lived, or where I lived. There's no way he could have gone out, killed her and buried her in her own backyard. There's just ... *no* way.'

She stopped and took a breath, jittery with the need to be heard, and believed. Her guilt was like a solid shape inside that bruised her whenever she said Johannes's name. Sergeant Cummings was taking rapid notes; Pam was watching with her fingers laced together and a pained expression on her face.

'Could Wyn have taken him there? To her house, I mean – could that be how he might have found it?'

'No. Like I said, he wouldn't come outside. One time she managed to get him to come out into the yard behind the hospital, but it was only for a second and then he ran back in. Besides, he would never have wanted to go where there were other people, and Wyn would never have tried to take him home to her family. They . . . He wouldn't have been welcome. He was our secret.'

'But she was trying to persuade him to come out?'

'Well . . . We were trying to help him get home, you see. But how could he, if he wouldn't leave the leper hospital?'

'He was a German soldier, is that right? An escaped prisoner of war.'

'Yes. He was Austrian, in fact. It was in the papers afterwards . . . He'd escaped from the camp at Larkhill, down near Stonehenge. He was . . . broken down, I suppose you'd say. All he wanted to do was go home,' said Frances. 'That's all he wanted.' Sergeant Cummings looked up briefly, then frowned and cleared her throat.

'And . . . you say you became friends. Did he ever . . . Was there ever anything that, looking back now through adult eyes, you might call . . . inappropriate? From him, I mean?'

'No,' said Frances, firmly. 'Never. And I'm not protecting him or . . . or whatever you might think. There was never *anything* like that.'

'Frances, that's simply not true,' said Pam. 'You told the police at the time how he'd acted, upon occasion, and—'

'I was wrong! I . . .' Frances shook her head. 'The way I said it – the way they heard it – I didn't know . . . They were looking for reasons to convict him, you must understand. They *wanted* it to be him! What he did . . . what I said happened wasn't the way it was. I can see that now.'

'After all this time,' said Cummings, sounding sceptical. 'What kind of behaviour, exactly, are we talking about?'

'He wasn't a pervert,' Frances insisted. 'He wasn't dangerous. He was just a frightened . . . *kid*. In the wrong place at the wrong time. He was hanged for being German!' Images flooded her mind – Wyn's blood in the backyard of the leper hospital; her torn clothing, her shoe. *Hush, little sisters!*

'All right,' said Cummings, calmly. 'If we accept the . . . *possibility* that Johannes Ebner didn't hurt Wyn, and wouldn't have been able to hide her in her own backyard if he had, then have you any idea who *did* kill her?'

There was the opacity in Frances's mind; there was her own feeling of shame, ill-defined but terrible; there were all the years in which she'd said nothing, making it all but impossible to say anything now. She shut her eyes, and fought it.

'I . . .' She shook her head in frustration. 'I think it was somebody known to her family. Or even . . . somebody in her family. I think it has to have been. Or perhaps a close neighbour. Somebody who knew exactly where to find her, and exactly where to bury her. Where nobody would bother to look, because they were all out searching the city, after her things were found behind the leper hospital . . .'

'Her things were found there?'

'Yes. Some of her clothes. One of her shoes. And . . . blood,' said Frances. At this, Sergeant Cummings gave her a steadily appraising look.

'So it seems likely Wyn was killed there? At the leper hospital?'

'That's what they said at the time, but . . . those things could just have been put there, couldn't they? And anyone could have trespassed there, just like we did. Couldn't they?'

'I can't possibly say without looking at the case file,' said Cummings. 'Why would the killer put them there?'

'So that Johannes would get the blame!'

'Who else knew he was hiding there?'

'Nobody.' Frances paused, seeing the sergeant's point. 'That is, not that I know of. We never told — we swore it to each other, and to him. Or . . . or perhaps that *is* where she died. Perhaps she was followed there. Perhaps she ran there to hide, if someone was after her.'

'Can you think of any reason why somebody in her family might have wanted to kill her?'

'*Wanted* to?' said Frances, bleakly. 'Why does anybody *want* to kill a child? Nobody does. Children are killed by neglect, by accident, or because ... or to keep them quiet about something.' She looked up and met the sergeant's gaze. 'Ask anyone around here what the Hughes family are like. Bill Hughes, her dad, and her sister, Carys.'

'Frances! That's hardly fair,' said Pam.

'But it's true!'

In the lull after Frances spoke, the tap dripped loudly into the sink, and Dog sighed at Pam's feet, and Cummings' pencil scratched to a stop. Her big eyes held Frances's, and didn't blink. 'Wyn was such a fragile little thing,' Frances said, quietly. 'I never really noticed when we were that age, because she had this big character ... this *strength* about her. She never got downhearted over anything. But she was small for her age, and far too thin. She was tiny. It wouldn't have taken much to kill her, not much at all. A child could have done it.'

'What makes you say that?' said Cummings, sharply.

'What? I don't know ... I just mean to say, she was more vulnerable than she seemed,' said Frances, feeling Cummings' scrutiny. The policewoman looked down at her notes, frowning slightly.

'You suggested that children are sometimes killed to keep them quiet. Keep them quiet about what?' she said.

'You're the detective,' said Frances. 'You'd know better than me – you must have seen it before. Something they've seen, or heard. Something that's been done to them.'

'I've not been on the force that long, actually,' said Cummings, colouring slightly. 'I've never ... I've not had to deal with a murder, yet.'

'I've been dealing with this one nearly all my life.'

'Well,' said Cummings, closing her notebook and tucking it back into her pocket. 'It's not much to go on. I'll . . . we'll talk some more, perhaps. It won't do to point the finger at her family with no evidence beyond the fact that they're poor—'

'It's nothing to do with them being poor!'

'You spoke of what *kind* of family they are, what they're like,' Cummings said, neutrally.

'I meant difficult! Given to drunkenness, and . . . violence.'

'Plenty of people will have known where she lived, after all. I take on board what you say about Ebner, though. I'll take a look at the case report, and see what he had to say for himself at the time of his arrest. If I find anything untoward, I'll keep you informed. In the meantime, if you think of anything else . . .' She gave Frances a look so penetrating that Frances felt her face grow warm. 'If you remember anything else that might be significant, perhaps you'll let me know. Discreetly.'

'I will,' said Frances. She'd already decided to say nothing about Percy Clifton. There was nothing she could usefully say.

Once Cummings had left, Pam cleared away the tea things while Frances sat at the table, staring, lost in thought. She realised that what she'd said about Wyn — that she was a fragile little thing, small for her age and far too thin — was also true of Davy. It wouldn't take much to kill him, either. She felt weak again, and shut her eyes against a wave of pain. Gradually, she became aware of Pam's silence, and the abrupt way she was doing the washing up.

'Are you all right, Pam?'

'Why wouldn't I be?' Pam said, curtly.

'You'll chip the teapot.'

'Bugger the teapot.'

'What is it?'

'You could have spoken to me.' Pam turned from the sink with her hands on her hips. 'You could have told me.'

'Told you what?'

'Everything you've just told that policewoman! About not thinking it was Johannes Ebner that killed Wyn. About thinking it was one of the Hughes lot. How could you think that, all these years, and not say? How could you be friends with them, thinking that?'

'I ... I tried to tell you yesterday! And ... we've not been *friends*, exactly ... But I didn't know, Pam! And I *couldn't* say before. I've never been able to talk about it, and that's why ... perhaps that's why I've never been able to forget about it. And it was only finding her now ... it's only *where* she was found that has finally given me a way to *prove* it wasn't Johannes.'

Something in her desperate tone gave Pam pause, but then she folded her arms and shook her head slightly.

'It *was* him, Frances. Of course it was him! He was a fugitive, a desperate man. You said so yourself. He was hiding in the very place Wyn was killed ... perhaps he thought she was going to give him away, somehow? You don't know!'

'I do know, Pam. I *do* know. There's more. There's more that I ... don't know. That I need to *remember*.' Frances put her head in her hands, and Pam stared at her with a pained expression.

'What do you need to remember?' she said.

'I'm trying.'

'Oh, Frances!' Pam sat down beside her and took her hand. 'You could have talked to me, any time you wanted. I know you and your mum haven't always had the easiest time together, but we see eye to eye, don't we?'

'Of course we do.'

'You could tell me anything, you know, and I'd never think any the worse of you.'

'You can't say that. You don't know that.' Frances took a

deep breath. 'I have to go out. I have to post notices about Davy, and . . . see Carys,' she said, getting up.

'But you'll be back for supper?'

'I'm not hungry.'

'Frances, wait.' Pam stood up as well. 'All we wanted – Cecily and me, and your mum and dad – all we wanted was for this not to be the only thing your life was about. Wyn disappearing, I mean. Being taken like that. All we wanted was for you to be able to move on from it, live your life and be happy. And . . . I'm sorry. I'm sorry we didn't make that happen.'

'You couldn't,' said Frances, surprised. She gathered Pam in and hugged her. 'You couldn't have.'

Once she'd checked at home, and at the ruins of Springfield Place, Frances changed from bus to bus, visiting as many rest centres as she could find, leaving her notices, finding nothing. The centres were starting to empty out as people found places to stay with friends and relatives, or went in as lodgers elsewhere. There was a growing sense of the bombings being tidied away, dealt with and moved on from, that only heightened the desperation of Davy remaining missing. Sick with dread, Frances went to Beechen Cliff Place to report her failure to Carys and Nora Hughes, but Carys seemed too weary, too unsteady, to berate her wholeheartedly.

'Give me a hand packing up,' she said, flatly. 'Make yourself useful. The house is coming down the day after tomorrow.' Frances hesitated. It was getting late, the shadows darkening between the houses and the ruins. She wanted to leave, and was honest enough with herself to admit she'd far rather have gone to look for Owen than stayed there with his sister. Not seeing him all day had made the day longer. But Carys was staring at her blackly, so she nodded.

'All right. I can help for a bit.'

They started in Carys and Clive's bedroom, working in silence, putting things in boxes and bags. Frances heard a noise outside, and from the window saw Fred Noyle picking through the debris in the front yard, still wearing his gas mask. He was half-hearted about the task, kicking resentfully at the rubble, bending now and then to turn something over, or throw a stone. In his mask he was a strange, gnome-like figure, like something from a dark fairy tale. *No stone was left unturned.* The policeman's words whispered to Frances again; she saw the dank place with the stripes of sunlight, and this time a sense of panicked searching came with it. But perhaps that was her search for Davy, bleeding through – the resonance of old feelings with new, the spread of an indelible mark on her soul. She shook herself, unable to make sense of it.

'Is Fred afraid of a gas attack?' she said, groping for reality.

Carys paused, straightening up. She'd been pulling blankets and other things out from under the bed – her sewing basket; a string bag of outgrown children's clothes; a crate of empty pickling jars.

'What?' she said.

'Fred, always in his gas mask. Is he worried about the Germans dropping gas shells?'

'He just likes to wear it,' said Carys. Her face was crimson from bending over, thin strands of her hair flopped over her forehead. She swayed and took a sudden step to one side, and Frances wondered if she was dizzy from getting up, or simply drunk. It was hard to tell.

'Where will you go?'

'In with Mum and Dad for now. After that I've no bloody clue. There's a horse and cart coming for this lot tomorrow. The brewery where Dad works has got an empty shed it can go in for now.'

'That's good. Your dad sorted it out?'

'Mum did,' said Carys, shaking her head. 'Not heard from Dad since the weekend.'

'Oh,' said Frances. Carys didn't seem at all worried about him. Perhaps it was normal for him to disappear for days at a time; perhaps they were hoping he was gone for good. 'Have you heard from Terry and Howard lately?' she asked. Carys's other two sons were in the army, as was Frances's brother Keith. Keith was a machine engineer based in Algiers, repairing all kinds of army vehicle; he wasn't front-line infantry like the Noyle boys. Terry Noyle was only seventeen, but he'd lied about his age to join up when Howard was conscripted. Now Carys, like Susan Elliot, waited eagerly for letters addressed in her sons' writing, and in terror for a telegram.

'Yes. They write,' said Carys. 'Get on with it, will you? You're no help standing there, gawping out the window.' Frances gave up on the conversation.

Carys returned to pulling things out from under the bed, Frances to wrapping the contents of the dresser in newspaper, and packing it into an old tea crate. It was unsettling to know that, very soon, the room in which she was standing would no longer exist. Number thirty-three, into which she and Wyn had trespassed to try on Carys's corsets – back when Carys was still a beauty, Wyn was still alive, and Frances was a diffident child, hovering by the door. Carys and Clive had taken over the lease when Aunt Ivy died, even though she'd died because there were cracks in the chimney flue rising through the bedroom, which had leaked fumes while she slept. Clive had made the necessary repairs; you couldn't wait for landlords to take care of things like that. But now the foundations were compromised, according to the council's building inspector. There was a crack running down what had been the party wall with number thirty-two that Frances could have fitted two fists into. Her senses were tuned to any movement beneath her feet, any shifting, sagging or rumbling. She was poised, again, after all those years, to bolt for the stairs if necessary.

Opening a drawer, she picked up Clive's comb, shaving brush and razor but paused before wrapping them. She turned and drew breath to ask if she should leave them out, for Carys to keep with her, but the words froze on her lips. She had no idea when Clive had last been in Bath, when he'd last been to see his wife and the remaining two sons they had at home, and she didn't want to remind Carys of his absence. She looked over at Carys's broad hips and back, bent over, reaching for something out of sight. She'd carried seven of Clive's children to term in the end, not the ten he'd claimed to want. Two more had died in infancy, and three other pregnancies had miscarried late on. So of the twelve children they'd conceived, only five remained – possibly only four, if Davy was gone. If Terry or Howard died in the war, that would just leave Fred, lurking about in his gas mask, and little Denise, living with Owen and Maggie. Perhaps Carys would want Denise back, if that happened. It was a cruel thing to do to a child, Frances thought – to pass it about like a parcel. Just as she had passed Davy to the Landys, the last time she saw him. Flinching, she wrapped Clive's comb and shaving things in wretched silence.

Everything was dirty, and it wasn't just dust from the bombings. A layer of grime covered everything, the greasiness of coal smuts making it cling, and hairs stick. It was the dirt of a long-term lack of care, of wilful neglect – just like Davy'd had, in the early days. Frances's hands were filthy, and she itched to wipe them, to wash away all trace of the place – the human remains of Clive and his absent children, and of Carys's degeneration. From the same drawer, she fetched out a pressed glass dish containing a few bits and pieces: blunt razor blades, a bent tie pin and several plain shirt buttons. She was about to wrap it when a painted button caught her eye — a child's wooden shank button. It was incongruous, and she was trying to make out the design — green, red and black — when she spotted something else, and stopped. A flash of chipped yellow paint, a few traces of green, and a shape so familiar it made her catch her breath. A tin daffodil brooch, just like the one she'd bought Wyn for her last Christmas. Carefully, she picked it up. It was smaller than the one she'd bought Wyn — or was it just that her hands were so much bigger now? Frances turned it over. The back of it was plain metal, the pin a little bent from use. It couldn't be the same one; of course it couldn't. Her fingers trembled slightly. But when she turned it over again, there it was: the line across one of the leaves where it had got bent over, and the paint had cracked along the crease. Owen had done his best to bend it back, but it had never gone back like new; you could always see the damage. Frances knew exactly when it had happened, and exactly how.

The room blurred around her, and her skin prickled as though somebody were standing right behind her. The brooch felt too heavy in her hand. Carys gasped and swore her way out from under the bed, and stood up, pushing back her hair. 'There!' she said. 'That's the last of that lot. What's the matter with you?' But Frances couldn't answer her. She simply held out the brooch for her to see, and for a moment both of them were silent. Carys's wheezing breath smelled of gin and cigarettes; her eyes were lost beneath furrowed brows as she looked down at the brooch. Frances could hardly breathe at all, because it felt like there was a bubble behind her ribs, ready to burst. In the end Carys looked up, her eyes guarded. 'Wyn's old brooch,' she said, in an off-hand way that was utterly unbelievable.

'I . . .' said Frances, swallowing. 'I didn't think any of her things still existed — I thought your dad got rid of everything.

How come you have this? It was . . . she was always wearing it. She always wore it.'

'Not always,' said Carys. 'Our Denise found it one day, so I said she could keep it. Wyn wouldn't have minded.'

'Where did she find it?'

'How should I know? You know what kids are like. In their room, I expect – what used to be my room. You two were always in there, messing about, so I expect it fell off her one time.'

'But she . . . she *always* wore it. She'd have said something if she'd lost it,' said Frances.

'Well, obviously she didn't, did she?' Carys snapped. 'Now stick it in with the rest and let's get cracking.' But Frances shook her head, closing her fingers around the brooch. Its metal edges were sharp against her skin.

'I'll . . . I'll keep hold of it. I'll give it back to Denise, if it's hers now. I mean, I can give it to Owen, to give back to Denise.' For a moment they stared at one another, and Frances tried to read Carys's expression. Somewhere deep in her eyes, behind the mask of alcohol and bluster, Frances thought she saw fear. A flicker of fear. Carys didn't press Frances, or try to take the brooch; she didn't even look at it again, and she didn't argue in any way.

'Take it, then. Hardly matters.' Carys picked up the crate of jars and headed for the stairs.

Frances finished what she was doing, moving slowly, paying no attention to the task. She heard Carys shout to Fred to come in and help. She looked out, saw him pull off his gas mask and scratch his fingers through his sweaty hair. The room felt strange, even the air she was breathing. Her head ached, and wherever she looked she saw Wyn, walking away from her with sun in her hair and her body strung tight with emotion. She fought to remember when that had been; why

Wyn had been upset, where she'd been going and why Frances hadn't gone with her. Trying to place the memory was like trying to step on her own shadow. She gripped the brooch tightly, until it began to hurt, and when she opened her hand it had made small cuts on her palm, drawing a little blood, and the sight made the memory sharpen. She remembered what she'd wanted to say to Wyn's retreating back. The words had been right there, teetering, but had somehow never got said. *Wyn, come back!* A shout, a desperate one; yet she hadn't said a thing.

'Come back,' she whispered, touching one fingertip to the yellow flowers. But it was far too late.

When she went downstairs sometime later, Carys was sitting at the kitchen table with a bottle and a glass in front of her. She held the glass tightly in one hand, even though it was empty. Frances had lost track of how long she'd been upstairs, but it had got very dark outside; she had no idea how much Carys might have had to drink in that time. Carys looked calmer, distant, half-asleep, and after all her years of drinking it took a lot for that to happen. It was a dangerous state. Frances stood opposite her, Wyn's brooch in her pocket.

'What about my Davy?' said Carys, peering up at her blearily. 'What about him?'

'I'll find him,' said Frances.

'Ha! Like hell you will.' Carys slurred the words. 'He's *dead*. You . . . you left him to get killed.' Frances was silenced; all the questions she'd wanted to ask were bullied out by the sudden clear memory of Davy's tiny hand in hers, and the smell of him when she'd given him a bath, and the way his face sometimes lit up when she found something he liked – a perfectly round bird's nest, lined with moss; a hedgehog out foraging in Magdalen Gardens; an extra-large strawberry from one of the allotments in Alexandra Park.

'Please don't say that,' she managed, with difficulty. 'He's not dead. He's wandered off . . .'

'I *will* say it, since it's true!' said Carys, bitterly. 'Not like Mum, keeping on for all those bloody years that Wyn was still alive somewhere. Well, I think my Davy's *dead*. I think he was blown up by that bomb. Because you were supposed to look after him, and you didn't. That's what I think.'

'Carys—'

'What? What are you going to say that's going to make that any better?' Carys swayed slightly in her chair, her eyes gleaming. She reached for the bottle and tried to pour herself another tot, but most of it missed the glass. 'What are you going to say?' The words were a slurred mess.

'Is that why you're not even looking for him? Because you've given up?' said Frances, her anger building. 'You're supposed to be his mother—'

'I *am* his mother! No "suppose" about it!' Carys banged her hand down. 'And what would *you* know about being a mother? Hm?' She gave Frances such an ugly stare that Frances had to look away. 'I heard your husband kicked you out because you couldn't even have any kids. Well, don't go thinking you're a better mother to my boy than I am, 'cause you're not. You don't know a damn thing about it!'

'He didn't . . . it wasn't like that,' said Frances, shaking. Her throat was very dry, and she tried to swallow. 'I know I'm not Davy's mother, but I do . . . love him. And I *am* going to find him. I won't give up,' she said. Carys grunted, drinking the gin down.

'Good,' she said, breathing hard, and messily. 'Good. Go on. I hope it ruins your life, like you've ruined mine.'

1918

'Hush, little sisters!' The pallid man who probably wasn't a ghost after all spoke strangely – with an unfamiliar rhythm, and very quickly. Frances stayed at a safe distance, holding hands with Wyn; she was still ready to run should he make any move towards them. But he didn't. They stared at one another for a while, as though both needing time to decide if they were friend or foe. Once Wyn had caught her breath and her shoulders had relaxed, she turned to Frances.

'He doesn't *look* like a leper,' she said.

'Or a ghost,' Frances conceded, warily.

'*Ein Geist?* Did you think I was a ghost?' said the man, his head bobbing up a little further, birdlike. He disappeared from the window and opened the door.

'Of *course* not,' said Wyn, with impressive disdain. 'But... have you seen any at all, in there?'

'No.' A rapid shake of his head, never taking his eyes from them. 'No ghosts in here. Only me, and spiders.'

'No lepers?' said Wyn.

'Leper? What is this?'

'Never mind,' said Wyn with a small sigh. She turned to Frances. 'It's just a *person*,' she said, deeply disappointed. Frances was deeply relieved.

'What do we do now?' she said. If there was somebody living in the leper hospital then it wasn't particularly mysterious any more, it was just a house. 'Shall we go?' she suggested. Wyn thought about it.

'We could still look inside,' she said. 'None of the boys

have ever been inside, that's what Owen said.' Wyn squinted at the pale man in the doorway. 'Can we come in?' she said. The man's face twitched nervously, he swallowed, and seemed to think fast.

'Do you have food?' he said.

'No,' Wyn admitted.

'*Ach*. Yes, come, come.'

Now that the threat of the supernatural had lifted, Frances was interested to see inside. She hoped it would still look as it had when it was last occupied, which she supposed was centuries before. She hoped it would be untouched – ancient clothes and cups and brooches, bones even; small, everyday treasures for her to pick up and touch and smell. The building was a shell, however – two small rooms downstairs and two upstairs, empty except for all the mummified flies, a buck-toothed rat skull and a pervasive smell of damp. Only the twisting stone staircase bore any imprint of the medieval lepers Owen had told them about. As they went up, Frances forgot about spores and put her feet into the deepest part of each worn tread, trying to feel a whisper of those past lives. Upstairs, they peeped out at Holloway through the narrow pointed windows.

'Isn't it strange to be on this side looking out, for once?' said Wyn. It was; like being on the wrong side of a mirror. The upper rooms had bare floorboards, and wall cupboards with dusty shelves gnawed to powder by woodworm. Everything else had been robbed out at some point in the past, and Frances could sense Wyn's growing boredom.

They went back down to where the strange man was waiting nervously in the lean-to, which was much newer than the rest even though it was falling down all the same. There was a mat of old newspapers and a rusty vegetable oil can full of water, where the man was living.

'You are looking for something, I think,' he said, scratching at the back of his left hand, where the skin was scabby and red.

'Not really,' said Wyn. 'We thought there might be ghosts in here, but there's nothing.'

'No. Only me.'

'How come you live in here? Nobody's supposed to live in here.'

'I am not living here, I am . . .' He trailed off, wrapping his arms around himself, looking around as if seeking the answer. He was very thin, with fair hair, not quite blond, brown eyes and slanting cheekbones in what was trying to be quite a round face. His head looked too large for his body. He twitched. 'I am just a visitor. My name is Johannes. I saw you before, I think. You came once before, yes?'

'Yes.' Wyn shrugged. 'We just wanted to see.'

'What are you called?' he said, and Wyn smiled because he pronounced the *W* as a *V*.

'I'm Bronwyn, but everybody calls me Wyn. This is Frances.' She hooked her thumb at Frances, who hung back, shy of the stranger. Johannes smiled, but then a look of fear chased it away, quick as a flash. They heard the creak of a passing cart out on Holloway, and the carter's voice raised in encouragement as the horse laboured up the hill. Johannes shrank back into the corner, snatching in a breath, eyes darting, and Frances felt her heart soften. How could she be afraid of him when he was so frightened himself? When a familiar sound made him start like a rabbit? 'It's only a horse and cart,' she said. 'Nothing to be frightened of.' Wyn squinted at him, tilting her head to one side.

'Are you *hiding* from somebody?' she demanded.

Johannes didn't answer at once. He bent down for the old oil can and drank some water, then wiped his mouth on his dirty sleeve. Frances saw bits of twig and grass caught in his hair, and that the laces of one of his muddy boots had snapped. He looked at them and then away, seeming in an agony of indecision.

'Can you keep a secret, little sisters?' he said in the end, blinking too much, trying to smile.

'Yes,' they said, in unison.

'I *am* hiding here. I need to hide here. But I need something to eat. Can you bring me something?'

'Who are you hiding from?' said Wyn. Frances was already thinking about what she could bring him to eat, but it would be hard when she already had to bring things for Wyn – she handed over all the snacks her mother dished out, and spent all her pocket money too. She wondered if Wyn would be willing to share.

'I am hiding ... I am hiding from the men who want to catch me, and keep me prisoner,' said Johannes. It wasn't really an answer, Frances thought, but it was enough for Wyn, whose interest grew as her imagination filled in the gaps.

'You'd better keep out of sight, then,' she said, sagely. 'We'll come back and bring you something.'

'You will? You promise this? It has been many days since I had food.'

'I said so, didn't I?'

'You are kind ... you are very kind girls. But, please, you must not talk about me to anyone. You must be silent, like small mice.' He put a finger to his lips – a finger that shook. 'You must hush, little sisters.'

'Course we won't say anything,' said Wyn, carelessly.

They decided to try to steal something from Nora Hughes' kitchen first of all, since Frances's mother had already given her a slice of pork pie to keep her going until supper, and Wyn had wolfed it. But it was risky, and the mission didn't go well. Wyn's father was in his usual chair, between the fireplace and the door to the back room, and as they tried to sneak past him, he reached out and grabbed Frances's wrist, blinking owlishly at her.

'You don't look like one of mine,' he said. Her whole body froze at his touch, and she almost cried out. It was the first time he'd ever touched her. She managed to shake her head. 'Well? Whose are you, then?' he said, but Frances couldn't reply. Her mind and her mouth emptied completely, so great was her fear of getting the answer wrong. She simply stared, slack-jawed, until Bill glanced over at Wyn.

'Is the brat half-witted?' he said, the lilt of his accent still almost musical, despite the roughness of his voice.

'This is my friend Frances,' Wyn told him, coming to stand by his chair and patting his shoulder lightly. Bill stared blearily at Wyn, and Frances was shocked to see tears flood his eyes. Just then, Carys came in, carrying a bundle of washing, and watched from the doorway as their father ran the back of his hand tenderly down the side of Wyn's face, then pinched her chin between his finger and thumb.

'*Fy merch hyfryd*,' he whispered. Frances was dumbstruck, and Carys's face darkened. Bill gathered Wyn into his lap and hugged her tightly, burying his face in her hair. He sobbed, and rocked her gently, and Wyn sat quietly, limp and obedient in his arms.

Once she was released, Wyn and Frances headed for the back door, but Carys stopped them.

'Don't go running about out there making a racket. Mum's upstairs having a lie-down, and Dad needs to sleep it off.' Carys paused. 'You might think you're his favourite, but it's not because you're anything special, Wyn,' she added, stonily. Wyn didn't reply; she watched her sister with an angry, wounded expression, waiting for whatever she would say next. Carys stared down at her and didn't blink. 'You're no better than the rest of us. It's only because you remind him of *them*.

And he's drunk, that's all. Here,' she said, kicking the bundle of laundry towards them. 'Take this along to Grandma's and chuck it round the back there for washing. Poor Clive's still stuck trying to fix our washhouse floor, and I don't know when I'll be able to get in there. Dad was supposed to be helping him – fat chance of that,' she muttered, tucking a wayward lock of hair back into her bun.

'But we were about to—'

'Don't argue, just get on with it.' Carys rolled her eyes. 'Make yourselves useful for once.'

They did as they were told, lugging the heavy bundle between them along to Parfitt's Buildings. Wyn was quiet, frowning, and Frances worried that once the floor of the Beechen Cliff Place washhouse was repaired the newts would stop coming. Afterwards, the mission to steal food was abandoned without a word – it would be difficult with Carys about, and downright dangerous if Bill Hughes caught them. Suddenly aimless, they wandered down to Bath Deep Lock, at Widcombe. They sat on the sun-warmed wood of the top gate and watched the water spout through the leaky gates, splattering through swathes of weed into the empty lock chamber fifteen feet below them. Frances was still shaken by being grabbed by Wyn's father – the speed and strength of his arm; still shaken by the way he'd then hugged Wyn, and cried. He was so changeable, so impossible to know. She'd been worried that he'd crush Wyn in his arms. She felt she had to say something about it – that it would be wrong to just change the subject as though nothing had happened. But she didn't know what to say.

At first, Frances hadn't given Wyn's bruises a second thought – she herself often had skinned knees and scabby elbows – but over time she'd realised that a lot of them came from Bill. Like Carys's occasional split lips and flaming cheeks; like Nora Hughes' more regular blacked eyes, and Owen's sudden, tearful sprints from the house, leaving shouts and banging doors behind him. And then there were the times when Bill swayed slightly on his feet, smelling of beer and wearing a lost expression on his face, like he had no idea who or where he was. On those occasions he would let Nora sit him down and give him tea, and sometimes he would cry, just like today. That, to Frances, was the worst thing of all – seeing those hard eyes empty out, and tears trickle through the black and white stubble on his cheeks. The Hughes children might fetch a beating for taking more than their fair share; for making too much noise; for pestering, getting underfoot; for using the last sheet of paper in the outhouse; for anything that could be considered wasteful – like opening a door in winter, and letting out the precious warmth. Frances simply couldn't imagine having to live like that, in the shadow of such threat.

Wyn stared down at the splashing canal water in silence, and Frances felt embarrassed on her behalf – for the awful thing Carys had said, and because her father was so strange and mean. But she was curious too.

'What did your dad say to you just then? Was it Welsh?'

'Yes. He said "my lovely girl".'

'That's nice, isn't it?' said Frances. Wyn didn't reply. 'Carys is really horrid sometimes,' Frances went on. Wyn peered across at her, and nodded. 'What . . . what did she mean when she said you remind your dad of "them"? Who's *them*?'

'I'm not supposed to know,' said Wyn, resting her chin on her bent knee. 'Mum told Carys once she was old enough, because she said she had a right to know, and that it helps to explain things, and then Carys told me to be mean because she doesn't like it that I'm his favourite.'

'Told you what?' said Frances, rapt. Wyn squinted at her, and just for a second Frances felt a hundred miles from her. Wyn's gaze was that of a stranger, someone she couldn't possibly know. As quickly as it had appeared, the look was gone. Frances swallowed, shaken.

'Dad had a whole other family, before he had us,' said Wyn.

'What do you mean?'

'What I said.' Wyn picked a dandelion and threw it into the water. The yellow flower swirled for a second before the water pummelled it under. 'I went round to Auntie Ivy after Carys told me, and she told me all about it.'

'Will you tell me?'

'Okay. But you can't tell *anyone* else.'

'I swear I won't,' said Frances.

'When he was young, Dad lived on a farm in the hills in Wales, and he was married to a woman called Kathleen. They'd been in love since they were children, and after they got married they had three children called Emlyn, Gavin and Genevieve. The boys were dark-haired, like Dad, and Genny was fair-haired, like Kathleen. And like me. Then, one year, they all died; all but Dad. Emlyn was eleven and Gavin was eight, and they both died of the flu. Then Genny, who was six, drowned by accident in the stream that ran by the farm, and Kathleen was so broken-hearted she hanged herself.'

Wyn paused, but Frances could only stare, silenced by the story. She had no idea what to say. 'After that, Dad left Wales and never went back. He came here and married Mum, and had us.' Wyn shrugged, and picked another dandelion to destroy. 'I once heard Carys ask Mum if Dad loved his first family more than us,' said Wyn.

'What did your mum say?'

'She didn't say anything. They both just went really quiet.' Frances thought about that for a moment, and said nothing because it sounded so bad for Wyn and Carys, for Owen and baby Annie. And for Mrs Hughes. She wondered if Bill Hughes would look different the next time she saw him, now that she knew about the other life he'd lived, and all the grief he'd suffered. It was such a strange thought; it made everything feel a little unsteady, like being up too high and looking down. With a pang of guilt, she was glad it wasn't *her* father in the story.

The next day, Bill Hughes was arrested for causing an affray at work, and when Frances came home from school she overheard her parents in the kitchen, talking about not letting her play with Wyn any more. Frances held her breath to listen, her pulse speeding anxiously.

'Now then, Susan, poor Bronwyn can't be held responsible for the man,' her father said.

'Of course not, and I don't say that at all, Derek. I know it's not the child's fault. But Bill Hughes is a nasty piece of work and this latest thing just proves it. He broke the man's jaw with a single blow – over some slight that wasn't even meant, as I heard it.'

'He'll go up before the magistrate now, and no doubt get a fine. Perhaps that'll steady him up a bit? He can't afford to keep doing it, after all.'

'But this is hardly the first time, is it? You know that. I heard that Frank Little only keeps him on at the brewery because he's too scared to sack him.' There was a long pause.

'He's no danger to the girls though, is he? You can't think that,' said Derek.

'I don't know. I just don't know about that,' said Susan. There was another silence.

'It'd break our girl's heart if she couldn't play with Wyn,' said Derek. 'We can't do it, Sue. They're tight as peas in a pod.' And though her mother sighed, that seemed to be the end of it.

Frances felt giddy with relief, but she remained uneasy. She wasn't at all sure that Bill Hughes wasn't a danger to them. Her mother only ever spanked her when she'd done something really naughty – albeit usually inadvertently. Like the time she filled the privy downspout with pebbles to see what would happen, and the answer was that the privy flooded. Her father had never once hit her, and she couldn't imagine having to live with the knowledge that he might, at any moment, and for no reason at all. She understood all the more what Pam had said about Wyn's fearlessness being necessary, and could easily believe that Bill Hughes' employer might be too frightened to sack him. It seemed to Frances that only two people she knew of *weren't* afraid of Bill Hughes – Wyn was one, and the other was Clive Noyle.

Frances felt sorry for Clive. He'd had to ask Mr Hughes' permission before he could get engaged to Carys, and in marrying his sweetheart he was getting a horrible person for a father-in-law. But Clive, miraculously, didn't seem to mind too much. He spoke to Mr Hughes in the same jovial, relaxed kind of way that he spoke to everyone, which always astonished Frances. Clive wasn't a Hughes, so perhaps he didn't know what might happen if Mr Hughes had cause to get upset. Frances wondered if someone ought to warn him about that, but it certainly didn't seem her place to do it.

'All right, Mr H?' Clive would greet him, cheerily, if they passed on the path or in the front room, adding something like: 'How's your good lady wife today?' To which there was usually no reply. 'I can help you fix that, if you like?' Clive would say, having squinted up at a gap in the roof tiles, or down at a rotten piece of skirting board, or into the chimney flue when it wouldn't draw. 'Won't take us long if we get stuck in.'

'Mind your own bloody business.'

'Right you are, Mr H.' And if Clive caught Frances watching, he'd roll his eyes and wink. Frances thought this treatment was very unfair, since Clive was only trying to help. She wanted him to offer to help her with something, so that she could accept and be grateful, though she would no doubt blush and turn shy if he ever did.

Frances didn't feel sorry for Wyn, though. It was impossible to feel sorry for Wyn, who never seemed troubled by anything other than her growling stomach. She never got afraid, and she never, ever felt sorry for herself. Frances was surprised to find that she was sometimes sorry for Carys, however. Carys wasn't always mean, and Frances decided that she *had* to be nice, deep down inside, because of how Clive adored her. But Wyn clearly *was* her father's favourite, and nobody could blame Carys for resenting that. It was cruel that his precious few moments of tenderness were reserved for just one of his offspring. One Saturday, Frances saw Carys and Nora at the bottom of Holloway – they came out of the Workman's Rest as she was waiting outside the grocer's for her mother, who was in buying Rinso and custard powder. Carys was sobbing, cradling her nose in both hands.

'He doesn't mean it, love,' said Nora, trying to see the damage. Frances hoped that they'd go past before her mother came out and saw what Bill Hughes had done again.

'He bloody does! He does mean it,' said Carys. She didn't have a handkerchief so was using her sleeve, and it was bloodied and slimed. 'Not our fault they all died, is it? It's not our bloody fault we're not them! Why did he even have us?'

'You'll be away from him soon,' Nora said, sadly. Frances tried to melt into the wall but Carys spotted her, and pinned her with a baleful look. There was a great deal of Bill Hughes in Carys, and his frightening glare was one of the things she'd inherited.

Wyn almost never cried, so it was shocking when she did; like on the day they planned to go back and see Johannes with what scant food Frances had managed to accumulate. It was three days since they'd first met him; Frances had been fretting that he might have starved to death. Already, she felt the weight of their responsibility for him, because they'd said they would go back. Wyn was distracted, less bothered. She weighed next to nothing – skin and bones and a rope of pale hair. Other people's hunger was not her first concern. When Frances went to call for her she came running through from the back room just as her father was coming down the stairs. She half collided with him, then couldn't get out from under his feet quickly enough, so he shoved her out of the way. Not that hard, but hard enough to send her flying. Frances watched in horror. There was a huge clatter as Wyn crashed against the fireplace and into the fire irons, and she screwed up her face in pain as she landed, hitting the knobbly bones at the top of her spine against the edge of the hearth. But she didn't make a sound. Bill carried on to his chair and sat down as though nothing had happened; he didn't even look at Wyn. White-faced, blank-eyed, Wyn got up and tottered past Frances, out of the house.

'Wyn! Are you all right?' said Frances, following her friend. Wyn nodded, though she kept rubbing at the back of her neck, and looked very pale. After hearing the story about Mr Hughes' first family, Frances had tried to feel sorry for him. But while she could feel sorry for the Bill Hughes in the story very easily, the sorriness wouldn't transfer to the Bill Hughes she knew now – the one in the fireside chair with the snarl of black hair, the stony eyes, the ready fists. The one who'd throw his own daughter – his favourite – across the room, for no reason at all. She hated him, in fact, and she was scared. Until that moment, Wyn had always seemed so tough, so unbreakable. Halfway up Holloway Wyn stopped and looked down, and it was then that she burst into tears. 'Does it hurt?' said Frances, stricken. Wyn wasn't supposed to cry.

'Look! It's ruined!' said Wyn. 'I've ruined it.' She was looking down at her daffodil brooch. One of the leaves had got bent over when she fell, and the paint was all chipped off along the fold.

'Oh! Oh, we'll fix it – I'm sure we can fix it,' said Frances, urgently, noticing that Wyn said 'I've ruined it', not 'He's ruined it'. Wyn wept wordlessly. 'We'll ask Owen – Owen'll help us,' said Frances.

Still looking down, still touching the bent leaf of her brooch with the fingers of her left hand, Wyn carried on walking. Frances went by her side, wishing she could think of something to say, and some way to help. In silence they climbed down into the leper hospital yard, and in silence they knocked on the back door and let themselves in. Inside, there was a smell of sweat and something rancid, faint but unpleasant. Johannes was hunched on his newspapers, knees drawn up, face hidden in his arms, and he didn't look up until Frances crouched cautiously in front of him, laying out what she'd managed to beg, buy and filch: a meat paste sandwich, a wrinkled apple, two hard-boiled eggs and one of Pam's cheese scones. Johannes stared at the food as though he might be seeing things, then grabbed the sandwich and began to stuff it into his mouth. As he chewed, he burst into tears, and this, finally, seemed to touch Wyn. Her own face was tear-streaked and strangely immobile as she went to sit beside him. She patted his shoulder, peering at him as he continued to eat.

'It's all right,' she said, as his face got messy and wet. 'It's all right. You'll be all right.' Wincing, she leant forwards and rested her chin on her knees, and as her hair fell around her shoulders Frances saw a ferocious blue bruise spreading across the back of her neck, and down between her shoulder blades. 'I've got horrible pins and needles,' said Wyn, to nobody in particular. 'All down the left side of me.'

Frances didn't know whether to stand or sit, or what to say. She sat, in the end, feeling useless and excluded for not being as thin, or as hungry, or as sad as either of them. It was a lonely kind of feeling. The stone floor was cold and dirty; she heard sparrows chattering in the gutters outside, and the breeze was dropping the last pink petals from the Judas tree into the yard to rot. Wyn's eyes followed each piece of food as Johannes ate it; she stared so intently that he noticed, once his tears had stopped, and offered her one of the eggs. To Frances's amazement, Wyn shook her head. 'It's all right,' she said. 'You have it.'

'You are kind to me, little sisters,' Johannes said, when all the food was gone. 'I thought I would die. I thought I could die here.' He was shivering, and sounded sleepy. 'You have saved me.' At this, Wyn's eyes showed wonder, and pride.

'Did you hear, Frances?' she whispered, when he tipped his head back against the wall and seemed to fall asleep. 'Do you think it's true? Do you think we saved his life?'

'He could have gone out and found some food for himself, I suppose,' said Frances, uncertainly. 'I wonder why he didn't?'

'Because the bad people would catch him. He said so,' said Wyn, watching Johannes, rapt. Frances sat and thought about it all – about Johannes crying, and Wyn crying, and the bruise on the back of Wyn's neck and the way her father had knocked her flying and then just carried on to his chair as though nothing had happened. She felt cross and altogether inadequate – she wanted to help them, and make things better, but she didn't know how. What she didn't feel was any danger. She didn't know how danger could hide, the way it could lurk. She only knew about the kind of danger Bill Hughes represented – real, obvious, immediate. She couldn't imagine somebody like Johannes being a threat – not with the way he flinched, the way he'd wept. She didn't know yet that people, just like animals, didn't have to be angry to be dangerous. It could also be because they were desperate, and afraid.

6
Thursday

Four Days After the Bombings

Frances woke from broken sleep to a rainy morning, and a letter from her husband. Pam opened the back door to let Dog out into the garden and water dripped with a soft percussion from the door jamb onto the step. It pattered on the leaves of the hydrangeas outside. Frances stepped out for a moment and felt it spot through the shoulders of her shirt. She took a deep breath and realised that the smell of smoke had finally gone. It smelled like an English spring again – damp stone, earth and greenery; the mild spice of privet and laburnum blossom.

'Aren't you going to open it?' said Pam, as she came back in.

'I am. Though I can't think what he's got to say,' said Frances, sitting down at the table. She'd left wet footprints on the tiles, but Pam didn't comment, or tut, or run to fetch the mop as her mother would have done.

'No. What could a man who's been away for months on end possibly have to say to his wife?' Pam said, drily. 'Perhaps you should go up to the farm and see Judith at some point, what with all the drama. And we're out of eggs.'

'I'd rather not.'

'Don't be such a baby. She's all on her own up there.'

'She's got the useless land girls. And she hates me.'

'Of course she does. She can't blame her only son for what happened, can she? And in any case, you're the one who left, so you get the blame. That's just the way it works. And you left Judith as well, when you left the farm. How do you think that felt?'

'Well.' Frances thought for a moment. 'I think she was pleased, actually. It proved her right about me.'

'Oh, stop feeling sorry for yourself. I know she's difficult, but you left Joe, and you didn't give her any grandchildren. You can hardly blame her for having the hump.'

'I haven't got time to visit her now,' said Frances. 'I need to keep looking for Davy.'

She skimmed Joe's letter, unwilling to let him into her cluttered mind. She let his reprimands glance off her without sinking in, and allowed her eyes to drift away to a thrush that was beating a snail to death on the path outside. She thought of the bleached snail shells that scattered the leper hospital yard, nothing inside them but dirt. One day she and Wyn gathered up as many as they could, for some game Frances couldn't remember now. In her mind's eye Wyn lined them up to be counted, lips pursed in concentration, her daffodil brooch pinned to her chest. The daffodil brooch was in Frances's pocket now; she was preternaturally aware of its shape and the barely-there weight of it; aware that finding it again was momentous in a way she couldn't quite grasp. *Wyn, come back!* Those were the words she never said, and she wondered what would have happened if she'd said them. She wanted to tell Sergeant Cummings about it.

'Well?' said Pam, as Frances laid the letter down in silence. 'There's been no trouble, I hope?' She was putting her raincoat on over her Woolworth's uniform. Dog watched her sadly, knowing she'd be gone for hours. 'He's all right?'

'He's all right. Tells me off for not sending a telegram after the bombings, but otherwise I think he's just bored.'

'Bored? I doubt that. Being down the mines is a dangerous business.'

'Well, he says it's the same every day,' said Frances, tonelessly. Pam paused, giving her a steady look.

'He still wants to patch things up, I suppose? Don't give me that look, Frances, I'm on your side. You were unhappy. It took guts to leave him – millions don't. But you *did* marry him in the first place, and you can't expect him to take it all lying down, not when he didn't do a thing wrong.'

'I just . . . wish he would.'

'If wishes were horses, I'd sell a few of mine and not have to go and do this shift at Woolies. See you this afternoon? It's liver and onions for supper. You might take Dog with you, if you're going out. And I haven't seen the pet meat man since before the bombings – if you get the chance, could you go down to Cole's and pick up some bits for him? Not whale meat though, he won't touch it and I don't blame him. Use a coupon if you have to, the poor beast's had nothing but rusk for days.'

Once Pam had gone, Frances hunted out an umbrella and Dog's lead, then set off for the hospital. The mongrel trotted alongside her in a businesslike manner, ears pricked. He gazed at ruined churches, water tanks, flattened street shelters and discarded furniture with equanimity. Only the bomb crater in the centre of The Circus seemed to trouble him. When Frances paused at the fluttering tape, Dog barked and barked at the patch of sky caught in the muddy puddle down in its depths. She heard boys' voices; the scuff and thud of a game of street football. Some kids were playing nearby, in Brock Street, but the echoes Frances heard were from years before – Owen kicking his football against the wall of the leper hospital while Frances was inside. It sent a shiver over her skin. *Hush, little sisters!* She turned away abruptly, and let her husband enter her thoughts to quieten the rest for a while.

She couldn't remember exactly when her relationship with Joe changed from friendship into something more. She hadn't thought anything of him, particularly, when they were little. He was just a boy; less awful than most, but still a boy. For a long time after Wyn's disappearance, Frances hardly went out at all. All through that autumn and winter, and into the spring of 1919, she went to school, and then she went home. Now and then to Aunt Pam, now and then to Mrs Hughes. She didn't play, she didn't explore. The end of the war – all the street parties and celebrations – passed her by. Only her father's return – thinner, older than he'd been, but still smiling – made an impression. But the following summer she began to roam out of the city again, in search of escape – from all the places Wyn wasn't, and, most of all, from the way she felt.

She liked to be high up, looking down on Bath, small and far away; she would try to feel the same way – small and far away. She tried to feel as though she'd left everything bad behind, down on Holloway; wilfully, she detached herself from it all. She walked for miles, and in doing so encountered Joe Parry again. She couldn't remember when it was, or even how old she'd been. Perhaps ten, by then, perhaps eleven. Her walks often took her past Topcombe Farm, and she'd seen him at work many times – waving a crooked stick as he walked their small dairy herd in to be milked, or walking it back out again; wrestling a sheep onto its back and holding it while his father trimmed its feet or drenched it with a funnel and tube. Then one day she bumped into him when he was out shooting crows, tramping the fields with his air rifle cradled over one arm.

Joe was two years older than Frances and didn't seem like a child any more. She felt older too – not like a grown-up, but not like a child; she didn't know where that left her. He wore a canvas coat so stained that the stains had become its colour; he smelled of sheep grease, hay, earth. His trousers were tucked into his boots, and he tied string around his legs beneath his knees to keep the rats and spiders out. Frances had a nightmare about that, that night. Being invaded by spiders and biting rodents; having them inside her clothes, inside her skin. She woke from the dream with a gasp and a racing heart, but was careful not to cry out. She often had night terrors after Wyn vanished, and her mother had been forced to her bedside so many times that she'd grown weary of it, even slightly resentful. Frances had taught herself to wait silently, eyes straining into the darkness, until the dreams faded.

There was something about Joe that was reassuring, and easy. Perhaps it was that he didn't smile too much. He wasn't grim or bad-tempered, but there was a quiet, undemanding seriousness about him; he didn't make jokes or act up, so she wasn't obliged to smile or laugh. He liked to walk, just as Frances did; he liked finding the traces wild things left behind – tunnels worn through bramble thickets by badgers; fur and antlers shed by fallow deer; the reek of a fox. Quietly, gradually, they became friends again.

'Goodness, how you've grown,' said Judith Parry, flatly, the first time Joe took her home for tea. Frances was twelve by then, almost as tall as Joe and awkward with it. Tea at the farm was not like tea at Woodlands with Pam and Cecily. There were no cakes or scones, no matching cups and saucers. Joe would pour them mugs of tea and they'd take them outside to drink in the barn, or to the front of the house, where an old iron bench was rusting garishly through its white paint.

Frances liked the long view down Smallcombe from that bench – the scatter of Bath's houses in the distance. The farm was a different world to the one she lived in, and Joe was different to everyone else she knew.

'Your mum doesn't like me,' she said, on one occasion. Joe grimaced but didn't deny it.

'She says you're a "strange child". She thinks you're not right in the head any more.' He was always open like that, always honest. He shot her a quick smile over his shoulder. 'What does she know?'

'What if she's right?' said Frances, with a leaden feeling.

'So what if she is? Who's to say "not right" is wrong?' said Joe. Frances said nothing for a while.

'You should come down for tea at my house some time,' she said, feeling she ought to offer. She was relieved when he shook his head, looking uncomfortable.

'Thanks, but I've no time for it, really, what with all the work here.'

'That's all right,' said Frances. 'It's better here, anyway.'

'Is it?' he asked, and Frances shrugged, peering down into her cup.

'Everyone down there still looks at me funny. Even my parents. Like I might vanish any moment, too.'

'Why would you?' said Joe. Frances shrugged again.

'I don't know.' She looked away because she *did* know. Some instinct told her that what had happened to Wyn *could* still happen to her. Her mind shied away from the thought. It was the first time she'd ever lied to Joe, but it wouldn't be the last.

They first kissed when Joe was sixteen and Frances fourteen; sitting in the lee of a fallen beech on Claverton Down, on an autumn day when the cold wind sounded like the sea. It wasn't Frances's first kiss; she'd had others, even before Owen pushed her away, and others since as well. Defiant, unhappy kisses. But it was Joe's first kiss, and Frances did it because she knew that Joe had wanted to kiss her for a long time. It sometimes felt as though people wanted all sorts of things from her, most of them impossible. 'Chin up. Why not make some new friends; try a bit harder. It's time to leave it all behind you, Frances.' This her father said, after an almighty tirade from her mother about Frances's intractable silences, her lacklustre approach to everything. He said it kindly – he was always kind to her – but it had made her feel like a failure, and sad that he didn't understand. So she kissed Joe because Joe wanted her to, and because, for once, she could oblige.

His nose was cold and damp, and his hands rough and strong where they grabbed suddenly at her coat and arms and face. His mouth, which had been so familiar before, became a strange thing, entirely unknown and capable of things neither one of them really understood. Her own fingers were numb from the cold, but her stomach clenched oddly during the kiss.

'Was it all right?' he asked, breathless, when they broke apart. He had a shine of saliva on his bottom lip; his eyes looked different and there was a flood of colour in his cheeks.

'I don't know,' she said, truthfully, but when he kissed her again she didn't stop him. They weren't an item after that; far from it. They were still friends, but they sometimes kissed. Sometimes she stayed down in the city for days and days, and when she saw him again he was silent and angry, so she walked by herself instead. She kissed other boys; she didn't know if Joe knew that or not. If he'd asked her she'd have told him, but perhaps he had the good sense not to ask when he didn't really want to know.

Once, when Frances went looking for him, she overheard Judith say: 'I don't know what you see in her, Joe. She's hardly a beauty – face like a stone wall since her little friend died. I don't think she's quite right.'

Frances thought about that for a long time. A few months previously she'd also overheard Cecily say to Pam: 'The poor thing has such a look in her eyes! Like an old woman who's lived through a war. Don't you think? It's heartbreaking. Not at all like a little girl any more.' So perhaps this was how everybody ended up, and it had just happened to Frances sooner – that things which had once made her laugh no longer did; that her face felt too heavy to smile; that there was a barrier between her and the rest of the world through which nobody could see, and across which nobody could reach.

Stirred from memory by Dog tugging at the end of the lead, Frances hurried on up Bennett Street, passing behind the charred shell of the Assembly Rooms, where stalactites of molten lead hung down from the shattered roof. The fire brigade had run out of water to douse the flames. Then she halted in front of what remained of the Regina Hotel. The huge building had been sheared in two, so neatly that what remained looked like a giant doll's house, ready to play in. She saw several floors of mantelpieces, each with a mirror or picture above it; in one case a coat still hanging on the back of a door, and a candelabra still on a shelf. In the ruined half the destruction was total, and Frances was surprised that anybody had come out alive, especially from the downstairs bar, where the nurse had said several people had remained when the sirens went off. Frances pictured Percy Clifton lying underneath it all, and couldn't place the feeling she had. An odd ache in her knees, a sympathy pang of dread and fear, but also the nagging feeling that it might have been better if he'd been left in there to die. Had he been awake? Had he felt his face begin to scorch as the flames got nearer, and heard the thud of falling stone around him? She shivered, and tried to turn away, but Dog refused to move. He barked furiously at the empty street behind them, in the direction from which they'd come, straining at his collar, tail trembling but not quite wagging.

'What is it?' said Frances. Dog stopped barking but continued to stare, but Frances couldn't see anyone. Her skin prickled; she felt again that sure feeling of being followed, of being watched, and not kindly. 'Come on.' She pulled Dog to heel, and walked away quickly. She'd once read that dogs could see things that humans couldn't. Things like ghosts.

The chaos at the hospital was barely any less. Frances looped

Dog's lead through a radiator pipe in the foyer, rubbed his ears for a moment then left him there. A ward nurse telephoned through to the Bristol Infirmary for her, and when there was no news of Davy in either place, Frances did her best to suppress her despair. She *couldn't* collapse again, like she had the day before; she needed to keep going. Carys's terrible words echoed in her ears: *What would you know about being a mother? You don't know a damn thing about it.* However true it was, it had caused a spark of defiance to kindle. She might not be his mother, but she *did* love him, and she was responsible. And she *would* find him, even if not there, in that place and moment.

Frances went to the end of Percy Clifton's bed, drawn there yet again by something she couldn't quite define, and saw from his chart that he had a slight fever. The patients either side of him had changed since she'd first visited, but Percy hadn't been moved. She sat uneasily on the hard chair at his bedside, and the man in the next bed smiled at her. His leg was plastered and up in a sling.

'Hello there,' he said, cheerfully. 'Looks like it might brighten up out there, doesn't it?' He tipped his head at the window, and the steady downpour of rain. Frances nodded, but couldn't find any small talk. It was the first time she'd actually sat at Percy's side, nearer to his level; she stared at his profile, tense to her very core – if he moved, she knew she would jump up at once. The slope of his jaw, the kink at the bridge of his nose and the curve of his chin. For a second there was something desperately familiar there, but then it was gone. His cheeks sagged back towards his ears, his chin down towards his collarbones; there were broken veins across his nose, and a short scar beneath his lower lip. She stared and stared.

Percy's breathing seemed faster than usual, and appeared to work his chest slightly more. In moments of quiet on the ward she thought she could hear a rattle in his lungs. The pink flush on his skin had deepened; he looked shiny again, like when he was first brought in, and she thought he might be sweating. Suddenly, Frances was fearful – that he was sickening, worsening, and would die. She stood abruptly, looking around for a nurse or a doctor, and the man in the next bed watched her curiously. Percy Clifton mustn't die yet. She suspected that he was somewhere in her mind's dark waters, somewhere deep down; she needed time for him to surface. He was like a forgotten word, stuck on the tip of her tongue; a tune she couldn't quite sing. Scenes from a dream, vanishing in morning light. She looked down at his hands, limp on the sheet with the fingers slightly curled. She thought about touching one of them but couldn't bring herself to do it. She wanted his attention, and at the same time didn't think she could bear to have him look at her. But if he died before she'd spoken to him, before he'd spoken to her ... The thought made her clench her teeth. She leant forwards slightly.

'Mr Clifton?' she said, so tentatively that the words were barely audible. She cleared her throat and tried again, feeling foolish and conspicuous. 'Percy,' she whispered. The name was foreign to her, but something shifted. She saw the toes of her shoes beneath her bent knees, heard a rustle of dry leaves; there was hot sunshine, a smell of nettles and something else, she realised ... *something else* ...

The man in the neighbouring bed cleared his throat; Frances jumped, and the memory vanished.

'You're not his wife then – or his daughter?' he said. 'Sorry – don't mean to eavesdrop, but it's hard not to in here. I'd just assumed you were, you see.' Frances shook her head, then a thought occurred to her, since the man was clearly the talkative type.

'You don't happen to know if anybody else in here came from the Regina Hotel, do you?' she said. The man smiled.

'That's where he copped it, is it? Well, him and me both.

I'm Victor, by the way, Victor Spurrell. Poor bloke, looks like he had it far worse than me – I was staying there, you see. I'd gone up to me room, and as luck would have it, that was in the half left standing. I broke me leg running down the stairs – don't know if that's good luck or bad.' He paused to reflect. 'Good, I suppose,' he said, more soberly.

'Do you know this man?' said Frances, pointing at the sleeping figure beside her. Victor shrugged.

'What's his name?'

'Percival Clifton. Percy, I suppose.'

'Name rings a faint bell . . . There was a fellow in the bar all night, trying to get people to play him at cards – any game, he kept on saying. Any game, I don't mind, as long as you don't mind making it interesting. A gentleman gambler, I supposed; well dressed, nicely spoken. He might have said his name was Clifton, but I can't be sure. Looked a bit older than this fellow here, as I remember it, but it's hard to tell, isn't it?'

'So . . . do you think this could be him?' said Frances. Victor studied Percy obediently, then gave a helpless shrug.

'Sorry, pet, I couldn't say. Not with his head all wrapped up like that. Didn't know at the time that I'd have to remember any of them, did I? I just wanted a quick brandy after supper, that was all. There was the gentleman gambler, and a younger man – though not *young*; a bit of a spiv, if you know what I mean – something a bit shifty about him, like he might know a chap who could get you anything you wanted. That kind of fellow. The ladies seemed to find him charming, and I suppose he was a good-looking bloke, though gone to seed a bit. Perhaps he was offering to get them nylons – he looked that type. My Carole would find anybody charming that could get her nylons; she's been putting gravy browning on her legs for months.'

'Percy Clifton could be the spiv, then?' said Frances. Victor looked again, but shook his head, helplessly.

'I just couldn't say. Sorry.'

'Who else do you remember? Were either of those two with anybody? Did they say where they were from?'

'No, and I don't think they were with anybody. There were plenty of married couples of a certain age, perfectly respectable, and the younger ladies I told you about – shouldn't have been in there on their own, in my opinion. There were two titled ladies, a Lady King down from London to escape the Blitz – *there's* a cruel irony if ever I heard one – and Lady Shand, from Newport. You should have seen the two of them, eyeing each other like a pair of buzzards.' He chuckled. 'There was the vicar – he and I shared a table at dinner since we were both on our own. Woodmansey, his name was. Only lived round the corner, on The Circus, but he said the cook at the Regina was one of the best. Paid for that meal with his life, he has. If only he'd stopped at home for beans on toast instead.'

Victor shook his head sadly, curling his fingers around the edge of his sheet, and Frances began to doubt that he could help her.

'So you can't tell me anything about *this* man? You don't remember him at all?' she said.

'Well, I can only apologise,' said Victor, perplexed. 'It was a funny sort of night, all told. But you've told me his name already, haven't you? Percival Clifton.' Frances shut her eyes in frustration.

'But this *isn't* Percy Clifton,' she said, realising the truth of it.

'It's not?'

'No! Because I don't know a Percy Clifton! But I know this man. I *know* I do!'

'You've lost me, pet,' said Victor. 'Heads up!' he added, in a loud stage whisper. A frowning nurse – Frances thought she recognised her from before – was stalking towards them.

'What's all the racket?' she said, tersely. 'Madam, I know

these are extraordinary times, but we do need to begin restoring some kind of order around here. Visiting hours are two till four. I'm afraid you'll have to leave now.'

'He looks worse,' said Frances, gesturing towards Percy. 'And his temperature's up. Has he got an infection? Is he going to be all right?' Still frowning, the nurse put the backs of her fingers to Percy's cheek, then took his pulse. Frances felt her own pulse ticking in her throat. Then the nurse lifted Percy's exposed eyelid and peered into his eye, and Frances caught a flash of sightless iris, a gleam of moisture. The sight jolted her.

'A slight infection, possibly,' the nurse said. 'Most likely the effects of the smoke he breathed in – it can cause irritation to the lungs and airways. I'm sure it's nothing to be concerned about. We'll be keeping an eye on him, don't you worry. Rest is what he needs, so, please, off you go.' Frances turned and walked towards the door, undone by the sight of Percy's eye – a glimpse of rich brown in a bloodshot white, seen for only a second, but shocking because it was exactly what she'd expected to see.

When Frances got back to Woodlands, she found a note from her mother pushed under the door, and her heart leapt at the sight of her tidy, painstaking handwriting. She hurried to Magdalen Cottages, and into the kitchen, and there were her parents – her father washing his face in the sink and her mother scouring scale out of the kettle with a stiff brush – and for a second it was as if nothing out of the ordinary had happened, and everything was as it had always been. The thought gave Frances a pang of longing to return to before the bombings, when Wyn was still lost and Davy was not, and she could carry on, day by day, thinking little, feeling little. But there was no going backwards, only onwards towards a chance of reprieve; a hope of redemption. She was going to cause upset, in the coming days – of that much she was certain. Susan jumped around with a little cry, then hushed herself, and Frances saw that she wasn't quite forgiven yet. She crossed the room and hugged her mother.

'Sorry, Mum.' She noticed how small her mother seemed, how fragile. 'I'm sorry I didn't go with you, and I'm glad you're back safely.' After a second's hesitation, her mother hugged her back.

'That cut's healing up all right, isn't it? Any word on the lad?' she asked, scrutinising Frances at arm's length. Frances shook her head.

'I'm still looking,' she said. She glanced at the floor where she'd seen his footprints, but Susan had swept it clean. 'He'd been in here,' she said. Susan looked at her, wide-eyed. 'After the first night of bombing, I found his footprints. He came looking for me, or for food. He'd climbed up and got the biscuit tin down from the shelf, and he'd looked for food in the cupboard. But . . . I've not seen any sign of him since.'

'Oh! I did wonder if someone . . .' said Susan. 'And you think it was Davy?'

'I know it was him.'

Derek dried his face then came to squeeze her shoulder. He looked exhausted; brown rings beneath his eyes turned his face lugubrious. Frances hugged him tightly.

'It's so good to see you, Dad. Are you all right?'

'I'm fine, love. I've been asking everywhere about the boy,' he said. 'Telling them to keep an eye out.'

'Thank you for that.' They sat at the kitchen table with tea, and for a moment none of them seemed to have much to say – or so much that they didn't know where to start.

'Your room's still out of action, I'm afraid, what with the ceiling down,' said Derek. 'But you can bunk in with your mum for a bit, and I'll take the floor.'

'Don't be daft, Dad,' said Frances. 'I'll stop on at Pam's a bit longer. You need your sleep at the moment.' Derek looked relieved.

'Are you sure you don't mind?' said Susan.

'Of course I don't mind.' As she said it, Frances realised how much she would rather go back to Woodlands than come to live at home again. Home made her feel as though she were trudging backwards; it made her feel a failure.

'Can't say I'm heartbroken.' Derek smiled. 'My back's killing me.'

'You've been back to work, have you? That's good,' said Susan.

'Yes. But it seems wrong, when I still haven't found Davy.' Her parents exchanged a look.

'Well,' said Susan, a little too brightly, 'I think it's good to get back to normal. Not to ... dwell on things.' She didn't look directly at Frances. Puzzled, Frances's cheeks grew warm.

'What is it?' she said.

'What's what, love?' said Susan, smiling evasively.

'We're just worried about you. That's all, pet,' said Derek.

'Why should you be? I'm fine.'

'It's all been such a terrible shock. I mean, you being out in the bombings, and Davy being ... going missing; and then with Wyn ... being found. We're just worried that it's ...' Susan trailed off, sending her husband an appealing look.

'You won't remember how you were back when she went missing,' Derek said, gently. 'You'll remember it happening, of course, but you won't remember how *you* were. It took you a long time to ... bounce back. For a while we ... we weren't sure you were going to. And we know it must be hitting you hard, now. Her being found, bringing it all back.'

'But you needn't let it, Frances,' said Susan, reaching to take her daughter's hand. 'You needn't let it get to you. It's ... it was all a very long time ago. And nothing's changed, really.'

She sounded almost desperate for it to be true, so Frances didn't have the heart to contradict her.

She stayed for a while, and helped her father hang a front door he'd bought from a man whose house was in ruins. The door was Harrods green, which meant that the man had saved up, probably over the course of his whole lifetime, and managed to buy the house. Almost nobody did that, in their district.

'He's got nothing left at all?' Frances asked, quietly. She couldn't imagine how it must feel to lose everything you'd worked for like that.

'Not a thing, poor old sod,' said Derek. 'But he's got a daughter in Wells and she's taking him in, so that's something.' Derek told her about the places he'd been that day – how the rescue crews were still digging, still trying to find survivors in the ruins.

'And have you found any?'

'Not since yesterday,' he said. 'All we found today were bodies. I think too much time has passed for there to be much hope now...' He looked at her gently, and Frances looked down.

'But you'll keep trying, won't you? There's not *no* hope.'

'No. There's not no hope.'

'Kids are tough. They don't always go where they're supposed to go – like into shelters, or cellars,' she said. There was a long pause, and she wondered if it sounded as obvious to him as it did to herself that she was clinging to the idea of finding Davy out of sheer terror. That the time left in which there was a hope of finding him alive was trickling away, like a clock winding inexorably to a stop. She couldn't bring herself to tell him about the faceless man who'd snatched Gordon Payne from Dolemeads the year before.

'That's better,' said Susan, as the new door swung shut. She took a big, gulping breath and turned away. 'We're lucky, aren't we?' she said, sounding strained. 'Still got this house, still got each other. Not like some folks.' Her teacup rattled into the sink and Derek went to stand behind her. He rubbed her shoulders as she burst into tears.

By early afternoon the rain had cleared, leaving the streets slick and dark; clouds moved fast across the sky, huddled tight together, and the air had the tang of wet ash. Frances waited outside the police station, surrounded by traffic noise – buses, trams, and a few motor cars; the crackle and splash of wheels through puddles; the clop of horse-drawn delivery wagons weaving carefully through it all. She had sent in a message for Sergeant Cummings, claiming the need to see her at once on a personal matter. She put her hands deep in her pockets, trying to stifle her growing sense of urgency. She needed a breakthrough of some kind; a step, however small, towards understanding. There was so much in her head she could hardly think straight – remembered words and unspoken ones, and half-formed images that wouldn't coalesce. Then Cummings emerged, adjusting her belt between her curves, hanks of fluffy hair escaping from her hat.

Frances moved to intercept her, stepping into her path so that Cummings pulled up short, looking harried.

'Mrs Parry, it's you! What's happened – are you all right?'

'Yes, I'm fine,' said Frances. Cummings exhaled, her shoulders dropping.

'When your message said it was a personal matter, I thought my mum ...'

'Sorry! Oh, I'm sorry. I just didn't want your boss to know it was me. That you'd agreed to look into Wyn's case for me.'

'Right. I see.' Cummings took a deep breath. 'In future it'd be better if you waited for me to come and find you at home. Any word on young Davy?'

'No. Did you check up about ... about missing children? Kidnapped children?'

'Yes, and there have been a small number. Most of them runaways who made their way back eventually. No mention of Gordon Payne, though his dad's got a record as long as your arm.'

'Owen said they didn't talk to the police when he went missing.'

'I'm not overly surprised about that. But how on earth were we supposed to find out who took him if we'd no idea it'd happened? If families on the wrong side of the tracks don't talk to us, how can we help at all?'

'No, I know. But . . . did you find anything that might make you think . . . it had happened before, or since?'

'A serial child-snatcher, you mean?' said Cummings, gravely. She shook her head. 'No. But, as I said, we've hardly got the full picture. It's far more likely that Davy's lost, Mrs Parry. Or been killed. I'm sorry, but it is.'

'Well,' said Frances, swallowing. 'Well, if he's lost, he can be found. I . . . I wanted to show you something else. Do you have time?'

'Yes, a little. What is it?' said Cummings. Frances reached into her pocket for Wyn's daffodil brooch.

'It's this.' She held it out in the palm of her hand, picturing how much bigger it had seemed in Wyn's hands when she'd first pinned it to her cardigan, lit up by firelight at Christmastime. It seemed a hundred years ago, and yesterday. It seemed, again, impossible that Wyn was dead, that her hands would never grow any bigger than that. Impossible that Frances could stand there holding Wyn's brooch, when Wyn herself had gone. Cummings took it carefully, and studied it.

'This was Wyn's?' she guessed.

'I gave it to her for her last Christmas. She loved it . . . she always wore it. I never saw her without it. I know it's the same one by the way the leaf's been bent over, there – see where the paint's cracked? She *always* wore it.'

'So how come you have it?'

'I found it yesterday, in Carys's bedroom.'

'That's Carys Noyle, Wyn's elder sister?'

'Yes. I was helping her pack up – her house is going to be demolished. She said her daughter Denise found it in what used to be Carys's room. Wyn and I used to go in there all the time,' Frances explained. 'Wyn liked to try on her sister's clothes. Carys says Wyn probably dropped it in there at some point.'

'But you don't think so?'

'I . . . It made me remember something. The last time I saw Wyn, it . . .' The memory jarred, clashing with what she had always said, with what had become the accepted truth of it. 'I'm *sure* Wyn was wearing it then. That was the day before she disappeared.'

'You're sure?'

'If she'd lost it she would have said. She'd have been upset; she'd have said something.'

'But you gave it to her, so perhaps she didn't want to upset you by telling you, if she'd lost it?'

'No . . . Wyn wasn't like that. She didn't hide things . . .' Frances trailed into silence, remembering how Wyn had changed as that last summer had gone on. She *had* been different. Frances frowned.

'Did you see her wearing it the day she disappeared?'

'Nobody saw her the day she disappeared. Except the person who killed her.' Frances's heart picked up, the way it always did when she was lying. She was puzzled, because she didn't think she was.

'So . . . how do you imagine it came to be in her sister's house?' said Cummings.

'Somebody took it from her. Or, if she did lose it, it must

have happened . . . violently. The pin's still good, see? A little bent but still sharp, and the catch still works, so it wouldn't have fallen off easily.'

'An argument with her sister, you think? Would they have come to blows, though?'

'God, yes.'

Sergeant Cummings handed the brooch back to Frances, and gave her a piercing look.

'You don't have a good opinion of her family, Mrs Parry,' she said. 'But I'm afraid this doesn't necessarily prove anything. Wyn might have lost it, or dropped it, at some point before she died. You said you didn't see her wearing it immediately beforehand.'

Frances took a breath, looking down at the brooch for a moment. *Wyn, come back!* Her own silent words. *Hush, little sisters!* She shook her head.

'I thought it might . . . I thought it might convince you.'

'Convince me of what, exactly?' said Cummings, not unkindly.

'That it wasn't Johannes! That . . . something else happened. At her home.' She paused. 'Have you had a chance to look at the report on Wyn yet?'

'Well, no,' said Cummings. 'Give me half a chance – it's not as though we're short of work in there, you know.'

'I know. I'm sorry. I just . . . I feel we need to . . . strike while the iron's hot, you see, and . . .'

'Mrs Parry.' Cummings shook her head. 'The iron's been cold for near on twenty-four years. I'm not sure I understand the urgency . . .'

'Yes. Of course. It's just that . . . I just feel that *now* is the moment. And perhaps the real killer might disappear out of reach, now she's been found. Or perhaps . . . resurface.' She pictured Carys's hard, watchful gaze; had a memory of Wyn's small body sailing across the room to crash into the fireplace. She felt the shadowy figure following her, the watching eyes. She saw the man who was not Percy Clifton, lying in his hospital bed. *Hush, little sisters.*

'Mrs Parry, you must understand that the hopes of finding enough evidence to convict a different killer – if there was one – after all this time are... beyond slim. Only a heartfelt confession would do it! I only suggested I take a look at the report because... well. To be honest, I'm starting to doubt the wisdom of my having said anything.'

'Yes. I'm sorry. Please don't... I mean, please do look at it, won't you? I need to know how she died. How exactly, I mean.'

'You *need* to know?'

'Yes. It might help, you see. To piece it all together.'

They stood tight to the wall as an ambulance rumbled past, sending out clouds of exhaust. Sergeant Cummings appeared to be weighing up the wisdom of something. She scrutinised Frances for a long moment, then raised her eyebrows.

'I have the strongest feeling you aren't telling me everything, Mrs Parry,' she said. When Frances said nothing, she sighed. 'All I can tell you as yet is that there was no sign of a life-threatening injury to her skeleton. Inspector Reese had a doctor look her over at the mortuary, for the updated report. Wyn's neck wasn't broken and her skull was intact, no signs of a blow to the head.' Cummings glanced at some passers-by, as though feeling conspicuous. 'She had several old breaks, but the bones had knitted a long time before she died. Her collarbone on the left side; her right arm and her right wrist.'

'Yes.' Frances shut her eyes briefly. 'The collarbone was Owen, her brother. It happened when she was very little, before I knew her, but she told me about it – it was wholly accidental. They were bouncing on their Aunt Ivy's bed, and Wyn got thrown off. She landed against the window sill. He was so much bigger than her – well, everyone was. But he would never have meant to hurt her. The right arm was Carys, her sister. She caught us in her room, going through her things, and she wrenched Wyn's arm. Twisted it badly. I don't think she meant for it to break, but it's hard to tell with Carys. She's always had a dreadful temper. I . . . I don't know about the wrist. Perhaps it was before I knew her . . .' Frances thought for a moment, then shook her head. 'Bill Hughes knocked them all about. I'm surprised she only had those three broken bones.'

'Good grief,' Cummings muttered.

Frances thought for a moment.

'If she was hit on the head – or if she hit her head – hard enough to kill her, would it definitely have left a mark on the bone?' she asked.

'I think so, yes. But I'll check with the doctor.'

'I remember from back then – and from the newspapers – that . . . blood was found in the yard of the leper hospital. Will the report say how much, do you think? I mean, whether it was just a little, like she'd cut her lip, or . . .' Frances paused, swallowing. Cummings was watching her with that same look as before, partly shrewd, partly perplexed. 'And I know some of her clothing was found there, but not *what*, exactly.' Frances trailed off, feeling hot and nervous. Cummings left a long pause, as though waiting for whatever Frances would say to fill it. 'I just need to be *sure*,' she said.

'Sure of what, Mrs Parry?'

'Of *how* she died. Of where. And whether she was . . .' Frances fell silent. She couldn't bring herself to say it, and she could see questions forming in the policewoman's eyes.

'Mrs Parry, *please*. What is it you're not telling me?' said Cummings, keenly. 'Do you remember something about it all?

Is that it? Something that you've . . . perhaps not spoken about before?' She thought for a moment. 'Something you don't *want* to remember, perhaps,' she murmured. Frances couldn't speak, so she shook her head. Cummings waited, then pursed her lips. 'Well. The newspapers aren't a bad place to start, actually. I suppose the library will have an archive of *The Chronicle* from back then? If you wanted to do something, you could go and do some research—'

'I wouldn't need to go to the library,' Frances interrupted. 'Mrs Hughes cut out everything about it. She's kept it all.'

'Well, then. You could look for . . . anything you missed at the time.' Cummings gave her a steady look. 'Perhaps something might . . . spark a memory.'

When Frances knocked at number thirty-four later, there was no reply. She stood a while surrounded by the ruins, staring at Carys's doomed house. Her stomach was hot and empty; she felt light-headed, and fought to summon the energy to walk her beat around the rest centres one more time. Then Owen appeared, and saved her. He smiled when he saw her; still a beautiful smile, even if it had lost the width and glee it'd had in boyhood. It was more rueful now, more resigned, but it still put creases in his cheeks, just like when they were small. Right then, it was the only smile that could possibly have made Frances want to smile back. He was wearing a khaki uniform – baggy trousers and shirt, slightly too short in the arm and leg, belted and booted and pockets everywhere; and a garrison cap at a jaunty angle.

'Hello, Frances.' He took off his cap, then looked embarrassed. It was far too polite, far too formal a gesture for them, but he couldn't undo it. He looked down at the hat, then gave a little laugh, and let it dangle self-consciously from one hand. Frances's heart squeezed, and she smiled.

'Don't you look smart,' she said.

'Private Hughes of the Fifth Somerset Battalion – Bath City – Home Guard, Stothert & Pitt Platoon, at your service, ma'am.' He clicked his heels together, and performed a sloppy salute.

'As you were, soldier.'

'I just thought I'd stop off on my way home, see how Mum is.'

'There doesn't seem to be anyone at home.' Frances looked at the blank windows. 'Unless she saw me coming and hid.'

'Don't be daft. How are you? You're a bit pale.'

'I'm all right. I missed lunch, that's all. I've been back to the hospital today, and they called through to Bristol, but there's no news. I was about to go round the rest centres, and—'

'Frances,' said Owen, touching her arm. 'Nobody expects you to spend every minute of every day hunting for him. You'll wear yourself out.'

'Well, I can't do nothing; and Carys . . . Carys has given him up for dead.'

'I know.' He sighed. 'And she's hitting the bottle again, like that'll help.' Frances nodded, and a silence grew between them.

She dropped her hand into her pocket, curling her fingers around Wyn's brooch again. She could give it to Owen to return to Denise right then, but she knew she wasn't going to. She wanted to keep it – not for herself, exactly, though she felt it was safer in her care, but as evidence of something. She wanted to ask Denise Noyle where *exactly* she'd found it. And suddenly she wanted to tell Owen about Percy Clifton – or rather, not Percy Clifton. The unidentified man. She wanted to tell him everything she suspected, everything she was trying to do. That she had a core of confused, unbearable guilt at the heart of her, linked to Johannes's death but also, somehow, to Wyn's. That she had memories she was fighting to dredge up;

that she had been to the police; that she was being followed. She wanted to have him on her side, but the landslide of words caught in the back of her throat, and she wasn't quite ready. She didn't know enough; she wasn't sure enough.

'I was thinking about you today,' she said instead. 'You and that pilfered football of yours that you were never without.'

'Really?' Owen smiled again. 'It wasn't pilfered, I'll have you know. I found it, fair and square. What in heaven's name made you think of that?'

'Whatever happened to it? I suppose you can't even remember now.'

'Are you having a laugh? I've still got it.'

'You have not.' For some reason, this cheered Frances enormously.

'I have. Come along and see sometime, if you don't believe me. It's a good ball, that. It's lasted out many a game with my Nev, and it'll do for many more with Colin yet.'

'I remember you kicking it against the side of the leper hospital. I looked out and saw you; you didn't know we were in there.' At the mention of it, Owen's face fell.

'Nobody knew you were in there. I wish to God we had,' he said. Frances was silent. 'Whose idea was it for the two of you to go there?'

'Whose do you think?' she said, quietly. She didn't say that Owen had given Wyn the idea, with his stories. She didn't say that he was one of the small missteps that had led them there. She would never be that cruel to him. Owen nodded.

'She always had her nose in everything, did Wyn. Our Granny Lovett used to call her "mouse" because of it.' Owen looked away, knots at the corners of his jaw. 'We always end up talking about her. Every time,' he said, quietly.

'It's hard not to, now. But I've always thought about her, in any case. Haven't you?'

'Yes,' said Owen. 'But it does no good. I just wish...' He shook his head, and didn't say what he wished.

'It's good to see you, Owen,' said Frances, abruptly. She hadn't meant to say it, and felt her face flush. Owen smiled, but he looked troubled.

'Shall we get on, then?' he said.

'What do you mean?'

'To the rest centres. I'll come with you. We'll go via a café, and get you a bowl of soup or something.'

'All right,' said Frances, her relief like a wave. If Owen went with her, she could stand it. 'Thank you.'

Once they were walking and no longer face to face, the urge to talk was even stronger. Frances longed to spill out all her fears and suspicions, to straighten the rattling mess inside her head. Flashes of a dank, shaded place; bright sunlight; remembered fear and phantom smells. Wyn, walking away, furious. *No stone was left unturned.* But Owen didn't want to discuss it. Frances didn't want to keep secrets from him, and she didn't want to make him hear something he wouldn't want to hear, and there was no way to satisfy both of those desires. She was worried about the guilt that had burdened her since she was eight years old; the feeling of shame that had its sickening echo in how she now felt about losing Davy. She understood some of it, but not all; there were things she had lost, and she was determined to find them out – the whole truth. But there was a chance that doing so would mean pushing Owen away forever. There was a chance she had done something truly unforgivable. She pictured Owen's face closing off; imagined him turning away in disgust, and never smiling his lovely smile at her again. She wasn't sure if anything was worth that, and suddenly doubt sank through her like a rock.

7
Friday

Five Days After the Bombings

Nora Hughes came slowly down the stairs carrying a small, tatty cardboard box. It was another rainy morning; Frances could hear water gurgling in the downpipes and spilling out of the blocked gutters. It would be dripping through damaged roofs across the city, damping down the dust and soaking into charred timber.

'Here you go,' said Nora, but she hesitated before actually handing the box to Frances. Her face was a tangle of worried lines. 'Though I don't see what good it'll do, looking at it all again.'

'Thank you,' said Frances. 'I just wanted . . . I can't really explain. Because I was so young at the time, I suppose, I only saw a certain amount of what went on.' Nora nodded, and sank into a chair.

'I understand; it seems important to know. Not that knowing makes any difference.'

'Have you heard from Bill?' said Frances. A shadow of unease clouded Nora's face.

'No. Not yet.' She wrapped her cardigan around herself, tucking one side under the other as the damp crept into the room. 'That's normal, though. He'll surface.'

'Do you . . . do you think he knows about Wyn being found?'

'How should I know that?' said Nora, perplexed.

'Yes. Sorry. Have you been . . . have you made any decisions about the funeral?'

'I've . . . made a start.' Nora clearly didn't want to talk about it, so Frances dropped it.

'I could take this up to Woodlands, if you'd rather? Save me cluttering up your front room?' The air was turgid and oppressive, like Nora's palpable sorrow, and Frances was keen to leave.

'I'd rather you didn't, if it's all the same to you. Especially not in this rain.'

Nodding, Frances opened the cardboard box carefully. She didn't know exactly what she was looking for, and didn't dare tell Wyn's mother that she'd spoken to the police. She hoped to find out things she hadn't known, things that would make her remember what had happened. Though she recoiled from it, she needed to know exactly how Wyn had died – what exactly had killed her. Uppermost in the box was the latest small article from the *Chronicle & Herald*, about the discovery of Wyn's bones. Frances lifted it away, and caught her breath. Underneath was a grainy, indistinct image of Johannes. It had been twenty-four years since she'd last seen his face, now here he was, his head and torso, his arms out of sight behind his back, beneath the headline *Escaped German Prisoner Guilty of Child Murder*. There was his round, famished face on top of his skinny neck, his mouth slightly open, his eyes shocked and afraid. Frances touched her fingertips to the image, finding it hard to breathe.

She lifted out the article and read it, feeling her fury rise as she did. It called him an enemy agent; a perverted deviant; a slaughterer of innocents. *Ebner took advantage of the youngsters' naivety in the most evil and callous way, in luring them to do his bidding and serve his depraved purposes.* It announced his death sentence with a satisfaction that bordered on glee, and praised the work of the police in bringing him to justice. As if they'd had to do a damn thing, Frances thought. As if he hadn't been delivered to them on a plate, too frightened to resist. The injustice of it was so like a poison it almost had a taste, metallic on the back of her tongue, and shame made her head pound. She stared hard at his picture, trying to see it through the eyes of somebody who hadn't known him, and who believed what was said and written about him. But try as she might, she couldn't see anything but a persecuted teenager. *Depraved*, it said. Did that mean there had been evidence of something sexual? Frances scanned the article for more details, but there were none. Dark hints of grave things. Nothing specific about which items of Wyn's clothing had been found, alongside her shoe. She'd still been wearing her yellow cardigan when she was buried; Frances had seen the tattered remains of it clinging to her bones. The cardigan to which her brooch had always been pinned.

She put the article back, saying nothing. She was aware of Nora's steady scrutiny, and wished she were alone. Beneath the cutting about Johannes were several more about Wyn, covering the first frenzied days of the search for her, after the discovery of blood and clothing in the leper hospital yard; after Johannes's discovery and arrest, and his *refusal to cooperate*. No description of how much blood – whether it was enough to make them think she'd died there from a cut, or a stab wound. Frances remembered little of those days. She remembered being kept at home, and escaping to go and look for Wyn in the places they used to play. All the places except one. She thought back; saw a dank place with sunlight lancing in, and Wyn walking away, swinging her arms. *Wyn, come back!* She remembered being questioned for what felt like hours by a policeman with meaty breath, and telling him things just to make him stop. But of the aftermath, of Johannes's arrest and trial, she remembered nothing. She didn't know if her parents had shielded her from it or if she'd blanked it out. Then, one morning at the end of November, her mother had sat her down and told her that the bad man couldn't hurt anyone any more. It had taken her a while to understand.

The door opened abruptly and Carys hurried in, her coat held over her head against the rain. Frances's heart sank. Carys dropped a shopping basket to the floor and shut the door, chest heaving.

'I couldn't get any bacon again. Nor sausages. What's happened to all the bloody sausages?' she said.

'Never mind,' said Nora, soothingly. 'We'll make do.' Carys looked down at Frances, perching on a chair with the box of cuttings on her knees. 'Well, I'll be blowed,' she said. '*You're* here again. Fancy that.'

'Hello, Carys.'

'I don't need to ask if you brought Davy back with you, do I?' she said. 'Don't need to bother asking *that*, do I?'

'For heaven's sake! Give it a rest, will you?' said Nora. 'You're not helping, blustering on all the time. Frances is doing as best she can.' There was a pause, and Frances braced herself, but Carys seemed to deflate a bit. She let out a slow breath, shaking her head, then came to stand over Frances. She frowned when she saw the clippings.

'What are you doing?'

'I just wanted to look at these.'

'Why? What for?' Carys demanded.

'Just . . . because. I've been thinking about it all, I suppose. Since she was found.' Frances looked down. Carys's scrutiny was hard to bear; it felt different to normal, more intense, and she realised that Carys was sober. Frances couldn't remember when she'd last seen her with her wits about her. She had a creeping sense of danger, of the need to give nothing away.

The smell of Carys's wet hair and clothing was everywhere; her presence in the room seemed over-large.

'What are you looking for?' she said, coldly. Frances's hands began to shake.

'Nothing,' she said.

'Perhaps you shouldn't be looking, then?'

'Be a love and pop the kettle on, Carys,' said Nora, sounding strained.

Grudgingly, Carys grabbed up the shopping and went through to the back.

'It's funny, having her home again,' said Nora. 'Just like when she was a kid. I'm glad of the company, truth be told.' She lowered her voice. 'I was hoping Clive'd be down from London by now, what with all the work round here after the raids, and with Davy gone . . .' Her eyes drifted away from Frances as she said his name, and Frances felt the weight of blame. Nora shook her head. 'We sent word up about it all, and about the house coming down later today, but we've had nothing back so far.'

'London's not exactly a safe place to be, is it?'

'No, but we'd have heard if he was in any trouble. He always did like to show up unannounced and surprise her, so here's hoping.'

'But . . . you'd think he'd want to come, because of Davy . . .' Frances said tentatively. Nora pursed her lips.

'Clive barely knows the lad, truth be told. It's a crying shame. He's been more away than here since Davy was born, with one thing and another. Well, you know that. Not that there's much to know, with Davy, is there? Or was there, perhaps I should say,' she corrected herself, sadly. 'He was a simple little soul.'

'I can hear you, you know,' said Carys. She reappeared in the doorway, red-faced, eyes snapping. But then it all fell apart, and she started to cry. She looked so horribly vulnerable that Frances looked away.

'Oh! My poor girl,' said Nora, struggling up and attempting to hug her.

'Oh, leave off, Mum,' said Carys. 'God, I need a drink.'

Quickly, Frances flicked through the rest of the cuttings, looking for something – anything – that might have been missed by her or by everybody else; something that might cast a light into the dark places in her memory, or push something to the front. *Fears concerning the safety of missing Bath girl Bronwyn Hughes, aged eight years, have deepened following the discovery of items of the child's clothing, alongside blood stains . . .* There was never any more detail than that. Oblique references to violence and tragedy, to the rousing spirit of neighbourliness as people turned out to help with the search, to the consternation the crime was causing across the city. *Hush, little sisters!* Frances fought the urge to screw them all up – all the flimsy fragments Nora had kept all these years, that said nothing about *Wyn*, nothing about the truth, and were no help to her whatsoever. She stared at the picture of Johannes again, trying to recall all the times she'd been to see him. But the more she tried to see, the more the memories fragmented. Her hands were still shaking as she put the clippings away, returned the box to Nora and went to work, knowing she had failed again.

Excelsior Street was typical of Dolemeads – a straight, narrow street across which two identical brick terraces faced one another. It didn't look like it belonged in Bath at all, and might have been more at home in one of the big industrial cities up north. The walls were filthy with soot, the gutters choked with weeds, and washing lines criss-crossed between the upstairs windows. There were gaps here and there where the stray bombs had fallen the previous Easter – numbers three and sixteen were gone. The door of number nineteen was dark blue, and had thick lines of dust in its mouldings. The broken windows were covered with roofing felt and canvas, and it looked an even sorrier place than Beechen Cliff Place. Frances had never been there before. She couldn't picture Owen living there, but when she knocked, he opened the door, looking surprised to see her.

'I saw your mum this morning; she told me you had the day off, and were doing some repairs. I was just on my way back after work and I . . . thought I'd come by and see if you'd heard anything. Or needed a hand with anything,' she said.

'Right, well, come in,' said Owen.

The front door led into a small hallway, from which a narrow staircase ran up in a straight line, front to back of the house. Owen ushered her through a doorway on the left, into the front room. There was a threadbare rug, worn to the backing in places; an upright sofa covered in dark brown fabric; striped wallpaper; and a framed reproduction of *The Hay Wain* hanging on the far wall. The fireplace had a simple iron surround, and was choked with ash. Frances stared at everything, trying to picture his life there: a married man, with a wife and children. She felt like an intruder.

'Make yourself at home,' he said, making no move to sit down himself.

'Thanks,' said Frances. They stood facing one another, and for a moment neither one spoke.

There were traces of Bill Hughes in Owen. Owen was taller and rangier, but he had Bill's dark hair, the length of his face and the shape of his nose, though it was hard to tell now, given how crooked Owen's had got. Bill had broken it for him at least twice, over the years. But there was no threat about Owen; there never had been. Frances couldn't think of a single time he'd shown a temper, or been violent, or unkind. She wondered if Bill Hughes had been like that before he lost his first family, which would make it even more of a tragedy. As a child she had known, instinctively, not to trust Bill Hughes – his moods, his fists. In the exact same way, she knew to trust his son. She had always trusted Owen.

'I haven't seen your old man around much,' she said. Owen looked puzzled. 'I mean, since the second night of bombings. I've been around to your folks' house a couple of times, but not seen him.'

'He mostly keeps himself to himself, these days. He doesn't get around as easily as he once did – his back's shot. So once he gets settled in somewhere, it takes a fair amount to shift him.'

'You mean, in one of the pubs?'

'Yes, usually. Or at home – some days he just stays in bed. Sometimes he finds other beds to occupy, though God knows where. Or how.' Owen smiled briefly. 'Mum doesn't generally fret unless he hasn't shown his face for a fortnight or more. I think she likes the breathing space, now and then.'

'But . . . he might have been killed, mightn't he? How would you know?'

'Well.' Owen looked uneasy. 'Everyone round here knows him, and he doesn't go far. Someone would have been along to tell us. Besides, he's a tough old bird. It'll take more than a few bombs to kill him.' Owen put his hands in his pockets and looked around the room, dingy with the windows partly covered, and Frances didn't point out that more than 'a few' bombs had fallen. 'Did you want him for something?'

'Oh, no.' Frances shook her head. 'I've just been thinking about it all. How he was when we were little. Did he . . . did he ever find out about Johannes? Before Wyn disappeared, I mean. If he found out we used to take him things – food, and other things – he wouldn't have liked it, would he?'

'You bet he wouldn't,' said Owen, guardedly. 'But as far as I know, he never found out. Come through to the back, I'll put some tea on. Do you want tea? I think there's milk. It might have gone sour, mind you.'

'Have you got anything stronger?' said Frances. Owen glanced at the clock, saw that it was only two in the afternoon, and shrugged.

'Well, why not?' he said.

As Frances turned, a framed photograph on a side table caught her eye. Owen and Maggie's wedding portrait. Maggie was wearing a lace dress with a shallow V-neck and elbow-length sleeves; Owen a plain suit that almost fitted him, with a rose in his buttonhole. They looked nervous, cautiously optimistic. Maggie was short and slim, her face just slightly too hard to be called pretty, despite her smile and the circlet of tiny white flowers in her hair. The definite outline of a bump was visible beneath the midsection of her dress. Owen looked so young, so unmarked, that it touched some vulnerable, tender part of Frances, like the memory of a loss from long ago. Owen hesitated when he saw her looking at it, then tapped the glass over the baby bump with one finger.

'That's Nev in there. Dad got drunk at the wedding and picked a fight with Maggie's uncle. Luckily he fell over before he could do any real damage. Clive's lungs were bad that day, so Carys danced with some other bloke and Clive got all shirty about it; Annie threw a tantrum about God knows what, and drove Mum to distraction. In fact, all I can remember after saying "I do" is putting out fires. It was a proper Hughes affair,' he said, and Frances smiled.

The kitchen window was intact, and pallid light seeped through it. Frances glanced around at the narrow gas cooker, the small sideboard, the plates in a rack up on the wall. One leg of the table was broken, and propped up on two bricks. Children's finger paintings were pinned to the walls; a crocheted blanket hung over one of the chairs; and on the drainer, long-since dry, were four plates and matching egg cups printed with Beatrix Potter characters – Jemima Puddleduck, Tom Kitten, Mrs Tiggy-Winkle and Benjamin Bunny. Frances thought of Davy, who'd barely known what a plate was for when Frances first knew him, and her stomach pitched. Owen followed her gaze to the plates, and saw her expression. With a frown, he reached into a crate of beer in the corner by the sink, opened a bottle and handed it to her. 'Do you want a glass?' he said, but Frances shook her head.

'This is fine.'

'You're doing everything you can, Frances,' he said, gently. 'All the rest centres and hospitals know to look out for him, and get in touch. They've all got his details.' Frances took a swig of the beer, looking away because there was something about Owen's gentle expression that put her in danger of crumbling, collapsing.

'Dad says the hopes of finding anyone alive in the ruins now are almost gone,' she said.

'Well, Davy's not in the ruins, is he? He's hiding some-where. Or he's with somebody. Isn't he?'

'Yes. I hope so . . . unless he's with . . . somebody who means him harm.'

'I wish to God I hadn't told you about that.'

'But what if he is, Owen? What if . . . it's the same person who killed Wyn?'

'Come off it – after all this time? That's *not* what's hap-pened, Frances. Sit down, please. Just sit down for a bit.'

They sat opposite one another at the little table, the silence between them a strange one: not uncomfortable, but somehow expectant. Frances noticed a child's sketch on the table top – an aeroplane, the pilot in his oversized cockpit wearing a huge, crooked smile. Most of the pencil lines had been scrubbed away, but the indentations in the shellac remained. She ran her fingers over it, remembering the chalk figures Wyn used to draw in the leper hospital yard. 'That was Colin,' said Owen. 'Just a few days before the bombings. Maggie boxed his ears for it, and made him howl.' Owen smiled. 'He's got that streak in him a mile wide – the one that pushes back when he's leaned on. Whatever he's told to do, he wants to do the opposite. Maggie'd told him he couldn't draw on the table. So he drew that and said, "See, Mummy – I can."' He grinned.

'He sounds like a Hughes.'

'He's *definitely* a Hughes.' Owen picked at some ground-in dirt beneath his thumbnail; Frances noticed that there was dust in his hair, and all over his hands.

'How are the repairs going?' she said.

'All right, but I was ready for a break,' he said. 'I've worn my shoes out today. I went out to see Maggie and the kids in Bathford this morning, and tried to convince her there'll be no more bombs, and that I've got the roof watertight.' He took a steady breath. 'Now she's saying she'll be back when everything's cleared. All the dust and smoke is no good for her or the kids' lungs.'

'But . . . that'll be months – years!'

'It will.' Owen took a drink, and couldn't quite meet Frances's eye. 'I don't think she means it; just that she's not quite ready yet. It was good to see the kids, mind you.'

'I'm sure,' said Frances, sensing there was something Owen wasn't saying. When he looked up, she saw an appeal – the need to be heard, and understood.

'It's just . . . nice to come home to people that are pleased to see you,' he said. Frances nodded, thinking of Joe and feeling bad for him.

'You and Maggie have been married fourteen years now, is that right?'

'Yes. Since Nev was well on the way.' Owen looked away,

thinking for a moment. 'We had to give it a go, didn't we? The girl I'd banked on marrying had other ideas, so . . . And you can't regret these things, not when there are three new human beings to show for it, and every one of them a little gem.'

'Of course. And that's the whole point of marriage, isn't it? To build a family.' Frances wondered if she sounded bitter; she didn't mean to. Owen gave her a searching look.

'Not the *only* point, surely? There's companionship, comfort in your old age, all of that. Love. If you're lucky.' Frances didn't reply at once. She waited, hoping for the beer to loosen the knots in her stomach.

'Well,' she said, when the silence had gone on too long. 'Shall I give you a hand with whatever you were doing? Get the place fixed, so they'll come back sooner?'

'You don't need to do that.'

'Many hands make light work. I'd like to help.'

The children's room was as sparse as the rest of the house – at around eight by eight feet, it was barely big enough for any furniture. There were two mattresses propped against the wall – one for fourteen-year-old Nev and his brother Colin, the other for Sarah and their cousin Denise to share. There was a chest of drawers, much scratched and battered, and a few toys tidied away in a crate – jigsaw puzzles with flattened boxes, gone at the corners; a tin spinning top; several model cars and a train. On the wall hung a print of a white duck leading little yellow chicks towards water. Thrips had got in under the glass – black speckles on the board, each in its own small halo of stain. The ceiling had cracks like lightning bolts running from each corner to a jagged hole in the middle, and Owen had already cleared away the fallen detritus and swept the floorboards clean. Sparkles of light were visible through the gap, where the sky peeked through the roof tiles. Owen peered up at them.

'Well,' he said, ruefully. 'I *think* I've got it weathertight. Most of the tiles are back where they're supposed to be, but a lot of them are cracked, and want replacing. Which won't be till next month at the earliest, when I get paid and can get out to the salvagers. And I expect they'll put a premium on them, now every Tom, Dick and Harry needs them.'

'I suppose pinching them from bomb sites counts as looting, does it?' said Frances.

'I suppose.' Owen thought for a moment then shook his head. 'Wouldn't feel right, anyway. Taking from people who've lost everything as it is.'

'Yes, you're right.'

'Bloody German bastards. We should bill them for the lot.'

Frances winced. She heard it everywhere – cursing the Germans; loathing the Germans; making crude jokes about the Germans. Just like she remembered from childhood, and the first war. She supposed it was a pressure valve, an acceptable way for people to vent the fear and madness of it all. But she'd seen the way people who were usually kind and reasonable could turn savage, so it made her uneasy to hear that talk – it gave her a nervy feeling, as though something awful and unavoidable were about to happen. Even mild, knee-jerk remarks like Owen's bothered her – the unthinking unfairness, the casual injustice.

'Their leaders and ours decided to go to war. Not us, or them. And we're giving as good as we get,' she said, knowing she oughtn't bother. Owen sighed, irritated.

'Well, I don't know, Frances. They bloody well started it, and—'

'Hitler started it.'

'They put him in charge! And if we're not allowed to be angry with them about that, then how are we supposed to fight them?'

'I don't know.' Frances thought about it for a moment. 'I don't know.'

'Well, then.' They worked in silence for a moment. 'Don't go talking like that to just anybody, will you?' said Owen. 'People don't take kindly to it. You could be had away to a camp for enemy agents, if you aren't careful.' Frances didn't scoff at this, since he was probably right.

'I won't,' she said, wearily.

They turned their attention to the ceiling. First they had to knock back the remaining lath and plaster around the hole, to expose ceiling joists to nail planks to, and all of Owen's careful sweeping was undone by fresh showers of plaster and dust.

'I didn't think of that,' he admitted, coughing through the clouds and looking down at the mess. 'Waste of time tidying, wasn't it?'

'Yes,' said Frances. She smiled briefly at his crestfallen expression. 'I'll help you clean up afterwards. It won't take long.'

'Thanks, but you really don't need to. You've enough—'

'Well.' Frances couldn't say that she didn't want to go, or that being there made some of her confusion quieten, and steadied the anxious rattle of her thoughts. Though there were still things she couldn't say to him – things she would have to be very careful about suggesting – the simple fact remained that being around Owen Hughes was far better than not being around him. 'Well, you've helped me enough, lately,' she said, awkwardly.

'I don't need paying back for that,' said Owen. He paused, then smiled at her. 'But I won't turn it down. Grab the other end of that plank, then, and let's get cracking.'

They didn't talk as the hole was gradually patched over – an ugly, uneven repair that any self-respecting builder would take down at once, and do properly. There was just the work, the cooperation and the slight warmth of a second beer in their blood. Perhaps that was what made it seem as though years hadn't passed since they were last so at ease with one another; that made it seem as though it had always been that way. Slowly, the scent of them filled the small room – their bodies towards the end of a busy day, mixing with the smell of wood and plaster. Owen always had the smell of the Stothert & Pitt works on him – a machine oil and metal smell, strangely compelling, like the taste of a new penny. Frances let herself think of their kiss, an age ago, beneath the railway bridge up Lyncombe Vale. The memory of it was still vivid, she could smell the cow parsley in flower, and the mud beneath their feet; the damp bricks of the arches and the tang of sheep muck in the field beyond. And she remembered Owen, of course – the outline of him in the near-dark, and the taste of his mouth, fleetingly, before he'd pushed her away. Lips and teeth and tongue, with traces of booze and cigarettes. Like there would be now.

'Frances?' said Owen, to get her attention. 'Wool-gathering?' He smiled down from the top of the step ladder. 'Pass me that clawhammer again, would you?'

'This one? Here you go.'

'Are you all right?'

'Yes, I . . .' Frances gathered herself up; with a wrench, she let the memory recede. 'I've been to the police. About Wyn.'

Owen frowned. He fiddled with the hammer for a moment, picking bits of paint from the handle.

'To say what?' he said.

'To say that I . . . I think the investigation should be re-opened.' To this, Owen made no reply. 'They've agreed to look into it. Well . . . one of them has.'

'Right,' he said, neutrally. 'And why do you think they should do that?'

'You *know* why, Owen! Johannes didn't know where she lived. He was afraid to set foot outside the leper hospital . . . I finally told them what I should have told everyone twenty-four years ago. Johannes Ebner didn't kill your sister.' The words felt huge in the room. At the top of the ladder, Owen stopped fiddling and turned to look at her. His expression was one of sorrow and resignation, and – she saw it clearly – fear.

'I know,' he said.

'You – *what*?' Frances was dumbfounded. She'd expected to be told to drop it; to be told, again, that she was wrong. 'You *know*? What do you mean, you know?'

'I just . . .' Owen shook his head, coming down the ladder. A deep flush was creeping up his neck, and Frances guessed he wished he hadn't said anything. 'I mean, he *could* have done it. He was hiding right there, where she died. And he was in a bad way.' He shook his head. 'But . . . I mean, *why* would he? The last thing he wanted was to be discovered, right? Well, nothing made it more likely that he *would* be than snatching a little girl and leaving her clothes right on his own doorstep, did it? And I remember his face when they took him out of there. You probably don't – I don't remember you being around, and you were so young, anyway. But I saw his face, and he was just . . . petrified. And bewildered. Like he couldn't understand how he'd been found, or why, or where they were taking him.'

Frances shut her eyes and fought a wave of dizziness; she felt smothered by shame – shame she still only barely understood.

'Oh, God,' she whispered.

'Besides,' Owen went on, 'you *knew* him. Nobody else did, once Wyn was . . . once she'd gone. There was nobody but you to speak for him, and, well, you're speaking for him now. So who am I to say you're wrong? But Frances, he's *dead*. He and Wyn are as dead as each other. It's too late – what possible good can you do him now?'

'It isn't too late – it can't be too late!' said Frances. 'There *was* only me to speak for him.' She blinked back tears, looking squarely into Owen's eyes. 'And I said the wrong things. They only asked what they wanted to hear, and they . . . they used me against him. And I didn't defend him! I can't change that now, I know that . . . But the least I can do is find the person who *did* do it!' She struggled to steady her breathing. 'Because the *only* thing as bad as Johannes being blamed when he was innocent is that the real killer got away with it.'

'Frances,' Owen said, shaking his head. 'You can't possibly think there's any chance of finding out after all this time?'

'There might be. I can—'

'No, you *can't*! It's impossible!' Owen's voice rose, silencing her. 'You'll end up hurting yourself, Frances! You'll . . . drive yourself to distraction. It's *too late*!'

'But I . . . I remember things! Things I've never told anyone.'

'What things?' said Owen, after a heartbeat's pause. He looked worried, and Frances had the new, awful idea that he was holding something back; keeping something from her.

'I . . . I . . .' Frances struggled to put the images in some kind of order; to name places, and people.

Percy Clifton. The name was right there, on the tip of her tongue. But it would be pointless to say it, pointless to ask Owen whether he knew Percy Clifton. Of course he didn't; neither did Frances. In all probability, Percy Clifton was dead. The *real* Percy Clifton, that was – not the man lying unconscious in the Royal United Hospital. She needed him to wake up and talk to her, and give her answers. Her heart quickened at the thought. *Hush, little sisters! No stone was left unturned.* 'I think,' she said, uncertainly. She saw Wyn, walking away, angry; she wanted to call her back. Wanted to, but didn't. 'I think I saw Wyn the day she disappeared,' she said, fighting for clarity. 'I . . . I lied to the police. I don't know why! I can't *remember* why. Wyn came to my house, and asked me . . . something. I don't know what it was. I was upset. I . . . I sent her away. By herself. And I wanted to call her back – I remember watching her go, and wanting to call her back. But I didn't.' Frances put her hand over her mouth, as the significance of that coalesced, becoming clear to both of them. Tears burned her eyes. 'If I'd gone with her . . . if I'd called her back, she might still be alive!'

'Frances, no,' said Owen, stepping forwards, gripping her arms. 'None of it was your fault! None of it.'

A knock at the door made them both jump. Owen squeezed her arms once more, then went downstairs to answer it. Frances heard him talking, but not what he was saying. She was shaking, certain now that she had it right – that she'd sent Wyn away by herself, to meet her killer.

'Frances!' Owen shouted up the stairs. 'Get your coat on. We have to go out.'

'What is it?' She ran down to him, and he handed her a telegram. He didn't smile, but there was a new energy about him, an excitement in his eyes, and her heart leapt. She read the slip of paper quickly: *Message for Mr O W Hughes from EMS centre, Frome Rd House, Combe Down. Boy, 5-6 yrs, being treated for wounds, no identification. Found Bear Flat 30/4.* 'Oh . . .' she said, looking up at Owen. 'It's Davy – it *has* to be. They've found him!'

'Come on.' Owen passed her her coat.

The Emergency Medical Service hospital in Combe Down had taken over Frome Road House, the huge Victorian workhouse where thousands of Bath's poor had lived and died across the previous century. It had a formal front range, with a central portico dominated by a huge clock, and behind that, diagonal wings reaching away in the shape of a letter Y – the men's wing, the women's, the boiler house and bakery and infirmary. Frances remembered Cecily campaigning for improved conditions for the babies and toddlers there – she'd shaken a bucket and given speeches outside the Roman Baths. There was a bustle of vans coming and going – the kitchens were cooking meals with Ministry of Food rations and distributing them to the rest centre canteens. Frances had paid the bus fare for both of them because it was a good mile and a half up to Combe Down, all of it uphill, and she couldn't be patient. She and Owen walked straight in through the door beneath the clock, and hurried to the reception desk.

Inside, the ceiling reared away; there was a smell like cobwebs and church pews, though the place seemed spotless. The stone walls were bare; light came from tall sash windows, and, weakly, from a lonely glass lantern, hanging from a long chain high above their heads. Frances pushed her way through a small group of people having a debate at the front desk.

'I'm afraid you'll have to wait your turn, madam,' the receptionist told her, sharply. She was marooned in a sea of paperwork, and kept her hands splayed flat across it all as though it might fly into a blizzard otherwise.

'It's all right – we only want pointing in the right direction.' Frances pushed the telegram towards the woman. 'Children's ward, I imagine – unless he's been into surgery? We don't know how badly hurt he is, you see, or when exactly he was brought in.'

'This is your boy, is it?' she said, flicking her eyes over the message.

'My nephew,' said Owen.

'All right. Nurse Portree!' the receptionist called past them. 'Sorry to collar you, Nurse – can you help this pair?' The receptionist handed the telegram to a short woman whose huge bosom made her fob watch stand out all but horizontally. The nurse gave them a brief glance and a nod.

'Follow me, please,' she said. Frances glanced at Owen and smiled, ignoring his uneasy expression.

Away from the front desk, the peculiar hush of a hospital descended – the continual murmur of small sounds, far away and kept to a minimum. It echoed eerily through the barren corridors, and Frances couldn't wait to be able to take Davy out of there. Nurse Portree's heels rang against the tiled floor, and her shoe leather had a squeak.

'How is he, do you know?' Frances asked her.

'Fairly poorly, but he'll live, and nothing's broken. It was more a case of being without food and water for so long, I think. And he took a bit of a knock to the head as well; he seemed a little confused when he first came in, and we've had the devil of a time getting any information out of him. Quiet as a mouse.'

'Yes,' said Frances, her heart soaring. 'I'm afraid he isn't very talkative, even at the best of times.'

'Frances...' said Owen, cautiously. They walked further, into corridors with lower ceilings and less light. Frances glanced into the rooms they passed and saw camp beds in close ranks, each one made up with a single sheet and blanket. Makeshift wooden frames had been constructed around some of them, from which broken limbs were slung.

'His name's David Noyle, if you need to make a note,' she said.

'Let's wait and see, shall we?' said Nurse Portree.

He would have been well fed since he was found, Frances reassured herself, and he was awake enough to have shown a little confusion. She wished she'd had something of his that she could have brought in, to comfort him until he was allowed to leave, but Davy had never had anything much. He still had his mother, though – such as she was – and grandparents willing to take them in. With a flare of anger, Frances remembered all the times Carys had neglected him – shut him out or forgotten to feed him – because she'd passed out drunk somewhere. She couldn't help but worry about the home Davy would be going back to now. She couldn't help but wish things were different.

They entered a large room serving as the children's ward, and Frances found herself almost frightened by the thought of seeing Davy again – how it might make her feel, and how he might look with his injuries. Then she walked into Nurse Portree, who'd stopped and turned to them expectantly.

'Well, then?' said the nurse. Frances looked around, confused. They'd stopped at the end of the ward, by the very last bed, but the little boy lying in it wasn't Davy. She looked at the next bed along, but its occupant was a little girl, staring curiously.

'Shit,' Owen muttered, and Frances felt his hand on her shoulder.

'I don't understand,' she said. Nurse Portree picked up the boy's chart, frowning at it.

'Oh dear,' she said. Frances took a deep breath, momentarily lost for words. 'I'm very sorry ... it seems you might have had a wasted trip.' The nurse's cheeks flushed pink, and she looked contrite as she turned back to the small figure in the bed. The boy was freckled, with curly ginger hair and russet eyes. 'Since the telegram was sent out, somebody has been in to lay claim to the boy. Eric Cottrell, it says here. So at least we know who he is. That's a good thing, don't you agree? Would you like to sit down a minute?'

'No ... No, I don't want to sit down! I ... We clearly said, in all our descriptions – Davy has straight, *fair* hair, and *grey* eyes!'

'Now, I can understand you're upset, but we really can't have raised voices in here.'

'Frances, come on,' said Owen, trying to lead her away.

'No! We gave a ... a *very* good description of him ... It was very clear!'

'Well, I am sorry, but, obviously, there's been a lot of confusion lately,' said Nurse Portree, stiffly. Frances was suddenly so angry she could hardly keep it in. She was angry with Nurse Portree and her squeaky shoes; with blameless Eric Cottrell, for being in Davy's bed; with whoever had sent Owen the telegram. Most of all with herself for forgetting completely, for a blissful few minutes, the possibility that the anonymous boy might not be Davy.

With his face set, Owen steered Frances out of the ward and along to the refectory. He got her a cup of Bovril, which she left to go cold as Owen sat quietly beside her, staring into the middle distance. She realised that Davy had gone again. For a short while he'd been back at her side, safe, solemnly holding her hand with his attention drifting here and there, as it was wont to do – to an empty ginger beer bottle; a discarded newspaper; the furry nostrils of the scrap metal man's donkey, dozing between the traces. Such things had fascinated him. People came and went, tea was served, condolences given. It started to rain again – the smell of wet clothes drifted in with the visitors.

'Frances?' said Owen, eventually. 'Shall we go home?'

'Home?' she said. She realised she'd been crying; her eyes were itchy and swollen. 'And then what? Back to ... to waiting? To trailing around the rest centres when he's not *there*? Back to feeling that I've ... I've done the worst thing imaginable?'

'It isn't your fault!' said Owen, tightly. 'What do you want me to say? What do you want to do?'

'I want to carry on looking! I want to *find* him! Today – now!' Frances was shouting; people turned to look and she didn't care.

'Frances—'

'Because if I don't find him ... if I've done this thing, Owen – if I've lost him, and he's dead, then how ...' She fought for breath, her whole body shuddering. 'Then how . . . how can I *ever* live with that?'

There was a momentary hush in the canteen; Frances was aware of staring eyes all around, but it was Owen's – sorrowful, anxious – that she couldn't stand. Her chair scraped the floor as she got up, wiping her face with her hands.

'Frances, wait,' said Owen, but she hurried across the foyer and out into the rain. 'Frances!' he called again, jogging to catch up with her. Frances turned to him. 'All right, then,' he said.

'What do you mean?'

'You want to keep looking, so let's keep looking. Right now.'

'Look where?' she said, bleakly. Owen turned up his collar, squinting into the rain.

'I was thinking about that just now, inside. Places that you took him – all the places you took him. Anywhere he liked, or might remember. Anywhere he might have wandered to.'

'But . . .' Frances spread her hands helplessly.

'Look, he's not in any of the likely places, so let's look in some unlikely places. You told me Carys didn't know where he liked to play, so you tell me, where *did* he like to play?'

'He . . . he . . .' She tried to concentrate, to think. 'He liked going up Smallcombe, and to Topcombe Farm. He liked the hay barn. I took him a few times when I went to see Judith, soon after I left.'

'Then we'll start there. Yes?' Owen held her gaze, and, gradually, she felt a little resolve returning. She nodded.

'Yes.'

A fitful breeze whipped the rain into their eyes; it seeped in at their collars and cuffs. They cut across Claverton Down on footpaths then turned down Smallcombe Vale, one of the steep, green valleys that dropped southwards into Bath. They walked in silence, each lost in thought, slipping on the wet grass and mud. Frances halted as Topcombe Farm came into view, tucked into the hillside. A stream ran into a large pond beside it; an array of ancient sheds and barns stood around a neglected Georgian house. The breeze tore the skein of chimney smoke to shreds. Frances steeled herself for an encounter with Judith Parry, who'd never wanted her for a daughter-in-law, and would now never forgive her for leaving. Frances had done her best at being Joe's wife – a farmer's wife; she'd done her best to want a baby. But bringing a child into the world had always seemed such a frighteningly irrevocable thing, and the prospect left her cold. Children could disappear; they could break your life apart.

Owen followed her gaze.

'It was always strange, picturing you living up here,' he said. 'It didn't seem right, somehow.'

'I loved living here,' said Frances. Owen looked troubled. 'I mean, I loved the farm. The clean air, and the horizon being all the way over there, miles and miles away.' She'd loved the uncomplaining stoicism of the animals too, and how alive it all was, even in the middle of winter. The steam rising from the cows; the geese slipping on the frozen pond; the slew of mouldering hay in the barn, centuries deep, infested with rats, ticks and chickens. So different to the deadened streets of the city. 'I think that's why I agreed to get married in the first place.'

'It can't have been the whole reason, surely? You must have loved Joe.'

'No. I . . . I liked him. I said yes because he wanted me to. Because he loved me. I thought that would be enough; I thought it couldn't hurt to try. But I was wrong, on both counts.' Frances paused, thinking back. Another reason had been that Owen was already married to Maggie by then, but she couldn't tell him that. 'I thought I could leave the past behind me up here,' she said. 'My parents kept saying I should. But it turns out those things are part of you, and you take them with you whether you want to or not. But it felt like a good life, for a while.'

'Farming's hard though, isn't it? When you're not brought up to do it,' said Owen. Frances shrugged.

'I'm the right sort for it – I'm not bothered about a broken nail, a home haircut or the way you can never get shot of the smell of animals. I didn't mind any of that. And there was always something that needed doing; every day had a purpose.' For a while, living there, she'd felt differently about life. She'd felt the possibility of happiness. But as time had passed, she'd realised that she couldn't feel any differently about herself, or about Joe.

'So why did you leave? If you don't mind my asking.' Owen sounded uncomfortable. 'Did you and Joe have a falling-out?'

'No, no.' Frances thought for a moment. 'Joe deserved a wife who loved him. He deserved one that wanted to be a mother to his children. I made him miserable, and he deserved better.'

Frances set off down the hill before Owen could ask anything else, and soon heard him following. She went straight into the barn, casting her eyes around in the gloom. Davy had played in the haystack when they'd come before – grinning, giggling, covered in chaff; climbing up to jump and slide down, again and again. She scanned it for sudden movements, strained her ears for the rustle of a small body, hiding. Chickens crooned softly, flies buzzed; a mouse ran along a beam beside her.

'Davy?' she called. 'It's Frances... You can come out, now.' As though they'd simply been playing hide and seek. 'I've come to fetch you home. It's quite safe now...' Her voice trailed to nothing because she knew, simply *knew*, that she was talking to the rats and chickens, and no one else. Her heart sank. 'Come on, now, Davy,' she said again, weakly. Owen's footsteps rustled as he came up behind her.

'Nothing?' he said. She shook her head. 'Shouldn't we knock at the farmhouse, and let them know we're here?'

'Probably,' said Frances.

'Definitely, I'd say,' said Judith, from the doorway. Frances and Owen turned to find her peering at them down the barrels of her shotgun, which she quickly lowered. 'I thought you were thieves, Frances. I damn near shot you,' she said. Judith's face was gaunt, her eyes an unreadable black. Hardworking hands, all bone and sinew, held the gun tight.

'We're looking for Davy,' said Frances. 'He's gone missing. Can we check in the other barns?'

'That little boy you watch? The one you're so fond of?' Judith stared hard at Frances. 'Look where you like. I've not seen him,' she said, turning back towards the house.

'Well. She seems dear,' said Owen.

They searched everywhere, but found nothing. The rain got heavier; Owen hunched his wet shoulders to it, and Frances shivered as they set off back down the hill to Bath. On Holloway, muddied and quiet, they halted by the ruins of Springfield Place, where Frances had last seen Davy. It was bleak, utterly lifeless. The sky was darkening; they were both tired. 'Where next?' said Owen, staunchly, and Frances wanted to hold him tight.

'Owen . . . please go home. Thank you for . . . trying. Go and get dry, and have something to eat,' she said.

'Are you going to?'

'I . . . Yes. Perhaps not just yet.'

'Then I'm staying.' He pushed his hands deep into his pockets, and looked around. 'What about closer to home? You'll have looked in Magdalen Chapel already, I suppose. And the leper hospital.'

'What?'

'I . . . assumed you'd have checked in the leper hosp—'

'Why would he be in there?' Frances interrupted. 'He wouldn't go in there. I've never taken him.'

'Frances, what's wrong?' Owen frowned down at her. 'Have you . . . have you never been back there? Not in all this time?' he said. Frances shook her head. Owen turned to look at the chapel, and at the little cottage beside it, where Johannes had once hidden. Where Wyn had died. 'But . . . they're right *there*. If Davy ran out here, and it was dark and he was confused . . . mightn't he have gone into one of them? Gone in and either been too scared to come out, or not known where he was? We have to check.'

'All right.' Frances's throat had gone dry; dread took hold of her, as tangible as grasping hands.

Magdalen Chapel had a huge hole in its eastern end, and the walls were pocked with shrapnel wounds, as though giant worms had burrowed in. They checked beneath the pews and choir stalls, and in all the dark corners, and Frances was thrown back to the second night of bombing, and the soldier who'd died beside her – the smell of his blood. Her heart flung itself against her ribs.

'Are you all right?' said Owen. Frances nodded, not trusting herself to speak. They checked the graveyard, then stood at the side wall looking into the leper hospital yard. Dank, puddled, choked with weeds. Frances felt stretched, every nerve straining. Heavy drops of rain fell from the branches above. The last time she had stood in that spot it had been summer, and Wyn had been alive; Johannes too. 'This was how you used to get in?' said Owen. Again, Frances nodded.

'I . . . I don't think I can go in,' she said. It looked smaller, as things from childhood will. It looked completely different, yet exactly the same. *Hush, little sisters!*

'You don't have to, I can go,' said Owen. He hesitated, glancing at her. 'But . . . perhaps you should. Perhaps it would help. It's just a building, after all. Just a place.' He turned to look at the ancient hospital. 'Perhaps it might help you remember something,' he added, in a strange, flat voice. Frances tried to read him, but she couldn't keep her thoughts straight. So she climbed over the wall before she could change her mind.

She looked for chalk drawings on the paving stones; she looked for a pale face at the window; she looked for a small, quick figure with a streak of sunlit hair. She saw movement in the corners of her eyes and turned quickly, once, twice, trying to see. There was nothing but wet leaves and empty shadows. *Wyn, come back! No stone was left unturned.*

'Frances?' Owen touched her shoulder and she jumped round with a gasp. 'I'm here. There's nothing to be scared of,' he said, softly. 'There's nothing that can hurt you.' Frances wasn't at all sure he was right. Owen looked around. 'There were no hiding places out here in the yard? Nowhere he might be tucked, out of sight?' he said. Frances shook her head. She crossed to the back door. It stood open, six inches or so, and still had remnants of white paint on it. There was the same rusted handle that Wyn had touched – just waiting, all this time. Frances was breathing too fast; she felt faint, distant. The handle was cold in her hand, and she had to set her shoulder to the door to open it wider. Her first taste of the air within told her that something was missing. Damp stone, mould and spider webs . . . but Johannes's smell was gone. It had been everywhere, she realised – the smell of an unwashed body, and muddy clothes. Not a single trace of him remained; the emptiness ached.

'Johannes,' she whispered.

'What did you say?' said Owen. Frances couldn't answer him. 'Well, it seems empty, but let's check anyway.' Frances was aware of him speaking, but could hardly hear above the racket of blood in her ears. He took her hand, and she clung to him.

The downstairs rooms were dark, chill, quite dead. 'It's even smaller in here than it looks from the outside,' Owen muttered, no longer seeming to expect a reply. The stairs were so narrow that Frances had to let go of his hand to climb. She went slowly, putting her feet into the deepest part of the wear, just as she'd done at eight years of age; she felt a creeping sense of expectation – that there was something about the upstairs rooms she should remember, or perhaps didn't want to; an inward flinch she didn't understand. She stopped at the top, blocking Owen's progress; heart speeding, head full to bursting. *I promise never to tell a soul*. She gasped, hearing Wyn's voice, as clear as day.

'What's wrong?' said Owen. He was close behind her, in darkness; she shuddered at the anticipation of being touched. A man behind her, holding her head down; heat, fear; the smell of nettles. Forcing herself back into the present, Frances looked into the right-hand room, and a strangled noise came from her throat. *Johannes!* He was there – a thin figure, curled against the wall, just as she'd often seen him lie down to sleep. She opened her mouth but no words would come. She knew he was dead; he was a ghost, a haunting, just like they'd first imagined him to be. But then her mind caught up with her eyes; she saw more clearly, and hardly dared to believe what she was seeing. The figure was far smaller than Johannes had been.

'*Davy!*' she cried, running towards him, stumbling in haste.

Her hands and arms knew him at once – the weight and feel of him – as she gently turned him over and gathered him up. Joyful, incredulous sobs shook through her, over and over.

Owen fell to his knees beside them; he pushed back Davy's hair, and hurriedly checked his limbs, his body, for injuries. He was filthy, and limp, but he appeared whole. 'Oh, God,' Frances murmured, rocking him. 'Oh, God, I thought I'd lost you, Davy.'

'Bring him over to the window – I can't see a thing!' said Owen, and Frances obeyed, passing Davy to his uncle as she struggled to her feet. In the wan light from outside, his small face was deathly pale, his lips cracked and sore, hair matted with dirt. But he opened his eyes a little – a gleam of lucent grey. He stared at Frances, not seeming to see her. 'He's alive,' said Owen, his voice shaking.

'Hello, Davy,' said Frances. Tears slid down her face and she didn't bother to wipe them away. 'I bet you're hungry, aren't you? I bet you'd like a cup of warm milk.' With a small sigh through his nose, Davy shut his eyes again. Frances smiled across at Owen, and he put out a hand to cup her face.

'You were right,' he said. 'You were completely right, when anybody else would have given up. *I'd* given up! I thought he must be dead . . .' He shook his head. 'Let's get him home and warmed up.'

'Shouldn't we take him to hospital? He needs to have his medication.'

'Yes, you're right. Just to be on the safe side. Which one?'

'The EMS is closer. We can catch the bus again – or try to flag down a ride.'

Cradling Davy in his arms, Owen crossed to the top of the stairs, but when Frances turned, she saw something that stopped her in her tracks. It was the wall cupboard, with its sagging doors and worm-eaten shelves. 'Come on, Frances – what is it?' said Owen. She couldn't answer him. She was hearing other voices; she saw another dirty face, this one smiling – Johannes's quick, anxious smile. She saw a square of bright summer sun shining in through the window behind her. Only one of the cupboard shelves was still on its brackets, the others had fallen into the bottom of the recess. She knelt and began to lift them out. 'What are you *doing*, Frances? Let's go,' said Owen. The bottom of the cupboard was a foot or so above floor level; one of the planks had split, and part of it was missing. Frances pushed her fingers into the gap and lifted it out, light and powdery with rot. She stared into the dark space underneath, not knowing what she expected to find. A huge black spider on its back, desiccated legs curled in tight. Next to it a shard of metal, with shreds of a rag still wrapped around one end, to make a handle. *I promise never to tell a soul.* There was lettering on the underside of the plank in her hands. Thin scratches, wandering unevenly, as though written in the dark. Hardly breathing, Frances turned it to the light, until, suddenly, she could see it. A name, gouged by someone who'd hidden in that dark space, all alone. A name that sent a spike of agony through her heart. *Johannes Niklas Ebner.*

Frances dropped the plank and scrambled to her feet.

'Oh, no! Oh, no!' she cried, hands to her mouth as a wave of recollection broke over her head.

'What? What is it?' Owen sounded scared, his eyes were wide.

'I *told* them!' Frances said.

'Told who? What? I don't understand, Frances!'

'I . . . We swore we'd never tell, but I did! I . . . I *betrayed* him! And I sent Wyn here by herself. I . . . I knew she was coming here! The day she disappeared . . . I let her come alone. Don't you see? It's all my fault — it's my fault they're dead! *I* killed them both!'

1918

After their fourth or fifth visit to Johannes, when the food had made him stronger, Wyn and Frances discovered that he had a genius for making things. He'd made himself a small knife from a piece of scrap metal, with a rag wrapped round it for a handle, and whenever they went to see him, he'd made something to amuse them from bits of rubbish that had blown in under the door or down the chimney – stick men with moving arms and legs, their knee and elbow joints pinned with tiny slivers of wood; bits of dried grass plaited and twisted into hearts, clubs and spades; strips of old chip paper folded into planes, or swans, or cats. He presented each new thing with a flourish, holding it out on the palm of his hand.

'What do you say, little sisters?' he asked, smiling one of his wide, fleeting smiles. If it was a stick puppet or a paper cat, he'd make it walk towards them, and wave.

'We're not *babies*, you know,' said Wyn. But they were both charmed, and Frances wasn't too proud to take his treasures home. She had a wooden jewellery box, another present from Pam and Cecily, and since she didn't own any jewellery other than her christening bracelet, it was the perfect place to keep them. She hid the box under her bed, because she and Wyn knew, from the very start, that Johannes was their secret.

They'd never been specifically forbidden to make friends with strange men hiding in empty buildings, just like they'd never been forbidden to feed bears, or throw eggs at the King of Spain, but they had enough common sense to know that the grown-ups wouldn't like it, and that Johannes would be in trouble if he were found out – from their parents as well as the people who were after him. His fear of discovery was something they understood on instinct, without needing an explanation. They were city-bred children of the twentieth century, far removed from their primordial roots, but they knew a battle for survival when they saw one. They ran risks to get food for him – one distracting Pam and Cecily while the other pocketed a sandwich or a shortbread; watching the bins near the chip shop in Widcombe for when somebody dumped their excess batter or last few cold chips. Frances spent her pocket money on peanuts, broken biscuits, and end-of-day buns. And any sense of unfairness she might have felt about it was quashed by the vague shame she felt about the solidity of her own body, and the roundness of her cheeks.

'At home we have apple cakes, with cinnamon, and cakes made from fruits soaked with brandy . . . do you ever have those?' Johannes asked one day, when the measly cheese sandwich Frances had managed to bring, flattened in her pocket, had been eaten in two bites.

'Sometimes,' said Wyn, hedging. Wyn only got cake when she came for tea with Pam and Cecily, and since the rationing of butter, sugar and all sorts of things began earlier that year, there'd been no cake for either of them. They'd seen a poster in a shop window that neatly summed it up: *No Cakes, no Jam, no Sugar, no nuffin!*

'Warm, covered with cream,' said Johannes, shutting his eyes in blissful recollection.

Frances, always the more inclined to query and to worry, was gradually accumulating questions about him – where he came from, and where he might be going. Because he had to be going *somewhere*, she reasoned. Nobody could live in an empty leper hospital forever, only eating what was pilfered for him. It was cool and damp in there already, in summer; she dreaded to think what it would be like come winter. But she wasn't sure what, if any of it, she should ask; she didn't want to be rude.

'Johannes, where do you live, normally?' she said, eventually. He roused himself from his daydream of cake, picked a few crumbs from the front of his filthy shirt and ate them.

'Summer Rain,' he said, or something like that; he said it softly, with a frown. Frances and Wyn exchanged a look.

'Did you say "Summer Rain"?' said Wyn. 'I've never heard of it . . . where is it?' Johannes's face went through an extraordinary series of expressions, so that Frances wasn't sure if he was going to cry, or laugh, or shout angrily at them.

'It is far, far away!' he said, throwing his arms wide. 'At the rainbow's end, you know? Where everything is gold.' And then he laughed, but Frances still wasn't sure if he might not cry as well. Wyn watched him closely, and Frances saw her imagination working, taking hold of her.

'Johannes,' Wyn asked, very quietly, 'are you a prince in exile from a wicked imposter?' Johannes laughed again, and his eyes gleamed.

'Yes!' he said, delightedly, leaning towards her. 'Like in a story. Yes, little sister, I am the prince of Summer Rain!' He dropped his voice, conspiratorially. 'So you must never, never tell where I am, to anyone, yes? Or I will be captured!'

Johannes wore a matching shirt and trousers of dark blue canvas, frayed at the cuffs and hems and torn across the knees. He had cracked black leather boots with layers of mud worn into the grain, and when he took them off, the girls saw big, raw blisters on his heels and toes, as though the boots didn't fit him at all. Johannes wasn't handsome, exactly – he was too thin and pale – but his face was so mobile, and so ready to show feeling, that he *seemed* handsome. He had long fingers, and long legs with bulbous knobs for knees. He was filthy from head to toe and he smelt, but not too badly – it was an earthy, outdoors kind of smell. He moved in a quick, precise way that reminded Frances of how a bird moved.

'I have much need of . . . these things,' he said, catching the girls staring at his damaged feet. He tapped his ankle. 'Made of sheep. What are they called?'

'Socks?' Wyn suggested, giggling. 'You mean *wool*, not sheep.'

'*Ja*. Socks. You are bringing it? Is it possible?' he said. Frances gave Wyn a helpless look. There was no way either of them could go taking their fathers' socks without it being noticed. That only left thieving, and Frances had made her views on that quite plain. Wyn shrugged.

'If we got caught, we'd go to jail. Then we wouldn't be able to come any more,' she explained. Johannes nodded sadly.

'Yes, I see. It is better that you come.' He sat forwards, reaching to pull the boots back on.

'Leave them off, if you want them to heal,' said Wyn. She often went barefoot during the summer, since all her shoes were hand-me-downs and she had similar problems with blisters. The soles of her feet were tough and stained. Johannes shook his head.

'But if they come, I have to run. I must be ready,' he said.

'What will they look like?' said Frances. Johannes gave her a haunted look.

'Men without mercy,' he said, swallowing. 'Men in uniforms, with guns and ropes.'

'We have to help Johannes go back home, and take his rightful place on the throne of Summer Rain,' said Wyn, as they walked back down Holloway.

'He was only playing when he said that,' said Frances.

'No, he wasn't!' Wyn shot Frances a beseeching look, warning her not to insist that it was make-believe, and Frances was helpless to it. She nodded, though she wanted to talk about him in more practical terms – who he might really be, why he might really be hiding and what, if anything, they ought to do about it. 'Once he's crowned, he might marry one of us to say thank you, and make us into princesses. Don't you think? He might fall in love with one of us,' said Wyn, her eyes a little starry. Frances wasn't at all sure about that, so she just nodded again. Wyn swung her arms happily, imagining this new life which would be so very different to her current one. It was a clear, benign summer's day, warm but not hot. Frances knew her mother was making toad-in-the-hole for dinner, with baby peas from Pam's garden, and since she'd given her lunch to Wyn and Johannes, she couldn't wait. So she didn't blame Wyn for wanting to escape. Wyn wasn't going home to toad-in-the-hole; she was going home to Bill Hughes.

'Where do you think Summer Rain is, really?' said Frances.

'I don't know.' They both thought hard. The furthest Wyn had ever gone was Wales, and for Frances it was Minehead. 'Maybe it's in Scotland,' said Wyn. 'They talk funny up there – I heard a Scottish woman in the butcher's once. Maybe that's why Johannes talks like that.'

'Yes. Maybe.' Frances wasn't sure about that, either.

Frances did like having a secret – a proper secret, not like the little ones she and Wyn had always had, about Carys's corsets or the location of a den in Smallcombe cemetery. A proper secret that other people might actually want to know, and that *had* to be kept. She'd never felt so important before; it was exciting and nerve-racking at the same time, because having a secret came with the responsibility for keeping it. Before Keith came upstairs for bed each night, Frances fetched out her jewellery box and examined the things Johannes had made. She marvelled at the precise folds of a paper bird, or the way a stick man could seem alive, and have a personality of its own.

'That's pretty, where did you get it?' said her mother that night, appearing in the doorway so suddenly that Frances didn't have time to hide the knotted straw flower she was holding. Her heart lurched into her throat and she nearly burst into tears.

'Wyn gave it to me,' she managed to say, and the lie sounded so weak she was sure her mother would spot it at once.

'Oh, that was kind of her,' her mother said. And that was it. Frances could hardly believe her escape; it took a long time for her to calm down and get to sleep.

At the beginning of July, Magdalen Chapel held its annual bring-and-buy sale. The churchyard was small and crowded with graves, so the stalls spilled out onto the pavement and into the front garden of the house around the corner on Magdalen Road, where the woman who laid out the hymn books and laundered the altar cloths lived. The sun shone but the wind almost spoilt it – tablecloths flapped and billowed, threatening to scatter the displays of flapjacks, toys and home knits; the Judas tree tossed and shed seed pods over everything; people had to raise their voices to be heard, and the women frowned as their hats were tugged, and their skirts hobbled them. Frances normally loved bring-and-buys – the home-made honeycomb and lavender bags and felt hats. But this time the fun of it was ruined by being next door to the leper hospital – knowing that Johannes was inside, and that there were suddenly so many people who might see him, or somehow guess, or decide to go and explore. The thought of that made her stomach churn. She had no idea what would happen then.

When Wyn arrived with her whole family, Frances caught her eye, hoping to share the burden of nerves, but Wyn simply waved, excitedly, then took her mother's hand and dragged her over to the first table. Bill Hughes frowned at everything she pointed out.

'What the hell do you want with that?' he asked, when she held up a handkerchief with the initial *B* in one corner, stitched in red thread. 'Our Carys can do you a better one.' He snatched it out of Wyn's hand and threw it down in disgust. So it went with everything that afternoon – Wyn's excitement gradually waned, Bill's expression got uglier, and Mrs Hughes looked increasingly worried as she followed along with two-year-old Annie grizzling on her hip. Later on, Frances saw Mr Hughes bending over Wyn, speaking angrily right into her face. She saw the way his fingers bit into Wyn's bony arm, and later saw the bruises they'd left.

'Mr Hughes is horrible,' she said, sadly, to her own mother, who took a breath through her nostrils and thinned her lips.

'Yes, well. Why the man came at all is anyone's guess. To spoil everyone's enjoyment, I suppose.'

Derek Elliot would have gone to the allotment instead, if he hadn't been away at war. It was what most of the men did on a Saturday – that, or the pub. Mrs Elliot glanced down at her daughter. 'Why do you keep staring at the old hospital, Frances?' she said. Frances looked away hurriedly. She'd been wondering whether Johannes could sell the toys he made at the next bring-and-buy, and get some money to take the train home. It seemed the perfect solution – he could wear a disguise, or Frances and Wyn could sell them for him.

'I wasn't.' Frances looked the other way, and saw Carys and Clive seated on a bench by the wall. He was holding her hands in the air between them, like they were praying, and looking deep into her eyes. The sun was in their hair and Carys wore a soft smile, and they looked like a Valentine card. Frances tried to picture Wyn and Johannes looking at each other like that, when Wyn was older and Johannes was a prince again, but it made her feel strange. Then Owen and Wyn popped up from behind the bench, grinning, and threw a handful of daisies over the couple – a damp and shrivelled confetti. Clive laughed but Carys leapt up in outrage and went after her sister. Wyn skipped away, singing loudly.

'Carys, Carys, give me your answer do!' She glanced back over her shoulder, taunting, and yelped when Carys made a grab for her.

At the end of the afternoon, when the tea urn was empty and the unsold items were being packed away into baskets, Frances asked to stay and talk to Wyn. Her mother only agreed when she'd reassured herself that Bill Hughes had gone home.

'Make sure you're back for supper,' she said, and Frances nodded. Owen, Wyn and Carys had gathered around Clive, and Frances itched with curiosity. She went over to join them, admiring the way Clive's oiled hair shone bronze in the sun, and how handsome he was. It was no wonder Carys was different around him – gentler, happier. Frances would be happy too, if a man like Clive wanted to marry her. He had a canvas bag, and was rummaging in it with one hand.

'Now then,' he said. 'For Owen – for gallantry in the face of that thrashing you had on Tuesday – Will's Allied Army Leaders number fourteen, General Botha, and number twenty-eight, General Wingate.' He handed the cigarette cards to Owen, who took them, grinning. 'Which, if I'm not much mistaken, gives you the complete set of those.'

'Thanks, Clive!'

'And for Wyn, for having the prettiest smile.' Clive handed over the handkerchief Wyn had admired, with her initial in the corner, and Wyn gasped. Carys, Frances noticed, was already wearing a new pair of crocheted gloves; she gave her fiancé a guarded smile.

'You'll spoil them, Clive,' she said. 'And surely you can't afford to be buying all these presents?'

'Nonsense,' said Clive, straightening up. 'Don't you worry about it.'

He seemed to notice Frances for the first time, admiring Wyn's new handkerchief. A look of consternation filled his face. 'Frances! I didn't see you there. I . . . I'm rather afraid I haven't got anything for you this time.' Frances blushed crimson and felt too shy to answer; she didn't know what to say.

'Well, you hardly need to be buying things for the neighbours' kids as well,' said Carys. 'Besides, this one hardly goes short.'

'Well, now,' said Clive. He put his hands in his pockets and seemed a bit stuck for a moment.

'It's all right,' Frances said, wanting to rescue him. She smiled, in spite of her blazing cheeks, to show she wasn't in the least downhearted over it. Clive chucked her chin with his knuckles.

'Attagirl,' he said, which cheered Frances up so much she really didn't mind about not getting a present, or about the leper hospital being so close by. Wyn shook her handkerchief out of its folds and held it in pinched fingers, wafting it in front of her face as though she had the vapours, and Frances couldn't help but laugh.

Owen's most prized possession was a football – a proper leather one with a rubber inner. He'd found it in the high nettles behind the playing fields one lucky day, when he'd been looking for bottles to return to Bowler's factory for a few pennies.

'It might have been kicked there by a Bath City player, during practice,' said Owen. 'And given up for lost. I can train myself up properly, now.' It had got punctured several times, and been patched; it was dark brown, and in wet weather it soon got so heavy that it was like kicking a boulder. But it was a proper ball, and far better than any of his school friends had. When he led the pack out for a kick-about after school he was cock of the walk; at supper time he sauntered down Holloway with sweaty hair and an air of triumph – that was Owen at his happiest. Frances liked to watch him go by from inside the leper hospital, carefully keeping her head down. She liked to imagine his surprise if she were to pop up and wave, since she was somewhere he and his friends had never dared to go. He would think her brave then; he would be impressed.

She watched him go by one afternoon, while Wyn was trying to persuade Johannes to go outside.

'Just into the yard,' she said. Johannes shook his head incredulously, as though she'd suggested he parade down the street, singing.

'No, little sisters. I cannot be seen.' He shrank back from the door as though even the oblong of light shining through it were a danger to him.

'But nobody *will* see you,' said Wyn. 'It's just the backyard. Nobody can see into it except from the graveyard, and there's nobody there. I've checked.' To prove her point she went out into the yard and spun around. 'It's so nice and warm out here,' she said, coaxingly. When he didn't move she lost interest, sighed, and began to draw out a hopscotch court with a chunk of chalk she'd found. Frances sat down inside next to Johannes, and they watched through the door as Wyn found a suitable pebble and began to play, pointedly ignoring her audience. The sun caught her yellow hair as she turned at each end and stooped suddenly for her marker; she was wearing a frayed cotton pinafore and a white blouse that had belonged to Carys, many years before. Her bare feet made a soft scuffing sound with every hop, and she winced now and then when she stood on a stone. She looked beautiful.

Suddenly, a loud banging started up at the front of the building. Wyn looked up briefly, then dismissed the sound and carried on playing. The banging was almost rhythmical, but not quite. Johannes's eyes went so wide that the whites showed all the way round, and his face turned strange and empty.

'What is this?' he said, sharply. He surged to his feet, knocking Frances backwards. 'What is this?'

'I don't know,' said Frances, struggling up from the floor.

'You have brought them here? Hm?' Johannes whispered, voice shaking. His face filled with blood, flaring crimson. He grabbed Frances by the arms and shook her hard. 'You are telling them where to come?'

'No! I didn't!' Frances cried, stricken. The transformation was so sudden, and so complete, it was shocking; she thought of Carys's bloody nose, and Wyn knocked across the room. She'd never imagined that Johannes could be like Bill Hughes. Her heart hammered; his fingers hurt, and she'd bitten the end of her tongue. 'I promise!'

'Let go of her!' said Wyn, running in and pulling at Johannes's hands. 'We didn't tell anyone!'

'Then what is it? What is it?' he cried, letting go of Frances. He raised one arm for a moment, and Frances shut her eyes, certain he was going to hit her. But then he backed away, staring at them like they were snakes.

'I don't know!' Wyn stared back at him, eyes snapping with anger.

'I can't go back! I can't!' he began to say, over and over.

Frances ran upstairs and peered out over Holloway, and there was Owen, kicking his ball against the wall of the old hospital. Relief surged through her. Owen was frowning in concentration, deeply involved in his game. After one particularly straight, hard kick he raised his fists in imaginary triumph. When she'd caught her breath, Frances went back downstairs, cautiously, but Johannes had shrunk into a corner of the lean-to and was cowering, hands over his head. Frances had heard of somebody shaking like a leaf but she'd never seen it happen before, and she couldn't help but feel sorry for him. She could taste blood on her tongue, which was stinging, but she forgave him.

'It's all right,' she said, but the sound of her voice only made him flinch, and mutter words she didn't know. She backed away nervously, not sure what to do. 'Wyn!' she called. Wyn had gone back outside but she came to the door and peered at him, then at Frances, her expression wary and calculating.

'Let's go, Frances,' she whispered. Even that was enough to make Johannes whimper. Owen's ball banged and thumped against the wall; Frances prayed silently for it to stop.

'It's only Owen and his ball,' said Frances. 'Shall I just go and tell him to stop? I'm sure he—'

'No, Frances!' Wyn was firm. 'We can't tell *anyone* we come here, not even Owen. He'd only tell his friends, and then *everyone* will know.' She glanced warily at Johannes again. 'Let's just go.'

'But . . . shouldn't we help him?' said Frances.

'We can't help him, not when he's like that. It's better we go.' In Wyn's family, Frances supposed, men who were upset did unpredictable things. And they often did them with their fists. She thought of the way Johannes had shaken her, and the fury in his face. She ran her bitten tongue along her teeth, feeling the sore, raised lump. Still, it didn't seem right to leave him like that.

'I want to try,' she said.

'Suit yourself.' Wyn shrugged and went back to her hop-scotch. But she did it less enthusiastically, and with a frown.

Swallowing hard, Frances went and stood closer to Johannes. She really didn't know what she ought to do, and could only think of the way her mother soothed her when she had nightmares.

'There, there, Johannes,' she said. 'It's all right.' He didn't seem to hear her. She felt awkward, uneasy, but still sorry for him. It was horrible to feel afraid. Summoning all her courage, she crouched down beside him and patted his knee softly. He flinched, trying to make himself even smaller. 'It's really all right. It's only Owen – that's Wyn's big brother – kicking his football against the wall. He's not doing it on purpose; he doesn't know we're in here. I promise he doesn't. He just really likes kicking his football around – he does it even when he's by himself, like now. Johannes?' She patted his arm, and noticed that the shivering had lessened a little. He seemed to be listening to her at last. 'Owen's older than us, but younger than you,' she went on, for something to say. 'He's twelve. How old are you?' She'd been wondering, and hadn't been able to guess.

'*Neunzehn*,' Johannes whispered.

'What?' said Frances. Slowly, Johannes lowered his hands and peered at her from behind the cage of his arms.

'The sound,' he said, tearfully. 'The sound reminds me of other places. Other things. I thought they were coming in. I thought they had me.'

'Nobody's coming in, I promise. What does "noyn-zen" mean?'

'Nineteen. I have nineteen years.'

Frances gathered her skirt behind her knees and sat down. Outside in the yard, Wyn had stopped hopscotching and was drawing on the ground with agitated swipes of the chalk.

'What's it like where you live?' Frances said to Johannes. 'Summer Rain, I mean. Is it very far away? Wyn thought it might be in Scotland.'

'It is very far.' Johannes rubbed at his eyes. He thought for a moment, taking a shuddering breath. 'Not in Scotland. I don't know . . . I don't know where we are, so I don't know how far away. But it is a long way.'

'Is it over the sea?'

'Yes, yes. Over the sea,' said Johannes. His body loosened the more he talked, the shudders waned. 'It is a small town, not many people; very far in the east of my country. There are big hills to the south, steep, and covered in dark forests where wolves used to run.' He went on to tell her about the river, the quarries in the hills and the towering pinnacle of the church spire; the ancient fountain with its spouting faces, and the castle, built by a king two hundred years before.

'Is that where you were born?' said Frances

'*Ja*, my family lives there for many, many years. My parents, and my little sister Clara. She is not so much older than you two; her hair is like Wyn's. My father makes toys; he sells them at the markets at Christmas-time, and he sends them to a toy store in the city. His workshop is behind our house, smelling always of wood and paint and glue.' Johannes smiled at the thought of it.

'Is that why you're so good at making things? Because your father taught you?'

'Yes, yes, he teaches me. One day, when I go back, I will work with him again, and we will create many new things . . .' Johannes blinked, and swallowed. 'If he is coming back. If I am.'

'How will you get back, Johannes?' said Frances.

Outside, Wyn had stopped drawing and was listening, her gaze fixed on the ground. They heard boys' voices, and Owen's laugh, and then the banging of his ball stopped and the voices moved away down the hill. The sudden quiet was a relief, even to Frances. A blackbird carolled from the ivy on the graveyard wall, flies buzzed in the sunshine, and in the distance a train puffed and rattled into Green Park Station.

'I don't know,' said Johannes. 'One day . . . one day. There will be a way.'

'We want to help you,' said Wyn, finally fed up at being left out.

'You do help,' he said. 'Little sisters, I am thankful to you, for the food you bring. And I . . . I am sorry for before. I am sorry for saying you had betrayed me.'

'But how did you *get* here?' said Frances, trying to draw herself a mental map of where he belonged. 'If Summer Rain is over the sea . . . how did you get here?'

'I remember only walking,' said Johannes. 'There was a lot of fighting, big battles; and to arrive here, I walked. I was going to walk all the way to the sea, and get on a boat, but I never found it.' He shook his head, thought for a moment and then laughed. 'So I have been like a saint, hm? Or a magician!'

'That's daft,' said Wyn. 'It doesn't make sense. And we're miles from the sea!' Johannes shrugged, his gaze distant.

'That is what I did,' he said. Wyn looked puzzled and impatient.

'Come on, Frances. We should get home or we'll miss tea,' she said, standing up, brushing grit from her hands and knees. Frances rose obediently, reluctant to leave Johannes there.

'You could come to tea,' she said to him, knowing it was hopeless. 'We could tell them you're . . .' But she had no idea what lie they could possibly tell.

They didn't go home right away. Wyn led the way up Beechen Cliff, and they sat in Alexandra Park, picking the feathery grass seed heads.

'Here's a tree in summer,' said Wyn holding up a freshly picked stem. She stripped the seeds off with her thumb and forefinger and held up the bare stem. 'Here's a tree in winter. Here's a bunch of flowers.' She held out the pinch of seeds for inspection. 'Here's the April showers!' She threw the seeds over Frances's head, and they laughed.

'Do you think he's all right?' said Frances, and their laughter stilled at once. She rubbed at her arms, where faint bruises the size and shape of Johannes's fingers were appearing.

'Why?' said Wyn, squinting over the city's haze to the distant hills beyond.

'Do you think he's . . . I mean, he seems to get upset easily. Over nothing at all.'

'I don't know.' Wyn shrugged. 'Sometimes people get upset, that's all. And he *is* being hunted, and having to live like a poor person when he's used to living in a castle – you heard him say so just now.' Frances thought back, trying to remember hearing that, and to phrase what it was she wanted to say. Something about what happened when Wyn's father got that upset. Something about how thin Johannes still was, and that he wouldn't come out of the hospital, and didn't know where he was. Something about how it was starting to feel less fun to have him as their secret.

'Do you think . . . Do you think we should ask for help? For Johannes, I mean?'

'No.' Wyn eyed her, and Frances looked down, fiddling with the grass again. 'Don't you like him?' said Wyn. 'Don't you like going there to see him?'

'Of course I do.'

'Well, then. We can't say *anything*, Frances. We *promised*, and he's our friend.' Wyn wore her beseeching look until Frances nodded. It was the word 'friend' that did it. Of course they were Johannes's friends, so of course they had to keep their promise to him. 'Promise you'll never tell a soul,' said Wyn. 'I will too. We'll say it together. Ready?'

'I promise never to tell a soul,' said Frances, with Wyn's voice overlaying her own.

8

Saturday

The staff at the EMS hospital lifted Davy out of Owen's arms and carried him away with such unspeaking efficiency that it made Frances nervous.

'I'm going to get a message sent down to Carys and Mum,' Owen said, leaving her to wait in the shadowy corridor. She stood, fidgeting; she walked to and fro. With Davy out of sight she worried that she'd got it wrong – that they'd found some other child and she'd only dreamt it was him. But the doctor came out to speak to her only a few minutes later, and he smiled.

'It's nice to be able to give good news for a change,' he said. 'David's going to be perfectly fine. He's undernourished, and he's very dehydrated, but we were able to wake him and there's no sign of any injury, and we've given him his pheno-barbital. We'll keep him in tonight to be on the safe side, but you should be able to take him home tomorrow. He'll need to be kept warm, and rested. And your son needs to put on some weight, Mrs Parry.'

'Yes, I know. Only, he's not my son... Owen's gone to send them a message.'

'Well,' said the doctor, raising his eyebrows. 'Then I shall tell his mother, too. Try not to look so frightened, he'll be right as rain in no time.'

'Thank you, Doctor. Can I sit with him for a while? Until they get here?'

Davy slept, perfectly still but for the subtle rise and fall of his ribs. Frances held his small hand in hers, feeling its softness and warmth. His fingernails were filthy; the skin scabbed here and there. She wondered whether, having dropped down into the leper hospital yard, he simply hadn't been able to climb back out. It was far harder to do from the lower side, and she hated to think how trapped he must have felt. Or perhaps he'd had a seizure, an absence, and hadn't remembered afterwards where he was, or how to get out. He wouldn't have shouted for help because he hadn't been raised to expect help to come. She said silent thanks for the wet weather since the bombings – the drips and puddles he'd have been able to drink from. Then she simply sat, watching, hardly daring to look away in case she *was* imagining him. Owen returned with Carys and Nora and they hurried in, stifling their voices as they leaned over Davy's bed. Nora smiled and smiled, dabbing her eyes with her fingertips. She pulled Frances into a short, fierce hug.

'Well, I can hardly credit it, Frances,' she said, and Frances nodded. But it was Carys she wanted a word from. A single word, or a gesture. A look. Something to say she was forgiven, even if she wasn't likely to be thanked. But Carys simply stood beside her son, crying messily and reeking of spirits. Frances saw the doctor stiffen when he smelt it. Owen came to stand beside Frances, he wrapped an arm around her shoulders and squeezed. Frances wanted to turn towards him, bury her face in him, sleep there.

Before long the doctor told them to go home and let Davy rest. They took the bus back down the hill, and, in bed at Woodlands, Frances slept deeply, dreamlessly. She woke to a surge of relief so powerful that it washed out everything else, just for a while. But the things she'd remembered at the leper hospital soon crept back in – the source of the nameless shame she'd felt for so many years. A part of it, in any case – she knew there was something more, something worse. Sunshine and fear; the smell of nettles; a waking nightmare. Pam had gone to work, and as she sat alone in the empty house, Frances tormented herself by imagining the week Davy had spent alone, afraid, starving; hiding in the leper hospital in such a terrible state, just as Johannes had done. Davy was so little, so frail, to have suffered such an ordeal. She promised, silently, to make it up to him; to never let him feel frightened again. When she saw him, she would tell him that she'd searched and searched for him, and hadn't given up. He would be discharged from the hospital soon, and the last thing Nora Hughes had said, when they parted, was that she and Carys would collect him. She'd said it gently, but firmly nonetheless, and Carys had still refused to even look at Frances.

She took the bus to the RUH, where the man who wasn't Percy had not moved. She didn't know who he was, she only knew the feeling he gave her. The revulsion. She sat stiffly on the bedside chair and fought to remember him, and where he fitted into it all; why he'd appeared in dreams of half-forgotten fear. Frances leaned towards him, turning her head to listen. His breathing was even more laboured; the muscles of his stomach and ribcage worked hard beneath the sheet. When he exhaled there was a faint bubbling at the very bottom of the breath – a little wet catch of sound. Frances sat back and stared hard at his face. His eyes seemed more sunken, his jaw slacker, and the hair at his temples looked damp. There was a white line of dried saliva along his bottom lip, and the lip hung down a little, giving a glimpse of teeth that needed cleaning. The sight disgusted Frances. She glanced across at Victor, the man who'd also been at the Regina Hotel, but he was fast asleep. The spiv and the gentleman gambler – those were the only single men he'd remembered seeing in the hotel bar. Percy

Clifton had been one of those, Frances guessed. And this man, lying in front of her, had been the other.

She sat watching him for a long time. The hospital ward was calmer now, as the panic of the immediate aftermath of the bombing eased. The flood of new admissions had slowed to a more normal trickle – people who'd tripped and twisted an ankle in the blackout; housewives who'd cut themselves chopping onions; men who'd jabbed their feet with gardening forks, digging for victory; children who'd fallen out of trees. Frances cleared her throat.

'Can you hear me?' she said, quietly, watching for any sign that he could. 'I know you're not Percy Clifton. Do you even know who Percy Clifton is? Or was?' Her voice had risen against her will. She glanced around, feeling horribly conspicuous; feeling that same conflict she'd felt before, of wanting him to wake up and see her, and praying that he would not. 'I'm not going to go away,' she whispered. 'I am going to keep coming back until you wake up. And then you're going to talk to me. You're going to tell me the truth.' The man lay prone, vulnerable, before her. She felt no power, but no pity either. She noticed that the eye behind his good lid had begun to flick restlessly from side to side. As though she were giving him nightmares.

Number thirty-four Beechen Cliff Place now ended with the painted party wall it had once shared with number thirty-three. Frances stared at the gap. Carys's house was a pile of rubble, the broken blocks of the front and back walls poking out like teeth. All that remained of the room where she'd watched Wyn trying on her sister's make-up was the stained distemper of the inside wall, now exposed to the world. It was a desolate sight; it seemed a heartless, heedless thing to do to somebody's home. Frances knocked at number thirty-four, and waited as footsteps thudded down the stairs inside.

'I said, *I'll* get it,' said Carys, close behind the door. She opened the door a few inches and glared out, and Frances didn't like her expression. She looked lofty, almost triumphant. 'Yes?' she said. 'What brings you here?'

'Well, I—' said Frances, taken aback. 'I've come to see Davy. To see how he's getting on.'

'He's fine, thank you.' Carys began to close the door.

'Wait – can I come in and see him, please?'

'No,' said Carys. She stared at Frances, her face a flat mask of hostility. Frances stared back, as she began to understand.

'But I . . . I found him, in the end! And he's going to be fine!' she said, her voice rising.

'You can hardly expect credit for finding him when it was *you* that lost him in the first place,' said Carys. 'He was lost nearly a week! I've no call for a child minder who lets that happen, have I? So you've no business here any more.'

'Carys—' Nora's voice came from inside, pained and tremulous. Carys ignored it.

'Please – please let me come and see him. Even if you don't want me to watch him any more,' said Frances. The growing realisation that Carys was serious gave her a panicky feeling. She didn't trust Carys to hug Davy, or wash him; to make sure he had something to eat every day, and his dose of pheno-barbital. She didn't trust her to love him enough.

'No, I don't think so. Now why don't you clear off and leave us alone?'

Carys tried to close the door again, and in desperation Frances stuck her foot in it.

'Please don't do this!' she said. 'You can't!'

'I'm his *mother*! And who are you? You're no one! So, I

can do it, and I *am* doing it! We don't need your help. Davy doesn't need you!'

'Yes, he does! You're his mother, you say? You didn't even look for him when he was missing! You didn't even know where he liked to go! You did nothing but drink yourself stupid, like you always do! So he *does* need me!'

'Please, stop,' Nora shouted from within. 'The pair of you!'

'Oh, you think you're so bloody special, don't you? You think I'm a bad mother – you always have! Think we're worthless, don't you – talking to the police about us, telling tales ... You don't know the *half* of what I've sacrificed for my kids! You haven't a clue! So get your bloody foot out of the door or I'll break it!'

'How did Wyn's brooch end up in your house, Carys? Answer me that! How did it get there, when she wore it *every day*?' Frances hadn't known the question was coming.

'What? What are you on about?' Carys's eyes gleamed in her ruddy face.

'You know *exactly* what I'm on about! And every time I mention her you find some reason to shout or send me away – you find some way to avoid talking about her!'

'Did it ever occur to you that I send you away because I don't *like* you? Because I don't like you hanging around here, judging me all the time? Because you're causing my mum so much grief with your constant bloody stirring, you might just give her a heart attack? Well, if you want to talk about Wyn, why don't we talk about how you didn't have the sense to tell anyone there was a bloody *German* hiding up there! How you held your tongue – even after she'd disappeared! Who knows how long he kept her alive before he killed her – if we'd known where to look, we might have found her in time!'

'That's ... that's ...' Frances couldn't get her breath, and her thoughts scattered. The accusation shocked her because she felt the truth of it in her bones. She felt the shame of it. 'You're . . . you're doing it again,' she managed to say. 'Dodging the question—'

'Oh, just bugger *off*, Frances!' Carys shouted. She leant on the door until the bones in Frances's foot began to creak, and Frances was forced to pull it clear. Then the door of number thirty-four slammed shut, and she was left to stare helplessly at the peeling paint.

Frances walked back to Woodlands half-blinded by guilt and anger. She heard voices in the garden and paused, keeping out of sight inside as she looked through. Sergeant Cummings was outside with Pam; she was in plain clothes, with her cloud of blonde hair fighting to escape from its pins. She wore no make-up, even outside work, but she didn't really need to. Her skin was flawless, pink in the cheeks, and her eyes were clear and bright. Pam was showing her around the garden, shielding her eyes against the sunshine while Dog scouted around their feet. The paths and steps between the garden's terraces were furred with moss, and there was new growth everywhere. Not just the crocuses and tree blossoms of early spring, but grass between the paving stones, and leaves on the flowering currant, and cowslips the colour of custard along the foot of the hedge.

'Well, you are lucky, Mrs Elliot,' said Sergeant Cummings. 'It wasn't till the war broke out that I managed to get a bit of ground to garden. But I'm not supposed to grow anything *nice*, of course. Nothing that flowers, just cabbages.'

'It's a lot of work for one person, mind you,' said Pam, folding her arms. 'I ought to have turned more of it over to veg, or got a pig, but, you know, every time I see one of those irritating posters of Potato Pete, I just dig my heels in. Why the government feels we need to be spoken to like children, I'll never know.'

'What about Doctor Carrot?' Cummings smiled.

'*Honestly*,' said Pam. They stopped near the apple tree and Pam pulled a twig towards her. The blossoms had dropped, and the stubby new leaves were vibrantly green. 'It had a good blossom, but I wonder if the apples will taste any different this year... Silly, I know.'

'It feels as though everything must be tainted by it, doesn't it?' said Cummings. 'But I'm sure they'll be delicious.'

Frances made her way down to them.

'Hello,' she said, noticing their faces change when they saw her – Cummings' becoming more serious; Pam's opening up, but turning a little sad.

'Ah, good, you're home, Frances,' said Pam. 'Needless to say, Sergeant Cummings came to see you, not me. I'm afraid I've beaten you to it, and told her about Davy. I couldn't help it.'

'It's such wonderful news,' said Cummings. 'So many stories from the bombings aren't having such happy endings.'

'Yes. It *is* wonderful,' said Frances, but she was thinking about Carys slamming the door in her face, refusing to let her see Davy, and it was hard to sound upbeat.

'Well,' said Pam, uncertainly, 'I'll leave you to it. Come on in as soon as you'd like tea. Or lunch.' She left them, and Frances and Sergeant Cummings sat on the bench, squinting out over the sunlit garden to the city beyond. Cummings cleared her throat.

'I worked very late last night. They like to leave me to file all the paperwork at the end of the day, since I'm a woman, so I fetched up the report on Wyn's disappearance.'

'Can I see it?'

'No. But I've read it, and I took note of the key points. I'm still not... I'm still not sure I should be telling you about it. But it's a very old case, after all, and... I'm relying on your discretion,' said Cummings. Frances glanced across at the sergeant.

'I'm very good at keeping quiet,' she said.

'There are some things I can tell you, but, Mrs Parry, if you know *anything* . . . if you have some theory, as I suspect you do, as to who really killed the child, then I need your word you'll come to me with it, not go off and . . . try to do anything yourself.'

'Please call me Frances. Mrs Parry doesn't . . . sound like me. It never did, really.'

'All right, then.'

Frances thought for a while.

'I don't have a theory, but I . . . I've been remembering some things, from back then. And I think there's more to remember. I think perhaps I *know*.'

'Yes.' Cummings nodded. 'I thought that might be the case.'

'Do you think you could make Inspector Reese do anything about it, if I did remember?'

'Well, that would depend on what you told me, and what other evidence there was. Whether there was enough to persuade him of the possibility of a good outcome, should we reopen the investigation. I'm sure you can understand that we'd have to have more to go on than memories from when you were eight years old.'

'Yes, I understand,' said Frances. 'Nora Hughes let me look through all the newspaper clippings she'd saved.'

'Was there anything useful in them?' said Cummings. Frances shook her head.

'Not really. A picture of Johannes. I . . . I hadn't seen his face in twenty-four years. He looked just as I remember him. So young, and so scared.' She paused. 'There were . . . hints . . . about depravity. I couldn't tell if that was just the papers turning a phrase, or . . . Did they mean the general depravity of a murder, rather than the *specific* depravity of . . .' She couldn't bring herself to say it. To ask if Wyn had been raped. 'Will you tell me what was in the report?' she said. Cummings gave her another long look, then took a breath.

'The bloodstains in the yard adjacent to the leper hospital were minimal. Drops and smears.'

'So, she didn't die from . . . from being stabbed? Or battered?'

'Or if she did, it didn't happen there. The clothing that was found . . . The clothing amounted to one shoe, her drawers, stockings and a torn section of her skirt.' Cummings spoke quickly, as if to make it less awful, the implications less horrific. Frances shut her eyes, feeling sick.

'Everything from the lower half of her body.'

'Yes. Again, this might not . . . It might not mean what it appears to mean at first glance.'

'But it might.'

'It might. It was certainly indicated in the report that the investigating officers suspected a . . . sexual motive for the crime. But without Wyn's body there was no way of knowing how she was killed, or if she was . . . assaulted first. We'll *never* know for sure.'

'But they suspected Johannes of . . . raping her?'

'Johannes was . . . he was questioned at length. But he never confessed to the killing. He said he'd heard footsteps outside, Wyn's and others, and that he heard some other noises.' She paused and checked her notes. 'He heard what sounded like heavy breathing. But he didn't dare look out, and then it all went quiet again.'

'Oh, God.' Frances swallowed. 'He heard it happen.'

'Perhaps. Or perhaps he was lying, and he attacked her.'

'On his own doorstep, when what he feared most of all was discovery? Then took her and buried her in her own backyard, unseen by anyone, when he had no idea where she lived and was too afraid to go out?' said Frances.

'How can you be so sure that he didn't know where she lived, Mrs— Frances? I know you've told me your reasons for thinking that, but you were eight years old. Forgive me, but you were too young to have understood everything that was going on around you. You can't know what was . . . in his head. He wasn't in his right mind.'

'He was frightened – I *saw* how frightened he was. He would never have been able to go out, to follow her home or whatever. But he wasn't deranged.'

'I read what you yourself told the police about him. That he hurt you on at least one occasion, when he thought he'd been discovered. That he assaulted Wyn, too.'

'No, no – it wasn't *assault!* It wasn't.' Frances's frustration built. 'They twisted what I said! I didn't know they'd do that – I didn't know what they were getting at! They made it sound bad, but . . . He just . . . he sometimes got so frightened, he panicked. He didn't know what he was doing.'

'Deranged, some might say?' said Cummings, softly. 'And perhaps Wyn told him where she lived herself. Perhaps she described it to him.'

'No, she never did. He never asked.'

'Perhaps on one of the occasions when Wyn went to see him by herself?'

'But she didn't go there by herself.' Frances hesitated. *Wyn, come back!* She took a deep breath as the memory of a huge unhappiness welled up inside her. 'There was one time, maybe. But she wouldn't have told him. He wouldn't have asked.'

'According to Ebner's statement, Wyn often went to see him by herself, especially in the last few weeks of her life.'

Frances stared at Cummings, shocked into silence. Even now, twenty-four years later, the pain of betrayal was sharp.

She and Wyn weren't supposed to have had secrets from one another, and Johannes was *their* secret. But Wyn had lied to her, and gone without her. *I promise never to tell a soul.* Frances shook her head. Clearing her throat, Cummings continued. 'Ebner claimed that Wyn seemed different on those visits. She seemed anxious, and was very quiet. He said she appeared to be hiding.'

'Oh, Wyn,' Frances breathed.

'Unfortunately for Ebner, his admitting that Wyn used to visit him by herself only served to condemn him all the more.'

'But why would she? *Why?* And why wouldn't she tell me?'

'I couldn't possibly say. And I'm afraid that, at this point, nobody can. She was eight years old. Children don't always understand—'

'I think they *do*,' Frances said adamantly. 'I think they *do* understand. I just don't think they necessarily know what to do about it.' She thought hard, summoning her friend to mind – how she was, who she was. 'Perhaps . . . perhaps whoever killed her – *if* she died at the leper hospital . . . perhaps they followed her there. Or perhaps they knew she went there . . . so even if she died somewhere else, they knew to put some of her things there to make it look as though Johannes did it.'

'It's possible. But there's simply no evidence of that.'

'But it's possible.'

'There was the blanket Ebner had been sleeping on as well. It had hairs on it, confirmed by an expert to be Wyn's.'

'Of course it had her hair on it! It came off her bed – she gave it to him!'

'Frances,' said Cummings, gently. 'Shall I tell you what I gather from what I read in the report? I gather that Ebner was a disturbed young man, in a desperate situation, who developed unnatural feelings towards a little girl who used to visit him, often by herself. I gather that he had ample means and opportunity to kill her, deliberately or otherwise, and that you can't possibly know whether or not Wyn had told him where she lived. And you can't possibly have been expected, at that age, to fully understand everything that was going on, or that Ebner was a threat.' She put her hand lightly on Frances's arm. 'I know you don't want to think it was him. I know he was your friend. But the simplest solution is often the right one.'

'But not always.'

They sat in silence for several moments. Frances could tell that Cummings had all but made up her mind, and she didn't know how to get her back.

'Why don't you tell me what it is you've remembered about it?' said Cummings. Frances nodded, and took a deep breath.

'I lied to the police,' she said. Cummings frowned. 'I told them I hadn't seen Wyn the day she disappeared, but I did see her. She ... she came to my parents' house to call for me, and asked me to go off with her. But I was ... It was late, and I was ... upset with her. I can't ... I can't remember why exactly. Things were ... Something had gone wrong. I was upset, so I ... I sent her off by herself.' Frances glanced up at Cummings, to make sure she understood the significance of this.

'Sent her off where? Where was she going?'

'To the leper hospital.'

'You mean ...' Sergeant Cummings shook her head minutely.

'She wanted me to go with her, but I let her go on her own. And then she was killed.' There was a lump like a stone in Frances's throat, impossible to swallow. 'But the thing is, Sergeant, when I saw her, when I sent her away, she was wearing her brooch.'

'The one you found at her sister's house the other day?'

'Yes. She was wearing it. I'm certain of it. I remember

looking at it, and feeling sad because . . . because she was so happy when I gave it to her – she said I was the best friend she'd ever had. But at that time, we'd all but fallen out. And I wanted to call her back!' Frances fought to keep her voice steady. 'I wanted to call her back, and say I'd go with her. Or tell her not to go – I don't know. But I didn't. I let her go.'

'Frances, you clearly feel that you're somehow to blame for what happened to Wyn, but you aren't. You were a little girl.'

'But I was *there*. I was part of it. There were so many times I could have said something that might have stopped it. But I didn't.'

'What do you mean? What times? What could you have said?'

'I . . . I don't know exactly.' Frances thought hard, but the words had been spoken on impulse, and stemmed from something she couldn't yet grasp. 'I could have told a grown-up about Johannes. We could have got him some help. Do you know, recaptured prisoners weren't punished, overly much? They were just sent back to their camps. He'd have been safe. And . . . it was the middle of 1918. The war was about to end. He'd have made it home. If I'd spoken up, he'd have made it home. And perhaps Wyn would still be alive, too. But the only time I spoke about him was after she was dead, and I . . . I told them where to find him. He had a hiding place in the leper hospital, and I told them *exactly* where to find him. I *betrayed* him! I handed him to them. Don't you see – I could have prevented it all!'

Frances started to cry; she couldn't stop herself.

'Oh, dear – please don't cry!' said Cummings, patting Frances's arm. 'Mrs Elliot!' she called out to Pam.

'No – I'm fine,' said Frances. 'I am. It's just . . .' She shook her head, forcing herself to calm down. *No stone was left unturned. Hush, little sisters!*

'I think that's probably enough for today,' said Pam, appearing by her side and taking her hand.

'Yes, you're—'

'No – please. I'm fine. Please, let's finish talking.'

'Well...' said Cummings, uncertainly.

'Thank you, Pam, but really, I'm all right.' Frances wiped her face, struggling to order her thoughts. 'Don't you see how important it is that I found Wyn's brooch at Carys's house? Carys never wants to talk about Wyn. She always fobs me off when I ask anything, or gets angry. But Wyn was wearing her daffodil brooch the day she disappeared—'

'But that still doesn't mean she was wearing it when she died, Frances,' said Cummings.

'What?'

'You say she was going to the leper hospital by herself, and that perhaps somebody followed her there, and killed her. But you don't know for sure that she actually went straight there, right after you saw her. Do you? She could have changed her mind and gone home, or gone to play somewhere else.'

'But—'

'I understand you being angry at the Hughes family for the way Wyn was treated as she was growing up,' said Cummings.

'It's not that.' Frances shook her head. 'Of course I'm angry about it. But it's more than that... I *saw* Wyn get knocked about. I saw her get... thrown across the room!'

'I know you did. And it sounds awful, it really does.'

'You're going to say it doesn't mean anything. That it's not proof,' said Frances. Cummings gave a small shrug.

'So, you think it was her sister?' she said.

'I—' Frances couldn't answer. She thought of the man in the hospital. She thought of her nightmares; the smell of nettles and something *else* – another smell; of the way Owen had back-tracked, flustered, after saying he believed it wasn't

Johannes who'd killed his sister. 'I don't know,' she said, help-lessly.

'Did something happen to make you remember seeing Wyn that final time?' said Cummings, and Frances nodded.

'It was when I went back to the leper hospital, looking for Davy. I saw Johannes's hiding place – the one I told the police about. I saw . . . He'd scratched his name into the wood. It was the first time I'd been back there in all this time and it . . . I suppose it took me back.'

'Yes. Retracing one's steps, places, smells . . . they can be quite powerful.' Cummings folded away her notes and stood up. 'You might try carrying on with that – go back to some other places from your childhood, see if anything else occurs to you. I'll see you again soon.'

'Wait! If . . . if Wyn *was* raped – if that's why she was killed, and if it *wasn't* Johannes, then . . . then *that* man walked free. And he's been free all these years,' said Frances. A look of profound unease filled the sergeant's face.

Once she'd gone, Frances stayed on the bench feeling somehow precarious, as though small cracks were appearing at the edges of the world, and she wasn't sure of her balance. She felt abandoned, left behind, and thought it might be Wyn's abandonment of her she was feeling. By keeping things from her, by going alone to see Johannes. What else had Wyn not told her? *Had* she told Johannes where she lived? Had she managed to coax him to go outside? Had she told someone else about him, and broken their promise to each other completely? Frances rubbed her tired eyes as Pam came to sit beside her, handing her a mug of tea and a cheese sandwich on a plate.

'I take it that didn't quite go as you'd hoped?' she said.

'Not exactly.' Frances smiled sadly. Pam studied her briefly, then looked out across the city. 'It was all so long ago, Frances. You've found Davy – isn't that cause for celebration?'

'Carys wouldn't let me see him. She says she won't, not ever again.'

'What?' said Pam. 'Oh, curse the wretched woman! She was probably drunk – she'll change her mind as soon as she needs help with him, don't you worry. Come on, eat up. Let's go up to Beechen Cliff.'

'Why?'

'Don't you want to see the king and queen? They're going up the cliff for a view of the damage. We'll collect your mum on the way – come on, I won't make you wave a flag.'

'You go.' Frances shook her head. 'Sorry, Pam. I just don't feel like it.'

'Please yourself.' Pam stood back up with a sigh. 'Don't . . . don't get lost in this, will you, Frances?' she said.

'I'll be all right,' said Frances, because there wasn't much else she could say.

On her way to the pub in the evening, Frances sensed her shadow again – the same, now familiar feeling of being watched, like an unwanted touch on her skin, making her shudder. She stopped, and the footsteps behind her took a second to halt after she did. She stood in the middle of the street, blind in the blackout darkness, the blood thumping loudly in her ears as she strained to hear movement behind her. She turned about, eyes scanning, but could see nothing. Deprived of information, her eyes played tricks on her – conjuring movement and shapes where there turned out to be none. She wanted to run but couldn't bring herself to turn her back on whoever was there. Following her; watching her. Ever since Wyn had been found. She took a deep breath.

'I know you're there,' she said, as steadily as she could. The darkness swallowed her voice; the silence seemed to be listening. 'What do you want?' Her voice sounded thin compared to the thudding of her heart. Far away she heard other voices, and a short bark of laughter, and she longed to run towards them. 'Was it you?' she said. 'Would I know your face, if I saw you now? Was it you?'

She waited a few more seconds for a reply, and even though there was only silence, only the dark, she knew she wasn't imagining it. 'I'm not scared of you,' she said, trying to believe it. 'I'm . . . I'm on to you.' She remembered Dog tugging at the lead, barking at an empty street behind them. In daylight and in the dark, her follower was there. And she realised, too late, that she had just threatened them. Her stomach fluttered as she turned and walked on, quickly, fighting the urge to run, and she reached the doorway of the Young Fox with a flood of relief. The long room at the back of the pub had a skittles alley built of polished woodblock down one side, and a match was in full flow. It was crowded, the din even louder than normal, the faces even redder with drink; a defiant outpouring of merriment against the fear and grief of the bombings. Frances ordered a large brandy and stood cradling it in a corner until her hands stopped shaking. She couldn't unpick it all – the person following her; the man in the hospital; Carys having Wyn's brooch, Owen's reticence. However she shaped it, it wouldn't make sense, but she knew it was all to do with Wyn's death. With the things she remembered, and the things she'd forgotten; with the killer being free all the years that had followed, and still being free.

Owen was on the skittles team, so Frances sat down to wait while he played. She drank her brandy, and then another, and began to enjoy being lost in the crowd. The alcohol blurred her thoughts; the heat from all the bodies made her sweat. Her father was also on the Young Fox's team, which was beating the team from the George down on London Road. Every ball was met with a roar; the tables were laden with smeared glasses, the air thick with smoke. Her father slapped Owen on the back after he sent the skittles flying and Frances felt a pang she was coming to know – almost nostalgia, almost regret. An old, familiar feeling of missing out. She sat pressed between strangers and tried not to think, since all her thoughts made her feel wretched. In the Saturday night ruckus it was easy to feel like one of many, like one of the crowd; nobody noticed that she was there by herself – for a while, not even Frances.

The table top was scattered with spent matches, and they made her think of Johannes's treasures. She tried to remember what had become of them, but their fate was lost in the maelstrom of that summer. Had she thrown them out herself? Had her mother found them in her jewellery box, and destroyed them? She had no memory of them going, or of when she last saw them. One moment everything was fine, and the box was full of charming things, then at some point later nothing was fine, and the box was empty. She tried to recall what the last thing he had made them had been, but it was impossible. Go back to old places, Sergeant Cummings had suggested. Places that might stir memories. The man in the hospital was like a place she'd used to go – he had that same nagging familiarity, that same power to rouse feelings she'd felt long before. She tried to think where else she might go, since the leper hospital was the only place she hadn't returned to since she last saw Johannes. But as she thought about that summer, pushing the burnt matches around on the table, making shapes and destroying them, another place came to mind. It came with a shiver of cold; a sickening stirring of the blackest thing in the darkest corner of her mind. The place was Warleigh Weir.

'Penny for them?' said Owen, sitting down beside her. Frances looked up, surprised that time had passed and the skittles match was over.

'Oh, they're not worth that,' she said. 'Did you win?'

'Weren't you watching? We trounced them.'

'I just . . . lost track.' Frances could tell from Owen's eyes that he'd also had a few. His skin had a sheen from the heat, and end-of-day stubble cast a shadow along his jaw; his hair was a sweaty mess, and the smell of metal and oil was still on him from the works. Frances found herself too aware of the nearness of him, assailed by a sudden, intense wanting. She could look at anybody else in that crowded place and not really see them, not really notice they were there, but when Owen was near she couldn't help but notice him. He seemed more real than everybody else.

'I saw you over here all by yourself, watching everyone,' he said. 'How come you don't sit with one of these gangs of women?'

'I don't know any of them; I was waiting for you.' Frances looked away, wishing she had things to say that would make Owen smile. 'I went to see Davy earlier, but Carys . . . won't let me see him any more.'

'She what?'

'That's what she said.' Frances expected her anger to return, but the brandy strengthened her sorrow instead. 'Then I got angry and I . . . said some things to her. About Wyn. We had a bit of a row.'

'Oh, dear,' said Owen. He took her hand, and perhaps he only meant to squeeze it once then let it go, but somehow their hands stayed clasped together, down below the table where nobody would see. He tightened his grip and didn't let go.

'Do you think you could talk to her about it?' said Frances. 'I just . . . I can't imagine not seeing him any more. Even if she doesn't want me sitting for him . . . I can understand that, I suppose, given what happened the last time. Even if she doesn't want that, I could at least go round and see him sometimes.

Perhaps walk him back from school . . . I don't know. Will you talk to her?'

'I'll try,' said Owen, carefully. 'But you know my sister.'

'She'd listen to you though, wouldn't she? They all do.'

'Perhaps, once the dust's settled a bit. Best to let her calm down first.'

'But what about Davy? She . . . sometimes she doesn't give him any supper, and she forgets to bath him and wash his clothes, so he smells and then they pick on him at school, and—'

'Shh, Frances – he'll be all right. He will. He's living with my mum now, isn't he? She's not going to see him go hungry, even if Carys is on a bender. Is she?'

'No. That's true,' said Frances, feeling some of her worry ease, even if the pain of separation remained.

'Fancy another?' said Owen, tapping her empty glass.

Owen was a while at the crowded bar, and when he sat back down his smile was odd, and he looked away when he spoke.

'So, what was it you said to Carys about Wyn?'

'Oh,' said Frances. She shook her head, remembering how Owen had been when they last spoke about it – how she'd got the feeling he wasn't telling her everything. With all her heart, she didn't want that to be true. 'I just . . . It was just . . .' She put her hand in her pocket, where Wyn's brooch was hidden. She could show him, tell him that Wyn had been wearing it the day she disappeared, wait for him to make all the same arguments Cummings had made. She left it where it was. 'I was just angry with her about the way she'd given up on Davy, and not even helped look for him. I suppose I accused her of knowing something about what happened to Wyn.'

'What do you suppose she knows?' said Owen.

'I don't know. I just . . . With Wyn being found at home, in

her own backyard . . . I *know* it wasn't Johannes! And I just . . .'
She shook her head again.

'You think Carys knows? Why would she? Do you think we *all* know?' Owen sounded shocked.

'No! Of course not. But . . . Owen, if you *did* know something . . . or if you had a hunch . . . you'd tell me, wouldn't you?'

'Course I would,' he said, looking down at his pint. 'Will you tell me what it was you remembered in the leper hospital?'

'I remembered . . . where Wyn had been going, when she came to call for me the day she disappeared. She was going to the leper hospital, and she wanted me to go with her. And I remembered Johannes's hiding place – and swearing never to tell anyone about it.'

Frances told him about being upset with Wyn, and sending her away by herself; about telling the police exactly where to find Johannes. Owen listened with a frown.

'Come on, Frances – you were kids! You were bound to have fallings-out. And of course you had to tell the police where to find Ebner! Whether you'd promised not to or whatever. You did the right thing. And they'd have found him anyway, sooner or later.'

'Maybe not. Maybe he'd have had a chance to get away, if I hadn't told them.'

'And maybe that would've been the wrong thing to happen. He could have done it, Frances.'

'Sergeant Cummings thinks so too. But I don't – I *can't* believe it.'

'The police still think it was him?' Owen sounded relieved.

'At the moment. Unless I can find out something else.' Frances took a swig of brandy and felt it burn down her throat. Her head spun gently. 'Do you remember that time we all went to Warleigh Weir?' she said, then wished she hadn't.

'We went lots of times.'

'But I only went with you once. Me and Wyn. You had your school friends there, I can't remember their names.' She waited, but Owen merely shrugged. 'We swam for hours, and we had a picnic.'

'Possibly . . . why?'

'Oh. No reason.' Frances downed the rest of her drink, and thought for a while. 'I remember being terrified your dad would find out we were taking things for Johannes – we took a few bits of food, and Wyn took that blanket. Can you imagine what he'd have done? Especially since we were stealing for a stranger – a *German*. He'd have been furious.'

'He'd have had your guts for garters.' Owen nodded. 'Remember that time I pinched his fags, and sold them off to my mates? I was saving up for football boots – as if I'd ever have scraped enough together.'

'I don't remember that.'

'No? Dad pitched a fit. Scared the hell out of me – out of all of us. He was getting ready to blame Clive for it, and Carys was pulling such faces at me, so I bought a replacement packet and confessed what I'd done.'

'And he shook you by the hand, and said "Well done for owning up, son?"'

'Not exactly.' Owen laughed. 'My nose has been crooked ever since.' He shrugged. 'He was no picnic. But it wasn't all his fault.'

'Yes, Wyn told me about his first family.' There was a pause, and Owen took a drink.

'He'd have been furious about Ebner. But he didn't find out, did he? And anyway, he couldn't touch *you*. And Wyn was always his favourite; he'd never have hurt her.'

Frances didn't reply at once, confused because she knew Owen had seen Bill being rough with Wyn, and dealing her blows, just as he had with all of them.

'It wasn't normal, you know,' she said quietly. 'What you all had to put up with . . . that's not normal. My dad never once raised his hand to me. And Wyn was so small . . . so fragile.'

'*Fragile?*' said Owen, trying to make light of it.

'Physically, yes, she was. You know she was.' Owen's smile faded.

'I know,' he said. 'And I know it wasn't normal.' He drew in a breath and opened his mouth, but whatever he'd been about to say, he thought better of it. The din of the pub went on around them; Owen sat lost in thought, and Frances was sorry. A short while ago he'd been happy, laughing with his friends, and she had ruined it. In the midst of all her uncertainty, Owen felt like one sure, safe thing. She'd done without him for years and years but now couldn't remember how, and the last thing she wanted was to be a source of grief to him. She wanted to forget about it all, and to let Owen forget about it all. She wanted to forget everything except the way Owen had once made her laugh, and the way it had felt when they'd kissed. The room spun around her and she swayed, knocking the table so that the glasses rattled. 'Come on,' he said, standing up. 'It's too bloody hot in here.'

He led her out onto Old Orchard. The night air was crisp and it cleared her head a little; enough to know she might care tomorrow that people had seen them leave together, but that she didn't care just then. She could feel the race of her blood all round her body; she had a sensation like floating, and wanted, for once, to act without thinking. In the dark she took Owen's hand again, and brought it to her lips, tasting salt and smoke. She couldn't see his face, just the faint gleam of his eyes reflecting the night sky.

'I wish—' she said, but didn't finish, because there were too many things to wish, and she didn't know how to put words to her sudden yearning to sink into him until there was nothing left of herself at all. It was an instinct more than a feeling, something innate; like the feeling of safety he gave her. She turned her face up to his, felt their noses brush, then their lips.

'Frances...' Owen leaned back, just a fraction. He tipped his head so that their foreheads touched instead of their mouths. 'Oh, why *now*, Frances? Why did you have to come back now, and stir it all up when there's nothing to be done?'

'Come back?' She shook her head. 'I never went anywhere. I never will. I'll end up one of the leper hospital ghosts.'

'No, you went away. You got married. It was all left behind, and finished. I made myself not think about you.'

'I expect it was easy enough.'

'No.' He shook his head. 'No, it was hard.'

Frances put her hands up to his face, and shut his eyes with her fingertips. His arms wrapped around her and she felt the strength in them, the muscles and bones beneath his clothes, pulling her close. When they kissed there was something desperate in it, something that had been gone for so long they'd forgotten how much they needed it; Frances remembered the feeling from a long time before. Owen held her so tightly she could hardly breathe, and she didn't care – she wanted to drown in him, she wanted oblivion; she wanted to go to his house, to his bedroom, and lose herself there. But Owen broke the kiss off, and her mouth felt cold where his had been.

'We can't, Frances,' he said. 'I've got Maggie, and the kids. You've got Joe—'

'No, I haven't got anyone,' she said. She tried to kiss him again, pushing her hips into his.

'Christ, Frances, please... I can't do this. You're drunk—'

'I don't care.'

'Well, I do, and I'm half-cut too; we're not... we're not thinking straight.'

Stung, Frances took a step backwards. She shivered as

reality came crowding back in all around. Owen let her go, and the sudden loss of his touch was a shock. She felt foolish and unwanted, just like the first time he'd pushed her away.

'Of course,' she said. 'Sorry.'

'Don't say sorry!' He tried to take her hands but Frances snatched them away. 'What do you want, Frances?' he asked, earnestly. 'What is it you want?'

'I want...' It amazed her that he couldn't tell; that it wasn't obvious *he* was all she wanted – him, and to forget about everything else.

'If we weren't married,' he said, desperately. 'If it wasn't for that, and the kids...'

'Yes. Well. I should get home.'

'Maggie would take them, you see, if I ever... She's said so before, when things weren't good between us. She'd take them off somewhere. Hold on – wait. Tell me what you *want*. Please, Frances.' The way he said it made her pause. There was something he wanted to hear, but she didn't know what it was. She felt too raw, too uncertain.

'I want...' She didn't dare finish the sentence. Tears ached in her throat, and she swallowed them down. 'I want your help. I *need* your help.'

'Frances.' Owen sighed, and she wished she could see his expression. Her head was still spinning, only now it made her feel sick. She backed away, stumbling on the cobbles. If he didn't want her, then she wanted to be away, and she didn't care if Wyn's killer was waiting for her, out in the darkness. 'Of course I'll help you, if I can, but I don't know what you want me to do,' he said at last, but by then Frances was hardly listening. 'At least let me walk you back,' he said, as she hurried away.

1918

August began with a stretch of hot, dry weather, perfect for swimming in the canal and climbing trees to laze in the dappled light. It was the school holidays, so Frances and Wyn had long days in which to roam the hills like feral things, grass-stained and sunburnt, and having to take food to Johannes seemed more of a bind than it had before. They knew he relied on them so they kept on going, but they both found it harder to simply sit with him, doing nothing.

'Johannes, what would you do if anybody else came here?' Frances asked one day. The thought gave her a frisson of vicarious nerves, and Johannes looked alarmed.

'People are coming?' he said.

'No, I don't think so. I mean, I don't know. It's not very likely, especially in the nice weather. Everyone's doing out-door things.' The boys were too busy constructing rope swings in riverside trees to bother with old buildings. 'But what if they did?' She thought of the time before, when he'd thought Owen outside was someone trying to get in. How he'd shaken her, and shouted; how his eyes had emptied out. She wondered if Johannes would attack, or try to run.

'I would hide,' he said.

'Where? There's nowhere to hide in here,' Wyn pointed out, and it was true – there was no furniture to crawl inside or behind; there weren't even any doors to hide behind. Johannes looked at each of them in turn.

'But, you would not tell anybody to come here, would you?'

'No, of *course* not,' said Wyn, impatiently. She stood up with a sigh. 'It's only in case. Come on. We'd better look until we find somewhere you could hide.'

Frances rose obediently.

'There are places you could hide out in the yard,' she said, hopefully. 'There's all those long weeds in the far corner, and there's the old coal hole...'

'No! I cannot,' said Johannes.

'Don't be stupid, Frances,' said Wyn. 'He can hardly go outside to hide if someone's coming *in*, can he?' Stung, Frances went upstairs to search by herself. She peered into the chimneys, to see if they were wide enough for Johannes to crawl into, but it didn't look possible. She opened the wall cupboard in one room, and looked at the ancient, wormy wood. She was about to give it up as too obvious when she had a thought. The bottom of the cupboard was at her knee height, and through gaps in the planks she could see the darkness of a void underneath. She dug her fingers into one of the gaps and pulled, and the plank came up easily enough; she lifted another one and revealed the space underneath. She could see the floor joists, with dust and dead insects in between. 'What are you doing, Frances? Oh – that's a good place,' said Wyn, appearing behind her. 'He could just about fit in there, and put the planks back over himself. Johannes! Come and see!'

They did a trial run – Johannes wriggled into the void, carefully keeping his weight across the beams and not between them. Then, lying on his back and with a bit of manoeuvring, he pulled the planks back into place above himself.

'No one would ever know you were there,' said Wyn. 'Would they, Frances?'

'No. Nobody would ever think to look,' she said. Johannes pushed a plank to one side and grinned up at them.

'*Buh!*' he said.

'Well, that wasn't very scary!' Frances laughed.

'I am not scary,' he said, levering himself out, brushing off the dust. '*Sehr gut.* This is very good. Thank you, Frances.'

'Well, we'll go now,' said Wyn. 'If you ever think someone's coming and it's not us, you just have to come in here.'

'Yes. Thank you, little sisters. But . . . you are not telling anyone to come here?' he said. Wyn heaved a sigh and rolled her eyes.

'We've already said not, about a hundred times.'

From the outside the old hospital looked as deserted as ever. Frances reassured herself that nobody would ever think anyone was living there, let alone such a strange and interesting person. She didn't know why Wyn was so short-tempered with him, but then, she'd been in a strange mood that week – quieter than normal, and not as cheerful. Frances thought it might be the heat, because every so often Wyn would shake her head as though a fly were bothering her, and rub her fingers across her sweaty forehead, leaving dirty marks. She was clearly finding Johannes a bother, and Frances worried that she'd stop wanting to visit him. They walked up Prior Park Road, where there was a raised section of a stream, several feet above the road, channelled to run in front of some grand houses. Big, scruffy ducklings paddled there, still cheeping in their baby voices; small trout hung in the water, weaving their bodies to and fro. Frances tried to think of a way to reignite Wyn's enthusiasm.

'I *wish* we could think of a way to help Johannes get home. But it won't be easy if it's over the sea, and they even talk a different language there.'

'Well, *obviously*,' said Wyn. She thought for a moment. 'We need a map,' she said. 'Has your dad got one? Or Keith?'

'Keith got an atlas for Christmas, and it's full of maps. I could look in it, if he lets me.'

'See if you can find Summer Rain. Then we can work out

how he should get back. And I . . .' Wyn broke off, chewing one thumbnail. 'I'm going to take him a blanket to sleep on. Mum's been airing out all our winter ones, so maybe I could snatch one off the line; she'll just think some other bugger's nicked it. He shouldn't have to lie on newspaper like a dog,' she said, warming to the idea. 'Not when he's an important man.'

'Wyn, don't! What if you get caught?'

Frances was horrified. She thought of Wyn being knocked clean across the room just for getting under her father's feet, and was afraid for her.

'I won't get caught.' Wyn took off her cardigan and tied it around her middle, checking, as she always did, that her daffodil brooch was still fastened. She leant on the railings and stared down into the water.

'But what if you do, though?' said Frances. 'Your mum's bound to notice. What if she tells the police? What if she tells your dad? Imagine how angry he'd be.'

'I'm not scared of the police, and anyway, no one will know it was me.'

'I don't think you should,' Frances persisted.

'Well, I'm going to,' said Wyn, and Frances knew it was pointless to go on. The more resistance Wyn faced, the more she pushed against it.

'But then we'll take it to him together, won't we?' said Frances. 'It can be from both of us . . . like all the food's been. You won't go without me?'

'Course not,' said Wyn, very quickly. They headed for home, and when they reached the steps of Magdalen Cottages Frances's mother gave them a wave from the front window. 'See you, then,' said Wyn, trotting off with a small, thoughtful frown.

*

At Warleigh Weir, near the Claverton pumping station, the River Avon split into a wide, lazy braid, with a meadow in the middle where dairy cows grazed and swung their tails. The canal and railway ran along just to the west, and there was a curved weir down which the water ran in a sparkling curtain. Warleigh was a good walk east out of Bath, down a steep lane from the Warminster road and then across the water in a little ferry boat, which was pulled along a rope by a gnarled, elderly man. They had to go in three loads because it was only a small boat and there were so many of them – Frances and Wyn and Owen; Carys and Clive; Aunt Ivy and Cousin Clare, and Owen's school friends, Tom and Noah. Frances was relieved that Wyn's parents hadn't come with them – not that she minded Mrs Hughes, she just minded Bill Hughes a lot. They'd invited Joe Parry to go with them too, but he'd had to stay and help his parents on the farm. Frances felt sorry for him; he never complained, but she could tell he'd have liked to come. He'd looked hot, itchy and fagged out, and rarely seemed to have much fun.

'Well, it's not *our* fault,' said Wyn, when Frances remarked upon it. That wasn't the point, but Frances didn't argue. Wyn leaned over the side of the ferry boat as they crossed, trailing her fingers in the water and staring down at her broken reflection, in spite of the ferryman's order to 'sit steady'. 'We could be going to Summer Rain,' she whispered to Frances, as they got off at the other side. 'Over the water to faraway places.' She sounded wistful.

It was so hot the grass seemed to steam, and Ivy and Carys spent a long time debating where to spread the picnic blankets. Frances was carrying one of the baskets of food and it was cutting into her hands, and kept banging her knee. She eyed the river longingly. The water was greenish but quite clear; it shone in the sunshine, almost too bright to look at, and beneath the surface long weeds waved like ribbons in a slow wind. Carys had rolled up her sleeves and her dark hair was unravelling from its combs. There was colour high in her cheeks as she fought to keep her temper, and Clive sauntered along in her wake, wearing a straw boater, carrying a deckchair for Ivy, and smiling at the rear view of his fiancée. Once they'd settled on a spot – part sun, part shade, not too near the water, not too near the railway tracks – and the blankets were down and Ivy was installed in her deckchair, the girls were allowed to swim. Owen and his friends had already disappeared – tearing down to the water and leaping in. They didn't need to wait for permission because they were twelve years old, and boys; their voices, loud with laughter, rang out across the meadow.

'Heads I take forty winks,' said Clive, tossing his silver dollar. 'Tails I swim all the way to Bristol.' He caught the coin and peered at it, then grinned. 'Marvellous,' he said, lying back in the splotched shade of a horse chestnut and tipping his hat over his face.

'Fancy a paddle?' Clare said to Carys, who nodded and began to take off her shoes and stockings.

'You two girls mind how you go,' said Ivy, as Wyn and Frances stripped down to their vests and knickers. 'Stay together, and no falling down the weir.'

'We will,' said Wyn. 'Hurry *up*, Frances.'

'Watch out for the pike, nipping at your toes,' said Clive, drowsily.

There were lots of other swimmers and picnickers at Warleigh that day, but the meadow was large and there were plenty of places to swim, so it didn't feel crowded. The air was cooler by the river and tasted of damp ground; where the bank shelved in shallowly it had been churned muddy by bare, wet feet. Frances and Wyn walked out along the top of the weir, away from the bank, until they felt far from safety and supervision. At first the water was bitingly cold, but it soon seemed soothing and fresh. Frances looked down, amused by how big and white her feet looked.

'See, it's only really bad at first, like I said. Just like everything,' said Wyn. She took Frances's hot hand in hers. 'Ready?' Frances nodded. They turned to face the deeper water upstream of the weir, putting its sloping face behind them. Taking huge breaths and pinching their noses, they leapt.

The water whooshed over Frances's head and gurgled in her ears. It went through her hair and under her clothes, both shocking and wonderful. She lost Wyn's hand and surfaced through bubbles, spluttering and laughing and rubbing her eyes, not minding that her feet were tangled in weeds or that she'd swallowed some greenish water. Wyn was grinning as she came up, her hair slicked to her head, making her look younger, thinner, and smaller. Her eyes sparkled, though, and Frances realised that they hadn't for some time; that she hadn't seen Wyn's gap-toothed grin in quite a while.

'Let's swim upriver, and see how far we can get,' Wyn said.

'All right,' said Frances. The current was slow, with the river at its summer low, so it wasn't too hard to swim against. When they got tired, they went closer to the bank where they could rest, holding onto reeds or low-hanging branches of blackthorn and willow. Damselflies zipped around them, and moorhens swam jerkily away. At one point a pair of swans came in to land, flying so low over their heads that they felt the buffet of their wings, and saw the sunshine glowing through their feathers.

Before long, they'd swum out of sight of Warleigh, and all the other people. A train steamed slowly past, on its way into Bath, and when they waved to the guard he waved back. Wyn was shivering by then, her bottom lip wobbling uncontrollably. She looked impossibly white, like milk. 'Let's get out for a bit,' said Frances. They clambered onto the bank to sit in muddy puddles of their own creation, and the sun immediately warmed them.

'Johannes would love this,' said Wyn, resting her head on her knees and shutting her eyes. 'If he wasn't scared to be outside, I mean. Wouldn't it be good if he could swim back to Summer Rain? I hadn't thought of that before.'

'It's probably a bit far,' said Frances.

'I know that, but it would be good if he could. Nobody would think to look in the river, would they? He wouldn't leave any tracks.'

'I suppose not.'

'He could be as free as us! We could swim all the way to the sea if we wanted. Right now! Couldn't we? We don't ever have to go back, if we don't want to.'

'We don't!' Frances laughed, but she was troubled by Wyn's sudden eagerness; that she seemed to mean what she said, when Frances couldn't imagine wanting to leave home. 'We could swim to France!' she said, to hide her worry. 'And marry French fishermen, who'll think we're mermaids.'

'Marry a fisherman?' Wyn sounded appalled. '*You* can, if you want. I'm going to marry a rich man.' She thought for a moment. 'Do you think Johannes really is an important person where he comes from?' Frances stopped laughing, and didn't answer for a long time. She hated to lie, and there was clearly a point where make-believe became lying. She wasn't quite sure where that point was any more.

'I don't know,' she said, in the end. Wyn opened her eyes to look at her – a narrow gleam between her eyelashes. Somehow it was clear to both of them that Frances had debunked the make-believe, which made it difficult for Wyn to pretend any more, either. They sat in silence for a while, as the delight and possibility of the moment before ebbed away. Frances felt the sun scorching her skin, and her scalp itched as the river water dried.

'I'm going back,' said Wyn, at last. She slithered back into the water, and Frances followed even though she'd said *I*, not *we*. Swimming downstream was much easier, and they seemed to fly along.

'Look how fast we're going! We *could* be mermaids,' said Frances. 'Or otters.' But Wyn ignored her.

The picnic consisted of a large rabbit and potato pie to share, cheese sandwiches, tomatoes and lemonade, and in the afternoon they played a game of sardines with the boys. Wyn was quiet, and didn't smile very much, but when Frances asked her what the matter was, she only shrugged, and looked cross, so Frances shied away from asking again. But she knew when Wyn was upset, and she knew when there was something she wasn't saying, and it stole what was left of the fun from her day. She didn't really want to play sardines, but Owen begged them, since you needed enough people to play it properly. Frances's heart wasn't in it; she even began to wish it was time to go home. She found a good hiding place, in a shady thicket of elder and hawthorn beside an old cow byre, eased her way past the nettles and hunkered down to wait to be found. Flies buzzed around her, and her dress was stuck to her back where her hair had dripped onto it. She seemed to wait an awfully long time. The feeling of wanting to go home grew and grew; she almost gave up and came out of hiding several times, but she didn't want to let everyone down and spoil the game. So she stayed there in the leafy shade, half hoping to be found quickly so it would be over, and half hoping to stay hidden forever, so no one would notice how wretched she felt.

Time began to behave oddly, and Frances lost track of how long she'd been there. The insects buzzed and her neck ached from hunching; she was hot and still a little hungry, and thirsty too; she felt drowsy but at the same time her heart was thumping oddly, and after a while she really couldn't tell if she *wanted* to stay where she was or was simply unable to move. Eventually she heard Wyn shouting her name, and emerged on wobbly legs only to be told that they'd given up on her the game before, and that this time she was supposed to be seeking, not hiding, and was therefore the loser. Frances didn't even have the heart to protest such blatant unfairness. Her head ached and her knees were bruised from kneeling; she had nettle stings and she couldn't look at any of them, not even Wyn. Her insides felt swollen up, too big for her body, and she knew that if she spoke, something would start to spill out, uncontrollably.

'Good Lord, but you've managed to get filthy!' her mother exclaimed, when Frances got home at the end of the day. She held up Frances's dress as Frances rinsed the weed from her hair in a bucket of water. Her sunburnt shoulders were stinging.

'I went swimming too,' said Keith. 'We went to the *best* place – a secret place, not boring old Warleigh. I bet I had more fun than you did.' Frances didn't contradict him.

'That's enough, Keith. I'm sure you both had lots of fun.' Susan was scrubbing at the back of the dress with a stiff brush, frowning at the stains. 'Honestly, Frances – what *is* this you've got all over yourself? And this vest will never be the same again.' She tutted, and Frances lowered her head so that the water filled up her ears, and made her shiver, and her mother's voice turned muffled and strange. She wanted to go to bed and not think about the day; she wanted it to be tomorrow, a different day altogether. She was so tired she didn't want to talk, or eat, or anything. She sat mute while her mother put slices of cucumber on her pink shoulders.

'You'll wake up covered in slugs,' said Keith, smirking

at her. The sun hadn't burned him, just brought out more freckles across his nose.

'Keith, if you can't say anything nice, don't say anything at all,' said Susan. Frances dreamed about the slugs, though – slithering all over her, covering her with slime; more of them appearing for every one she picked off.

Johannes had asked them to bring a newspaper and read it to him, so Frances pinched her mother's old copy of *The Bath Herald* out of the basket by the fire, and took it with her when they went to see him a few days after the trip to Warleigh.

'Can't you read?' Wyn said to Johannes, incredulously.

'Certainly, I can,' he said. 'But not in English. Reading and speaking are most different things,' he explained, when they looked puzzled.

'Well, what language do they speak in Summer Rain?' said Wyn. Johannes looked quickly at each of them; he blinked twice, and swallowed.

'Austrian,' he said, tentatively, and Frances felt a knot in her stomach loosen. Austrian. Not German. She'd started having uneasy thoughts. Britain was at war, after all; could Johannes be somebody who wasn't meant to be there at all – could he be the enemy? The Hun – a German spy? They were every-where, Owen said. She had no idea what a German looked or sounded like, but given the sort of thing she'd overheard about them murdering women and children as they marched across Belgium, she pictured them tall, snarling, and blood-soaked. She'd thought about mentioning it to Wyn, but lately she'd begun to second-guess everything she said before saying it, in case Wyn wouldn't like it. In any case, the war was far away, in other countries. There was no way a German could have come to Britain without anybody knowing, and a spy wouldn't be hiding in the old leper hospital. A spy would be in

London, where the important people were. 'It should be called *Summerlish*,' said Wyn, and Johannes laughed.

'You are right, little sister. So from now on, we shall call it that.' He had a lovely laugh, light and bouncy, and it was very rare to hear it. Wyn beamed, her narrow chest swelling, and Frances felt a little bereft. She looked away, and saw something that shocked her.

In the corner of the room was a navy blue woollen blanket, much darned where moths had got at it, but still good and heavy. She recognised it – it had covered Wyn's bed throughout the winter. Wyn had stolen it, like she'd said she would, and she'd brought it to Johannes by herself. Like she'd said she wouldn't. The betrayal hit Frances like a thump in the stomach, sudden and shocking. Her fingers shook as she opened the newspaper and stared down into it. Johannes hadn't asked her to start reading, but she needed something to do, some way to evade the horrible spotlight she suddenly felt herself under – the shame of being in pain, and the fear that others would see it.

'What's the matter with you?' said Wyn, so innocently that Frances couldn't look at her.

'Nothing,' she said, the blood roaring in her ears.

Frances was a better reader than Wyn. As she got started on the front page, Johannes shook his head, and put one hand out to stop her. He had his mouth full; a hard-boiled egg bulged in his cheek.

'Not news, please,' he said.

'But . . . what then? It's a *news*paper.'

'Nothing about the . . . fighting. About death. Is there something nice in it? Something normal? About . . . people. A church. Or the football team.'

'Owen says Bath City are rubbish at football,' said Wyn.

'But he's still going to join them once he's old enough. He says he can turn them around.'

'Your brother? He says so?' Johannes grinned around his mouthful. Frances turned to the back pages and started to read about the team's latest defeat – reported in heroic terms, none the less, because so many players were away with the war, and what was left was a mixture of older men, those in reserved occupations and those unfit for service. Johannes shut his eyes and tipped his head back against the wall to listen to her. When she'd read about the football team Frances looked back through the paper until she found a report on an annual charity lunch in aid of the abbey choir, and read that as well. Then a story about a new school that was going to be built, and the rescue of a small child from the canal at Bathampton. Wyn sat with her knees drawn up, fiddling with the frayed edges of her cuffs and rubbing at spots of mud on her hem, which only ever made them worse. Frances just wanted to keep on reading and reading, because while she was doing that she wasn't having to think about where Johannes had come from, and how long he could stay in the leper hospital; she wasn't thinking about Wyn coming to see him by herself, when she'd promised she wouldn't; and she wasn't thinking about Warleigh Weir.

Sooner or later she ran out of nice stories to read, and all that was left were reports about local men who had died or were missing at the front. She didn't want to read them any more than Johannes wanted to hear them, even though she was sure, in her heart, that her father would never come to such harm. The thought of him brought on a wave of longing – for his big hugs and his steady presence, his silly jokes and the rumble of his voice coming up through the bedroom floor after lights-out. She folded the newspaper, still unwilling to meet Wyn's eye. She had no idea how to act, or what to say; the situation was alien – feeling wronged by her friend, feeling unhappy with her.

'Thank you, little Frances,' said Johannes, making Frances jump. She'd thought he was dozing, as he often did once all the food was eaten. 'You will do this again, next time, perhaps? You are reading very well.'

'If you like,' said Frances, too dejected to enjoy the praise. Wyn was a silent, watchful presence she could feel without having to see. There was a long pause, and Frances found herself fighting back tears.

'Frances is the best reader in our class,' Wyn announced, suddenly.

'Is it so?'

'Yes. Miss Gould – that's our teacher – always chooses her first of all, to stand up and read. And she always says "First rate, Frances" when she finishes.'

'This is good, Frances,' said Johannes, and Frances's cheeks flamed. She knew Wyn was only saying it to make it up to her, and she was torn between being pleased and feeling that it didn't make up for it at all. 'I like to read too. At home, I mean. And to learn languages – I learn them fast. The wife of one man in my town was from London, and she came to my school to teach us English, and I was the best. My father and I are going to travel further, to other countries, taking our toys and models . . .' Johannes's voice faded, his face turning tired and bereft. 'These were the plans we made,' he finished, so quietly it was hard to hear him.

The girls caught his sadness the same way they could catch a yawn, or a fit of the giggles. Wyn sighed and worried listlessly at her clothing again. House martins were nesting under the eaves of Magdalen Chapel, swooping to and fro with boundless energy; the day was warm, bright, full of colour, but Frances suddenly felt hopeless, and it was almost unbearable to be cooped up there. She couldn't just go, though – not until Wyn said. She was trapped. The trouble was, Frances was worried. She couldn't help it, and it was getting worse all the time. She was worried about her mother or Keith finding out where all the extra food she'd been taking was going. She was even more worried about Wyn's father finding out what they'd been up to, and that Wyn had taken the blanket. She was worried that Wyn was still treating it all as a game when, for Frances, it no longer was. The fun kind of excitement had passed, and what was left was the reality of it – that Johannes needed them, and that he wasn't a normal person, and that there seemed to be no end date to his stay. She glanced at him. He'd picked up the newspaper and was fashioning something from one of the pages. He was nice, and not dangerous, she knew that; but she also knew that there was something wrong. It was hard to put her finger on it, but perhaps it could be summed up simply – that he oughtn't to have been there at all.

He was not 'the enemy', that much she had already con-cluded to her own satisfaction. And yet, now and then, with no warning, she was beset by a horrible feeling – a creeping, trembling sensation that felt like the onrush of tears. She remembered what had happened to Mr and Mrs Smith just the year before; she'd heard her parents arguing about it. Mr and Mrs Smith ran a small flower shop up on Bear Flat, but it turned out – though nobody seemed to know how this had been discovered – that Mr Smith's real name was in fact Schmidt, and he was from Germany. And even though he'd lived in England since he was four years old, people who'd been his loyal customers for years ransacked his shop, and the police were forced to take him away to a camp, in their wagon with the bars on the windows, to prevent the people ransacking Mr Smith as well.

Frances didn't like to think what would happen if they

found Johannes and mistook him for a German. He wasn't from England, and the war cast a kind of shadow on people who weren't from England. And then there was the way he refused to leave the leper hospital. Admittedly, nobody else wanted to live there, but Frances was fairly sure that somebody would mind, in any case, if they knew. She had no idea how to explain any of what she was feeling to Wyn, when Wyn still talked about helping Johannes return to Summer Rain by various fantastical means – a hired ship; the horse owned by the landlord of the Traveller's Rest, which had once been a racehorse and was still lithe and handsome even though it was old – so that he could marry her one day, and take her far away from Beechen Cliff Place. When Wyn had decided on something it was pointless trying to change her mind; Frances could only wait and hope she'd do it herself at some point soon.

Wyn broke the quiet, getting to her feet.

'It's far too nice to stop indoors,' she declared, to Frances's great relief. 'Come outside, Johannes. Just for a moment. You're as pale as Granny Lovett, and she's *dead*. Come on.' She held out her hand to him, but he shook his head. Wyn sighed sharply through her nose. 'Tell him, Frances. You can't stay in here forever. You just can't. You'll *never* get home if you won't set a foot outside. Will you?' she demanded, as though suddenly impatient with him, or even angry. She clamped her jaw as she waited for a response, making her overbite more apparent and her top lip pop out.

'I think Wyn's right,' said Frances, apologetically. Johannes was looking at Wyn as though she might attack him. Perhaps he thought she was going to, or that it was a trap of some kind. 'It's really all right,' Frances added. 'It's so hidden out there, nobody will see you.' But Johannes didn't move; his body had gone as tense as a bowstring.

'Johannes.' Wyn folded her arms angrily. 'Come outside!

There's nothing to be scared of. And if you don't, we'll never visit you again. Will we, Frances? I swear, we won't. You'll have to starve.'

Frances didn't think Johannes would do as Wyn said. She was still trying to guess which was the stronger – Wyn's will or Johannes's fear – when he got slowly to his feet. He was breathing hard, trembling all over. He took a few steps forwards to stand in the doorway, bracing himself against the jamb. Frances felt nervous on his behalf, but Wyn looked triumphant. 'That's it,' she said. 'Go on!' Johannes looked down at her.

'How can I get home, if I won't go outside?' he said, and Wyn nodded. Johannes took one step outside, and then another, until he was clear of the doorway and standing in the yard under the wide blue sky. Wyn clapped her hands, which made him flinch.

'Hoo-bleedin'-ray!' she said, a phrase Owen had taken to using. Frances followed Johannes cautiously, but Wyn pushed past them both to skip about the yard, throwing her arms out wide. 'See! There's nothing to be afraid of,' she said. Johannes didn't answer her – his eyes raked left and right, searching, and Frances couldn't tell what he was thinking or feeling. After a while he tipped his head back, turning his face to the sun like a flower; he shut his eyes, swaying slightly.

'*Nichts zu fürchten*,' he said. He took a deep breath. 'Nothing to fear. I am telling to myself that this is the same sun they see at home; the same sun my mother is seeing, this very day, and my little sister Clara. Perhaps my father, too.' He swallowed, his Adam's apple bobbing wildly, then shuddered and opened his eyes. With a gasp, he turned to look at something Frances couldn't see; then he shook his head. '*Nein*. I cannot,' he said, and fled back inside in three long strides.

Left on their own out in the yard, Wyn's face fell and the

air of victory left her. Frances still couldn't quite look at her, but she didn't want to go back inside either. She was suddenly deeply, horribly unhappy. She felt lonely, and unwanted; she wanted to go home and be by herself, but she also wanted to be with Wyn, and for things to be how they'd used to be. She didn't want to have to keep coming to the leper hospital, but she was terrified that Wyn would stop wanting to come. She wanted to help Johannes, but she didn't want to have to. It was the summer holidays, and they were supposed to be having fun. Trying not to cry, she turned to follow Johannes back inside and Wyn pushed past her, angrily.

'Well,' said Wyn, in a teacherly tone. 'That was a start, but you're going to have to do a lot better.' She stood over Johannes, who'd sunk to the floor in his usual corner. She put her hands on her hips and didn't give an inch, even though Frances was shocked to see tears brimming in Johannes's eyes.

'Wyn, don't be mean,' she said, cautiously. Wyn glared at her.

'It's for his own good, Frances,' she said.

'The things I have seen, little ones...' said Johannes, brokenly. 'You cannot know this, I know. You cannot know the things I have seen. The things that have been done.' He shook his head, and even though his face was turned towards them, it seemed to Frances that he wasn't seeing them at all, he was seeing far-off things. Other people, other places.

'It's all right,' she said, uncertainly.

'Please, little sisters. You would not leave me to starve. You would not bring the soldiers here. Please, I beg you, please.' The tears rolled down his cheeks, hanging in drips from his jaw, and his face was strangely immobile. At last, Wyn sighed and went to crouch beside him. She patted his arm.

'We won't leave you to starve,' she said.

Johannes's face crumpled. With a whimper, he gathered

Wyn into his arms and hugged her tight. Over Wyn's shoulder Frances could see his eyes screwed shut, his eyelashes wet. Wyn braced her hands against his shoulders in surprise, then pushed back against his hold, to no avail. Frances thought of the time she'd seen Bill Hughes hug her like that – long arms wrapping right around her skinny body in a hold she could never have broken in a hundred years. She thought of the way Wyn had simply hung there, patiently waiting to be released. How wrong it had seemed; how dangerous, somehow. The sight of Johannes doing the same thing made her knees ache, and her stomach churn.

'Clara, *Schätzchen, wie ich dich vermisst habe*,' he whispered, and a second later Wyn began to struggle. Her feet pedalled against the floor, hitting Johannes's legs, scrabbling, kicking; she turned her head side to side, craning away from him, and beat his shoulders with her fists. They went on like that for a few seconds, seconds that seemed taut and strangulated. Frances stared, paralysed by the strangeness of it; conflicting instincts told her to run and to help. Then Wyn's voice rang out, shockingly loud.

'Get *off* me!' The shout burst out of her, a sound Frances had never heard before – strident, utterly furious, panicky underneath. '*Get off me!*' Startled, Johannes opened his eyes and released her. He looked confused as Wyn struggled to her feet, breathing hard. She glared down at him for a moment with a look of such outrage that Frances was sure she was going to kick him or hit him.

'Wyn,' said Johannes, hoarsely. He raised a hand against the attack he also foresaw. 'I am sorry, Wyn. I forgot . . . I forgot.' In silence Wyn turned and stormed away, and Frances was left, bewildered, in her wake.

She caught up with Wyn on Holloway, walking slowly as though she didn't know where to go. 'I don't think he meant to upset you,' she said, uncertainly. Wyn shrugged. Her eyes were still wide, her face set. Frances was going to say that the people Johannes was hiding from must be very bad, and the things he'd seen must be very frightening, but the words got stuck, and what did come out was completely different. 'You said we'd take him the blanket together.' Her cheeks burned again, and she kept her eyes fixed on her walking feet.

'I know,' said Wyn. She sounded careless, a little distant, and for a terrifying moment Frances thought that was all she was going to say. 'But I couldn't. I had to wait for the right moment to take it, when I wouldn't get caught. And then I had to take it straight away, didn't I? What else was I supposed to do with it? I came to your house but you were having tea, I saw in through the window. It's all right for *some*.'

'Oh.'

'So there. I didn't *mean* to go without you.' So Frances felt foolish again; a bit better, but still worried, and guilty about the tea she'd been having. She wanted to talk about the worries, but she knew Wyn wouldn't listen, and wouldn't have any practical solutions. The mood of their visits had changed, and she could tell from Wyn's frown that she knew it too – it was undeniable. Frances knew how quickly Wyn could get fed up with something; how fast she could drop it and suggest something new. Especially now Johannes had upset her with his hug and his refusal to go outside. What would happen to him then? Frances had no idea.

'Don't you think we should tell someone about Johannes, now?' she ventured. 'He's been there so long. Weeks and weeks. Maybe Aunt Pam? She might know what to do, and—'

'No, Frances!' said Wyn, pleading and commanding at once. 'He's our secret. You promised!'

'But . . . but how long can he just stay in there? Doesn't he need a proper place to live?' said Frances, desperately. Wyn had no ready answer to that.

'He's a grown man,' she said, eventually. 'It's up to him what he does, and when he decides what to do, he'll tell us.' Wyn looked across at Frances, and waited for her agreement. 'Won't he?' she pressed. Frances shrugged, then nodded. 'There, then. If you tell, I ... I won't be your friend any more.' It was the first time Wyn had made such a threat, and Frances felt it like a wound.

She tried to stop worrying. She wasn't used to being the one who knew better, or decided what should be done. She wanted to be like Wyn, and absolve herself of all responsibility, but she couldn't. They were the only ones who knew about Johannes, so they were the only ones who could do anything about him. So she remained anxious, and undecided. She started to chew at the skin around her fingernails, until it got sore and bled. After a few days her mother examined the damage, turning Frances's hands over in her own, her face stern and troubled.

'What's the matter, Frances? You've never been a chewer – what's it all about?' she said.

'If she keeps on, she might chew one of her fingers right off,' Keith observed.

'Thank you, Keith. Well, Frances?'

'Nothing. I don't know,' said Frances, wishing more than anything that she could just blurt it all out. But she could never betray Wyn and Johannes like that, not when she'd promised. Her mother gave her the steady look that always seemed to see right through her, and Frances hung her head.

After they'd eaten, Frances had to put on the cotton gloves her mother wore for cleaning the windows, and keep them on even when she went to bed, to stop her chewing. They smelled unpleasantly of vinegar, and Frances lay awake for a long time, tense and unhappy. She couldn't work out what had happened to the summer – why things that should have been fun had turned out not to be; why things that had once been fun no longer were; and why it felt as though Wyn was a long way away, even when she was right there in the same room. She had a bad dream one night, and wet the bed. She hadn't wet the bed for years, and was horribly ashamed, so she dragged the sheets down to the lean-to and was attempting to wash them when her mother came down.

'What on earth are you up to, Frances?' she said, and Frances burst into tears. 'Oh, love, hush, now.' Her mother hugged her, looking worried. Frances had a terrible, foreboding feeling that things had changed and would never go back to the way they'd been. A feeling that something very bad was going to happen.

9
Sunday

Seven Days After the Bombings

Frances woke with a sick stomach and a thumping head, assailed by images of the previous night – kissing Owen, and being pushed away again. They made her wince to her very soul, and left an ache of loneliness. She didn't know when she'd become the kind of woman who got drunk and threw herself at married men; she didn't know how she could ever face Owen, or how they could possibly get back to normal, after that. Gingerly, she sat up. It wasn't *married men*, she thought, in plaintive mitigation. Only Owen. She shut her eyes again, humiliated at the thought of people having seen him leading her out of the pub, stumbling drunk. Her father had been in there somewhere. She got dressed slowly, without moving her head any more than she had to. She tried not to think about Owen, the feel of him or the taste of his mouth. She felt bruised on the inside; she was teetering on the brink of something, and couldn't risk a fall. She thought it might be despair.

Retrace her steps, Cummings had suggested. There was the leper hospital, there was the man in the RUH, and, she'd realised yesterday, there was Warleigh Weir. There had to be a reason she'd never gone back there after her day trip with the Hughes family; there had to be a reason the thought of it made her mind twist away. She would have to go there to find out, and she *needed* to find out – she needed to know it all, however bad it was. If the killer knew her, and was watching her, then she was certain, in turn, that she knew the killer. She paused, caught by her reflection in the mirror. Her eyes looked shadowy and tired; her mouth sad, almost bitter. Everything that had stood between her and feeling it all too much had been stripped away. Looking after Davy; living at Topcombe Farm, and being married; Wyn being distant, barely mentioned; the monotony of everyday life: it had all gone. She had no armour left, she was defenceless, and she had to know what her part in it had been; she had to understand why she felt the way she did – the shame that didn't only stem from her betrayal of Johannes. It had shaped everything since, she realised; every step, every thought and word, every mistake.

The church bells struck ten across the city as Frances waited in the ruins of Parfitt's Buildings, along from Beechen Cliff Place. The day was cool and clear, the low sun blinding. Eventually, Nora Hughes emerged and walked slowly down the path with her shopping basket over her arm. Frances had hoped to see Davy at her side but there was no sign of him. Perhaps it was too soon to expect him to be out. She followed Nora quietly, and once they were out on Holloway she touched her arm to stop her. Nora uttered a small cry of alarm as she turned.

'Frances! Dear God, don't go pouncing on people like that!' Nora pressed a hand to her chest, and Frances heard the wheeze of her breath. She was grey-faced, her eyes rimmed with pink. Frances worried at once that she wasn't well; that Davy might lose her too. 'You near enough stopped my heart.'

'Sorry, Mrs Hughes, I didn't mean to startle you,' said Frances. 'I just wanted to ask how Davy was getting on?'

'Oh, he's coming along well.' Nora smiled. 'Such a dear little thing. He's been up and about; very quiet, same as always.' She looked at Frances, and her smile faded. 'He was asking where you were. Carys took it hard.'

'Oh.' Frances's heart clenched. 'Do you think ... do you think she might let me see him? I know she said not, but perhaps she was just angry ...'

'I don't know, Frances.' Nora looked at her sadly. 'Davy going missing like that scared her. And she's always felt guilty about you looking after him, and being so patient with him when she isn't. She knows he's been happy with you; happier than at home, sometimes. That'd be hard for any mother.'

'Yes, but ... isn't it more important that he's been happy?'

'I don't expect you to understand, Frances, what with not having kids of your own.'

'Of course,' said Frances, flatly. 'How could I possibly understand? But, please ... would you talk to her for me? Please?' Nora looked dubious. 'Would you try? I just ... I miss him, you see. Very much. I hardly got to see him at all after we found him, and I—' She broke off helplessly. 'Even if she doesn't want me to look after him any more, I could just pop round and say hello.'

'I'll try, Frances, but—'

'She's just using him to punish me!' Frances's face flushed hotly. It felt horribly unjust, even though she suspected it was not.

Mrs Hughes looked uncomfortable, and thinned her lips before speaking.

'You shouldn't have kept on about Wyn!' she said, tersely. 'You shouldn't have asked her about that brooch – I heard you. Making it sound like she did something wrong! You don't know, Frances ...' She took a breath. 'You were just a little girl when we lost Wyn. You don't know what it was like for us. *We* weren't kids; we had no excuses. We were supposed to look after her! We felt so bad that we'd failed her, it was like a ... a sickness. And we lived with it the only ways we could – Bill got rid of every last trace of her, like she'd never been born.' Tears sparkled in Nora's eyes. 'I let my heart break, and I let it stay broken. Carys... Carys blamed herself for every mean thing she'd ever said and done to the kid, and got angry – angry with us, angry with herself. Owen set himself to keeping us all going.'

Nora fell silent, her shoulders high and tense, hands gripping her bag, and Frances didn't know what to say. People pushed past them on the narrow pavement, peering curiously.

'I'm sorry,' Frances said.

'We're all sorry,' said Nora. 'But if you can't let it go ... if you can't let *her* go, how are we ever supposed to carry on? No one can live like that, Frances.'

'I want to – I do. It's just...' Frances shook her head. 'I *know* things, things I can't remember. Things that might be important. I know that I ... I feel responsible for what happened. But I don't know *why*, exactly.'

'Responsible? How could you be?'

'Did Wyn ever tell you about Johannes? That we visited him, I mean. That we took him food?'

'What? No, of course she didn't! We'd have put a swift stop to it if she had.'

'Yes. Of course.' Frances knew she should let up, but she couldn't. 'But do you think ... anybody found out about it? Bill, for example? Or maybe Carys? Or perhaps ... did anybody notice things had been taken, and realise what was going on? Have you ever asked Carys?'

'I just said, we didn't know! What are you getting at?' Nora looked cornered.

'Nothing, I just wondered—'

'Well, I wish you'd *stop* wondering, Frances! I wish you'd bloody well leave it alone! Haven't you heard a word I've said?' She turned to go, but Frances caught her arm.

'Please will you talk to Carys for me? About Davy? Please?' Nora stared at her for a moment, then relented.

'I'll try, if the moment presents itself. But if you go on at her about Wyn, then that'll be that.'

At the foot of bed five, Frances had a moment of pure panic. The patient occupying it was no one she'd ever seen before. He was young, blond, and had his arm in a sling. He was also wide awake, and watching her curiously. He cleared his throat.

'All right, then?' he said, nervously.

'Who are you?' Frances demanded. 'Where's the man who was in this bed before?'

'I'm afraid I ... I don't know,' he said. 'Sorry.' Frances stared at him, her heart speeding. She couldn't think of any reason the man who wasn't Percy would have been moved other than that he'd died. Other than that she'd been too slow, and was too late.

'He can't be dead! He *mustn't* be!' she said.

'Sorry,' the young man repeated, helplessly, but Frances had already turned and was hurrying to the end of the ward, where the nurses had their room.

'Hello?' she said, abruptly, putting her head around the door. 'Percival Clifton. He was here ... he was in bed five all week, and now he's not – where is he? Is he dead? Where have you taken him?' Her voice had ragged edges; the hangover still had her head in a vice.

'That's quite enough of that,' said a gaunt woman in a ward sister's uniform. 'Mr Clifton is not remotely dead. And who are you?'

'She's his only friend. She's been in all week, visiting him,' said a young nurse, whom Frances vaguely recognised.

'Well. Take her along then, please, Nurse Wells. But do

calm down, won't you,' the sister said to Frances. 'There's really no need to flap.'

Percy had been moved to a smaller room with only four beds, where it was quieter, warmer, and each of the beds was hidden from the next by a tall, folding screen on wheeled feet. None of the men moved, none of them seemed to breathe; the stillness was unnatural. The back of Frances's neck prickled, and she had the unnerving sense of being surrounded by dead men.

'Here he is, see,' said Nurse Wells, too brightly.

'Why has he been moved?' said Frances.

'Dr Phipps was just a little concerned about his chest – he might have developed pneumonia. We've brought him in here for a bit of peace and quiet, and to keep a closer eye on him, that's all.'

'I was told before that . . . that the brain can be starved of oxygen during a fire.'

'That's right, yes.'

'So if he wakes up . . . if he does, there's a chance he could be . . . damaged?'

'Well, let's cross that—'

'Can't you just tell me?'

'All right,' said Nurse Wells, taken aback. 'Yes, there's a chance of that. We're giving him penicillin for the chest infection, and we'll know more in the next couple of days, I should think. What he really needs is rest, and time to recover. The best thing you can do is let him have that,' she said.

'All right,' said Frances. 'I'd just like a couple of minutes.'

'Five minutes,' said Nurse Wells. 'I'll be back to check.'

There were no chairs in the smaller room, and Frances leaned over the man to see his face square on. It felt like an aggressive pose, but at the same time like leaning out over a high cliff, or over a dog that might jump up and bite. He actually looked better, she thought; his colour was a little more normal, his skin not as shiny, his breathing not as loud. But then she realised that was only because his breathing was so much shallower – a scant lift of his ribs, barely anything at all. Like he'd almost decided not to bother, and was waning. Her hands moved before she could stop them. She clutched the front of his hospital pyjamas and felt the warmth of his body underneath.

'Wake up!' she whispered. 'Don't you *dare* ...' His breath nudged her face, tainted with decay and thick, stale saliva. Frances recoiled, horrified. Her insides lurched; she tasted the bitter contents of her stomach and had to swallow it down, stepped backwards and gasped as something touched her. She turned around and caught at the screen, almost knocking it over before she got hold of herself. Then she stood shuddering for a while, her own breathing the loudest thing in the room.

Sergeant Cummings had left a message for Frances at Woodlands, so she turned right around when she got back.

'What about your lunch? It's already gone as dry as old leather,' said Pam.

'Sorry. I'll have it later,' said Frances. Pam sighed, looking concerned.

'Are you all right, Frances? I feel as though I've hardly seen you in days.'

'Sorry, Pam. I'll be back later.' She left before her aunt could say anything else, and walked westwards. It had clouded over, and drizzle made everything dreary as life went back to a forlorn kind of normal. The houses in Oldfield Park were turn-of-the-century; terraces with a single bay window and a front door set back inside a small porch. Some had hydrangeas and dormant roses in their small front gardens, most just had weeds and last year's thready herbs in cracked clay pots. Frances found the café Cummings had suggested – a green awning and steamed-up windows – and went inside. It was crowded, but the chatter was subdued; Cummings was at a small table towards the back, reading the paper with a pot of tea in front of her. She waved Frances over.

'You're just in time,' she said. 'I was about to give up and go home.'

'I was up at the hospital,' Frances said, without thinking. Cummings frowned.

'Oh? Is everything all right?'

'Yes, I—' Frances was unsure how much she should say, but she realised, as she sat down, that she trusted Sergeant Cummings. 'There's a man there. A patient. I . . . I found him last week, when I was looking for Davy. I don't know who he is. I mean, they think his name's Percy Clifton – that was the name on the ID card he was carrying. But I don't think that's who he is. I *know* I know him from somewhere.'

'Why would he have somebody else's papers?' said Cummings, picking it apart at once.

'I don't know. He was at the Regina Hotel when it was hit . . . Another man who was there told me there was a shady character in the bar that night, on his own, and the nurse told me he was brought in with a lot of cash on him. His clothes were burnt so they threw them away, but I looked at his shoes – they're second-hand, I'm sure of it, and all but falling apart.' She paused, glancing up at Cummings. 'I think . . . perhaps he was picking pockets. Perhaps neither the cash nor the papers were his.'

'Yes, perhaps.'

'There's only one Percy Clifton living in Bath, and it's not him. They've checked.'

'So whose papers did he steal?'

'Some other Percy Clifton's; someone from out of town, staying at the hotel.'

'What makes you think you know him? If you don't recognise his face, I mean?'

'Well, he was in a fire. Part of his face is burnt, and he's
all bandaged up. It's hard to see him properly. And he seems
to me to be . . . someone I knew a long time ago. Maybe.' She
shook her head slightly. 'Perhaps I'm going mad.'

'I doubt it, you seem quite sane to me,' said Cummings,
thoughtfully.

'I'm not so sure,' said Frances, wearily.

'Have some tea,' said Cummings, testing the pot with the
flat of her hand. 'I'll order fresh. And how about a sandwich?
You look a little . . . pasty.'

Once she'd had something to eat and drink, Frances felt
better. She looked up at Cummings, whose face was rosy in
the warmth of the café.

'You know you told me to go back to old places – places I
used to go with Wyn, that last summer she was alive? Well,
that's what he feels like. This man who isn't Percy. When I
look at him, it's like I'm *trying* to remember something . . . But
the harder I try, the more it escapes me. It's infuriating. What
do you think I should do?'

'Keep trying.' Cummings shrugged. 'What else can you do?'

'I suppose so.'

'Well. Let me tell you why I asked to see you today.'
Cummings' expression turned serious, and Frances felt uneasy
at once. 'Something you said last time we spoke got me thinking. You said that *if* Johannes was innocent, and *if* Wyn was
killed for a . . . sexual motive, then the true perpetrator has
remained at large. Who knows, he might still be out there
today.' Cummings looked down at her hands. 'The thing is,
from what I've learnt, men like that . . . a criminal of that kind,
I mean, with those unnatural drives, is very unlikely to stop
offending of their own accord. I began to wonder about the

possibility of there being more victims. So I . . . I had a look back through our records. And I found something.'

'What?' said Frances, tersely.

'Who, rather. Lesley Rattray. Does that name mean anything to you?' said Cummings. Frances shook her head. 'Lesley was nine years old; she lived here in Oldfield Park – not far from where we're sitting now, on Canterbury Road.'

'*Was* nine years old?'

'Lesley was found dead about a hundred feet from her home, in the alleyway that ran along behind the gardens. This was in September of 1924, so it was six years after Wyn was killed. Lesley had been . . . raped, and strangled.'

Frances had a feeling like pins and needles across her back and chest, and fought down a wave of nausea. 'Are you all right?' said Cummings. Frances nodded once. 'Her killer had used his hands rather than any kind of ligature. There were never any suspects, and no arrests were ever made. Whoever . . . whoever did that to Lesley got off scot-free.' Cummings sounded grim.

'God,' Frances whispered.

'Yes, where was he?' Cummings muttered. She hesitated, then reached into her pocket and took out a piece of paper. 'I'm not saying the two cases are linked. I still think Johannes Ebner was most likely responsible for Wyn's death. But . . . such a person *cannot* be allowed to escape justice. I've transcribed Lesley's mother's statement, and if you can stand to read it . . . perhaps there might be something in it – something you might spot, that nobody else would.' She looked apologetic, and Frances took the piece of paper.

Lesley never said anything about a man being too friendly, or trying to grab her, and I never saw anyone loitering about that shouldn't have been there. Lesley wasn't acting any different, she was her normal self. She was shy of strangers, and not much of a talker, but she was always happy and smiling. She liked to have her little pet projects and lately it was toads. There's a pond out the back of our road, on the rough ground where they're building the new houses, and it was full of all sorts of things. Lesley loved playing there even though I told her not to. I didn't want her playing near the building work, as accidents do happen. And I didn't want her getting all muddy and coming home with toads in her pockets. A few days before she was taken the men filled that pond in, and all the creatures came teeming into the gardens along our side of the street. Lesley kept going along the alleyway trying to catch them, no matter how many times I told her not to. She was just her normal self, right to the end. I told her off the day before it happened, I called her a mucky tike. She was a bit upset after that but nothing out of the ordinary. The morning it happened she was supposed to go and visit my sister, her Aunt Pauline, because I had an appointment with Dr Calloway. I sent her along in her good jacket with the ladybird buttons, and a skirt that was brand new, and I put her hair in plaits. I thought she'd go straight to Pauline's, and not go out looking for toads wearing her best things. She had made the trip by herself many times before and knew the way. Only she never arrived at Pauline's and it was when Pauline came around to see where she'd got to that we went out to search for her. She was a good girl really.

Frances had a lump in her throat when she finished reading; she could feel Mrs Rattray's despair and regret, even through the bland tone of her official statement. *I called her a mucky tike. She was a good girl really.*

'Poor, poor thing,' she murmured.

'Yes,' said Cummings, quietly. 'So . . . is there anything in it? Anything that . . . rings a bell? Anything at all?'

'I . . . I don't know.' Frances refolded the paper but didn't give it back right away. 'Perhaps.' She shut her eyes and searched. Something had fidgeted in her back of her mind – the memory of a dank, shady place with sunlight streaming through the gaps in the door. *No stone was left unturned.* 'I'd have loved those toads too,' she said, absently. 'Though newts were my favourites.'

'Frances?' Sergeant Cummings was leaning towards her, intently. 'There might be no connection whatsoever. You said to me that children are sometimes killed to keep them quiet. Didn't Johannes have a very big secret that he needed both of you to keep?' She stared at Frances and wouldn't let her go.

'Yes.'

'Couldn't he have thought, for some reason, that Wyn was going to give him away?'

'I . . . I don't know.' *Come outside!* Frances heard Wyn's angry voice, clear as day, and she flinched. *Johannes, come outside! If you don't, we'll never visit you again!* Her heart began to pound. *Get off me!*

'So,' said Cummings, eventually. 'As I said, there may well be nothing to connect them. But keep hold of that, if you want to. I don't need it back. It was only . . . a thought. But if anything does occur to you, let me know.'

'I'm being followed, I think,' Frances said. Cummings had been standing up to go but she paused, frowning.

'What?'

'Someone's been following me, ever since we found Wyn's body.' She looked up at Cummings. 'Ever since I started saying it wasn't Johannes.'

'You think?'

'I'm certain of it. I keep hearing footsteps that stop when I do. Whoever it is set my aunt's dog barking when I had him with me one time; and I saw a movement once, a quick movement, like somebody hiding when I turned round. And I can... I can feel it,' she said. Cummings was silent, staring down at her. 'I'm sure Wyn's killer was someone local, someone who knew her. Well... if they knew Wyn, they knew me, too.'

Cummings pulled on her coat, still frowning in thought, though Frances couldn't tell if she believed her or thought her delusional.

'Be very careful, Frances,' she said. 'Don't go out alone at night, will you? I'm sure it's... nothing. It's easy for the mind to play tricks, during the blackout. But even so.' She waited until Frances had nodded before she left. Frances sat by herself for a while. There *was* something in Mrs Rattray's statement, and it was gnawing its way in – finding a place in her sunken memories, where it was too dark to see. Like Percy Clifton; like the damp, shaded place, and the smell of nettles on a hot, painful day. Like the feeling she'd had when Wyn's bones were found – the exact place and depth of them; and the fear that clouded her memories of Wyn's last summer, lingering like smoke after a fire. It was all just waiting for her to join the dots. *The men filled that pond in. Toads in her pockets. Get off me! No stone was left unturned. Hush, little sisters!* Frances took a deep breath and tried not to fight. The truth was like a furtive movement in the corner of her eye that froze when she turned to look for it. So she would try not to look, until it came nearer; she would lie in wait for it, and she would go to Warleigh Weir.

Frances took the bus out along the Warminster Road, and got off at the top of Ferry Lane. The narrow lane led down to a humped bridge across the canal, a level crossing over the railway, and the stone steps where the little ferry crossed the

Avon. Even though it was Sunday afternoon, the drizzle and the bombings meant that Frances was the only person waiting to cross. The little boat was still pulled across by a ferryman and rope, but it wasn't the elderly man she remembered from the last time. She supposed he must have died. The river was quick after all the spring rain, as deeply green and glossy as before. *We could swim all the way to the sea if we wanted . . . we don't ever have to go back.* She remembered Wyn trailing her fingers in the water, and the burn of the sun. Why hadn't Wyn wanted to go back?

'Not much of a day for a picnic,' said the ferryman, as he took Frances's twopence.

'No.'

'All by yourself?' he said. Frances glanced at him sharply, then nodded; he was only trying to be friendly, but she was on edge. 'Well, you know where I am, if anything goes amiss,' he said, as he handed her out at the other side.

Frances walked out into the middle of the island between the two arms of the river. The gentle roar of the weir was constant; her feet were soon soaked, and tiny flecks of rain caught on her eyelashes. She looked about, wrapping her arms around herself. It was all as she remembered it – lush grass spotted with cow pats; stands of trees here and there. A few people were walking their dogs, but there were no swimmers that day. She went to stand on the bank by the weir, and watched the white cascade for a while. Then she stared upstream, where she and Wyn had swum. She should have been happy. It should have been an idyllic day out, and they should both have been happy, but they hadn't been. Neither of them.

'What *was* it, Wyn?' she said, under her breath. 'Why weren't you happy? Why wasn't I?' She remembered feeling rejected by her friend; feeling shut out. She remembered being worried about Johannes by then, but it was more than that. She'd had nightmares – had they begun before the trip to Warleigh, or afterwards? As she turned and walked back towards the stand of trees where she thought they'd set up the picnic, she remembered walking back from their swim. The feeling of ill-defined desperation, and of wanting to go home. She stood as near the spot where Ivy had sat in her deckchair as she could surmise, and looked around again.

She saw the hills all around, veiled grey by the rain; she saw a farmhouse on the eastern bank of the river, and soft new leaves on the horse chestnut trees. And then she saw it. Perhaps a hundred metres away, in the middle of the meadow, was a thick clump of brambles and elder, growing over something. Frances's stomach plummeted. Warily, she walked towards it. It had been a small shed or cow byre, or something like that; all that remained were the stone footings and some rusted shards of a corrugated roof. The rest had gone; sunk back into the earth. *Hush, little sisters!* Frances remembered playing sardines with Wyn and Owen, and Owen's two friends; she remembered that she hadn't wanted to play, and she remembered hiding beside the ruined hut. *Get off me!* Her skin prickled; she was cold all over.

She remembered the sun on her back, and cramp in her legs and neck. She couldn't breathe properly; she couldn't look up, and could only see her own toes and the dead leaves on the ground. The smells of nettles and hot earth were strong, and there was another smell, too. Something familiar but unexpected. Frances concentrated, but she couldn't place it. She'd been very, very frightened – she could feel the echo of it now, tightening her chest, making her legs shake. Then she knew: somebody had come and found her in her hiding place. The memory surfaced in a shocking rush, like the violent expulsion of something her mind could no longer tolerate. Somebody had come and found her. Tears ran down her face; she wanted to turn away but she couldn't move. Just like the last time. Somebody had found her, and hurt her. But however hard she tried, Frances couldn't see who it was. Her head was held down. She saw her toes over her bent knees, and she smelt nettles.

The sky was darkening when Frances forced herself to give up. The rain had flattened her hair to her head, and hid the tears that kept coming – tears of anger and frustration, and old pain. She was stiff with cold and shivering as she walked back to the ferry. The boatman took one look at her face and took her across in silence. She had no wish to hurry back to Woodlands, to Pam's concern and well-meaning questions, so she decided to walk rather than taking the bus – it was about three miles, up Claverton Hill, down Widcombe Hill. A lonely walk through the failing light; little traffic went past, and the trees of Claverton, then the houses of Widcombe, seemed watchful and unfriendly. It was almost dark by the time she got down to Widcombe Parade, where she'd bought Wyn's daffodil brooch. She halted, feeling hollow. The only person she wanted to see was Owen, and knowing that she had made that all but impossible sent her close to despair again. It felt like weeks since she'd seen him; if she turned right, she could reach his house within minutes. She remembered the touch of his hands, holding hers – the warmth and security of him – and she longed for it.

Bereft, she turned left instead, and walked slowly back towards Woodlands. At the corner of Alexandra Road she became aware of footsteps ahead of her, which then stopped. She froze, nerves tightening. She hadn't heard a door open or close, and the person couldn't have simply vanished. She wondered if it was the person who was always watching her – perhaps now waiting for her to get nearer. Lying in wait for her to come down the steps from Woodlands, or go up them; poised to attack. *Don't go out alone at night*, Cummings had warned her. The shadows suddenly seemed sentient, and threatening. Skin crawling, Frances walked closer, making as little noise as she could, her ears straining for any other sound. Then a figure moved in front of her – a tall, barely visible shape.

'Who's there?' she cried, jittery with fear.

'Frances?'

'*Owen?* God, you scared me!'

'Sorry . . . are you all right?'

'Of course I'm all right.' Frances took a breath to steady herself, and the memory of the night before rose awkwardly between them. 'What are you doing here?' she said.

'I was . . . I was coming up to Woodlands. I didn't know if you'd be in.' His tone was so strange that Frances wished she could see his face. She smelt the particular smell of his Home Guard uniform – the cheap leather of the belt, the coarse khaki fabric.

'I've no idea of the time,' she said.

'It's about half past nine.'

'Is that all? Where is everybody?'

'Home, or gone, I suppose. Things aren't back to normal yet, are they? Things might never go back to normal.' He paused, and Frances knew what he meant. He sounded strained, and she was glad that the darkness hid her face. 'I've just come from Junction Road,' he said. 'They've got us guarding some UXBs – there's two of them there. Could go off at any time, the army lot say. I've been standing there, waiting for them to go up and take me with them. And I've been thinking.'

'Oh,' said Frances. She didn't know what else to say.

'I just wanted to——' Owen cut himself off. Frances heard the soft rustle of clothing as he fidgeted. 'I suppose I wanted to say sorry for last night.'

'You've nothing to say sorry for,' said Frances, heavily. He sounded strange, she decided, because he was embarrassed. She had embarrassed him, as well as herself. 'I'm the one who should be sorry, and I am. It won't happen again. I'm . . . I'm quite tired. I'd better get back. Goodnight, Owen.'

'Wait!' He caught her arm. 'I'm not sorry at all.'

'What?'

'I'm only sorry . . . I'm only sorry I stopped you.' There was a long pause after he spoke.

'Perhaps . . .' Frances's throat was so tight she struggled to speak. 'Perhaps you were right to.'

'Perhaps I was, but all day I've been thinking . . . All day I've been thinking that I don't care.'

'What do you mean, Owen?'

'Come back with me now, Frances.' He took hold of her other arm as well. 'Please. Come back with me.'

10

Monday

Eight Days After the Bombings

Morning light threw a bright oblong onto the cracked ceiling of Owen's bedroom. The street noise was very different to that at Woodlands, and sound travelled easily through the walls. Frances heard the creaks and muffled voices of the neighbours getting up for work, just as, in the night, she'd woken to the bass saw of distant snoring. She felt rested but heavy, an unfamiliar combination of exhaustion and serenity. Cautiously, she lifted her head to look at Owen. He was still asleep and she didn't want to wake him. The warm, solid length of him lying next to her was as alien as it was perfectly natural; the smell of him was both familiar and new. She studied the lean, flat muscles of his chest, and the scattering of dark hair that drew a V down onto his stomach. There was a silvery scar across the front of his right shoulder, and she didn't like not knowing how he'd got it. In sleep, his face lost the lines life had given it, and looked boyish again. Frances realised that she hadn't dreamt, once they'd gone to sleep; she couldn't remember when she'd last slept so well. She lay back and stared at the ceiling, feeling marooned from the real world and entirely happy to stay that way. Almost desperate to stay that way, in fact. Owen murmured something plaintive in his sleep, then turned over and curled one arm around her.

When he woke he looked at her searchingly, and Frances held her breath. She understood – she was looking for the confirmation of a shared memory too; for signs of regret, or fear, or resentment. She couldn't see any of that in him; at least, not in that first moment of waking. Instead he reached out and brushed his fingertips over the healing cut on her forehead, so lightly she hardly felt it. Then he kissed her, pushing his hands into her hair. Some time later, he got up to make tea, and brought it back to bed. They sat side by side in silence, sunshine catching the steam from their cups; the air had a chill, and Frances pulled the sheet high up over her chest.

'Are you cold?' said Owen.

'Not really. I'll live,' said Frances.

'That's a relief, then. I'd hate it if you didn't.' He smiled, then it faded. 'Won't your aunt be worrying where you are?'

'Yes. Hopefully she'll just think I've gone out early.'

'Frances, I ... God, I wish this had happened years ago! Before Maggie, and Joe. Before the kids came along. If only I'd worked up the nerve to say something to you. If only you'd said something to me.'

'You told me never to say "if only".' She smiled. 'Besides, I did try. Twice in my life I've ... made a pass at you. Twice you've brushed me off.'

'What? When?'

'Yesterday, and ... that time in Lyncombe Vale. Under the railway bridge,' said Frances. Owen frowned in confusion, until realisation dawned.

'You count that as making a pass at me? It was a hundred years ago!'

'Well. I remember it very well. I ... I was dotty about you. Handed myself to you on a plate,' she said, ruefully. 'Well, I tried to. But you didn't want me.'

'I didn't *want* you?' Owen turned towards her, perplexed. 'Frances, you were *fourteen* years old! And a bit drunk ... it wasn't right! I was eighteen ...' He shook his head. 'That's a

big gap, at that age. It wouldn't have been right. I thought...
I thought we had plenty of time, you see. Time for you to get
a bit older, time for... all the rest that was still to come, for
us. Or wasn't to come, as it turned out.'

Frances let his words settle for a moment. Owen was quiet
too, and when he did speak he sounded incredulous. 'Are you
telling me that's why you disappeared? Why I hardly saw you
after that, and you barely spoke to me for twenty years? Why
you went and married Joe bloody Parry?'

'Partly,' said Frances. She couldn't bring herself to look at
him. She felt like a child again, and foolish, but with an adult's
regrets gathering like clouds on the horizon.

'Frances...' He turned to her, and made her look at him.
'When I said before, a couple of days ago, that the girl I'd
wanted to marry wouldn't have me... that girl was you. I've
always... I've *always* loved you, you idiot.'

'I've loved you too,' said Frances, unsteadily, her throat
constricted. Happy; unbearably sad. Owen shut his eyes,
breathing in long and slow. 'I'm sorry I didn't tell you sooner,'
she said. 'But you got married, and had babies, and...'

'Christ, Frances.' He shook his head, eyes still shut; then he
reached for her again, and pulled her down with him.

When Frances woke for the second time, she panicked,
knowing she should be at work. A moment later she realised
she wouldn't move from Owen's bed even if it meant losing
her job. They lay curled together; Owen's arm was over
her hip and she could feel his breath between her shoulder
blades. It felt like home. She didn't let herself think that it was
Maggie's bed she was in, and Maggie's bedroom; the arms of
Maggie's husband. Maggie didn't seem real, and neither did
her claim to Owen; any more than Joe's claim over Frances
was real. Not when her heart had belonged to Owen Hughes

since childhood; when not having him had meant that she hadn't really cared who she got.

'This isn't real, is it?' she said softly, not knowing if he was awake and listening or not. His breathing was steady and slow. 'This is . . . this is a break from real life. I was standing next to a man when he died. On the second night of bombing. I'd been searching for Davy, and I got caught out. He was a soldier – there were three of them, and they took me in to shelter at Magdalen Chapel. He was . . . he was hit by shrapnel, and died at once. I couldn't see because it was pitch black, thank God, but I remember the smell of his blood. There was nothing anyone could have done to save him. He was there one moment, as alive as you and I, and then gone. Just like that.' She paused, wondering what it was she wanted to say. 'It was . . . *appalling*. How can anything matter, really, when that can happen to us? When we can simply cease to exist like that?'

'Some things matter,' said Owen.

Frances wove her fingers into his and pulled his arm tighter around her.

'Did you ever think about moving away from Bath?' she asked. 'I did. I do. I've stayed here because . . . I've stayed here because of you. And because of Wyn. Knowing that she was still here, somewhere, and needing to find her. Knowing that I've . . . That there were things I'd forgotten, and never spoken up about when I should have. I've been waiting, I suppose. But the sea . . . I'd like to live by the sea, I think. No more dreary streets, no coal smoke always catching in the back of your throat, no seeing the same faces every day, and doing the same thing, over and over, scraping by and feeling it's all . . . pointless.'

'We could live in a fisherman's cottage, up on a cliff,' said

Owen, and she felt him smile, his cheek creasing against her shoulder.

'Like in some Victorian romance.'

'If that's what you'd like.'

'I had a taste of it up at Topcombe, while I was there — living away from here, I mean. The fresh air and the . . . space. No crowds of people everywhere, all the time.'

'I can't imagine that. But I'd go and live anywhere, if it meant living with you,' he said. Frances smiled, heart aching. She took a breath, hating what she was about to say.

'I know you can't leave Maggie. I know you won't. I know your marriage vows mean more to you than mine ever meant to me, and I know how much you love your kids. But let's pretend, just for this morning.'

'Frances, I——' Owen sounded desperate.

'It's all right,' she said, even though it wasn't, even though she could feel the pain growing and tears creeping up on her, starting as a quivering deep in her chest. She squeezed his hand tightly. 'I'll love you anyway.'

'I'll love you too,' he said, with such despair in his voice that Frances couldn't speak again for a while.

When her tears had stopped, she lay in Owen's arms, overwhelmed by the longing to be free from it all; free from the mundane — her job at the station, her failed marriage, her childhood bedroom at Magdalen Cottages; free from walking the same streets she'd always walked and seeing the same things she'd always seen. Free, most of all, from the way she felt. The pernicious sense of guilt and shame, of having made the wrong choices, and been treacherous; of having cheated herself, and others, out of the chance to be happy.

She thought hard, and tried to believe that it wasn't too late, that she could start over — shed it all like an old skin and live differently, feel differently, *be* different. If she could only excise the memories that plagued her, wash them out like grit from a wound. She'd been a child – that's what she'd been told, so many times. A child was not responsible. Nora Hughes' grief for her daughter was real; as was Carys's, after her fashion. Frances's questions about Wyn could be unwelcome simply because they stirred up that pain. Wyn might have lost her brooch while rifling through Carys's things, after she'd been to call on Frances. Lesley Rattray might have been killed by a completely different man. Percy Clifton could be Percy Clifton, a stranger, nobody she knew. The rest might be in her mind – her memory playing tricks on her, disordered by the trauma of losing her friend. It *could* be true that Johannes had killed Wyn; and if it was true then she'd been torturing herself for nothing.

Neunzehn. Johannes had been nineteen years old, and damaged. Frances could see now what she couldn't see back then – how broken he'd been, how shattered. Who knew what a person who'd been through such things was capable of doing, even without meaning to? A person who'd known so much chaos and fear and death. *Neunzehn*. Barely more than a child; a brutalised child. What if Wyn *had* visited him more times than Frances knew about, as Cummings had said? What if she'd told him where she lived, and tried to badger him into leaving the leper hospital – what if she'd threatened to turn him in, or to abandon him, if he refused? What if she'd talked about marrying him, and confused him? Frances pictured him: tall and thin, his head looking too big on his neck, like a pumpkin on a stick; his eyes filling so readily with fear, with kindness, with humour. The way panic could take over him, driving out reason. She pictured his newspaper bed with Wyn's blanket folded neatly alongside it; the little toys and models he'd made them, and his rusty old can of water.

Frances gasped, her eyes snapping open. 'What's wrong?'

said Owen, at once. He'd been awake, just like Frances. Lost in thought, just like her.

'We never took him water,' she said, the realisation jarring through her, cold and sickening. She sat up abruptly.

'What? Who?'

'Johannes! We . . . we never took him water. Only food. He had this old can, and it was always full of water.'

'I'm not following you, love,' said Owen, sitting up beside her, and Frances wished she wasn't thinking of Johannes, and could feel the joy of hearing him call her 'love'.

'Don't you see?' she said, stricken. 'There was nowhere in the yard it could have come from. He . . . he *must* have left the leper hospital to get water!'

'I suppose so,' said Owen, grimly. 'There's the old horse trough over the road – that's fresh spring water. Perhaps he got it there,' he said.

'How can I . . . how can I not have thought of that before?'

'I don't understand, Frances – you told me Johannes was innocent. You were so sure!'

'But what if I was wrong? All these years . . . What if I was wrong? Oh, God.' She shut her eyes and pulled her knees up to her chest. 'I wish it would stop!' she cried. 'I wish it would all stop!'

'*Shh*, Frances, it's all right! You're safe . . . I'll keep you safe! It's all right,' said Owen.

'Is it? How can it be all right? How can I ever leave this room when it's all just . . . waiting for me – like always?'

'Then don't ever leave this room,' he said, trying to hold her. 'None of it was your fault, Frances. None of it . . . If I could only convince you of that . . .'

'You don't know. You don't *know* that . . . What if . . . I have nightmares. I *know* something. Something important!'

'Then *tell* me, Frances! Tell me anything – everything!'

Frances tried. She tried to think of the right words, and then to form them, to make them come out of her mouth, but they wouldn't. They hadn't twenty-fours years before, and they wouldn't now. Nothing froze your tongue like guilt, she knew. Nothing made it harder to speak than knowing you were to blame, and nothing made you more alone. It was hopeless. After a long silence Owen lay back, putting one hand over his eyes. He looked worried, unhappy, and Frances could hardly stand it.

'I have to go. I'm sorry, Owen. I'm so sorry. I've ruined everything – and I don't just mean today, this morning . . .'

'No. Don't you dare shoulder it all like that.'

'But it's true.'

'It's not. All we did . . . all we did was the best we could. If only we'd talked more, years ago, things might have been different. But we didn't, so things are how they are.' He sounded so flat, so tired. Frances moved away, swinging her legs over the side of the bed.

'Do you know when Maggie will be back?'

'No, I . . . She hasn't said.'

'I could . . . come back later.'

'Don't go now.' He took her arm. 'Don't go at all – why are you leaving?'

'I have to . . . I have to try to sort all this out.'

'How can you sort it out, Frances? After all this time? I *hate* watching you torture yourself like this!'

'But I have to try! Or I'll lose my mind! I need to . . . make sense of everything I've thought this past week. Everything I've thought for the past two decades. Please, Owen . . . I just can't *stand* not knowing any more.' She knew that as soon as she left, their perfect, suspended moment would be over. But then, it was already over. Owen was silent, so she could tell he knew it too.

'What if . . .' he said at last. 'What if you'd be better off not knowing?'

'No. Whatever it is . . .' She stared into his eyes. 'Whatever it is, I need to know.'

'Then I'll come with you,' he said, sitting up again. 'Wherever it is you're going.'

'No. I . . . I need to be by myself.'

'All right,' he said, hurt. 'Then come back when you can – as soon as you can. I won't go anywhere today, I'll wait here for you. So you'd better come back.'

'I'll come back,' she said.

Leaving Owen's house felt like an act of deliberate sabotage, but Frances had to do it. She knew where she was going, and was barely aware of the familiar streets as she walked there. Through Magdalen Chapel's graveyard, over the wall; dropping down, stomach churning, into the leper hospital's yard. There was the usual mess of leaf mulch and litter on the ground, and a watchful line of bored starlings along the ridge of the roof. She stood for a while in the narrow backyard, where Wyn's clothing and shoe were found, just a few feet from the back door of the sagging lean-to. Had Wyn been trying to get in, for safety? Or had she been running out, to escape? Frances hadn't dared to go there in the days after Wyn disappeared; she hadn't been allowed to join the search, though she'd escaped at one point and gone looking all the same. *No stone was left unturned.* Frances shut her eyes – she almost had it. Light was inching into the darkness. Sun on her back, nettles; the incapacitating grip of fear. *Come back!*

She felt like she was travelling in time, or that no time had passed; as though everything that had happened since had been a dream – or perhaps that her happy childhood leading up to that point had been only imaginary. She felt that the ground beneath her feet wasn't solid at all. Just like when Wyn's bones had been found, it seemed a mere crust that could easily shatter, and that beneath it lay a place as dark as death. She fought down rising panic, the panic of hearing that Wyn was missing, and that Johannes had been discovered. It bubbled up inside her, ghosts of a past emotion still strong enough to overcome reality; the same ghosts that had kept her silent then, and kept her silent ever since. Frances struggled for calm, and for clarity; she clenched her teeth and shoved the back door open.

She saw the place more clearly now that it was full daylight, and without the distractions of Owen and their frantic search for Davy. The building had continued its steady decay during her long absence – bindweed and ivy snaking greedily through cracks in the floor; flakes of rotted stone, and dust everywhere; a buddleia growing in the corner of the lean-to, and the wall behind it green with algae. Shreds of newspaper and garbage made her heart stutter, until she realised that they had simply blown in, and were nothing to do with Johannes. Rooks chattered outside in the Judas tree; she noticed the skeleton of a bird in the downstairs fireplace, its beak wrenched open in a silent cry. In the upstairs room where they'd found Davy, the room where Johannes had hidden, she picked up the plank on which he'd carved his name, and sat down with her back against the wall. *Johannes Niklas Ebner.* She ran her fingers over the words. It was the only proof, besides the grainy picture in the paper, that he'd ever existed. 'Oh, Johannes,' she breathed. '*Was* it you?'

Frances tried to think of reasons Wyn would have come to see him by herself, that last summer. Was it purely because she'd liked to be in charge? To do her own thing, sometimes? She'd been different; cross and distracted. Frances remembered her own worries, and the way she'd started having nightmares. She remembered their day at Warleigh Weir, and that somebody had frightened her badly. So badly that her mind had buried the memory of who it had been, and what they had done; just as it had buried the memory of sending Wyn away the day she went missing. Frances frowned. Was there something else about that last time she saw Wyn? Something still to be remembered? She'd felt distant from Wyn, as though something had come between them; she remembered the frantic feeling of sorrow that had given her. 'What was it, Wyn?' she whispered. 'What was happening to you?'

Frances had no way of knowing what had passed between Wyn and Johannes when Wyn had gone by herself. If he *had* been able to go out – and he must have, to get water – if Wyn *had* told him where she lived; if she *had* threatened him, or tried to bully him, in an attempt to better fit him into her plans of a glorious homecoming, and a marriage. Acknowledging it felt like despair, like the betrayal of everything she knew. Tears burned in her eyes, because it hadn't only been where Wyn's body was found that had convinced her of Johannes's innocence: his innocence was something she'd known all her life. It was a part of her, as hard and deep as her bones; it had been a large part of the guilt she'd carried ever since. *No stone was left unturned.* The exact place Wyn was found . . . the way Frances had asked, instinctively, for the police photographer to take pictures of the views from there, so that she could orientate herself. She *knew* those views. She had stood in that precise spot many times before.

Frances thought of Carys's hostility, and the way she had always deflected questions about her little sister – flaring into anger, sinking into drunkenness, storming out, slamming the door. She thought of Owen saying 'I know', when Frances proclaimed Johannes's innocence. He'd back-tracked afterwards, but he'd said it with a kind of resignation. As if he'd always known. *All we did was the best we could*, he'd said to her, just hours before. Had he been talking about more than their own failure to be open with one another? She pictured Wyn, knocked flying across the living room, crashing against the hearth; pictured her white, teary face the time Carys broke her arm; thought of her wanting to carry on swimming up the River Avon that day, all the way to Summer Rain. *What is this you've got all over yourself?* She heard her mother's voice, frowning at Frances's dress after the outing to Warleigh. The thoughts got louder, one on top of the other, a rising cacophony that roared in her head. The Hughes family had their problems, but they loved one another. They were loyal to one another.

Wyn's daffodil brooch was still in her pocket; Frances took it out and turned it over in her fingers. Wyn had always worn it. It could have been lost, or it could have been stolen from her. *All we did was the best we could.* Someone could easily have followed Wyn to the leper hospital, if she'd gone alone. Their secret place might not have been nearly as secret as they'd thought. *They filled that pond in. Hush, little sisters!* She saw Wyn walking away, angry and hurt. But was that right? Had she been angry, or had she been afraid? The walls seemed to crowd in around Frances; the ceiling to press down. She glanced at the derelict cupboard and saw Johannes smiling up at her from his hiding place, the first time he'd tried it out. *Buh!* It hadn't been him. She knew it then; she'd always known it. It hadn't been Johannes. She turned the brooch, letting its sharp points stab her fingertips. There had been somebody else; someone she'd banished to such depths that she could no longer see them at all. Wyn had been so fragile. It wouldn't have taken much to kill her; even a child could have done it.

Shivers washed through her, cold and nauseating. She shut her eyes and focused on the final time she saw Wyn: Wyn on the doorstep of Magdalen Cottages, asking her to come to the leper hospital. The afternoon sun making her glow, catching on her brooch and hair and eyes. Frances refusing to go with her. And before Wyn had turned to go up Holloway alone, she'd turned to look the other way – down the hill, towards her home. Frances held her breath. Wyn had glanced behind her, down the hill, and she'd frowned. And then she'd marched away and Frances, trembling inside, hadn't called her back. But before she'd shut the door, she had looked down Holloway as well, to see what Wyn had been looking at. She'd looked, and she'd seen – a figure, familiar to her, coming around the corner of Beechen Cliff Place. But no matter what she did, she couldn't make herself see who it was; she'd done far too good a job of forgetting.

Frances waited outside the police station for a long time. Repeatedly, she checked behind her for watching figures, and searched the faces of passers-by for anything familiar, and anything malicious in their eyes. She felt both hunted and hunter; desperate to keep hold of the memories she'd dragged up, but scared of them, too. Profoundly so. Towards the end of the afternoon, when it seemed as though most of the staff had left, she went into the station and gave her name as calmly as she could, asking for Sergeant Cummings. She felt horribly conspicuous, but the officer at the desk was young, and bored, and barely looked twice at her. Cummings gave her a startled look when she appeared, and ushered her through to a large, stuffy room set out in an orderly way with desks, filing cabinets, lamps and papers. The air had the metallic smell of ink, and felt over-used.

'Are you all right? Has something happened?' said Cummings, quietly. She cast a glance at the far end of the room where two men were deep in conversation. 'Sit down,' she said, to Frances. 'I'll pretend I'm taking a statement from you about something.'

'No, nothing's happened . . . that is, not much . . . I remembered something else. Or someone, rather.'

'Who?'

'I don't know.'

'Oh.' Cummings' face showed a tinge of exasperation.

'Somebody was following Wyn. I'm certain of it. Someone was bothering her. She was crabby, and unhappy . . . It *wasn't* Johannes, even though I think . . . I think he must have come out of the leper hospital, from time to time, to get water. Perhaps it was easier for him at night . . . But it wasn't him. I saw . . . whoever it was coming up Holloway behind her, the day she disappeared. For some reason, I can't remember who it was.' As Frances spoke she realised that she did know the reason – it was because of what had happened at Warleigh. To remember the one was to remember the other, and she'd buried it deep. She'd not wanted to look at it ever again.

Sergeant Cummings cleared her throat.

'You're now saying that Ebner *did* come out of the leper hospital? That he *wasn't* too afraid to?'

'Yes,' said Frances, her heart sinking. 'He must have. We never took him water, you see, and those final weeks were very dry. It hardly rained. He must have got it himself, perhaps from the trough across the road.' She stared at Cummings in appeal. 'I . . . I've only just realised it, but he'd have had no choice.'

'Frances . . . right from the start, the *only* thing you've had to convince me of Ebner's innocence was that Wyn's body was at Beechen Cliff Place, and that he was too afraid to have gone outside to get there! Now . . . now what is there to even *suggest* it wasn't him?'

'That I *know* it wasn't!' said Frances. Cummings took a deep breath. 'If I could please just see the file on Wyn's disappearance? There might be something in it. Something that will... *force* me to remember.'

'Frances.' Cummings shook her head. 'Don't you think it might be time to drop all this?'

'No! Please... I'm close. I know I am. And perhaps... perhaps whoever's following me knows it too.'

'That's if—' Cummings cut herself off, pressing her lips together.

'*If* someone's even following me?' Frances finished for her. 'I don't blame you for not believing me. I even thought myself, earlier on... what if it was Johannes? What if I'm wrong about him? It would be the simplest solution, I know.' She swallowed, her throat bone dry. 'But I *know* it wasn't him.' She stared at Cummings and saw her indecision. '*Please*. Let me see the file.'

Cummings chewed her lower lip for a moment. She glanced at her colleagues again.

'All right,' she said, quietly. 'But it'll cost my job if anyone ever finds out, you understand?'

'Thank you.' Frances exhaled in relief, though her heart had begun to speed. Cummings opened the bottom drawer, took out a faded brown file, the paper soft with age, and put it on the desk in front of Frances. Frances rested her fingers on it, and felt how thin it was. She glanced up at Cummings, who shrugged apologetically.

'It wasn't much of an investigation,' she said. 'They had their man, after all.'

'Of course they did. I... I gave him to them.'

'I've been over and over it, Frances. I really don't think there's anything in there that will help you... Well. I'll get us a tea, shall I? If anyone comes over, hide it under this.'

Cummings put a newspaper next to the file, then got up and left Frances to read.

It only took her about an hour to read it all. The Hugheses' statements were short and to the point – when they had last seen Wyn, what she'd been wearing, and that it was out of character for her to run away. That they'd had no knowledge of Johannes Ebner's presence in the city, or that the girls had made his acquaintance. There was Frances's own questioning by the police, written up by the officer she'd spoken to at home. Reading it turned the knife inside her. *The Elliot child attests that Ebner had been violent towards her on at least one occasion, and that his assaults included unwanted physical affection towards Bronwyn Hughes on at least one occasion.* The page shook in Frances's hands. She'd also told him that the last time she'd seen Wyn had been the day before her disappearance. She'd wiped the whole incident of Wyn coming to her house, going on alone, and of the figure following her, from the official history. She had done that – expunged any mention of the real killer from the record, and left Johannes entirely unprotected. The words blurred. She read Johannes's statement with her throat aching. *I have never harmed the children . . . I had no cause to harm them, they were of great kindness to me . . . I heard heavy footsteps outside of the house. I heard strange sounds, I did not know them. Also the breathing of a person, very loudly . . . I do not think it was the child herself.*

'Who was it?' Frances murmured. 'Oh, Johannes, if only you'd looked out, and seen.'

'What was that?' said Cummings. Frances looked up, startled; she'd forgotten that the policewoman was there. She shook her head, and noticed that her tea had cooled and gone scummy. She took a sip, regardless. 'Anything?'

'Not so far,' said Frances. There wasn't much more to read, and she fought against rising despair. She read the last two pages of the file — a simple log of people spoken to and evidence gathered — slowly, and twice, because she didn't want to finish and have found nothing. And then she saw something that made her pause. She put her finger beneath a single word, and looked up at the sergeant. 'Here,' she said.

'What is it?' Cummings leaned forwards to read the word. '"Miscellaneous"?'

'"Miscellaneous items". It says that material evidence gathered at the crime scene amounts to: "Items of the child's clothing, viz.: Torn section of fabric identified by Mrs N Hughes as coming from the victim's skirt; one pair of child's drawers; one pair of child's stockings; one child's shoe, also identified by Mrs N Hughes as belonging to the victim; & miscellaneous items recovered from the vicinity of the blood stains." What items?' said Frances. Cummings frowned, and read the section of text herself.

'I don't know,' she said.

'Is it . . . is it all still here? The evidence — her things?'

'Well, yes. They should have been kept, since they never found her body.'

'Can we look?' said Frances.

This time, Cummings didn't try to dissuade her. She cast another glance at her colleagues, but they weren't paying them any attention.

'Come on,' she said, standing up. She led Frances through a door at the side of the room, and down some stairs to a quiet corridor where the lights were out. Cummings tutted as she fumbled for the switch. 'You were never down here, right? Wait here a moment,' she said, once she'd found the lights. She disappeared for a minute, and came back with the key to a storeroom door. 'It'll have been archived,' she muttered, half to herself, as she went to the furthest part of the twilit room. Piled cardboard boxes muffled all sound, and the shadows between the high shelves were inky black. Frances wrapped her arms around herself, inexplicably cold. 'Here,' said Cummings, and Frances hurried to where she was. She'd pulled a box out onto the floor and had crouched down to open it. Frances knelt opposite her. She was afraid to see what was inside – Wyn's torn clothes, stained with her blood. Afraid of how they might make her feel. But she had to see.

Each item of clothing was labelled and wrapped in paper. Carefully, Cummings opened each small packet, revealing frayed pieces of grubby cloth, the blood stains on them faded to brown. Frances reached out to pick up the shoe but Cummings blocked her hand. 'Best not to touch anything,' she said. Frances thought about the other shoe of the pair, which she'd seen in the rubble of Beechen Cliff Place, still worn on Wyn's skeletal foot, and felt that same slip in time, that same shift in reality. Cracks appearing in what she thought was real, like hairline fractures deep in her bones. *Wyn, come back!* At the bottom of the box, underneath the packets of clothing, was a small, brown envelope with *Misc. Crime Scene* written across it in slanting handwriting. Frances reached in for it, not bothering to ask permission. 'Tip it into the lid of the box, not into your hand,' said Cummings. Frances did as she was told, untucking the flap of the envelope with hands that shook. A few small items slid out, barely making a sound. And when Frances saw what was there she stopped breathing for a moment, and her heart stuttered. Suddenly, all of her memories had a face; there was no hiding any more, for her or for Wyn's killer. 'What? What is it?' said Cummings. But Frances could only stare. Two cigarette ends, shrivelled and dry; a shirt button, entirely nondescript; and a coin. An American silver dollar, somewhat tarnished but still bright; the year of it, visible to Frances as she looked closer, was 1892. The year of his birth.

*

Frances ran all the way back to Excelsior Street, as the evening light was fading. It was Owen, before anyone else, whom she needed to tell. The truth was so shocking to her, so terrible and so urgent, that it was both real and unreal; she knew that telling Owen would be the test of it. But she stumbled to a halt at the corner of his road, because a pony and cart had pulled up outside number nineteen, and Maggie Hughes was overseeing the unloading of her children and their luggage from it. She wore a shirt tucked into a practical skirt, as neat as her figure – petite and economical; hard-faced but still almost pretty, now with white strands running through her dark hair. It had been years since Frances had seen her, and a flood of some anonymous emotion assailed her. Part of it was guilt, but another part was uglier, angrier; something territorial – the jealous hoarding of something she had no right to claim. She realised then how carefully, over the years, she'd made sure she never ran into Owen's wife, and how close she and Owen had come to being discovered in their first ever act of marital infidelity. The thought sent blood rushing to her face. But what she felt most of all, as she stood and watched Owen's family return to him, was grief. The snuffing out of a brief glimpse of true happiness. Owen appeared on the step, but Maggie said something and gestured inside, and they both disappeared from sight.

Owen's eldest son, Nev, was the spitting image of his father at that age. Frances watched with bittersweet nostalgia as he lifted his little brother down and went back for a box of their belongings. Sarah and Denise were feeding carrot tops to the pony, giggling at the tickle of its hairy lips. Denise looked a little like her mother, Carys, a little like Davy, and a lot like Wyn. She had limp blonde hair, a thin face and dimples in her cheeks. Without fully intending to, Frances walked over to them.

'Hello, girls,' she said, trying to smile. 'You're Denise, aren't you?'

'Who are you?' said Sarah, taking charge as the elder.

'I'm Frances Parry. I look after... I used to look after Denise's little brother, Davy.'

'Oh,' said Sarah, rapidly losing interest. 'Did you want Mum or Dad? I can fetch them—'

'No, that's all right,' said Frances, quickly. 'It was Denise I wanted to speak to.' She crouched down, putting herself at the little girl's eye level, and fumbled in her pocket for the daffodil brooch. 'I think this is yours, isn't it?' she said, holding it out. Denise looked at the brooch but didn't take it; she looked at Frances, uncertainly, then turned her face to the ground.

'Yes,' she said, guardedly.

'I found it when I was helping your mum to tidy up at her house the other day.' Frances tried to sound relaxed, but she could see she was making the little girl nervous. 'Your mum told me that... that you found it, is that right?' she said. Denise put one finger in her mouth, and nodded. 'Well, that's all right – it's finders, keepers, after all,' Frances reassured her. 'Did you know that this is a very special brooch? It used to belong to your Auntie Wyn, when she was just a little girl.'

'But I haven't *got* an Auntie Wyn,' said Denise, mumbling around her finger.

'No... that's right. She's not around any more. But this was hers, so it's very precious. I'm sure she'd be happy that it's yours now, but... will you promise me you'll always keep it safe, from now on? There's a good girl,' said Frances, when Denise nodded. 'Now, can you tell me something, please? Can you think back, really hard, and tell me where you found the brooch? Can you remember?'

Frances held her breath and waited, but Denise shook her

head, twisting on the spot. 'You won't be in any trouble, I promise,' said Frances.

'At home,' said Denise.

'Yes. Yes, I thought so. But do you remember whereabouts at home? Can you tell me which room? Was it . . . was it hidden away, perhaps? Maybe in a drawer or a cupboard? Or was it on the floor, perhaps under the rug?'

'Daddy said I could keep it.'

'Yes, I'm sure he did.' Frances swallowed. 'And you can, but can you remember where it was, Denise?'

'What's all this?' Maggie appeared from inside, looking suspicious; Denise went over and hid her face behind her legs. 'Who the hell are you?' said Maggie, and Frances knew she'd missed her chance.

'I'm . . .' Frances stood up, and had to pause for breath. 'Sorry. I'm Frances Parry. I look after Davy Noyle, and I've been helping Nora and Carys since the bombings.' The half-truth slipped out easily enough.

'Oh, right,' said Maggie. 'You two get on inside and help the boys,' she said, and the girls obeyed her at once. Frances had to bite her tongue to stay silent; she suspected she would never see Wyn's brooch again.

'I just came to give something back to Denise, something I found while we were clearing out number thirty-three. A brooch.'

'Oh,' said Maggie, easing up. 'Well. Thanks very much.'

'It's . . . You're welcome.' For a moment, the two women stared at one another, then Owen appeared in the doorway and Frances took a step back at once. The sight of them side by side caused an actual pain in her heart, a sharp ache, both hot and cold.

'Well, we'd best be getting on,' said Maggie, pointedly. 'Cheerio, then.' Frances met Owen's eye for a fraction of a second, just long enough to register the distress there; the horrible reality of the situation. She looked away in case she gave herself away, and she knew she should go, and leave him to his life. But she couldn't.

'Owen . . . can I talk to you for a minute, please?'

'What about?' said Maggie.

'It's . . . there's . . .' Frances swallowed. 'There's somebody in the hospital. A patient. Somebody I think . . . I think you know.'

'There's what?' said Owen.

'At the RUH. I . . . I found him last week, when I was look-ing for Davy. Please would you . . . I think you should come and see him. Please.'

'What's she on about?' said Maggie. Owen looked worried.

'Who is it, Frances?'

'Please will you just come with me, and see him? It's im-portant.'

'He hasn't got time to go off now – we've just this second got back, and there's lots to get sorted—'

'Leave off, Mags,' Owen said, firmly. 'I'll be back before long. Come on, then.' He nodded to Frances.

They rode the bus across Bath in near silence. At one point, Owen took a breath and turned to her.

'Frances, I . . .' he said, but didn't seem able to finish. Frances just shook her head. She couldn't speak until he'd seen the unconscious man. Until he'd confirmed what Frances thought – what her instincts had told her from the very beginning, and the evidence at the police station had confirmed. If she said anything, she might say everything. Owen looked more and more anxious as they arrived at the RUH, and Frances led him to the small room where the man lay in his bed. He was flushed and deflated – his body sinking into the mattress, his face shrinking back between the ridges of the skull underneath. He was dying. Frances didn't even need to ask; the nurse's steady, stilted expression confirmed what her eyes told her. He smelled of stale sweat; the dressings around his head and over his right eye had been changed, and were stark white against his pink and yellow skin. 'He's been waking up, ever so briefly,' the nurse said, quietly. 'As of last night. But with the fever running so high I'm not sure he's much of an idea what's going on. Best not to get your hopes up, I'm afraid.'

'I see,' said Frances, tonelessly. She didn't have much time. When the nurse had left, she pulled the screen around the three of them. Her heart was jumping high up in her chest. 'Well?' she said to Owen.

'Well, what? Who is it?' he said, looking at her rather than at the dying man. 'What's going on, Frances?'

'Please, look at him. And then tell me,' she said. Owen frowned, confused, but he did as she asked. He looked down at the man, and turned his head to one side as though he was going to shake it. But then he froze.

'Hang on,' he said, looking closer. 'What in hell's name . . .' He gripped the man's shoulder with one hand, and Frances hated to see them touch. 'But this . . .' Owen looked up at Frances, shocked. 'This is . . . it's *Clive*!' he said, his voice tight with emotion. 'What's he doing here – why weren't we told he was here? Why didn't you say? What the hell's going on, Frances?'

Frances shut her eyes. She saw him down at the bottom of Holloway, on the corner, as Wyn walked away, alone. Carys's handsome husband, who'd always been kind, and fun, and smiling. She saw him watching Wyn. Following Wyn. And she knew it was him who'd come and found her at Warleigh Weir. She knew what it was she'd smelt that day, along with the nettles and the summer ground, and she felt sick. When she opened her eyes Owen was staring at her, and he looked almost angry. 'I'm going to send a message down to Carys, and I want to talk to the doctor—'

'Wait!' Frances took his arm as he passed. She swallowed. 'It was him, Owen.'

'What was him?' Owen shook his head. He was no dissembler; he never had been. Frances saw that his confusion was real, and was profoundly relieved. Whatever he'd thought, he'd had no idea about Clive. Frances wanted to hold him close, and spare him from it.

'He killed your sister, Owen. He killed Wyn.'

There was a hung moment in which they were both silent, both still. Then Owen let out an incredulous huff of air.

'Don't be ridiculous,' he said, shaking his head, but as he absorbed the look on Frances's face, he paled. 'What ... how can he have? Why? Frances, why on earth would you say that?'

'I've ... I've always known. But I forgot – I made myself forget. I was too frightened. I couldn't ... I couldn't stand it. I didn't know what to do. And then it was too late, and ... Johannes was hanged.'

'Clive would never have hurt a child! He *loved* us kids. I know he's ... fallen off the straight and narrow, over the years, but he's ... he's always been like a brother to me!'

'Yes.' Frances nodded. 'I'd always liked him, and I trusted him. We both did.'

'So how can you *possibly* suggest he'd have hurt Wyn?'

'Because he ... he hurt me, too.' Frances needed to sit down. Her knees felt spongy; she gripped the rail of the bed for support. Owen was staring at her, incredulous. 'The day we all went to Warleigh Weir, to swim and have that picnic. We played sardines, remember? I hid in the undergrowth by the fallen-down cowshed. I was there for a long time, and ...

Clive came and found me there. I only got a glimpse of him as he came along behind me, and then he . . . he held my head down, so I couldn't look. But I'd already seen him. I knew who it was, and I . . . I smelt him. The Bosisto's Oil. Eucalyptus. I . . . I didn't understand. I didn't know what to do afterwards, and he just . . . he just went on as normal. Like nothing had happened.'

Frances stared at the limp figure in the bed. Finally, she understood why he had always made her skin crawl. Why he'd turned up in her nightmares – or rather, why he'd always been there. Owen was silent for a long time, and Frances saw that he was shaking.

'Are you saying that he . . . that he *raped* you?' His voice was little more than a whisper.

'No,' said Frances. 'No, he . . . he held me down. He put one hand over my mouth, and the other hand . . . the other hand on me, and he . . . rubbed himself against me. Until he . . . finished.' *What* is *this you've got all over your skirt?* Frances couldn't look at Owen. The humiliation was unbearable; the shame no less excruciating for being misplaced. 'I couldn't breathe, I thought I was going to suffocate . . . I was so scared. I remember the sound of him wheezing. Then he just . . . went away again. I stayed there for a long time, and when I came out I didn't know what to do or what to say. And he was just the same – smiling, joking, flirting with Carys. Flipping that bloody coin of his. I felt . . . I don't know what I felt. I just knew it was very, very wrong, and I wanted to go home. I didn't know what else to do. His . . . stuff was all over the back of my skirt. Jesus Christ, I remember my mum scrubbing at it, trying to work out what it was.' She stopped, her stomach churning. 'I suppose I got off lightly, in some ways. He knew I wouldn't say anything, you see. He *knew* that I'd seen him, but he knew I was scared and shy and . . . horribly embarrassed, and that I wouldn't be able to tell anyone. But Wyn wouldn't have kept quiet, would she? Wyn wasn't scared of anything. He knew that.'

Owen was staring at the floor as though he couldn't bring himself to look at either one of them. His hands were fists at his sides, and the corners of his jaw were knotted with stress. Frances leant over Clive.

'Wake up,' she told him. In the pause that followed she heard the weak bubble of his breathing. The pneumonia was slowly drowning him. She grabbed his hand and jabbed her thumbnail into the webbing between his first two fingers, grinding it in as hard as she could. 'Just *wake up!*' she whispered furiously. Clive made a high, plaintive sound, and moved his head fractionally. Frances gasped, digging her nail in harder, not caring if she hurt him; *wanting* to hurt him. He opened the one eye he could, just a little. Frances saw the iris she'd glimpsed before, when the nurse had examined him; bronze-brown, like fresh conkers. She dropped his hand, and her nail had left a deep purple welt. Clive kept his eye on her, watching her dully. 'Do you recognise me?' she said. She leant closer to him, staring hard, but he showed no comprehension. 'We've found Wyn's body. I know exactly where you buried her, and I ... I know you killed her.' She paused, struggling for control of herself. The brown eye opened a little wider. Frances thought she saw fear in it; she thought she saw shock, and recognition. 'I'm going to tell everyone,' she said, choking on the words. 'I'm going to tell *everyone* what you did!'

Clive murmured again, a wordless sound that might have been an attempt at speech. He looked away across the room as if longing for escape. 'You ruined my life,' said Frances. 'Look at me, damn you!' Clive turned his head slowly, obediently. 'So you *can* hear me,' she said. His chest rattled, but he was too weak to cough. 'I wish ... I wish you could have faced justice – public justice, I mean. I suppose this is justice, of a kind; you lying here like this. But it's not enough. Wyn *trusted* you! We both did. I *saw* you. I saw you following her . . .' She shook her head. The eye with the brown iris blurred behind tears, and Frances was sure she saw guilt there, stark and terrible. His face was a mask of it. 'You've no right to cry,' she said. 'None at all.'

'You saw him following her?' said Owen, in a strange, rough voice. Frances stepped back from the bedside, and turned to look at him.

'The day she disappeared. The last time anyone saw her – except for *him*. He was following her up Holloway, towards the leper hospital . . . I wouldn't go with her.' Frances felt tears roll down her face. 'I let her go on her own. Because of *him*. If I . . . if I'd gone with her like she wanted,' she said, forcing the words out. 'If I'd gone with her, she'd still be alive.'

'I can't . . . I just can't . . .' Owen pushed his hands through his hair, then covered his mouth for a moment. He shook his head violently. 'I have to go.'

'Owen, wait! Please stay!' Frances cried, stricken. But Owen shook his head again, and wouldn't look at her. Then he turned away.

1918

The first sign of any trouble was an apologetic knock at the door, halfway through the morning of the thirteenth of August. It was a Tuesday, and Frances was sitting at the kitchen table making a birthday card for her father, for which Cecily had donated coloured paper, glue and some faded silk flowers that were no longer wanted. As she cut and pasted, Frances tried to imagine how far the finished card would travel – miles and miles, over the sea to wherever her father was. She wished she could go with it. When he got back she was going to ask him if he'd been to Summer Rain, or if he knew where it was. She looked up, surprised, when her mother brought Mrs Hughes into the kitchen.

'Frances, Mrs Hughes is asking if you've seen Wyn?' said her mother. Mrs Hughes' smile was tremulous, and Frances felt her face go hot. Sweat prickled under her arms. She knew that something was wrong. 'Mind your manners, Frances – speak up when you're asked a question,' said her mother.

'I saw her on Sunday. We played at the allotments, and then she went home for tea,' said Frances. She didn't say that Wyn had come calling on Monday too, nearly at bedtime. Her mother had been out the back, Keith upstairs in their room. She didn't say that she'd refused to go out with Wyn; that she was hurt, and confused; or that Wyn had said, crossly, that she was going to the leper hospital with or without Frances, and that it had made her want to cry.

She'd felt frantic as Wyn gave up and walked away; she was going to call her back, but Clive had been coming up the hill behind her, and she'd had to close the door in case he saw her. She couldn't bear for him to see her. Fighting back tears, she'd run through to the backyard and stayed close to her mother as she took the washing in. Now Frances worried that Wyn was in trouble for going out at that late hour.

'Well, it's just . . . she skipped off out again after her tea last night, and . . . she never came back,' said Mrs Hughes, her eyes on Frances, wide with hope and consternation. Frances didn't say anything. 'She's never once done that before. She never stops out all night,' she added.

'Well, Frances?' her mother prompted her, impatiently. 'Do you know where she might be?' Frances shook her head, wishing she could disappear. She looked down at the half-finished card, but it seemed rude to carry on with it when Mrs Hughes was just standing there, waiting, so she put her pencil down.

Nora Hughes had a muddy brown bruise around one eye, and a cut on her lip with a thick, black scab, like a beetle. She could look very nice, when the sun was on her face and she was smiling – she and Wyn had the same mouth, with the lovely, pouting top lip – but that wasn't very often. Frances couldn't tell them about the leper hospital. It wasn't the same as telling them about Johannes, but it was *almost* the same – they'd be bound to find him if she told them about it. She felt desperate relief at the thought – that Johannes would be looked after by grown-ups from then on, not by her and Wyn; that it would all be over, and not a secret or a burden any more. But Wyn had said she wouldn't be her friend if she ever told anyone, so Frances said nothing. She was sure that was where Wyn would be, which meant that she'd get bored sooner or later, and come out. She chewed at the skin around her left thumbnail. It was already torn and sore, but it gave her something else to think about, and seemed to ease the worry a little bit. 'Frances, do stop that gnawing!' her mother snapped.

'I don't know, Mrs Hughes,' said Frances, in a small voice.

Mrs Hughes went away and Frances continued making her card, but her heart was no longer in it, and there were knots in her stomach that made it hard to concentrate. The knots stayed there all day, and she couldn't think about anything for more than a few seconds without the thoughts stuttering to a halt. She would normally have gone to call for Wyn after lunch, if Wyn hadn't called for her, or she'd have waited for her in Magdalen Gardens. They'd never needed to arrange to meet up or play – they'd always just met. But that day, Frances didn't want to go and call. The idea of Wyn not being there if she did was too horrible. So she played in her room, and in the backyard, and she helped her mother knead the bread dough and chop the onions for supper, and she kept quiet.

The following day, a policeman came. Frances's mother sat him in the front room and made him have a cup of tea, which made the policeman look embarrassed. He took his helmet off, and his hair was damp underneath. Frances watched warily from the doorway until she was called forwards. The man had bright blue eyes with shadows underneath them, and Frances thought he was quite handsome until she had to go and sit by him, and could smell his breath. It was metallic, like the smell of raw meat, and she didn't like it at all.

'Now, Frances,' he said, in a strong Bristol accent. 'You're Bronwyn's best friend, aren't you? Jolly good,' he said, when she nodded, though he looked so stern she couldn't imagine him ever finding anything jolly. He opened his notebook and held his pencil over it, poised. 'I should like very much for you to give me a list of all the places the two of you like to play. All the places you can think of where she might be hiding.' It wasn't a request, it was an order; Frances knew the difference well enough, and she began to panic. Surely she had to tell him about the leper hospital, and about Johannes? Surely she couldn't be expected to disobey or lie to a policeman? She didn't know if you could be sent to jail for doing so, but it seemed likely.

'I don't know,' she said, wretchedly, chewing her thumb again, tasting blood. The policeman blinked at her, then raised his eyes to Frances's mother. He looked somewhat at a loss.

'It's all right, Frances,' said her mother. 'You're not in any trouble. Just tell the nice man where you and Wyn most often go.' Her mother sounded frightened. 'Like the new park on top of the cliff. You like to go up there, don't you?'

So Frances nodded, and began to name all the places she could think of – all the places that *weren't* the leper hospital. Topcombe Farm; Smallcombe cemetery; the Deep Lock; Broad Quay; the chip shop in Widcombe Parade. The policeman wrote down everything she said, and Frances couldn't tell if she was helping Wyn, or herself, or Mrs Hughes, or Johannes, or nobody at all. She had no idea what she should do, what was happening or was likely to happen next. When she finished her list the policeman fixed her with his steady blue gaze.

'Did Bronwyn ever mention running away from home? Did you ever talk about that? Perhaps as a game?' he asked. Frances shook her head. Swimming to Summer Rain, yes, but not running away. Wyn wouldn't, not for real; Frances knew that in her bones. At least not without making an exciting adventure of it, and plotting to take Frances with her.

'No. Wyn would never run away,' she said.

'Right you are,' said the policeman. 'Now, Frances. I hope you realise how very important this is? We need to find Bronwyn. She's not old enough to be out on her own in the world, however grown up you might feel. So. It's very important indeed that we find her, so that no harm can come to her. Do you understand? Good.' He stood up. 'And there's nowhere else you can think of where she might be hiding?' He stared down at Frances, and in his height and his uniform he seemed a terrible figure; one against whom she had no chance. She twisted on the spot, in an agony of indecision, then burst into tears. Her mother rushed forwards and knelt down in front of her.

'What is it, Frances? Oh, do just say! What *is* it?' she said.

'But it's a *secret*!' Frances blurted out, and was immediately sorry.

The policeman stayed for another half an hour, threatening, cajoling, promising and commanding Frances to speak, but she wouldn't. It was too much; she couldn't think, so she simply cried, and the more she cried the more her head ached, and the easier it was not to even hear the man at all. Her mother sent him away in the end, and put Frances to bed for a nap, like a baby. When she woke up, time seemed to have changed somehow. Everything was wrong, and out of kilter. It felt like a game that had gone on too long, like nobody was doing what they were supposed to be doing, and life was no longer how it was supposed to be. There was a buzz of activity out on Holloway, and neighbours kept dropping by to talk to her mother. Frances eavesdropped outside the kitchen.

'. . . still no sign of her. Can't say I blame the poor thing, with that father of hers . . .'

'Now, Linda, we don't *know* . . .'

'And you still haven't managed to get your Frances to talk?'

'Well, *I* can't join in the search, I've to stay here with Frances,' her mother told one caller, in a harried tone of voice.

'The whole district is out looking. One of her family is stopping at home in case she turns up there. They're taking it in turns.'

'Well, she's not going to just turn up, is she? She's been snatched – pretty little thing like that. I'll be keeping my Katy in till they catch the man, I can tell you that.'

After a while, Frances couldn't stand to listen any more.

'You know where she is, don't you?' said Keith, as they lay in bed that night. 'If you know, you *have* to say. Don't be an *idiot*, Frances. If she's just hiding somewhere to get attention she's going to be in *so* much trouble when they find her – and you will be too, for not saying.' Frances didn't sleep a wink. In the morning she asked to go out and help look for Wyn.

'Fat chance!' said her mother, who looked fraught.

'But she's *my* friend.' Frances began to cry again; her eyes were red and swollen from it. Her mother crouched down in front of her and took her by the arms.

'You're to stay here with me and Keith. If you want to help, you can tell me what this secret of yours is. *Please*, Frances.' Her eyes bored into Frances's until Frances felt suffocated. Sobbing, she twisted out of her mother's grasp and bolted through the door, ignoring the shouts that followed her. She wanted to go the leper hospital and ask Johannes if he had seen Wyn, but she didn't dare – there were far too many people around. She was sure she could feel her every move being watched, and she knew she didn't have much time. So she went up Jacob's Ladder instead, to the top of Beechen Cliff, puffing for breath but not staying long because she knew that Wyn wasn't there. Then she went to Smallcombe cemetery, and then to the Deep Lock, but the certainty of not finding Wyn followed her everywhere.

Finally, she went to Wyn's house and crept into the back-yard. It felt horribly wrong to be there without Wyn. She was still afraid of Mr Hughes, and of Carys, but her new, nameless fear was far bigger and it blotted out the others. She looked in the fetid privies and the coal shed, and then in the washhouse, where everything looked wrong, even the floor. Then she heard a voice outside, and froze.

'Wyn? Wyn!' Hurried footsteps came nearer. 'Oh, Wynnie,

is that you? You'll get such a walloping from you dad, for making us worry like that!' Mrs Hughes appeared in the wash-house doorway, her face full of a light that guttered out when she saw Frances. She took a deep breath as her eyes gleamed. 'Oh. Oh, go *home*, Frances! You're not supposed to be here,' she said, and turned away. Shaking, Frances did as she was told. She didn't want Mrs Hughes to see her. She didn't want *anyone* to see her. She wanted to disappear, just like Wyn.

By the third day, Frances was lonely and sluggish. It felt like there was a wall between her and the rest of the world, between her and all the other people. She wondered if it was because she couldn't talk any more, or if she couldn't talk *because* of the wall. The two were tied together, hard to unknot. She was very tired but couldn't fall asleep. The policeman came back and said it was 'of critical importance' that she impart any other information she might have. He said that Wyn's life possibly depended upon it, and, finally, Frances realised that if Wyn didn't come home at all then it wouldn't matter whether or not she would still be Frances's friend; and if nobody went to the leper hospital, including herself, then Johannes would have no food. So she told them about the leper hospital, and as she did it felt as though something was tumbling down inside her – a long way down. When the policeman came back later, grimmer than ever, and asked who was living there and where they would be, Frances said that Johannes wouldn't have *gone* anywhere, and was probably in his secret hiding place. She described where it was, and let the memory of the words vanish at once, like steam from a teacup. And then, finally, he left her alone.

Tuesday

Nine Days After the Bombings

Frances didn't sleep. As the sky paled to grey she gave up, and crept downstairs to sit at the kitchen table. There she waited, trying to decipher how she felt. Seconds ticked by, steady and slow; they became minutes, then an hour. Part of her felt better, calmer; she was happy to wait because she had nothing to do, and no idea of what came next, and that was far better than thinking that things would simply go on as before. But she wasn't sure what she would do if Owen didn't believe her, or if he turned his back on her. If nobody believed her. She'd been so set on reclaiming her memories, on finding out the truth, that she hadn't really thought beyond that. She felt curiously light, but she longed to see Owen, and to talk to him. She decided that as long as he believed her – even if nobody else did – it would be enough. Blackbirds carolled out in the garden; when she heard the squeak of Pam's bedsprings, and the floorboards creak as she got up, Frances put the kettle on.

After breakfast she went out for a walk, past Beechen Cliff Place and Excelsior Street, but in neither place did she have the courage to stop and knock. She had no idea what she would have said to any of them.

'You haven't been to work in a while,' said Pam, when Frances got back and joined her out in the garden. Pam, wearing a canvas apron and gloves, was hoeing weeds out of the vegetable bed. Frances fetched a trowel and knelt down to help.

'No,' she said. 'I suppose they might fire me. Perhaps not, with the bombings. I'll find out soon enough.' The air was rich and earthy; she felt dew soak through the knees of her trousers. Her job seemed deeply unimportant just then. Pam gave her a measured look, squinting in the sunshine.

'You do plan to tell me, at some point, don't you?' she said. 'What's been going on, I mean.'

'Yes. Very soon.'

'But you're all right, are you?'

'I think so. I think I will be.' Frances kept her eyes down, and reached to pull a dandelion.

'Not like that! You have to dig the buggers out, else they're back before you know it.'

They continued in companionable silence, and as she worked, Frances sifted through the things she'd remembered, all the little things that had pestered her, hinting at memories she couldn't reach. She now knew the significance of each and every one; as though, having shifted the main obstacle, everything else had surfaced of its own accord. She could see the whole picture; nothing lay in shadow any more. She gazed around at the profusion of leaves and flowers growing almost visibly each day. Davy should have been there, helping them, or just exploring in his own quiet way. Getting some fresh air and sunshine, and looking forward to a good lunch. The sadness was solid in the pit of her stomach. She hoped that Mrs Hughes was looking after him; she hoped he was doing well, and wasn't still shaken up by the bombings. Didn't people always say that children bounced back? Frances wondered how to persuade Carys to let her see him again, but then she realised, with a jolt of deeper chagrin, that her accusations against Clive – Davy's father – would only make that less likely than ever.

Some time later, when they heard someone climbing the steps to the house, Frances got up and brushed herself down.

'That'll be for me. I hope,' she said.

'Put the kettle on, then, while you're at it. I'll be there in a minute.' Frances touched her aunt's shoulder as she passed. She was ready to talk to Sergeant Cummings; she knew exactly what she wanted to say. But when she opened the door it was Owen on the step, and the sight of him caused her a rush of joy, and doubt, and fear. A kind of sweet, desperate anguish.

'Come in,' she said, when he didn't speak. Owen reached for her instead, pulling her into his arms.

'I'm so sorry,' he said, the words muffled against her hair. 'I'm so sorry I left you there with him like that. I just ... I couldn't take it in ...'

'It's all right. I understand.'

'It's not all right! I should have stayed with you. I should have ... done something.'

'What could you have done?' They broke apart, and Frances smiled tentatively at him. He looked pale, exhausted, but there was a deep, slow fury in his eyes.

'I could have killed him. That's what I could have done,' he said. Frances shook her head. She felt dizzy with relief.

'Does that mean ... you believe me?' she said. Owen's expression turned quizzical.

'You have to ask that?' he said. 'Of *course* I believe you.' Weak with relief, Frances threw her arms around him, and held him close.

She made a pot of tea, and Owen sat down at the table without being asked, frowning in thought. Frances sat down beside him.

'I thought ... when you said you knew it wasn't Johannes,'

she said, 'I thought it meant you *knew*. And then you were so strange and cagey about it . . .'

'No, I—' Owen shook his head. 'For a while I thought . . . perhaps it had been my old man.'

'Really?' she said. Owen nodded.

'I've wondered about it, since we found her where we did. Not that he'd have done it on purpose – I don't think that. He loved Wyn. He loves us all, deep down. But you know what he's like, especially when he's been drinking. I wondered if . . . if he'd knocked her down the stairs, or something like that.' He looked down at his hands. 'An accident. And maybe Carys or Clive had helped set it up so it looked like she'd died at the leper hospital. If Wyn had told them about going there, or if they'd found out.' Owen spread his hands, looking up at her in appeal. 'None of us would have wanted to hurt her. Not even Carys,' he said. Frances didn't reply. She thought of Wyn's broken arm, and Carys's uncontrollable temper. There were things she wanted to say about Carys, but she hadn't yet worked up the nerve. 'Then . . . for a while . . .' He looked at her cautiously.

'What?'

'For a while I wondered whether you'd . . . When we found Davy, and you said that you'd killed them both . . . Only ever by accident! Frances, I know you would never intentionally hurt anyone . . . But, this guilt you've been feeling, and the way you can't remember everything . . . I thought . . .'

'You thought I'd killed her?'

'No! Well, maybe. Or that you'd seen what happened – maybe you'd seen Johannes do something; or there'd been some sort of accident while you were playing there, and he helped you . . . move her, and bury her.' He looked at her in appeal. 'I would never have thought the worse of you, Frances. You were so little when it happened.'

'Is that why you discouraged me from trying to find out? From trying to remember?'

'You'd gone to such lengths to forget, I thought it'd be best if it stayed forgotten. I didn't want you hurting yourself ... or blaming yourself, any more than you already did.' He squeezed her hand tightly. 'Are you angry with me? For even thinking it?'

'No,' said Frances. 'No, it's all right. For a second, yesterday – when I went back to the leper hospital ... for a second I wondered the same thing myself. I could tell there was something you weren't telling me, Owen. You've never said anything about it – about me, or your dad.'

'Well, I didn't know anything for sure.'

'If you had, would you have said something?'

'I ...' Owen sighed. 'I don't know. I was just a kid too, don't forget, and they're my family. If I'd known the truth about Clive ... by God, I've had said something about that.'

'Are you sure? You loved him like a brother. Have you ... have you told Carys yet?' said Frances. Owen looked shame-faced. He shook his head.

'I didn't know what to say. I've told her he's in the RUH – she's up there with him now. Mum, Fred and Davy too. Carys didn't even know he was back in Bath; none of us knew.'

'Davy's up and about?' Frances's heart lifted. 'Did you see him?'

'Yes. He's fine, Frances. He's just fine.'

'Did you ever wonder ...' Frances paused, wanting to tread carefully. 'Did you ever wonder why Carys sent Denise to live with you? Her, and not one of the boys?'

'She just ... you know what she's like. With the drink. She just couldn't cope.'

'But Denise is as good as gold, you told me. And she ... she looks just like Wyn.'

Owen was saved from having to answer by another knock at the door, and by Pam coming in from the garden.

'Owen! Hello,' said Pam, crossing to open the door. 'Goodness, it's like Piccadilly Circus here this morning. Do come in, Sergeant Cummings.' The policewoman smiled as she wiped her feet.

'Hello again, Mrs Elliot,' she said. 'Morning, Frances.'

'Thank you for coming.'

'I had to invent a call about a disturbance,' said Cummings. 'And I felt very shifty as I did, but I'm looking forward to hearing what you've got to say – what it was about that American coin we found that set you off.'

'Yes, I'll tell you,' said Frances. 'This is Owen Hughes, Wyn's brother. Owen, this is the police officer I told you about. The one who's been looking at Wyn's case.'

'What's all this?' said Pam, as Owen and Cummings shook hands.

'Pam, I . . . I've remembered a lot more about the summer Wyn disappeared. I want to tell Sergeant Cummings about it, but it . . . it won't be easy for you to hear. If you want us to go somewhere else to talk, I'll understand,' said Frances. Pam looked anxious, but she set her shoulders.

'I'm staying here, and so are you,' she said.

'I'll stay too. If that's all right,' said Owen. Frances nodded, and they all sat down in uncomfortable silence. Frances felt a familiar jangle of nerves as she began to speak.

'I did what you suggested, Sergeant,' she began. 'I went back to the places Wyn and I went that summer. And it worked.'

Staring down at her hands, Frances told them what had happened at Warleigh Weir, and that she'd seen Clive following Wyn the day she disappeared. Her story met with resonant silence; she was aware of Owen tensing up beside her, clenching his fists and his jaw. She risked a glance at Pam and saw her mouth open in shock, and tears in her eyes. 'I simply couldn't make myself remember who it had been ... that it had been Clive ... until I saw his coin. His silver dollar – you must remember, Owen? It was a present from his uncle in America – it was struck the year Clive was born, you see. He carried it around in his pocket all the time. He always had it. He used to toss it to make the silliest decisions, and make us laugh ... He must have dropped it when he attacked Wyn, because it's there, in the same box as her clothes and her shoe, in the police station. They found it where she was killed, but I suppose they didn't need to think about it too much, because they had Johannes. Perhaps the cigarette ends and the shirt button are Clive's, too, but there's no way of knowing. Certainly, Johannes never had any cigarettes.' Frances paused. 'When I saw it ... I remembered who it was I'd tried so hard to forget.

'Wyn was different that last summer – distracted, bad-tempered, dreaming of escape,' she went on. 'When he was arrested, Johannes said she'd been visiting him by herself for weeks, and he thought she was hiding from something. Or from someone.' Frances paused. 'It must have been Clive. Clive was following her. And then ... then Johannes heard strange noises outside the leper hospital. It's all there in his police statement. He heard ... he heard it happen. He distinctly remembered the sound of laboured breathing.' She looked at Owen, but he couldn't meet her eye. 'Clive's asthma. Wyn was trying to hide from him but he followed her there, and it was the ideal place for him to ... attack her. Completely abandoned – or so he would have thought.' Frances had to stop and take a deep breath. 'With me, I think it was just a case of ... the opportunity presenting itself. It was Wyn he wanted; Wyn he couldn't leave alone. And she was so fearless ... Wyn wasn't afraid of anything, but perhaps ... perhaps, like me, she just didn't know how to tell anyone what was happening.

Perhaps she didn't fully understand what was happening. Or what was going to happen.'

'Oh, *Frances*—' said Pam, sounding stricken.

'No, please – let me say it all, first,' she said.

Frances glanced at Sergeant Cummings as she took out the transcript of Mrs Rattray's statement, and unfolded it on the table. 'There was another little girl. Lesley Rattray,' she said, for Pam and Owen's benefit. 'She was attacked and killed in September of 1924, in Oldfield Park. This is her mother's statement.' She cleared her throat, and read it out to them. 'I knew the first time I read it that there was *something* in what she'd said . . . Clive's a brickie. There was a new row of houses being built right behind where Lesley lived; her mother says a pond got filled in, and Lesley liked to go and catch the toads. Well . . . I remember Clive bringing home frogs or toads for Howard, when he was little. I heard him say they were from a pond at work that they'd had to fill in – it *can't* be a co-incidence. Carys was very pregnant with Terry at the time, and Terry was born in October, 1924.'

'Jesus Christ,' Owen muttered.

'And there's something else. When I was helping Carys pack up her house and I found Wyn's brooch, I also found a button. I'd all but forgotten about it, because of the brooch and what it might mean, but I remember it now. It was a child's button, from a coat or something like that. It was red, black and green . . . Mrs Rattray says that Lesley was wearing a jacket with ladybird buttons. Is there any way to know if Lesley had any buttons missing?'

'Yes, possibly. It should be in the report,' said Cummings, keenly. 'In fact, since the case was never solved, the clothes she was wearing should still be in storage. Where is it now? The button?'

'I wrapped it up and packed it away with the rest. It'll be in a shed at the brewery now, but you could get at it – the police could, I mean. They were in Clive's dresser drawer – Wyn's brooch and the button. Denise found the brooch, and Clive told her she could have it. But he must have taken it back at some point. Because he wanted to keep it.' Frances paused. Talking about it was draining, but at the same time it felt like the setting down of burdens. Like the final sprint before she could rest.

'The day after Wyn went missing, I went out to look for her. I didn't expect to find her, because I thought she was at the leper hospital with Johannes. But I knew . . . I knew something was wrong. I went to Beechen Cliff Place, and I looked in the washhouse, where we used to play. I noticed the floor . . . Clive had relaid it earlier that year – do you remember, Owen? It had been very uneven, the stones all loose, but he put it back perfectly. But when I went in that day, some of the stones were wrong.' A damp, shady place, with sunshine streaming through the gaps in the door. *No stone was left unturned.* 'Some of the cobbles were the wrong way up – undersides up, so they looked paler than the others. Don't you see? She was already under there! Wyn was . . .' Frances swallowed. 'Wyn was already buried under there. And not many people would have had the strength or skill to take that floor up and relay it again so perfectly. So *almost* perfectly. When we found her, I knew the place was familiar. I *knew* I'd stood in that spot before. He buried her under the washhouse floor, and by that time the backyard had already been searched. Nobody would have bothered looking again.'

'But how can he have done that without somebody seeing him?' said Owen. 'The whole south side of Bath turned out to look for Wyn, and—'

'They weren't looking round the back of Beechen Cliff Place. Not after the first day. And somebody always stayed at number thirty-four in case Wyn turned up there. Clive took his turn – he was there alone at some point, long enough to ... to fetch her from wherever he'd hidden her, and bury her. Perhaps he rushed, or it was getting dark, and that's why he put some of the stones back wrong. But once he was inside the washhouse nobody would have seen him, anyway.'

After a pause, Frances continued. 'I started to have night-mares that summer. I started to chew my fingers; I chewed them till they bled. I was worried about Johannes, and how we would ever get him out of there; I think I'd figured out that he might be a German soldier, and I wanted to tell someone. I wanted to tell *you*, Pam, so he would get help, but Wyn wouldn't hear of it. And I ... I *knew* something was up with Wyn, but ... even after what happened at Warleigh Weir, I couldn't make the connection. I was too confused – it felt as though *I'd* done something wrong. I've been trying to forget that day ever since, and I started to forget about it almost at once. Because I couldn't bear to think about it.' There was a long silence, and Owen reached for her hand.

'You were eight years old,' said Cummings. 'It wasn't your fault.'

'I could have saved them both. Wyn and Johannes. If I'd told somebody about Clive, and what he'd done to me – even if I'd only told Wyn, it might have changed everything. It might have given Wyn the push she needed to speak up about him, and made it impossible for him to go near her. And if I'd owned up to the police about seeing her the day she dis-appeared – and seeing Clive following her ... that might have spared Johannes. But I threw him to the wolves, because I couldn't ...' She shook her head in helpless distress. 'I *couldn't* bring myself to admit what had happened. Even to myself.'

'Frances, you mustn't ... you *mustn't*—' said Pam, dis-traught.

'But it's *true*, Pam. I just have to find a way to live with that.'

Suddenly, Owen burst up from the table.

'He was the best man at my wedding, for Christ's sake!' he cried, eyes focused on the past, on memories that were re-writing themselves. 'He was like a brother. We all loved him!'

'Of course you did,' said Frances. 'Carys loved him; Wyn too. That's how he got away with it.' She searched for some way to make it easier for him, but there wasn't one. 'What do you think?' she said to Cummings. 'Is there enough? Can you talk to Inspector Reese, and get the case reopened? I want him punished. He *should* be punished.'

'You're damn right he should,' said Cummings. She thought for a moment. 'I'll try my best. If we can get our hands on that button, and prove that it *was* Lesley's – perhaps her mother could identify it . . . With the dollar coin, and your testimony, it might be enough, but I can't promise you anything. The guvnor's almost absurdly stubborn about admitting a mistake, especially when—' Cummings was cut off by more footsteps outside, and a loud banging at the door.

'Frances Parry! I've a bone to pick with you!' came an angry shout. Cummings and Pam looked up, alarmed, and Owen looked at Frances.

'Christ, that's Carys,' he said.

'Wyn's sister – Clive's wife?' said Cummings.

'That's her,' said Pam. 'Brace yourself.'

'You'd better let her in,' Frances said to Owen, standing up. She was so used to feeling that she had done wrong by Carys, it was hard to convince her mind to feel the reverse. As Owen opened the door, the sight of him took the wind out of Carys's sails for a moment.

'What are *you* doing here?' she said. 'Why aren't you at work?'

'Some things are more important,' said Owen, grimly. Then Carys saw Frances.

'*You.* I want a bloody word with you!' She marched in, her face a curdled red mess, eyes glassy with rage. Cummings stepped in front of her.

'You'll moderate your tone, Mrs Noyle, or you'll leave again this instant,' she said, evenly. Carys stared up at her, dumbstruck. Her eyes took in the police uniform, and, faced with Cummings' air of immovable authority, she backed down.

'Why are the sodding rozzers here?' she shot at her brother.

'What do you want, Carys?' said Frances. Carys gave her a savage look.

'I want to know why my husband's been lying in the hospital for over a week, but I've only just heard about it – when *you've* been going to see him most days since he was taken in.' She took a breath, and Frances caught the familiar reek of cheap gin. 'I knew my brother probably hadn't just *happened* to go in and find him, like he said.' She sneered at Owen. 'So I had a word with the nurses, and now I want to hear from you what the hell's been going on!'

Frances studied Carys for a moment. All her anger and her drinking; the way she lived a constant battle, pitting herself against everything and everyone round her. It had to be an exhausting way to exist; one she wilfully persisted in, as though she needed the distraction.

'I know it sounds odd, but I didn't recognise him at first,' she said. 'I had a feeling I knew him, but I wasn't sure . . . It's been years since I saw him. Years and years since I spoke to him.' She thought back, trying to remember if she'd ever spoken to him again after Warleigh. She didn't think she had. 'I needed to remember something, you see,' she said, quietly. 'Something about Wyn's last summer.' Something in her tone caught Carys's attention. She watched Frances intently, and Frances was sure she saw unease behind her eyes.

'Spit it out, then,' she said, less stridently than before.

'The way you were when I found Wyn's brooch in Clive's things . . . The way you reacted every time I mentioned her name . . .' Frances shook her head, wondering.

'Did you know, Carys?' Owen interrupted. 'Have you known all along?' His face showed disgust, and disbelief. Carys glanced from him back to Frances, seeming to struggle.

'What have you been telling him?' she said.

'I've told him what I know,' said Frances, quietly. 'I've told him the truth about Clive.'

'Why *did* you send Denise to live with Maggie and me?' said Owen. 'Why not one of the boys? They were much more of a handful.'

'I don't know what you're getting at . . .' Carys began confidently enough, but then the bluster seemed to collapse out of her and she couldn't finish. She reached out and steadied herself against the worktop, looking shell-shocked – eyes wide, mouth sagging.

'Carys,' said Owen, desperately, incredulously. 'How could you? How . . . how *could* you?'

'How could I *what*?' she shouted. 'He's my *husband*! He's the father of my kids!' She broke into convulsive sobs but only for a moment, then she looked up again, staring bitterly at Frances. 'Whatever stories she's told you, they're not true,' she said. 'She's been buttering you up since we found Wyn, I know. Telling you all sorts, making moon eyes at you.' Carys sneered in disgust. 'Offering you a bit on the side,' she said.

'What?' said Owen, flushing crimson. 'How did you—'

'It was you,' said Frances, realising. '*You've* been following me all week! When you said, the other day, that I'd been telling tales to the police . . . I didn't think anything of it, but how else could you have known? I thought ... I thought Wyn's killer was watching me.'

Carys stared at her in mute fury. 'Why?' said Frances. 'What did you hope to see me do? Did you want to speak to me about it?'

'No, I didn't want to bloody well *speak* to you about it!' said Carys. The two of them stared at one another for a long moment, and Frances thought about it.

'No. You wanted me to stop looking. Didn't you? You wanted to frighten me off.'

'I wanted you to ... I wanted to know what you'd been saying! And to who! All this nonsense – all these lies!'

'She's not lying, Carys,' said Owen.

'Well, it's hardly a surprise that she's got *you* convinced, but she doesn't *know*! She wasn't there!'

'Frances knows enough! He ... he messed around with her, too!' Owen cried.

'With *her*?' Carys's face writhed with disgust. 'I hardly think so! She was an ugly little spud when they were kids! He'd never ... he'd never ...' She shook her head.

'Mrs Noyle, if you have reason to suspect your husband of—' Cummings began.

'I've got nothing to say to *you*,' Carys spat. 'I've got nothing to say to *any* of you!' She pointed a shaking finger at Frances. 'You leave me alone, do you hear? My Clive's ... he's ... he could die! If I catch you *near* me again, you'll wish I hadn't.'

Carys left the door open behind her, and Frances sat down abruptly. She looked across at Sergeant Cummings, who let out a pent breath.

'So, now you've met Carys,' said Frances, faintly.

'She's good reason to be upset,' said Owen. 'If she *has* known, all this time ... even if she's only suspected ... I can't imagine what that must have been like for her.'

'Yes, you're right,' said Frances. She thought about it for a moment. 'I can't believe she suspected anything back before they were married. But after what happened to Wyn, and as the years went by . . . When I showed her Wyn's brooch, she wasn't surprised. She must have seen Denise with it, of course, but perhaps the fact that Clive had taken it back again meant something to her. Perhaps Denise finding it at home in the first place meant something to her. Perhaps that was when she decided to send her to live with you, Owen. She might have been trying to protect Denise from her own father.'

'I spoke to a colleague of mine – only in the most abstract terms,' said Cummings, quietly. 'He's been on the force for thirty-eight years, and he's seen it all. He told me men like Clive sometimes marry widows with young children, in order to have . . . access to the youngsters.'

'Or women with sisters far younger than them, living right next door?' said Owen. '*God*. Poor Carys.'

'I'd better get back,' said Cummings. She shook Frances's hand. 'I'll do my best, but please try not to get your hopes up. I'm afraid not everything you've come up with can be taken into consideration, legally speaking. But we'll see. If I have anything to report, I'll let you know at once.'

'Thank you, Sergeant,' said Frances. 'Thank you so much for helping me.'

Pam hugged Frances for a long time once Cummings had gone, but she didn't seem able to speak. She smiled, tears in her eyes, and held Frances's face in her hands for a moment. Then she went out into the garden without a word.

'It's a lot for her to take in,' said Owen. 'It's a lot for anyone to take in. Are you all right?' He took Frances's hands, holding them close to his chest.

'I don't know,' said Frances, truthfully. 'How does that old saying go – ignorance is bliss? Well, I think it's wrong. I do feel better than I did, despite how ... how terrible it is.'

'I hate to go, but I need to talk to my mum. Carys will be in such a state ...'

'Yes, I understand. Of course you must go,' said Frances, reluctant all the same.

'I'm so sorry, Frances. I'm sorry for ... everything.'

'None of it was your fault. None of it is.' Frances's throat ached. 'When will I see you again?' she said. Owen shut his eyes, leaning his forehead against hers. He didn't answer for a long time.

'Soon,' he said, eventually, and Frances knew that he meant *I don't know*. She realised that, from then on, whenever they parted she would have no idea when she would see him again – when she'd be able to talk to him, or touch him. She fought back tears.

'Good,' she said, brokenly.

She watched until Owen's long figure was out of sight, then walked slowly back into the garden, every step one further from him. The night they'd spent together – the fragile mirage of the life they could have had together – felt like something she'd imagined. The weight of it was crushing her. Pam was standing motionless in the sunshine. She turned and attempted to smile as Frances approached, and Frances flung her arms around her, sobbing.

'Oh, *Pam*!'

'My dear girl ...'

'Pam, I ... I can't breathe! It's breaking my heart!'

'There, now, shh!' Pam held her tight.

'I can't *bear* it!'

'Of course you can. You must.' After a while, Pam set Frances back and looked at her, her face etched with grief. 'Dear Frances,' she said, taking out a handkerchief and wiping her niece's face.

'What should I do? What can I do?' Frances begged her. Pam shook her head.

'Oh, I'm afraid you can't do a damn thing, my darling. Unbearable things don't magically go away because we can't bear them. Believe me, I know.' She smiled, sadly. 'But you'll carry on, and you'll survive it, because there's no alternative.'

Late in the evening Frances drank some cocoa she could hardly taste, and didn't hear the wireless as it chattered away. She thought about the first night the bombs had fallen, ten days and a hundred years before; how the grief and shame she'd felt for losing Davy had jolted her back twenty-four years, to the first time she'd felt that way, and had stirred up memories long since obscured. Everything had changed since then. She could hardly remember what it had felt like not to know the truth, or her part in it all; not to realise she'd been in love with Owen all her life. That version of herself was a stranger to her now; her memories, her guilt, the things she'd survived – they *were* her. So much had been lost, and much had been found. Perhaps she was better off now, but she couldn't make herself feel happy. Not without Owen.

She pictured Johannes hiding in the cupboard in his last hours of freedom; carving his name into the wood as a way to prove – what? That he'd existed, she supposed. She imagined the moment of his discovery, the realisation that he'd been betrayed, and didn't let herself shy away from it. At least there was something she could do for him now, however small and inadequate it was. A telegram arrived, pulling her out of her thoughts. It was from Owen, and she read it three times, utterly unable to tell how she felt. *Clive died 6PM today. Carys at his side.*

12

Friday

Twelve Days After the Bombings

Frances still had her job, and after the morning shift she went to the library. She spent hours poring over a huge atlas and searching out every hiking map and guide book to Europe she could find. She searched and searched, both the maps and her memories – everything Johannes had told them about Summer Rain. She didn't remember much, only the things that had most appealed to her eight-year-old mind – a place far to the east, with darkly wooded hills, full of wolves and hunters, coming right to the southern edge of the village; a river to the north that froze in the winter; a toyshop; a castle; an old fountain, with stone grotesques that spat water, in the square outside the church. She knew it was in Austria, not in Germany, and she knew that it sounded like 'Summer Rain'. She looked up 'summer rain' in an old, foxed German dictionary, and decided that it couldn't be a direct translation – there was a hard *G* in the German word for rain.

She hunched over the table, running her finger over the maps, reading name after name until her eyes would no longer focus and her back was aching. Then, as the librarian cleared her throat significantly for the third time, she saw it. A village in the far east of Austria, as close to Bratislava as it was to Vienna; a village at the foot of a wooded spur of the Alps called the Leitha Mountains; a village that looked northwards, to the River Leitha. A village, the hiking guide told her, with a castle, and a fine old church dedicated to Saint Marien; a medieval fountain to the front of that, and a name that derived from the church's saint – Saint Marien becoming, down the passage of centuries, Sommerein. *Summer Rain*. Frances let out a long breath, and leant back wearily, keeping her finger on the map. She looked up at the librarian and smiled.

'I'd like to borrow this,' she said, holding up the guidebook.

'Reference only,' the librarian told her, curtly. 'We're closing now.'

'All right. Then I'll see you tomorrow.'

She told Pam about it as they sat down after dinner to listen to the Light Programme.

'And you're certain it's the place?' said Pam, dunking a digestive into her tea. Dog stared up at her, longingly.

'It *has* to be,' said Frances. It's just as he described it, and it's the only place I've found that could have sounded like "Summer Rain" to us.'

'Well, what are you planning to do now that you've found it?'

'I'm going to write to his family,' Frances said, quietly. 'I know I won't be able to send it till the war's over, but still. Better late than never, and God knows it's late enough. I want to tell them that I knew him. That I was there, and that he never hurt anybody.'

'Perhaps they know that already, wouldn't you think? He's their son, after all. Who would know him better?'

'I know. I just . . . I would want to hear it, if I were them. I want them to know he hasn't just been . . . forgotten about. Not by me, at least. And that I'm going to try to have him pardoned.' She took a deep breath, twisting in her seat to unkink her spine. Pam smiled.

'I think you're right,' she said. 'I think they'd like to know that.' She took a sip of her tea. 'And then what?' she asked, carefully.

'What do you mean?'

'Once you've written to them . . . then what will you do?'

Frances recoiled from the question. She still had no idea. She couldn't bear to think about life just carrying on – empty without Owen, without Davy. It was going to be a half-dead kind of a life; she felt horribly precarious, and horribly lonely.

'I've outstayed my welcome, haven't I?' she said.

'Oh, heavens, that's not what I meant at all!' said Pam. 'Really – you can stay as long as you like. I expect your mum misses you, though.'

'I expect she does. But I don't miss living there.' Frances stared into the smouldering fire. Smothered – that was how the thought of going back to live at home again made her feel. She decided there and then that she wouldn't do it. 'I'll rent a room, or something,' she said. 'I could share a flat with another girl, somewhere not too far away.'

'Well, if that's the case . . . what about with this old girl?' said Pam, a little awkwardly. Frances looked across at her. 'If you'd like to, that is. I won't be offended if you don't – I know an old biddy like me is probably not what you had in mind. But we seem to rub along reasonably well, wouldn't you say? There's plenty of space here, and I don't need much from you, just something towards food and bills.'

'But . . . are you sure? I thought you liked living by your-self?'

'I do! I did. Well. It's been nice having you around, and I wouldn't be sorry if you stayed for a while. But it's entirely up to you.'

'Pam, I'd love to. Thank you.'

'Well, that's settled, then.' Pam cleared her throat. 'Should I be expecting Owen Hughes to come calling?'

'No. At least, not in the way you mean. But I . . . I just don't know how to do without him,' said Frances, brokenly. 'I've done everything wrong! *Why* didn't I tell him how I felt fifteen years ago? Everything could have been different!'

'Frances, you did the only thing you *could* do, at the time. For whatever reasons, and regardless of whether it was right or wrong. That's all any of us do.'

'I *miss* him. It's been three days since I saw him, and I . . . I miss him so much.'

'I know – I do know how it feels.'

'But . . . you and Cecily always had each other.'

'Not these past twelve years, we haven't. And not to begin with, we didn't. And we had even more stacked against us than is stacked against you and Owen. For a long time after I was sacked from my position with her family, I didn't think she was going to come after me. I didn't think she was brave enough, or that she loved me enough.' Pam sighed. 'It felt like my life was over. But then, she did it. She turned her back on her whole life to be with me.' She smiled at the memory.

'But Owen will never leave Maggie! He loves his children too much – she'd take them away from him if he left, and never let him see them. If only we'd told each other years ago, instead of both marrying people we didn't really want!'

'Well, yes; that would have been far better all round. But it's easy to say, and the fact is you didn't. Perhaps you both needed to grow up first; perhaps you needed to . . . lay Wyn to rest before you could be with him.'

'And now it's far too late.'

'You don't know that!'

'I do! Of course it is. It's hopeless.'

'Stop that. You'll do what I did before Cecily and I were reunited, and after she died. You'll wait, and you'll love him, and you'll try to tell yourself that anything could happen.

Time passes, things change. Those kids of his won't always be as young as they are now; before too long they'll be able to decide for themselves whether they want to see their dad. And Maggie's a local girl – her family's all here, around and about. Where's she going to take them? Oh, I know he'll always do the right thing by them, and by her. He'll always look after them; that's who he is. But you might just find that he changes his mind about keeping the *status quo*, before too long.'

'Do you really think so?' Frances hardly dared to hope.

'All I'm saying is, don't sit there telling yourself all is lost, because none of us knows what's going to happen. And you're strong, Frances. My God, you're strong. And in the meantime, nobody can prevent you loving him. No one can take that from you.'

*

Dear Mr and Mrs Ebner,

Frances wrote, pausing as she reached for the name of Johannes's sister.

And Clara. I hope this letter finds its way to you, and I can only apologise that it has taken me so long to write. It will be even longer before I can send it, but once this war is over we can hope that life will return to something like normal again. My name is Frances Parry, and I knew your son, Johannes, when he was here in England in 1918. I was one of the little girls who befriended him while he was hiding in the city of Bath. My friend Wyn Hughes and I went to the place where Johannes was hiding to look for ghosts, but we found him instead. He was very thin and very frightened. I don't know the details of how he was captured on the battlefield, why he felt he had to escape from the prison camp, or how he made his way to Bath. I can't hope to find out any of it until after this war, when I can make enquiries without arousing suspicion. All I do know is that he was in a bad way – he was very afraid of capture, and what he wanted more than anything was to go home. He thought and spoke about it, and about you, very often.

For several weeks that summer, Wyn and I visited Johannes and took him food. We did this because we wanted to help him, and because, since we were just children, it seemed an adventure to have such an interesting, secret friend. We did not do it because he coaxed us to, or threatened us or made us afraid, as the newspapers here reported. That was just spiteful storytelling, because he was 'a German'. He made us little toys from scraps of paper and wood; I'm sure you know how good he was at that. He called us his 'little sisters'. I got worried, as time went on, that he shouldn't have been there, and that we, as children, had no clue how to help him get home. I can't tell you how many times down the years I've wished that I had told somebody – my parents, my aunt, or our schoolteacher. Somebody who would have known to alert the proper authorities. He would have been recaptured and returned to the prison camp, and most likely he would then have been sent back to you when the war ended, as all the others were. The war was so nearly over at the time. If only we'd known. I thought then that I would have been betraying him, but if I had only spoken up sooner, he would not have had to die. This is one of the greatest regrets of my life.

Another is that I did not speak up about a family member of Wyn's, a perverted man who assaulted me shortly before he assaulted and killed Wyn. I also believe he killed other little girls in the years since then, at least one other that I now know about. I was too frightened to speak up about him, *and now he's dead — he died just recently before I could make him face up to what he did. Wyn was not herself in the weeks before she was killed. I believe she knew that this man was wrong in the head, and I believe he may have been following her or making her feel worried. Johannes said the same thing to the police when he was arrested, but he was not listened to. It was all too late by then. So by my silence I let them both die when they should have lived, and I will carry the guilt of that with me all my days. People tell me that I was a child and must not blame myself, but the facts are the facts, and if I'd only had a little more courage none of it needed to happen.*

My purpose in writing, I suppose, is to tell you, in case you ever had any doubt whatsoever, that Johannes was only ever kind and gentle to me and to Wyn, and never once hurt either of us. He paid dearly and unjustly for his friendship with us. Johannes was no pervert, and he was no murderer. I am sure you never believed it, but I wanted to say that not everyone in England believed it either. I have been to the police about this and I intend to devote myself to having your son pardoned. It will be difficult at the present time, but one day, perhaps. I also hope to locate his grave should you ever wish to visit it. I wish I still had some of the small toys he made us, but I don't know what happened to them after Wyn disappeared. I would like to come and visit you, one day, if it were ever possible and you would permit me to. It's a selfish thing to ask, I suppose, since it's only for myself that I ask, but there we go.

We only found Wyn's body just recently, after a bomb fell near her home and disturbed the place where she was buried. I suppose by coming to see you I might feel like I've found Johannes again too, after all this time. I can't ask you to forgive me, but I hope to hear from you. It would be so kind of you to write back to me.

Frances read and reread the letter several times to make sure it said everything she wanted it to say. She wasn't sure if she should mention getting him a pardon – she'd seen Sergeant Cummings the day before, and Cummings hadn't looked hopeful.

'Inspector Reese won't hear of it,' she'd said. 'Not now, with everything that's going on. Not while we're at war with Germany, and especially not since Clive has died. He calls it a waste of resources. The evidence is tricky, even with the coin, you see. It could have been that Wyn pinched it from Clive at some point before she died, then dropped it in the yard herself – I know, I know, that's not what happened. But it *could* have been. I'm working on a warrant to go and find that button of Lesley Rattray's, and I'll keep trying – perhaps I'll even go over his head with it. He already dislikes me, so it won't do any harm. But I don't think there's much hope, at least not till after the war.' Cummings had shrugged apologetically. 'I could find out from the prison service where he was buried, if you like?'

Frances folded her letter and slid it into the envelope she'd addressed, with the help of the German dictionary, to *Ebner Family, The Toy Shop, Sommerein*. Then she simply sat and stared at it for a while, wondering when it would ever be sent. The last war had ended just three months after Wyn's disappearance; three weeks after that, Johannes had been hanged. Who knew when the present war would end, and what injustices would be done in the meantime.

She reached across the table for the *Chronicle & Herald* and opened it to read the name again. Pam had spotted it, in an article that was really little more than a list of newly identified bomb dead. *William Hughes, aged 76 years, of Beechen Cliff Place*. Bill Hughes. He'd died on the second night, in a pub on Kingsmead Street, over the river, and hadn't been carrying his

ID card. The only person Frances could think of who would have wept for him was Wyn. She wondered what Nora Hughes was feeling: sadness, but also — surely — relief. She didn't dare go down to Beechen Cliff Place to find out, and wondered if she should go and see Owen, to offer her condolences. She ached to go and see him. A hundred times a day, she thought of reasons to do so; a hundred times a day, she told herself she shouldn't. That it would only make things harder for him if she did.

There was a knock at the door, and Pam shouted down from upstairs.

'Can you get that, Frances? I'll be down in a tick.' Frances opened the door and was surprised to see Sergeant Cummings.

'Oh! Hello, Sergeant,' she said.

'Oh, no — I'm off duty. It's just Angela today,' said Angela, smiling. She'd twisted up her hair, and was wearing a green jacket and a skim of lipstick.

'Is there some news?' said Frances. 'Have you spoken to Mrs Rattray?'

'Not yet, no. I really feel I ought to wait for some official sanction, before I go along and upset her,' said Angela.

'You could tell her Clive's dead — she might like to hear that.'

'Dead just now, having lived a longish life of freedom?' Angela shook her head. 'No, she'll want more than that. Just like you do.'

'Yes, I suppose you're right.'

'Don't keep her out on the step, Frances, that's no way to treat a guest,' said Pam, appearing from upstairs, similarly smart and tucking her hair into her hat. 'Do come in, Angela. Or, in fact, I'm ready if you are?'

'Yes, all set,' said Angela, colouring slightly.

'Angela and I are going out for lunch, such as we can find,' said Pam, in a mildly defiant tone. 'Will you take Dog out? Give him a leg stretch?'

'Yes. Of course,' said Frances, taken aback.

'Thank you. Well then, shall we go?' Pam tucked her hand-bag over her left arm, and offered her right to Angela, who looped her hand through it in a pleased, self-conscious sort of way.

Frances watched them walk out of sight, chatting, then she shut the door and looked down at Dog.

'Well,' she said to him. 'There's a turn-up for the books. I'm afraid you might have a rival for my aunt's affections.' Dog cocked his head, and she decided to take him out for his walk right away. She didn't want to be alone with her thoughts in the empty house, and decided to call in on her mother, who'd been teary since Frances told her the full story. Frances didn't want to be coddled, and she didn't want her mother to feel guilty about what had happened. They had some way to go with that. It was a bright, benign day, with the promise of summer on the gentle breeze. Frances took a deep breath of it as she turned down the steps, and then she stopped. Owen was halfway up, looking like he hadn't slept in days. Wordlessly, he closed the gap between them, pulled her in and hugged her tight. He buried his face in her neck, and kept it there a long time. Frances shut her eyes and breathed him in.

'I mean, they can't stop us seeing each other now and then, can they?' he said, pulling away, speaking as though it were a conversation they'd only just left off. He held her face in his hands, searching her eyes. 'They can't stop us ... bumping into each other down the pub. They can't stop us being friends, can they?'

'No, they can't,' said Frances. 'Owen ...' She smiled, touching his cheek. 'It's all right, my love. It's all right.'

'No. I can't stand it.'

'It's going to be all right, really. I'll wait. I'm going to wait.'

'You shouldn't – I mean...' He shook his head. 'I wish I—'

'I know! I know all of that. You don't need to say anything, and you don't need to worry. About me, or any of it. It's going to be all right.'

'Promise me,' he said, sounding abject as he hugged her again.

'I promise,' said Frances.

'I've let you down, I know I have. All these years you've had to... to carry all that, all by yourself. Blaming yourself; too afraid to say anything. I let you down.'

'No. You didn't.'

They stood in each other's arms for a long time, spellbound, far from the world, until Owen was calm, and Frances realised that Pam was right – she *could* stand it. She would carry on because she had to, and the time she spent missing him would be worth the precious times when she got to be exactly where she was just then. When she could hold him, and take great lungfuls of him. It wouldn't be easy, but it would be honest, and it would be better than a whole life with anybody else. When they parted, she sat down on a step, with the scrappy moss and the campanula, and the lilacs and elders arching over her head. She buried her hands in Dog's rough coat, holding onto him for strength. When Owen reached the bottom step, he turned, lit up by the sunshine on Alexandra Road. He looked up at her for a long time before he walked away.

At ten the following morning, Frances answered a hesitant knock at the door to Woodlands and caught her breath.

'Oh,' she whispered, then dropped to her knees and held out her arms. Davy let go of Nora's hand and stepped into Frances's embrace. 'Davy!' she cried. 'Oh, I'm so happy to see you!' She'd forgotten how small he was, how thin; it was like hugging a bird or a starving cat. He smelt different, and she realised it was because he was clean, and had been given new clothes. He didn't answer her, but she hadn't really expected him to. She laughed as she examined him, running her hands down his arms and smoothing his hair where her hug had messed it up. 'Goodness, Davy, you had quite the adventure, didn't you?' she said, and Davy nodded solemnly. Frances blinked back tears, and rubbed her wet nose on the back of her wrist.

When she stood up again, Davy kept hold of her hand. Nora smiled, in spite of the sorrow in her eyes.

'Well then,' she said. 'I thought you'd be pleased to see him.'

'Oh, I am – thank you so much! But . . . won't Carys be angry?'

'She's gone off to stay with her cousin in Swansea.' Nora paused. 'I don't know how long for. Perhaps for good.' She shrugged helplessly. 'Left Fred and Davy for me to look after, she has. Not that Fred's a bother – he takes care of himself.' Nora took a breath. 'She couldn't cope with us knowing, you see. About Clive, and what he did.'

'I see.'

'Perhaps she just needs some time in a new place, to get herself sorted out, and then she'll be back – for her boys if for nothing else. I don't know,' said Nora. Again, Frances wondered how much Carys had let herself see, and how much she'd wilfully blinded herself to. She wondered whether her love for Clive had turned to hatred, or whether the anger and hate had been all for herself. Being addled with gin had probably come as a blessed relief.

'Did you . . . did you ever suspect anything? About Clive, I mean?' she said.

'No! No, I never did. I mean . . . I knew *something* was up between him and Carys, over the years. No man spends that much time away from home if all's well. I supposed it was her drinking, or that things had just gone stale between them. I just can't believe...' Nora trailed off, shaking her head. 'When I think of him and my Wyn, I just can't believe it,' she said, brokenly. 'I can't stomach it! Oh, why didn't you *say* something, Frances?' Nora's face crumpled, and tears brimmed in her eyes.

'I couldn't,' said Frances, quietly. 'I wish I had. But I couldn't.'

'Do you know, for all Carys's tears, I swear she looked relieved when he died. I *swear* she did.'

Frances nodded, reaching out to squeeze Nora's arm for a moment.

'Won't you come in for a bit? Have a cup of tea?' she said.

'No. Not today, thank you; I must get on.'

'I was very sorry to hear about Bill,' said Frances, with as much feeling as she could muster. She didn't want Nora to go so soon, and take Davy away again. Nora nodded.

'Yes. Thank you. It certainly won't be the same without him. It's all gone a bit quiet round our place, now. I should quite like to move on myself – that house has too many memories; there's too many people who aren't there any more. But where on earth would I go? Not the right time to give up a perfectly good lease, is it? Not with so many people homeless, and not enough places to go around.'

'Well...' Frances sought about for something comforting to say. 'You could get some lodgers in, perhaps? A family – there's plenty without homes, like you say. And you're welcome here for a cup of tea, whenever you like.'

'That's good of you to say, but I shan't make a nuisance of myself.'

'You wouldn't be. And I'll come calling, too – save you climbing up all these steps.'

'Well, then.' Nora adjusted the fold of her coat sleeve

beneath the strap of her bag, 'I . . . I wanted to let you know that Wyn's funeral is set for the fourteenth, at ten o'clock, down at St Mark's. I'd like you to be there, if you can be. There's not many of us left to show up for her.'

'Of course I'll come,' said Frances. Nora nodded sadly.

'You're a good girl, Frances. You always were.' She looked up at Frances, her careworn face softening. 'I've to go down now and talk to the vicar about the arrangements. I wondered if you'd watch Davy for me, just for an hour or two?'

'Of course I will,' said Frances, her heart lifting. 'Whenever you need me to.'

Wyn's mother turned and made her slow way back towards the steps, and once she'd gone Frances simply stood on the threshold with Davy for a while, needing a moment to gather herself. She felt too full of emotion to speak, or to move. She was unbearably happy and profoundly sad; she was hopeful and she was bereft. Davy watched a pair of doves on the ridge of the privy roof, bobbing their heads, courting. The sky was patterned with clouds – white striations against a Wedgwood blue. 'Well, then,' said Frances, at last, and Davy turned to peer up at her. There wasn't a mark on him, for all his ordeal; his grey eyes were clear and steady, his pale hair soft and limp for being clean. It felt miraculous to have him there, alive and well, his hand in hers. It felt like a reprieve. His eyes were the exact colour Wyn's had been; Frances didn't know how she could have failed to see it before. A fragment of her long-dead friend was there with her, in Davy; a ghost, as faint as a breath, and Frances knew she couldn't keep hold of it. So she let her go. The sun lit Davy's jug ears pinkly, and Frances reached out to tweak one gently. 'What do you think? Shall we go and find something to eat?' she said. Davy nodded at once, and smiled.

Author's Note and Acknowledgements

The Disappearance is a work of fiction, and as such is not intended to be a full or complete account of the Bath Blitz. I have, however, attempted to recreate the events as faithfully as possible. In some places, I have included the names of real people and specific events; for example, the Revd. Woodmansey was indeed one of the twenty-seven people to lose their lives at the Regina Hotel on the second night of the bombings; and a three year old girl found on Henry Street did die of her wounds without ever being identified or claimed. Oral accounts given by people who survived the bombings vary regarding the fate of the three soldiers of the Gloucestershire Regiment who took shelter at Mary Magdalen Chapel. I have chosen to include one version – that one soldier was killed by decapitation, one was injured, and one was left untouched. However, official records indicate that all three men lost their lives that Sunday night. They were: Kenneth Hill, aged twenty-one; Victor Phillips, aged eighteen; and William Pumfrey, aged eighteen. To aid the story, I have taken a few liberties with the exact architecture and layout of Mary Magdalen Chapel and the old leper hospital, now number 90 Holloway, Bath. All characters with speaking parts are entirely fictitious.

As ever, my sincere thanks go to my wonderful editors, Clare Hey and Laura Gerrard, for skilfully coaxing the best from the manuscript; and to my brilliant agent, Nicola Barr, for all her support and insight. My thanks to James for tea, patience, and guided walks around the south of Bath; and, as ever, to the whole team at Orion Books for their continued support and hard work.